She loc
"Hey,"
Whiskey."

Say What? Mr. Oh So Smells Good knows her name.

"Uh yeah. That's me."

She gulped the sudden knot in her throat. "Um, but I think you're lost. Restrooms are on the other side. Down the hall. In the back. Down the hall." Wait. She already said that. Didn't she?

She was light-headed and weightless and supercharged all at once. It made no sense other than her body short-circuited and then bolted with a supernova charge. Multiple tingles and aches flooded Willow's body, shivering from their impact.

His lips fought a smile as she stared, still in a trance, at his light, moss-like eyes.

"Not lost darlin'. Think you told Levi you wanted to see what I got. Not thinking you taking me to the restroom is what you had in mind. Unless, it's a dark hallway, in the back," he said in a deep, timber voice.

Oh my, whispered Halo.

Oh yeah, whispered Tails.

Still dazed and lost in his soft green eyes, Willow leaned forward, unaware she was doing it. A soft brush of his hand tucked a careless strand of hair behind her earlobe.

"You still with me Whiskey?" the warm breathing wall with beautiful green eyes softly asked.

Happy Reading

Loving Whiskey

by

Gracie Cooper

Martini Girl Bar Series, Book 1

This is a work of fiction. Names, characters, places, and incidents are either the product of the author's imagination or are used fictitiously, and any resemblance to actual persons living or dead, business establishments, events, or locales, is entirely coincidental.

Loving Whiskey

COPYRIGHT © 2022 by Gracie Cooper

All rights reserved. No part of this book may be used or reproduced in any manner whatsoever without written permission of the author or The Wild Rose Press, Inc. except in the case of brief quotations embodied in critical articles or reviews.
Contact Information: info@thewildrosepress.com

Cover Art by *Lisa Dawn MacDonald*

The Wild Rose Press, Inc.
PO Box 708
Adams Basin, NY 14410-0708
Visit us at www.thewildrosepress.com

Publishing History
First Edition, 2023
Trade Paperback ISBN 978-1-5092-4766-0
Digital ISBN 978-1-5092-4767-7

Martini Girl Bar Series, Book 1
Published in the United States of America

Dedication

This book is dedicated to my family for all your support. Thank you for believing in me and giving me the foundation to follow my dreams and not give up. To my Mama Llamas, thank you for all the adventures, laughs, memories, and inspirations. I'm sure more than one of us will have pink hair enjoying a Martini or two. To Morena Stamm and The Wild Rose Press for giving a girl with a dream a chance at making Loving Whiskey become a reality. To my boys who I hope one day will love books as much as I do (a mama can dream). Finally, to my husband who supports my book-buying habit without judgment. I love you to the furthest bookstore times infinity.

Loving Whiskey: A Martini Girl Bar Novel Playlist

Keep Up—RaeLynn
Champagne Night—Lady A
All My Favorite People—Maren Morris
Dude (Looks Like a Lady)—Aerosmith
Wrecking Ball—Eric Church
Blow—Ed Sheeran/Chris Stapleton/Bruno Mars
New Rules—Dua Lipa
Beautiful Drug—Zac Brown Band
Call Me Maybe—Carly Rae Jepsen
Love on Tap—Courtney Cole
Speechless—Dan & Shay (featuring Tori Kelly)
Wine, Beer, Whiskey—Little Big Town
Best Shots- Jimmie Allen
Bra Off—Raelynn
Jessie's Girl—Rick Springfield
Sway—Danielle Bradbery
Pill for This—Sam Derosa
Sucker—Jonas Brothers
Hell of a View—Eric Church
Loving You Easy—Zac Brown Band
This Is It—Scotty McCreery
Simple Man—featuring Jensen Ackles

Chapter 1

My Best Friend Sucks…Not Really

"He's a vegan. A vegan, Sofia. I won't eat a vegetable soup to save my life and you go and set me up on a blind date with a non-meat eater," Willow oozed with sarcasm at her soon to be ex-best friend Sofia Lago. She patiently waited in traffic to cross the Lion's Bridge in her vintage blue 2004 Honda Accord, twirling a loose strand from her long wavy chestnut hair. The afternoon heat blazed with vengeance through her lowered windows. She counted to fifteen, since ten would not be enough, and ignored her now ex-best friend's giggles, and *'Ay Mijas'* along with horn blaring idiots, who believed honking excessively would speed the sailboat crossing under the drawbridge, and eliminate the massive traffic cluster jam.

Willow sighed, reaching the projected goal of fifteen and continued to count to thirty. The new set goal.

Traffic in St. Augustine, sucked.

Her vintage Honda, with no air conditioner in dead summer in Florida, also sucked.

Her ex-best friend, with the cute accent, sucked. Well, not quite, but today she sucked.

Her dating life at thirty, really, really, really sucked.

Breathe Willow, encouraged the little angel named Halo on her right shoulder as she fluttered her wings rapidly by Willow's face.

"He couldn't have been that bad. Come on, *mija*, you both have a lot in common."

Willow rolled her eyes far back in her head, she thought she saw future sarcasm comments developing.

The little devil named Tails sat quietly on her shoulder, sun-bathing.

"You like to read, so does he. You want to go to Ireland. He's been to Dublin. You both love animals and—"

"Uh, *un momento por favor*. He loves animal," Willow exaggeratedly cut in like a B-Rated adaptation of her friend's mother. "As in he loves them so much that he refused to eat them. I love cats and dogs and bunnies and foxes and those cute furry bat things. However, I would throw down for a burger with bacon and blue cheese or a nice skirt steak. It mortified him I would eat a majestic animal like a cow or pig. Mortified, and yes, before you ask, he believes cows and pigs are majestic." Sofia's laughter echoed through Willow's phone speaker. Yes, phone speaker since her vintage Honda had nothing smart about it. The downside to owning a classic car.

"*¡Ay Dios Mio!*"

Willow rested her head against her hand, leaning on her door, hoping to catch any breeze from the festering heat.

"First and last time. He said we were not compatible. No kidding. He prefers to eat a ball of tempeh, and I prefer a plate of meatballs."

Dating really sucked.

It will get better, consoled Halo.

Tails snorted.

"Please stop. I swear I'm going to pee my pants," Sofia continued laughing uncontrollably.

"I'm not kidding. Thank the good Lord almighty there was hummus and pita chips."

"Stop, girl. Oh crap. I have to pee. Wait. Don't stop. Keep talking. Ignore the sounds in the background."

The sounds of clothes rustling and the stream of her friend's business echoed through the phone.

"You're lucky I've known you since we were five, or this would be weird and gross."

"It's not the first time I've peed around you."

"Oh, I know. Remember when we couldn't find a bathroom on South Beach during Spring Break? You popped a squat right next to a cop car. We were about to get arrested." Good times. Her adventures with her Martini Girls were never a dull moment.

"Hey in my defense," sounds of the toilet flushing and hands washing competed for her attention, "It was an unmarked car and the cop turned out to be hot."

"What was his name again?" More noises came through the speaker as Sofia dried her hands.

"Detective Fernando Padron," Sofia moaned dreamingly.

"Bet you he likes to eat meat."

"Oh, *mija*, the man definitely likes to eat."

Oh my.

Did he have a brother? asked Tails, suddenly interested.

"Cheese and rice," Willow said. A little confused at the sudden voices in her head.

"Seriously, give him another chance. He's handsome and charming. He's got that boy next door look. You never know, he might grow on you."

Willow thumbed her fingers impatiently on her steering wheel. "Mom said the same thing."

"Then what's the issue?"

"I don't want him to grow on me like some fungus. I want to see him and feel a lightning strike. Or feel like you can't breathe in that moment because you're caught up in the magic of seeing him for the first time," Willow whispered.

The sudden silence worried her. Especially from Sofia. She was never quiet.

"I get it. I think we all want that. But this is life, not some romance movie," Sofia said.

"I know. I'm still holding out for it. Just a little longer won't hurt, right?"

"Right." With a loud clap of hands, Sofia cheered "Boy next door is out. On to the next."

Willow smiled, grateful for the understanding, and reenlisted Sofia back to best friend status.

At last, the bridge opened, and the light turned green. The portable air conditioner kicked in.

"Finally, freaking hot as spicy meatballs."

Willow maneuvered through the bridge's traffic and pedestrians touring the vintage downtown area. She passed the city's trolley, waving at the guest and laughing at the smaller kids enthusiastically waving back at all the cars. She turned on Avenida Mendez, straight home where she planned on doing nothing but binge watch her favorite designer show and enjoy her functioning air conditioner until her shift at the bar started.

"Why haven't you traded your car in?"

Good question.

"Time. I don't have it. Between the bar and

preparing the bid on the new place and presentation for the partners, there's not enough time to haggle with car salesmen who'll most likely see me as an opportunity to sell me every extra package and car warranty available to womankind."

"In other words, you don't want to deal with a sneaky car salesman who's looking for a big commission check?"

"Exactly."

"You know you can go see my—"

"Don't say his name." She smothered a giggle. "Please don't tell me to go see your cousin, Vinny. I can't keep a straight face around him."

"First off, it's Vicente. Not Vinny," she said in her Cuban accent.

"Same crap," Willow teased, riling Sofia up.

"No, it's not. Second, he's a nice guy who has a crush on you."

"No. No way. Not happening." Oh, hell no. How could Sofia think it was a good match up?

"Uh, why not?"

"Because he does look like Joe Pesci. Not that it's a bad thing. Joe is a total in 'your face don't mess with me or I'll cut you' macho man, but I can't keep a straight face around Vicente without quoting the movie."

Oh man she loved that movie.

"And I mean this with no disrespect," Willow added. "But he's a bit old for me, don't you think? Besides, Milly still has a few more miles in her." She rubbed her hand over the overheated dashboard of her car. "She's been good to me since forever," Willow continued defending her vintage car.

"She needs to be put to rest like a bad hair day. You

have no A/C. Your radio only picks up one station. Your trunk opens whenever it feels like it. You can't open your passenger door anymore. You can't go over sixty miles an hour without it feeling like you are on an airplane about to take off and you have the inside of the roof held together with tacks," complained Sofia.

Willow silently nodded her head, not disagreeing with any of the facts.

A steaming string of muttered Spanish curse words floated through the sound waves of her phone. "I'm over it. What time are you working tonight?"

"It's Friday. I'm there at happy hour till closing. It's inventory and payroll day. I'll get in a little earlier," she said pulling into her driveway.

The good thing about home, it was also where Willow worked. The Martini Girl Bar was located downstairs of an old home she renovated, making the entire second and third floor her apartment, with a working air condition.

She loved the old building. The three-story Spanish inspired home still had walls standing from the original construction from the early 1800s. With a fresh coat of white paint and black trimming on the wrap-around porch on the second level and smaller deck on the third floor, Willow brought life back into the old girl. The original doors hung inside, along with many of the paneling, giving the place an old-world charm.

She slung her messenger bag around her shoulder, grabbed her phone and few groceries, and slowly trucked up the flight of private stairs to her apartment. A blast of cool air escaped into the Sahara Desert. Slight exaggeration, however, but try driving around Florida without air condition in the middle of summer. Willow dropped her messenger bag on the dining table and flung her sandals off her feet into the stairwell that led to the third floor. She stumbled into her kitchen, all while holding keys in her mouth and balancing the phone on her shoulders.

They continued discussing song sets and drink specials while she put her groceries away in her small galley kitchen. Part of the perks of living above the bar she worked at was being the owner. Well, part-owner. Her partner Fabian, better known as Fabulous Fab, was the Diva Hostess. Yes *Diva*, not Drag Queen. Fabulous Fab refused to be known as a Drag Queen, as she*, not he*, preferred to be unique, and crowned herself as Diva Hostess. As the Diva Hostess of the Martini Girl Bar, she was the ultimate Hostess and the bar's MC. Fab made rounds and mingled with the customers, reassuring everyone was having a Fabulous Fab time.

Willow was the Bartender. As in The Bartender. To her friends and family, she was Willow, but at the bar, they knew her as 'Whiskey, The Bartender.' All loyal customers knew Whiskey made a badass martini. But no worries, those who didn't fancy a martini (cardinal sin by the way) could sample their share of other badass mix drinks and beers.

"Are Lemon Drops the special?" Sofia asked, smacking her lips loudly over the phone.

After the hot infernal day Willow had suffered, for sure. "Absolutely. Lemon Drops are the special and since it's Friday, we are keeping it classy as usual. Fab and the staff have an amazing show tonight. Get your red high heels on."

Sofia squealed with excitement, announcing she needed to prepare for the night's festivities. Willow reminded her happy hour started at five o'clock and the show did not start till seven o'clock.

"*Mija,* it takes time to perfect perfection," Sofia said before hanging up.

Cheese and rice. Her friend was a nut job.

The sudden beep alerted her of an incoming text. It appeared Sofia had activated the Martini Girl call tree.

Sofia—*Get those red high heels out and be ready at 5—*

Fab—*Dress to the nine's ladies—*
Piper—*Awe Yeah—*
Skylar—*Getting my hair done now—*
Harper—*Yes, Yes, Yes—*
Luna—*…—*
Zoila—*I need a drink and my girls after the week I've had—*
Willow—*Car pool and take my extra parking spot—*

With multiple thumbs up emojis from the group and still no response from Luna, slowest texter in the world, Willow went back to finish unpacking her groceries and going through the music set. A quick check of the time showed there was still room for two episodes before she had to get ready. She grabbed a bottle of water and sat down, turning her show on. Her phone beeped again and again. She read through the comments and GIFFs, snorting unladylike and joined in occasionally. The group chat teased Luna for her slow responses to text messages. She glanced at the time again and did her usual check in with her mom.

"Hey sunshine. How's my Whiskey girl doing?"

Her mom adopted her bar name from the beginning. "I'm good, Mama. How are you doing? How's the weather over there?"

"Oh, it's blistering hot here in Texas. Have you talked to your sister recently?"

She muted the drama unfolding between the designers. Willow leaned back on the couch as her cat, Prim jumped up and demanded cuddles. "I talked to her earlier this week. Is everything alright?"

"Honey. I think this time everything has gone down to hell faster than Shakira can shake her non-lying hips. Call her Whiskey girl. Mila needs someone to reach out to her. You know your sister. She won't make the move herself."

"I'll call her. But you're good, right?"

"I'm fine, sugar. I merely want both my girls happy and for Shakira to admit her hips lied at least once or twice. You working tonight?"

"Ugh mom. You're so weird. Leave Shakira's hips alone. I'll call sissy."

Willow hung up with her mom, hesitating before dialing her sister's phone. The sounds of her sister's heartbreak crackled through the phone.

"Mila," Willow whispered softly, aching for her.

Soft cries echoed over the phone. "Mila talk to me," she implored, sitting up straight on the edge of her couch.

"It's over," Mila stated weakly. "I can't…" Her voice broke over the phone, "I can't anymore, Willow. I can't continue living like this. With his lies and pre…tending no…thing is wrong."

Willow closed her eyes. She thought of ways to eliminate her brother-in-law's body without securing a permanent sentence behind bars and limited wardrobe in an orange jumpsuit. "What happened, sissy?"

"She's pregnant," Mila simply said. "Can you believe that? After everything. I begged for us to start a family. He said he wasn't ready. But she's giving him that." Loud sounds of glass shattering sounded through the phone. Angry tears flowed down Willow's cheeks for her sister as she listened to Mila unleash turmoil at her home. "He's filing for a divorce. Bastard is stating irreconcilable differences. The worst part is I have proof to fight him in court and clean his ass out. I don't want anything. Nothing, Willow. Not a spoon, or frame, or stupid dish rag. I want nothing from here."

Willow stood up and walked to her spare room, making mental notes and adjustments. "Come home, Mila. You and mom. We will figure it out. Pack whatever you need and come back home. I'll tell mom the same."

Mila blew her nose, "You have a two-bedroom apartment. We won't fit in your place."

"Guess you and I will share a room like we did as kids. Won't be the first time."

"You hog all the covers," she complained.

"And you kick in your sleep, but we will make it work."

"I don't know if I can leave," she stated softly.

"Why?"

"He has control over our finances."

"It's joint. Take out enough money for you to travel and head home. Keep track of what you take and we will work out the rest with an attorney. Bring the proof you have in case he makes a big issue about the money. If he knows what's good for him, he won't say squat about it. I have someone that I know who can recommend an excellent attorney."

"Are you sure, Willow? I don't want to be a bother or intrude. It will be a short time. I promise to—"

"Mila," her soothing voice probed further. "You and mom are not a bother. Neither of you could ever be that. I'm super stoked to have you both home again. Sucks for the reason it's happening, but overall, I'm happy that you are coming home. I miss my sister. I miss mom. Come home. Please, Mila. Come home."

Her sister sniffed over the phone and released a shaky sigh. "Alright sissy."

"I'll call mom. Start packing. You can go to the bank and withdraw the money. Handle whatever arrangements at work and head to mom's house. Or I can research flights."

"No. I think us driving will be good. Mom has always wanted to do a road trip, and it gives me time to think things over and plan."

After they disconnected, Willow called her mom, sinking to the floor.

"Whiskey girl, tell mama all the drama."

"Douche bag Daryl is filing for a divorce. He knocked up some chick," she blurted, scarcely aware of her own voice.

"WHAT?" hissed her sweet spoken mother, whose southern drawl no longer flowed with honey. The venom poured from every curse word known to mankind as her mother described vicious ways of disposing her son-in-law. No doubt it would leave Ted Bundy blushing.

"Should I pack my shovel?" Willow teased.

"Willow Mae Lawson, there will not be much left of him to bury after I am done with that cheating sack of horse—"

"Mama."

"I swear to the good Lord and all the Saints, if I see him, I'm going to rip out his fingernails one by one—"

"Mama…" she tried again.

"And pour hot boiling butter…no…cooking oil, all over his pecker, and see how useful he'll be to that wanton hussy."

"Don't hold back mama," muttered Willow.

"Oh, I'm not. That's just the beginning," she said, laughing wickedly.

"Alright, Mrs. Hyde. This has been fun, but I need my Mama back."

"She's still here.

"I need you to pack."

After a few seconds of silence, a yelp of joy erupted from the phone. Willow pulled the phone away from her ear. "We are moving back? Really, Whiskey girl?"

"Yes, Mama. Mila is packing. I'm sending you some money through cash app. You remember how to you use it, right?"

"Sugar, be proud of your mama. I've become quite savvy with the internet ways."

"Oh dear lord, help us all."

"Leave the good Lord out of this. Besides, you don't have to send money."

"I'm doing it, anyway. Please take it and enjoy the road trip. Stop at New Orleans and have her take a few days to relax. She's always wanted to go there."

"I can cover us," her mama persisted.

"I want to. Please."

"Alright honey, but don't put yourself in a bind."

"I'm good, Mama. Call when you leave. I'll have my place set up and ready for you."

"Sure, honey. Let me give Mila a call. Make sure she doesn't need any help packing."

"If she needs me to fly out there, let me know."

"I will, sweetie. Go get ready for work. I'll take care of it from here."

Willow sat on the floor for another minute. She thought of her sister. Thought of her heartbreak.

Why was love hard?

In the beginning, Daryl was the perfect gentleman, coming in and sweeping Mila off her feet with his charms and good looks. He pursued her even when she didn't want to be pursued and won her heart over. After they married, he accepted a partnership at the firm and transferred to Texas. The transfer brought back a light in Mila's eyes that Willow had not seen in a while. Still, something was off with Mila. Call it sister-intuition. After five years in Texas, things changed and Mila's marriage turned from fairytale to happily-ever-never. The shadows slowly crept back into Mila's eyes and remained permanent residents.

Excited about having them home, she surveyed the spare room and made a mental checklist of items needed to be cleaned out and rearranged. Which included the closet.

Ugh.

The thought of organizing her dreadful closet alone was worth an orange jumpsuit.

Willow stood and glanced at the clock. Time to get ready for work. She turned off her television and walked to her room, preparing her outfit for tonight. An off the shoulder black Martini Girl Bar shirt and dark blue jeans, paired with red high heels.

Heels.

The sexiest thing any woman should have in her wardrobe besides lacy panties. Even then, Willow knew her limits and packed her cute, glittery black ballet flats.

Her phone rang again as she grabbed her towel. Her pulse raced, worried it was Mila. She glanced at an unknown local number.

"Hello?"

"Hello, *bella*. It's Vicente."

I'm going to kill Sofia, she thought to herself. "Hi Vicente. How are you?"

"I'm good, *mi amor*. What is this that I hear you need a new car, but you have not come to see me?"

Yep, definitely killing her. She sighed. Vicente had a habit of calling her pet names such as beautiful and my love. He was a sweet man. A good person with a good heart and a massive flirt.

"I haven't exactly decided if I'm going to sell it or keep it yet, you know. Milly is special to me," she said, placing the call on speaker while opening a text message to Sofia.

Willow—*I'm going to kill you*—

"*Pero mi amor,* you need an upgrade and I can provide that for you. Why don't you come by sometime this week and we can discuss it at my office? I'll order dinner and we can look over the numbers."

Sofia—*I don't know what you are talking about*—

She growled at Sofia's text, quickly shooting off a GIFF of a hairless cat hissing.

"That's nice, Vicente. I'll look at my schedule and let you know. I don't even know what kind of car I would get," she answered honestly.

A beep on her phone showed a GIFF from Sofia showing a priest splashing holy water at the screen.

"*Bueno mi amor,* you call me and I will make plans for lunch. You have my number and I have yours. *¿Si?*"

She sent her another GIFF of someone being buried

in a grave, and answered, "I will Vicente. Thank you again for calling."

"*Hasta luego, mi amor,*" he said, hanging up the phone as Sofia's text message came through with a GIFF of Morticia filing her nails calmly with a knowing smirk on her face.

"My best friend sucks," Willow muttered to herself, grabbing her towel.

Chapter 2

The New Guitarist

"I want a raise" were Lizzie, the waitress, demands as soon as Willow arrived in the office to start payroll. Under normal circumstances, they evaluated anyone asking for a raise. But, asking for a raise where at the end of last year, Willow made sure everyone received a raise and an additional bonus, took big melons. Especially someone who Willow was tired of their attitude and poor customer service.

It was laughable.

"I'm sorry, Lizzie, but raises are not being evaluated. We can address it later this year."

"I'm not staying without a raise. I've been here over a year and deserve one," she snapped back, crossing her arms over her oversized enhancements and staring down her nose.

"You've been here a year and got a bonus. You're not one of my seasoned employees compared to the others who have longer tenure. This is not corporate America. You have a baseline rate and work for tips. We have talked about your attitude with the customers. You give them crappy attitude, and that impacts your tips."

"I'm not doing this anymore. The Punch Bar is offering more. Lead Hostess with a split pot on bar tips. If you can't offer that or give me more, I walk, Whiskey.

I know my worth and I know you need me," she said firmly with a know-it-all smile.

Willow stood back, glaring at Lizzie and her escalated voice. She attempted to avoid having this conversation in the open in front of other employees. Definitely lemon drop martini kind of night, but with an added floater, because, why not? It's her bar after all and she could do what she wanted, which included canning the entitled brat.

"Do you want to wait for your paycheck, or should I mail it to you?"

Suck it and take your 'I know my worth's butt out of our bar, Tails said continuing to throw shade at Lizzie.

"You are seriously, like, not going to consider keeping me? Like at all?"

Willow tilted her head slightly, pretending to consider it, "Like no. Enjoy the Punch Bar."

Walk away, Willow. Walk away. She's not worth it, Halo continued to chant on her right shoulder while Tails yelled, *SOCK IT TO HER, WILLOW* on her left.

"Cody, let's go. The Punch Bar said they would hire you, too. Curtis knows how good of a guitar player you are. He will even give you your own set time."

Wait. What?

Willow turned to find Cody, her lead guitarist, packing his gear and avoiding eye contact while the rest of the band called out, telling him not to do it.

The Punch Bar was competition, like any other bar. But Curtis Merk, owner of The Punch Bar, was a sleazy snake, and everyone knew that. He was the shade in shady. Losing Lizzie would not hurt Willow but taking Cody, well, that sucked the big hairy ones.

"You're going to do this, Cody?" Willow asked,

hoping Cody would realize it was a mistake.

"I get my own set. Play my own music. Work my schedule and be with my girl. I can't turn that down, Whiskey," he said, sounding contrite.

"You can do that here. Except being with your girl. Sorry, Cody, Lizzie's out. Her worth isn't worth much to me. But if this is what you want, then do I mail your check, or are you waiting as well?"

Willow silently hoped Cody would reconsider. His shoulders hung over in resignation. His obvious decision made. He told her to mail it, but Lizzie spoke up and said they would wait, entitled enhanced barbie that she was.

Willow ignored Cody's soft whisper of her name and walked into the office and reviewed their time. Frustrated she had to balance out of sequence, she wrote on her ledger next to Lizzie and Cody's payroll "Sucks Big Hairy Ones". Immature and inappropriate for a business owner, but at this point she was having a moment and was considering changing lemon drops to straight vodka served with a sugar rim and lemon curl peel.

She printed their checks and placed them in their envelopes with their appropriate names and not the names Tails kept chanting and egging her on to write (Big Hairy Ones Cody and Sucks Big Hairy Ones Worthless Lizzie…again unprofessional and inappropriate but whatever it's that kind of day remember.) Willow walked out and handed them their checks to a non-eye contacting Cody and a snide Lizzie before they walked out holding hands.

United.

"Does anyone know a guitar player?" Willow asked no one in particular.

"Yeah, I might know someone. Let me call him," replied Levi, the drummer.

Willow walked back into her office and rubbed the side of her temples. This was going to be a long night. She pulled up her contacts on her laptop and found the name she needed. Her stomach knotted as the phone rang. She ignored the rantings of Tails. The little hellion kept sending her messages to ask Mateo over for a drink.

"Hey, Mateo, it's Whiskey. Um…I know it's been some time since we've talked. Hope you're doing good, but I needed to ask you for a favor. It's for my sister, Mila, actually. If you have a chance, can you call me? Okay. Bye." She hung up and shook her head.

"That sounded painful," teased Beck from the doorway.

"You have no idea. Is it wrong when you don't even have your Ex's number on your phone but you have it as a contact on your laptop? I mean, who does that?"

"Apparently you do," he joked. "Mila alright?"

Willow caught Beck's somber expression. He always had the same look when they spoke of Mila. She never understood why the pair ended things, but she remembered it was not easy for either of them. They both loved each other fiercely, and as quickly as their relationship sparked and lit up, it burned out in raging flames, burning them both. Neither had spoken to each other since then. When they were in the same room for long periods of time, old feelings raged and quickly resurfaced, causing volcanic eruptions requiring immediate evacuations of anyone in the premises.

"No. But she will be. She's moving back, Beck, and I know you and her…"

"Water under the bridge, Whiskey. If you're

worried, don't be."

"Good. Cause I might need you to help me make her husband disappear if he tries anything," she half joked with him.

Beck's teasing look turned serious. "He hurt her?"

Good to know he had Mila's back if she needed it.

"Not physically," calming the storm brewing behind his big, dark brown eyes.

Beck was naturally an intimidating man. Had always been since high school. Standing at six foot five, with dark shoulder length hair, eyes even darker with a slight cut above his eyebrow, which earned him a wicked look that many women swooned over. Not to mention his killer smile that could light the room up in a flash. The black ink he sported around his bicep peeked from under his, Martini Girl Bar, T-shirt. Her sister did not stand a chance against Becker James Reed.

He is delish, Tails said, smacking her ruby red lips fluttering her long lashes.

He's not The One, Halo snarked back.

But he could be The One right now.

Tails, be serious.

Oh, I am. He is sinful in every way.

Uh hello. I can hear you two and for the record, my sister Mila would not approve. Willow chastised herself and then rolled her own eyes for even having this conversation in the beginning.

Nodding his head, Beck looked around her office. "When is she moving back?"

"Soon. I'm hoping she takes some time and enjoys the trip. Take a few days and stay in New Orleans. Mama and Mila have never been, and its somewhere Mila's always wanted to go. I figured she can use the break and relax a bit."

"It's hot in New Orleans," he stated, raising his eyebrows.

"It's hot in every Southern State," Willow simply said with a smile as he sat down.

"Do you know what days they will be there?"

"Not yet. They'll text me when they leave. Why?"

"Let me know. My cousins own a B&B there. I'll ask if they have availability."

"I forgot you grew up there."

"Yeah," he said again, lost in thought as he looked at his phone. "Better get back and see if Levi's boy came through."

"Thanks again, Beck."

"Anything for you, Whiskey."

****

Besides a pair of red high heels and a lemon drop, nothing beat having Martini Girl time. Her girls arrived and secured their usual table near the bar. Willow quickly filled them in on the Cod-Lizzia drama.

"I can't believe Cody left with that tramp," fumed Sofia.

Willow served the first round of drinks, with the added floater, and joined them, as tradition before the rush.

"I didn't see that one coming either. I knew he was messing around with her, but I didn't think it was serious. You should have seen how he said 'my girl' when he spoke about her. I almost felt bad for him. He's a nice guy."

"Almost felt bad?" a knowing smile curled Sofia's lips.

"Well, yeah. I mean, even though he screwed us

over, I don't wish him ill will. Her not so much. I couldn't care less if she tripped over her six-inch heels and popped one of her fake tits. But Cody. Poor guy. It would suck if he left all of this for a skank with one tit." The girls spewed their drinks and laughed obnoxiously loud.

"*Ay Dios Mio*, I gotta pee," Sofia said, holding her stomach while laughing hysterically.

"You always have to pee. You have a bladder of an infant," chimed in Skylar.

"Who's coming with me?"

"I'm working."

"Not it," called Skylar.

"I went last time," piped up Harper.

"I live with you, by default, I'm out," proclaimed her cousin Zoila.

Piper and Luna looked at each and sighed. They faced off and in unison chanted, "Rock. Paper. Scissors. Shoots."

"Oh stupid scissors always get me," Piper mumbled, taking the loss. She swallowed the rest of her drink and grabbed her clutch. "Let's go, chick."

"Wait, I'll take her. You take my spot next time," Luna said hurriedly in a high pitch voice, suddenly jumpy.

Surprised, they all looked at Luna confused.

"Yo, Whiskey, heard from my boy. He's here if you want to talk to him or try him out. Dude's solid. You know I don't vouch for anyone but will for him," Levi said, approaching their table. All six foot four of him with startling blue eyes, short cropped blond hair, and tatted sleeve arms, standing confident at their table.

"Ladies, you all look beautiful as always," giving

them his devilish smile as he greeted each one individually. "Luna," he said her name in a low, possessive growl, "How are you, love?"

"Um, Sofia has to pee," Luna quickly vomited from her mouth before she grabbed Sofia's arms and dragged her down the hallway towards the bathrooms.

Willow watched her friend run away, clearly flustered by her small encounter with Levi. She caught Levi's eyes following Luna. A sparkle of amusement brightened his blue eyes. He focused his gaze back on Willow. "What do you want me to do with Colt?"

It's not everyday someone from her crew highly recommended anyone off the streets. Levi Reginald was not simply part of her crew; he was her third partner in the bar. He'd been loyal to her since the beginning and stuck with her through the highs and lows and even during the hurricane crisis and flooding they had the last two years. He was her bestie with a penis from the opposite team, and she trusted his judgment with no hesitation. If Levi vouched for this Colt guy, then an interview was unnecessary, but he would need to prove his talent.

Cody was a talented guitarist. He carried the band, and crippled them when he abandoned them. They all felt it, including Levi. Whether he admitted it.

"Let's see what your boy has got going for him."

He shook his head with a chuckle and chin up. "Thought you would give him something more challenging, like making a long isle-tini or a prissy Cosmo. Rocking out is going to be easy for him. You going to let him pick the song?"

The girls gasped at the prissy Cosmo comment, each taking turns spouting insults at Levi as he laughed them off. Willow thought about the song selection. They usually had a set they rehearsed, but occasionally they would throw in a song or two, solely to rock the room.

"Sure, have him pick what he wants as long as you're good with it."

He rubbed his hands together and winked at the girls. She caught him glancing back at the restrooms before he walked back stage.

Willow grabbed the empty glasses, asking the girls if the needed another round as the crowd picked up in the bar. She quickly refilled their drinks as Sofia and Luna made their way back to their table. A knowing smile teased Willow's face as she placed the drink in front of Luna before she turned and walked back to the bar.

She hurried along, pulling several bottles of water and placing them on the stage for the band. She caught Wes and Beck tuning guitars and chatting over the song set list. They both gave her a nod as she walked by.

She admitted her guys in the band were hot and no doubt the reason her bar was mainly female dominated when they played, but the guys did not seem to mind and, hell, they loved the attention. Fab marketed the bar around that. It was not just their hot band. They were proud to have established a safe-haven for women to come in and hang out and have a good time with their friends. They welcomed men as well. She did not discriminate. It was just a place where more women frequented than men did.

And they were proud of that.

Willow rounded the stage and ran into an unexpected brick wall. A warm, breathing, oh so good smelling brick wall. She looked up and got lost in hazel eyes.

"Hey," he muttered. "Sorry about that. You must be Whiskey."

Say What? Mr. Oh So Smells Good knew her name.

"Uh yeah. That's me." She gulped the sudden knot in her throat. "Um, but I think you're lost. Restrooms are on the other side. Down the hall. In the back. Down the hall." Wait. She already said that. Didn't she?

She was light-headed and weightless and supercharged all at once. It made no sense other than her body short circuited and then bolted with a super nova charge. Multiple tingles and aches flooded Willow's body, shivering from their impact.

His lips fought a smile as she stared, still in a trance over his light, moss-like eyes.

"Not lost darlin'. Think you told Levi you wanted to see what I got. Not thinking you taking me to the restroom is what you had in mind. Unless, it's a dark hallway, in the back," he said in a deep, timber voice.

Oh my, whispered Halo.

Oh yeah, whispered Tails.

Still dazed and lost in his soft green eyes, Willow leaned forward, unaware she was doing it. A soft brush of his hand tucked a careless strand of her hair behind her earlobe.

"You still with me, Whiskey?" the warm breathing wall with beautiful green eyes asked softly.

Halo flapped her wings rapidly, bringing oxygen back to Willow's brain as Tails strutted around in a short red dress and spike heels.

"You're Colt?" she whispered, awareness seeping back in as his lips extended with a knowing smile. His eyes darkened.

"Hell. My name on your lips and with those eyes,

makes me want to drown in them."

Cheese and freaking rice.

Halo's wings faltered as Tails slightly bent over, showing off lacy red underwear.

"Yo, Colt, you ready?" Saved by Levi.

Her eyes drifted down to Colt's lips. He lightly licked them. The sudden flutters in her stomach and pounding heartbeat grew as he winked at her before he looked over her shoulder. "Yeah, just introducing myself here. Let's show her what I got."

His firm hands rested on her hips from their minor collision. He gently squeezed before releasing her. She turned, her eyes following his stride. She took a moment to finally catch her breath.

"Holy spicy meatballs!" Sofia's voice broke through her trance.

Halo slowly glided down on Willow's shoulder, fanning herself.

Tails snapped her fingers changing into an even shorter and more revealing dress.

Neither of them took their eyes off of Colt.

Willow turned, locking eyes with her best friend who stood with Skylar. Both stared at Colt and then back at her.

"I…I um…that…that was Colt…the new guitarist."

"For real? Here I thought he was the plumber," Skylar smirked sarcastically.

"Of course, he's not the plumber. Why would I need a plumber?"

"Cause your plumbing is still shit in this place even if the drinks, music, and Panty Dropper Band are the bomb," she snapped back.

Ugh, Mother Father plumbing! That's it. Straight

Vodka Martini's going forward, yelled Tails.
****

I'm in trouble, thought Colt, watching Whiskey stand behind the bar working orders and laughing with customers as they filed in, filling in the tables, bouncing with energy for the music to start.

People crowded the two smaller tables closer to the stage next to the Martini Girls' table, as told by his new bandmates, and along the large bay windows facing the pedestrian sidewalk near the front patio. Two large farmhouse style tables divided the bar from the bay windows, giving more seating rooms for everyone to enjoy.

The patio was lit up with white lights hanging from the great oak tree. Scattered patio furniture waited for the patronage to join their secluded hideaway. For those who preferred a more relaxed and quieter evening. Not likely known on a Friday night at Martini Girl Bar.

The bar was classy and stylish, with many of its original old charm and simplistic farmhouse furniture.

Colt had come in twice before for drinks after hours with Levi and the guys. He heard them play before and knew of Whiskey, but coming up close to the woman was a sucker punch he was not expecting.

He had never had the sudden urge to pull someone in closer and taste them like he did with Whiskey.

Her eyes.

Her lips.

His hands had tightened on her hips. Not wanting to let go. Her faint gasp and tremble were his undoing. Then she was gone, back behind that bar with those liquid amber eyes.

Yup. Deep trouble.

"You ready for this, Colt?" Wes grinned, shaking his blond hair from his man bun, letting it fall forward and anywhere it wanted. He grabbed his guitar and moved into place, causing a wild scream from the crowd as his shadow appeared on his mark on the stage.

Adrenaline pumped in Colt's veins, feeling the old habit he kicked coming back to life. It had been a while since he played live music.

When Levi had asked if Colt was interested, his first reaction was to turn it down. Levi took it in stride and told him to think about it and filled him in on what happened with Cody Mills.

Cody was a good guy. Misguided by an opportunist bitch.

A story Colt was all too familiar with.

After thinking it over, the extra cash would help with Noni's care and Lucy. It was difficult caring for a seventy-two going on twenty-seven grandmother and a four-year-old going on sixteen niece.

This gig came in at the right time.

He had called Levi back within the hour of turning it down and told him he would be there tonight.

Here Colt stood now, strumming music, soaring through his mind as he prepared to go on stage. Excitement pumping, adrenaline surging and all he could think was he wanted a shot of whiskey.

Both the drink and the woman.

"Deep, deep trouble," he muttered aloud.

"You good man?" Levi checked in, drumsticks twirling in his hands, bouncing on his heels, pumped with excitement.

"Yeah, I'm good."

"Know what song you want to start with? Gotta

queue the guys."

Without hesitating, he turned to Levi. "What she like?"

Levi stopped bouncing, still twirling his sticks, reflecting. "She's into country, doesn't mind rock. The guys and I draw the line on that pop shit."

Only Levi would know right away who Colt was referring to. "Country, rock and pop. Thanks. That narrows it down."

Levi drummed a beat on his sticks as he walked towards the stage, laughing. "You know the gig's yours, man. Wouldn't worry too much. But you want to make another type of impression then Eric Church, Luke Combs, Jimmie Allen, Chris Stapleton. That's up her alley. As are Billie Eilish and Dua Lipa if you're brave enough to pull that off," he laughed again. His drums roaring to life as the crowd's cry ripped with excitement.

Beck walked by, grabbing his Bass, pausing in front of Colt. Beck's deep voice matched his instrument. "I know what happened with your band. Know you walked away, but not before they turned their backs on you first."

"Yeah, it's ancient history Beck."

"Don't matter. Cody turned his back on us. We don't do that here. You stick with us; we got your back."

Besides Levi, Colt's friends had been his previous band, Blue Nitro. They had all turned their backs on him when he needed them the most. Levi had been angry on Colt's behalf, especially since one of the band members, Maverick, was Levi's brother. Mav had swept in and took lead guitar and Blue Nitro, leaving Colt out to dry.

An unfortunate hard lesson learned. Money talked and that's the truth.

Colt stood, stunned as Beck walked on stage, causing another tsunami of cries and cheers.

Suddenly, the song he wanted to open with slammed into him, as did his second choice. Colt walked on stage, turning to the guys, huddling close to Levi as Colt discussed his first song choice and the second. He asked Beck and Wes to move up center on the second song. Collaborating was important as a band. It took hours of endless practice and sometimes years of playing together to read and feed off of each other's vibes while playing. They only had minutes. They agreed Colt would take the lead on the first two songs and see how the crowd reacted.

While discussing the two songs, they turned as someone cleared their throat. "Are you Panty Droppers ready?"

The guys snickered. "You better go over there, man. Fab does not come out on stage till it's time for the show to start," Levi warned.

Colt turned and walked over to meet the famous hostess. "Heard a lot about you. Name is Colton Royce."

"Hmm, so you're the pistol who has Willow all up in a tither."

Chapter 3

Cobwebs

"Who's Willow?" Confused why Willow would be in a tither because of him.

"Whiskey, handsome. Now you boys ready, cause this ebony beauty wants to shine," she said, waving her hands dramatically at her sequin black pants with a black and red off the shoulder satin blouse. The blouse wrapped around her neck with an outrageous bow. She finished her look with large studded black earrings and deep red peep toe stilettos.

Colt was easily six foot two and Fab matched him at eye level. She rocked the outfit.

"We're ready Fab," confirmation coming from the guys.

"Well, alright, handsome. Let's get this show started."

She adjusted her exaggerated bow and turned. "How's my hair?" running her hand through her bald head.

Colt chuckled as he shook his head at the dynamic relationship between the band and the *Diva*.

"Blinging as always," commented Beck. "Especially with those bedazzled pants. You make those yourself?"

"Handsome the fact that the word bedazzle is in your

vocabulary would have me questioning whether or not you play for my team, but since I know you have an eleven-year-old princess who loves to sparkle and shine and you are a wonderful daddy who allows her to sparkle and shine, I'll let that one pass. But if you are ever in the market for bedazzle jeans, hot stuff, let me know and Fab will make you look Fabulous.

Colt smirked. Beck winked at Fab and took his place on stage.

"Such a shame you all are straight. Hmm. You sure you don't want to try black? You know what they say, baby."

"Jesus, Fab," muttered Levi.

"Oh hell," Colt said, laughing.

Beck's shoulders vibrated as he laughed in his corner.

Wes groaned and made his way to his spot.

"Stay here, handsome. You're new blood and need to be introduced." Colt nodded as Fab smacked her ruby red lips at him.

Fab nodded, queuing Levi. The steady beat of his drums rumbled, causing the crowd to cheer and clap along. The room vibrated with energy. The music flooded the bar in waves. Colt stood on the sidelines, anticipation rearing its way back up again. He chanced a glance past the sea of customers. Eyes locking on Whiskey. She clapped along with the crowd, encouraging them.

Her brown hair shined between the flickering lights. Her off the shoulder shirt, with the initials MGB in the front and snug jeans with red heels, were driving him crazy. Her eyes turned back to the stage and locked on his, a soft smile teasing her lips.

She faltered and recovered the rhythm, eyes never leaving his.

"Completely in trouble," he muttered under his breath.

The crowd cheered as the drums suddenly stopped. He broke the trance and watched Fab seductively strut on stage. The sounds of her heels echoed throughout the bar as she walked, posing like a runway model with the MIC above her.

"Where are my Martini Girls at tonight?" she asked the crowd.

The bar erupted with ladies cheering and clapping.

Colt's eyes rounded wide, surprised by the crowd's reaction. He looked over to the guys on stage and they all shrugged with knowing smiles. He peeked over the curtain again and glanced at Whiskey.

Pride radiated from her eyes.

"And where are my brave men at tonight?"

A sudden explosion of howls broke through the cheers with whistles and laughter.

"That's right. Now, are we here to have a good time?"

The crowd roared, "No!"

"That's right, we're not. Are we here to have an awesome time?"

They echoed again, "No," louder this time.

Colt watched with amazement as Fab hyped the crowd. Why the hell would Cody give this up?

"That's right. We are here to have the…" and suddenly the entire bar chanted in unison with Fab, "best-time-of-our-life night!"

Levi's drums pounded beat after beat, sputtering sharp punchy booms in rapid successions. The sudden strumming of Wes' guitar and Beck's bass brought in the melody everyone was familiar with to Aerosmith's, 'Dude Looks Like a Lady.'

Wes and Beck sang the lyrics, trading in between, with Levi backing up, as Fab posed and sashayed around the stage, joining in and singing the first chorus line with them.

"Martini Girl Bar, are you ready to meet The Crew tonight?"

With a resounding, "hell yeah," and whistles, Fab moved along the stage as the band rocked on.

"Give it up for your waitresses and waiters, cause without them y'all would be a bunch of thirsty people," she announced as the staff came down the front of the stage, as practiced, enticing a round of applause from the crowd. Each doing a variation of dance and tricks with their trays and posing by their sections, hyping the crowd.

Before long, Wes and Beck began singing the second verse of the song and Fab joined in on the notorious chorus of the song,

"These fellas, you don't want to mess with. Give it up for our bouncers. You get out of hand; they hand your ass out!" The two bouncers simply stood in their position, neither moving or breaking a smile causing the crowd to cheer and clap louder for them.

Fab joined in with the band again, singing while the crowd joined in. "And these ladies don't need introduction unless you plan on drinking tap water from our shitty plumbing. Give it up for our bartenders."

Colt remained mesmerized as Whiskey stood up on the bar with Lacey, both stomping their feet, twirling their hair and swinging their hips seductively as they danced to the song. "Yep, big trouble," he muttered with a smile.

"And for our source of entertainment. Our very own eye candy. Our sexy band. *The Panty Droppers*." The lights came full on the stage as the guys continued to play the song. Each giving themselves an opportunity to play a solo and show off for the crowd.

"Give it up for Levi on the drums, Wes on the guitar, and Beck on the bass."

Colt took a breath, wondering if this was how they started every night, or just Fridays. Because holy shit, this was incredibly insane and genius.

Levi had mentioned Whiskey was smart at what she was doing. Major understatement. This was brilliant.

As the song came to an end, Fab continued to play her role. "We have got a treat for you all tonight. We got fresh blood. He's a pistol."

Levi snickered.

The sudden Oh's erupted from the crowd causing a small smile to tease Colt's lips.

"Martini Girl Bar, show some love for Colton Royce."

Counting backwards from three, he steadied himself and walked on stage. With steady hands, he adjusted the MIC and looked over the cheering crowd. "Ya'll give it up for Fab, she rocked it tonight, like those sequin pants." Winning another round of applause from the bar as well as a humble, "thank you," from Fab herself.

"Alright, handsome, show Whiskey what you got," she whispered to him, and she sashayed off the stage.

He caught sight of Whiskey mixing drinks and sneaking glances his way. A soft smile teased her sweet, full lips. "I hear we have some brave men here tonight?"

This brought many cheers and howls from the men.

"Awesome. I'm gonna need your help tonight, with the ladies permission, of course," he said with a charming grin, causing several sighs. "Ask one of them to dance. You never know if she by chance is the one who hits you like a 'Wrecking Ball.'"

****

The immediate strums of Colt's guitar resounded from the speakers as he sang the lyrics of one of her favorite songs from Eric Church. It was a sensual song of a man's longing for his woman. It was country music at its finest.

Hot.

Sexy.

Needy.

Hot.

Hot.

Hot.

She loved the song. Always ached to sing it as a duet. But listening to his husky voice sing through the melody, his growl when he punched through the chorus, made her rethink that idea.

Like dropping our panties? Inquired Tails

Oh my.

His sultry voice shot right through her core as their eyes locked while he sang the lyrics slowing the melody at the end and slaying her with the last words.

A stream of cheers rose as the couples dancing all paused where they stood and clapped. Colt's eyes never broke contact with her. A soft grin teased as he winked at her.

Why did it feel like the air conditioner was not on? Were they having issues with the darn thing too? Lord, it was all sorts of hot in the bar today.

Tails, you are burning up, warned Halo, who watched Tails light up with wanton lust as she hungrily stared at Colt. *Control yourself,* Halo warned.

To Willow's surprise, Wes and Beck joined Colt at the front of the stage. Colt ripped through his guitar, strumming along to the song 'Blow'. They each took turns singing their part, feeding off each other as if they had played and rehearsed for years.

The crowd all sang along. The Martini Girls danced by their table cheering loudly, swinging their hair like an eighties rock video. Even Luna got into the song, with her hands raised above her head as she swayed on her stool. And if Luna was rocking out, then that meant the Panty Droppers were stealing panties and taking names.

Whiskey fanned herself. The air conditioner had to be broken.

Halo stared at Colt as he strummed his guitar expertly. *Oh my.*

Stand in line, growled Tails.

The second song ended. Fab came back out on stage, fanning herself dramatically. "Who needs to change their panties, because, ladies, that was hot!"

Panties are overrated, shouted Tails.

Fabulous Fab was a 'no hold back, say it how it is' Diva kind of girl and the Martini Girl Bar loved her for it. "Do we want more of our Pistol or what?"

The crowd all shouted, "Hell Yeah." In between songs, the band switched leads between the guys to sing or they called up one of the crew to sing with them.

Willow encouraged her staff to perform and have fun with it. Some pushed for a chance in the spotlight, claiming it gave them higher tips. Who was she to say no?

"Hey, Whiskey, need another round of drinks for your girls' table."

"On it, Vet."

"Your girls are drinking like fish tonight," Vet chuckled.

"I'll let you in on a little secret," she said, pulling him closer. "They're mermaids."

"I knew it," he whispered back with a sly smile.

She winked at him and loaded his tray with the citrus drink and a bottle of water for Luna, knowing she was at her max drink capacity. Willow tossed around bottles and chatted up with the customers, stealing glances at the stage. On the last song, The Panty Droppers ended with a booming bang as the lights turned off and the radio sounded through the speakers, shuffling through songs picked by the crew. People stayed on the small dance floor enjoying the music, others went out to the patios or wondered around mingling.

Fab floated around posing and taking selfies like an A-lister, making sure people tagged her and the bar on their social media accounts. She handled their social media promos, and Whiskey appreciated that. Whiskey avoided social media, which drove her girls crazy when they could not tag her on photos.

She watched her Martini Girls tease and flirt with Vet and snap pictures. Shameless hussies. Vet was their youngest recruit, at only twenty-one. He started working for her at nineteen as one of their bus-boys. Once he turned twenty-one, she moved him up to be a waiter.

Tonight was a trial period for stage tables for the boy. Busiest section. The position would replace Lizzie. Willow needed someone to take over quickly, and he had taken on the challenge. He worked alongside Trixie, working the tables, running drinks quickly, filling beer orders when needed, and placing in the cocktail requests. She discussed the partnership with Fab earlier.

"Willow, they will either work well together, or he'll bend her over and spank her by the end of the night, or they hate each other. I'm thinking about the first two."

Thus far, the first part worked out which ruled out the last one. Hopefully, any spanking would occur after hours and not in her bar.

Skylar leaned over and kissed Vet's cheeks while Harper wrapped her arms around both of them, posing for Luna as she snapped a picture. Shameless hussies. All of them.

"Mind if I grab another water?"

Colt's voice jolted her unexpectedly, causing her to fumble with the glasses she was organizing. "Shoot, uh yeah. Sorry. Do you want it cold or room temperature?"

Amusement sparkled in his eyes. "Cold if you have it."

She retrieved two bottles of ice-cold water and opened the cap of the first bottle instantly. She watched, mesmerized, as he swallowed each gulp. Why was she staring? Why couldn't she stop staring? She should turn around. There were customers that needed help.

But he might want more water after he deliciously inhales the second bottle, said Halo.

Or he might spill his water all over his white t-shirt, added Tails.

Oh my. Halo sighed.

Oh yeah, moaned Tail.

Both of you shut it!

Kill joy grumbled Tails.

Seriously, why did she argue with herself?

"Whiskey?"

"Huh?"

Colt leaned over with concern etched on his face, reaching out to tuck the stubborn strand of her fallen bangs behind her ear. "Are you alright? You seemed to be lost in thought there for a second."

Cheese and rice.

Busted, Tails teased.

"Yes," her voice came out higher than normal. She cleared her throat, trying to control herself. "Yeah I'm good. Busy tonight, you know. You guys did amazing."

Nice recovery, cheered Halo.

Colt ran his fingers through his short dark hair, holding the base of his neck as he looked around the crowd. "Yes, we did," he agreed, joining in with her, laughing. "It's been a while since I played live. Felt unbelievable. I forgot how much I miss it."

"You were in a band before?" This was news to her. Levi mentioned Colt could play but never said he was in a band.

"Long story for another night, if you're up for it."

Say yes! Say yes! We need this! He's hot. He can sing. He's charming. And he's HOT! Plus, your Netherlands have more cobwebs than a deserted attic! Tails shouted from her shoulder.

"Sure."

Happy randy devilish conscious of mine?

Not till the cobwebs are gone. Tails smirked before licking her.

****

Colt watched with fascination the expressions change on Whiskey's face. He had never met someone whose emotions displayed all over their beautiful honey eyes. Her dark hair and fair complexion made them stand out brightly. The soft splatter of freckles he noticed across the bridge of her nose teased him to touch. She was mid height; he guessed she was five foot seven, and a body full of curves.

He had learned from Levi she was three years younger than Colt's thirty-three. She had an older sister, Mila, who lived in Texas with their mom. Whiskey was close to her mom and sister and spent a lot of her time off with them. Her dad passed away when they were kids. She was loyal to her Martini Girls. Dedicated to the bar and had a pet cat name Prim who's spoiled and probably was a dog in another life.

A banshee squeal came from behind him, rushing fast as octopus arms wrapped around him, embracing him tight, causing him to spill his bottle of water. He captured a set of wandering hands from moving to a no-touch zone and turned to the women.

"Oh, my goodness. You're Colton Royce. You played with Blue Nitro."

The one with loose hands squealed and jumped up and down on her heels.

"I knew it was you. Can we get a picture?" The lady asked, posing with pouty lips alongside her friends.

He graciously smiled, keeping their hands in check with his two, all the while he glanced back at Whiskey, who eyed him curiously.

"OMG, my co-workers are going to flip."

He wrestled his way out of their grasp and felt a light hand on his shoulder.

He found Whiskey signaling him. "Jump over."

Colt slung himself over the bar, leaning far back out

of the way, letting Lacey and Whiskey work, watching them continue to fill orders. He tried to stay out of their way, observing their quick methods as they swiftly grabbed bottles and freely poured rations of its contents into shakers or straight into glasses. Stir and shake another glass, begin another drink, or return glasses to the washing racks for cleaning. Lacey passed along an order to Whiskey, asking for a trade. Lacey came back to grab a row of shot glasses, rimming them with lime and salt, pouring chilled shots of Tequila into the glasses.

"What did you trade her with?" he asked, curious why someone would switch their drink order.

"It's a specialty martini. Whiskey does those. I always screw them up," Lacey said with a shrug of her shoulder.

Fascinated, he watched Whiskey grab a fancy martini glass with double stems intertwined. She wet the rim and dipped it in red sugar. She then, thinly, layered a circle of fudge all around the base of the glass, creating a tornado of chocolate. Lastly, she poured the hot pink concoction into the glass and adorned it with white chocolate shavings. She turned towards him and froze.

"You forgot I was here," he stated.

"Sorry about that. Things are a little busy and we're short a server tonight."

She reached past him and grabbed one of the cleaned bar knives and handed off the Red Velvet Cake Martini. He took a chance and gently reached for her arm, pulling her around.

"What can I help with?"

Their eyes locked. He pulled her closer. Her scent flooded his senses. He pulled her even closer. Her gaze lowered to his lips. She was feeling this as much as he was. Still, he pulled her closer. He inhaled deeply, drowning in her honey eyes. Eyes darkening and beckoning.

"Hell, Whiskey. You can't look at me like that. Not when we have an audience."

"Whiskey?"

Colt pulled back slightly. Their trance broken by the unwanted intruder.

"Got a large order, and Lacey is up to sing."

Colt reluctantly let Whiskey go slowly.

"On it, Nate. Lacey, go. I got this," Whiskey said to a smirking Lacey.

"What do you need me to do?" he asked again, groaning as Whiskey shyly bit her lower lip.

"Think you can pour a few beers for me and slice some limes?"

His eyes dropped to her lips and came back to her eyes. "Yeah darlin'. I can do that."

Before she walked away, he pulled her fully flushed against him, feeling every soft curve against his. "This is not over."

Chapter 4

Plumbing and Hickeys

Drip.
Drip.
Drip.

The sound echoed throughout her apartment a little after five in the morning. Her friends had slowly trekked their way to her apartment at one in the morning to spend the night, calling dibs on the guest room and pull-out sofa. Sofia raced to the master bedroom, collapsing on the bed, not bothering to remove her clothes as she kicked her shoes off and curled to her side, passing out. Luna grabbed the recliner in the living room, quickly changing, removing her makeup, brushing her long brown locks and placing her face mask over her eyes, snuggling into her plush blanket.

Skylar and Piper took the pull-out sofa next to Luna's chair, fussing over the blanket and making their plains to steal Luna's. Harper took the guest bedroom with Zoila. Willow left them behind and went back down to the bar.

As her friends settled in above her, Willow finished closing the bar and made her way to her room by two in the morning, quickly stripping down to boy shorts and a tank top and curling to her side of the bed, slowly pushing Sofia, the petite bed-hogger, over.

She thought of Colt, and his longing looks as they worked together while Lacey did her song sets. The casual way he had brushed alongside her when he reached out for beer glasses, or passed her bottles for drink orders he was familiar with. He even assisted with making simple drinks and poured out a few shots.

After Lacey returned, he'd stocked up their garnish center and cleaned up the area. He organized the clean glasses, restocking them in their rows and placed the dirty dishes in the power wash dishwasher and ran a cycle for them. Shortly after, he walked past her. He slid his hand on her lower back and added a little pressure as he leaned in close.

"Got to get going, darlin'." The promise in his eyes as he'd left had Halo blushing and Tails primping for when he returned.

Drip.
Drip.
Drip.
Ugh!
Stupid plumbing.

Quietly walking out of the bedroom, she checked the bathroom's faucets, then checked her half bath.

Nothing wrong there.

She checked the kitchen, noticing the sink dripping. She tightened the faucet and stopped the annoying melody. Her arms stretched above her head. She looked over at her friends sleeping in the living room. Skylar and Piper had a fuzzy warm blanket resembling Luna's. Willow snickered and bit her lip to quiet down. She quietly walked over to a trunk, used as a coffee table, and pulled out an extra fuzzy blanket, laying it over Luna.

"Those heifers stole my blanket," she whispered

sleepily. She burrowed deeper under her new warm blanket. "Thank you, Willow."

"I'll pour vodka in their coffee for breakfast."

Willow covered her mouth as Luna cheered quietly, "Yes" and turned over and fell back to sleep.

A low rumbling sound turned Willow's attention back to the kitchen.

What was that?

A dread filled sigh escaped her.

The bar.

Willow raced back to the room and grabbed an excessively large St. Augustine Lighthouse sweatshirt, zipping it up over her tank top and boy shorts.

Luna's head popped up, with one eye peeking from under her mask. "Willow, what the bloody hell?" she whispered yelled.

"I'll be back. I have to check out the bar."

"Now?" more whisper yelling.

'The plumbing," was all she stated, catching the one eye roll back before it hid behind the mask and under the blanket.

Willow loved this old house.

Adored it.

But the plumbing sucked big hairy balls.

It was in the budget for a full make over this year and, of course, the old girl could not wait for it to happen. The noise rattled louder as she walked inside the bar.

Cheese and rice, had it only been three hours since she was here?

The obscene clock hanging on the wall blared in bright red light 5:15 a.m. She sneered and flicked it off as she walked past the stage and behind the bar.

Everything seemed to be quiet there. She made her

way into the kitchen and turned the faucet on and off. She walked behind the bar, checked the small faucet and dish washer.

Then a sudden rumbling and clattering startled her.

She stomped angrily back across the hallway, flicking the clock off again as it stated 5:21 a.m. and made her way to the bathrooms.

There, the noise grew louder and louder in the hallway. She practically kicked the men's door open.

Nothing.

She slit her eyes and took a deep breath through her nose. She pushed opened the women's bathroom. There, a mini Old Faithful made its appearance from the sink. The toilet rumbled as blue water splattered and sputtered from the closed lid, dripping down the white porcelain façade, staining the seat and white tiles.

"Great," she raced towards the mini sink geyser, slipping along the way in her cotton slippers. Willow prayed a toilet geyser would not erupt. Who wanted to deal with blue Clorox water all over them at five in the morning? Or anytime for that matter.

"Oh, my goodness, Willow," Luna cried out from behind her.

"Can you turn off the water below or hold this here and I'll turn it off?"

Luna raced over in her satin pink pajamas blouse and shorts, eye mask pulled over her head as a headband, as she crawled under the sink, searching for the valve to shut the water off.

"Which way do I turn it?" she squealed as cold water flowed over the sink all down her backside. "Bloody hell. This water is cold."

Whiskey sputtered water as the sink continued to

water board her. "Lefty-loosey. Righty-tighty," she told her.

"What?"

"Lefty-loosey. Righty-tighty," she yelled again.

"What?" screaming with confusion, Luna pulled her head from the sink staring wide-eyed at her tortured friend.

"Turn the valve to the right for the love of humanity."

"Then just bloody say that," Luna snapped back, quickly climbing back under the sink cabinet and turning the valve. Once they shut down their geyser, they stood, studying the surrounding mess.

Willow prayed the toilet would not blow up on them.

"Christ. What happened and how can I join in the action?"

Luna's eyes bulged from their eye sockets at the sound of Levi's voice.

They both slowly turned. Two hard and fast breathing hot brick walls stared at them amusingly.

Willow dipped her chin down, silently fidgeting and squirming. Luna crossed her arms over her sheer and soaked pajama top and raised her head high, wiping water from her face, arching her eyebrow.

"The plumbing is crap, and we fixed it. If you'll excuse me," Luna haughtily replied, rushing past an amused Levi.

"What are you two doing here?" Willow asked, surveying the mess nervously, avoiding Colt's hazel eyes.

"Left my keys for the shop here," Levi replied, shrugging his shoulders carelessly as he walked down the hall towards the office where the employee's lockers were, leaving her alone with Colt.

Willow swallowed the sudden edginess she felt as Colt's eyes wandered over her, appraising her slowly. His eyes leisurely moved from her ballet slippers, up her recently shaved legs (thank goodness), to her soaked thin gray sweatshirt.

Slowly, he moved away from the entryway and prowled towards her. His dark charcoal T-shirt with darker wet spots on some other areas captured her attention.

"Did you get attacked by a possessed sink too?" she joked as he stood in front of her, his usually light green eyes dark. His brown hair was wind-blown. Oh man, his five o'clock shadow looked delightful.

Delish, chimed in her newly awakened hellion.

"We were running this morning," he stated, leaning closer, trapping her against the still wet counter, his hands on each side of her.

"Running?" she questioned. "You mean, for fun?"

He rubbed his nose against hers teasingly. Her breath caught. "Tell me you're wearing something more underneath this sweatshirt."

She closed her eyes, feeling breathless. Why was it hot in here again? "I've got stuff underneath."

"Stuff?" His hands looped behind her lower back.

A sudden shiver came over her. "Uh, I...uh...should go upstairs and change."

"Go out with me, Whiskey."

Yes. Yes. Yes, chanted Tails.

Desperate much? Halo snarked back

Ugh, the two of you are driving me to drink.

He pressed her closer. Her hands lay casually on his

chest. A sure sign her little devil took over her better judgment and had taken matters into her own hands.

His heart beat steadily. His chest rose and fell with each breath. She leaned forward, closing her eyes, unsure of what to do. His warm breath on her neck sent a delicious chill through her body as he teased her skin with his lips. "Say yes, baby," he whispered in her ear.

Willow pulled back. Eyes locking with his, lowering to his lips, staying a little longer. A soft gasp echoed from the entry way followed by a: "Is he going to kiss her?", "What? Who's kissing?", "You two are in the way. Let me see."

He groaned in frustration.

She peered over his shoulder at their nosy intruders. Skylar smirked while Zoila smiled shyly. Sofia shoved her head between their bodies, peeking through with her raccoon eyes.

"Girl, I'm going to tell you the same thing I told Luna with Levi. Just kiss the man so we can get some sleep," retorted Skylar.

Yes, kiss him. I want some tongue hockey. Tails grinned.

"Someone kill me," Willow said and face-planted in Colt's warm chest.

His hands cupped her face, bringing her eyes back up to his. "Let me help you clean up. I have to head out as soon as Levi gets his keys."

Reluctantly, they pulled away from each other and cleaned up the mess in the bathroom. He finished hanging the, 'Out of Order' sign on the door as Luna made her way back down in leggings and a Martini Girl Bar T-shirt. Her hair was pulled up high in a messy wet bun, her lips were swollen, and there was a love bite on her neck. Levi trailed behind with a Cheshire smile.

"Ready, Colt?"

Willow followed them out the door, stopping Colt. Levi called out his salutations and a specific, "Later, Love," to Luna, who ignored him and his chuckles.

What the what?

Colt turned. His head slightly tilted.

"Yes," she said simply, caught up in his smile before he pulled his phone out for her number.

He has such perfect pearly white teeth, said Halo.

Right because that's exactly what we noticed first about him, mocked Tails.

"I'll call you later, darlin'," he said with a wink, before he ran and caught up to Levi.

Ugh, so close, whined Tails.

Indeed, they were. The chemistry between her and Colt was nuclear. He was charming in a southern bad boy kind of way, with his devilish smirk and twinkling eyes. The rugged shadow of his beard and messy, dark brown hair attracted her even more. Not to mention he was tall, had nicely toned arms, and played the guitar that made any woman's kitty-cat feel envious. A definite panty change.

Let him play with ours! Tails whined.

Besides his mastery hand skills and boyish sexy-as-sin charms, she knew very little about him. She knew he had played in a band previously. Intrigued, she had looked up Blue Nitro during her break and discovered Maverick Reginald was the lead singer and guitar player. He was also Levi's older estranged brother. Willow wondered if Colt was part of the reasons the brothers' didn't talk. Or maybe there was a conflict over who would lead the band and that's why Colt was no longer with them. And it upset Maverick that Levi sided with Colt? Or maybe Colt honestly was a better player than Maverick, and that's why he's out of the band? Or maybe...

Or maybe you're fishing for something to be wrong with him when he's a perfect specimen of a man who can fiddle with our kitty and dust out the cobwebs. Give over sister. Halo and I have agreed. We're keeping him.

She noted arguing with herself was hard work, tiresome, and overwhelming.

Then stop. We win!

Cheese and rice.

Luna's arm intertwined with hers. Both still stared out the door at the men, who had muddled their brains, now recreationally jogging away. Seriously, who did that?

Both were lost in their own thoughts.

"You two have some serious explaining to do. Spill it," demanded an annoyed Sofia. Her black shoulder length hair was in disarray from her wild sleep. No one would share a bed with Sofia. As petite as she was, Sofia was a kicker, slapper, in your-personal-space-all-night, steals-your-sheets-and-pillow and possibly-knocks-you-off-the bed kind of sleeper. In other words, she was a five foot two tornado with crazy bed hair and raccoon eyes.

Willow faced the firing squad, wishing the bathroom would erupt again. She was pretty sure Luna was hoping for the same, since she picked at her immaculate clean shirt, ignoring the curious glares.

"Uh, hello? What's up with the hot tatted bodacious Levi and Southern Sexy Man Pistol?" Sofia grilled them in rapid successions of questions, stopping only to catch a breath before firing more questions.

"Oh, alright already," conceded Luna, tossing her hands up in surrender. She recounted the events quickly. Winded after her fast response, redness slowly crept up her neck, brightening her cheeks. Unable to meet anyone's eyes, she continued. "As you can see, Colt assisted with the cleanup. *El Fin*."

Willow agreed and nodded, hoping Sofia would accept the explanation and Luna's attempt to poor attempt use the little bit of Spanish she had learned over the years with Sofia. Unfortunately, as Luna stood to walk past them, a swift Sofia jumped in front of blocking her.

"Oh no, *mija*. No, *el fin*. You don't get to avoid every question I asked."

"I did not!"

"You sure did, girlie," agreed Skylar with a nodding Zoila.

"The both of you buggar off."

"No can do. If you would have kissed him when I told you, which was before Sofia woke up, you would not be in this position in the first place," proclaimed Skylar.

Willow's poor friend's irritation exuded, with hands tossed high in the air, seeking divine intervention.

We are not helping her. Yet, warned Tails.

You are right. One girl at a time, agreed Halo.

"Fine. He kissed me. Happy?," conceded Luna.

"Clearly," Sofia retorted.

"I want to know how long have you been sneaking around? When did it start? Did he use tongue? Does he taste as good as he looks? Was it a slow kiss or a toe curling I need to change my panties kiss?"

Sighing with defeat, a dreamy look passed over

Luna.

Poor Luna. She didn't stand a chance against Sophia.

"Well, as you all know, Levi has been forthcoming since the beginning and, well, he's progressed."

"And?" Sofia's eyes bulged.

"And...he's quite the flirt. Talks a good game."

"And?" they all said simultaneously, persisting.

Flustered, Luna raised her hand and ran it through her hair, forgetting it was up in a messy pony bun, getting her fingers tangled. "And...he tastes divine, and I already changed my panties this morning."

"I knew it," whispered Sofia, pulling out the nearest barstool.

Willow walked behind the bar. "Coffee or Mimosas?"

A choir of Mimosas sounded as Skylar, Luna, and Zoila grabbed stools next to a sad Sofia.

"I miss toe curling kisses," she whined.

Willow grabbed the flutes and mixed orange juice with a splash of cranberry and champagne. Each solemn friend clinked their glass and muttered a cheer.

Willow leaned against the bar, savoring her drink, ignoring the silent warning signs going off in her head.

"Oh, you didn't think I'd forget about you and Colt?" Sofia asked, turning to face Willow.

She inhaled the rest of her liquid courage. "Nothing happened. Besides, he works for me."

"Uh no, *mija*. He does not work for you. First, he's filling in till you find a permanent replacement. Second, that up against the counter moment did not look like nothing. Last, both of you were eye sexing all night. Seriously, it was like watching Jensen and Danneel on the red carpet together."

"Eye sexing?" asked Willow, amused.

"Yes," Sofia replied sternly. "It's too early for me to be crass. I'm keeping it classy since we're having mimosas."

"Whose Jensen and Danneel?" asked Skylar.

Willow, Sofia, Zoila and Luna gasped. "*¿Què?* You don't know Dean Winchester and his absolutely, totally bodacious I-hate-her-guts because she's so beautiful, and has great red hair sometimes, wife, Danneel?"

"No, Sofia. I don't know them."

"No puedo contigo."

Willow bit her lower lip and Luna snorted unladylike.

"Is someone going to translate and tell me who the hell they are so we can move on?"

"I said I cannot deal with you."

Willow raised her hand quieting Sofia. "Dean Winchester is a character from Supernatural. His real name is Jensen Ackles. Danneel is his wife."

"And the bloke is bloody hot," Luna stated with a hiccup.

"So is his wife," Zoila confirmed.

Sofia groaned miserably. "I wish I could hate her, but I can't. I follow her on social media and she is one of the coolest people on the planet. Plus, they have the cutest babies. And," she said, raising her hand in Skylar's face, "we don't put down other women. We support them. We lift them up. We celebrate them. We—"

"Yeah, yeah, I get it," mumbled Skylar, downing her drink. "So Willow here was doing the same thing with Colt? Eye-sexing. Like they do. You little freak."

It was abundantly clear Sofia's sexual deprivation

had divested her of any common sense. They made all efforts not to laugh and successfully failed. The girls all spewed their mimosas.

"Don't worry, Willow, she's just giving you a hard time. My cousin has been keeping a secret. She's been getting sexy messages all night from detective Fernando Padron," snitched Zoila.

"Wait, What? Are you freaking kidding me? You kept in touch with him?" Willow asked.

"Uh duh. You would know this if you would join the rest of society on social media. We follow each other. He likes my posts and pictures. He's even said he would like to come up and hang out."

Her best friend truly sucked big hairy balls. She had been holding out this whole time. What the H...E...double hockey sticks.

"Why didn't you tell me?"

She shrugged her shoulders shyly and lowered her head to the bar table. Sadness crossed over her eyes.

"I like him. Like, *really* like him, but he won't go there with me. The distance, he said, it's too far."

Skylar wrapped her arm around Sofia, pulling her close as Willow leaned over the bar and held Sofia's hands.

"Hey, no crying allowed at the bar," she quietly spoke.

A smile broke over Sofia's face as she leaned up and scrubbed away the tears and mascara staining her cheeks.

"How do I look?"

Willow shook her head at Sofia's seesaw emotions and looked over at Zoila, who remained quiet while Sofia confessed her crush. The worried glances made her wonder if the crush was more than Sofia had led on.

"We need a weekend getaway," Willow impulsively said.

"Hell yeah," cheered Skylar. "Let's do it. I can escape for a few days."

"I'm sure I can put time off at the bank," confirmed Luna.

"I'm flexible, so I'm in," chimed Sofia.

"I have this weekend off if you want to go, or I can switch my time with another nurse for another weekend. Let me know," assured Zoila.

Excited about their plans, they agreed to leave Saturday and return on Tuesday. This gave everyone time to make the arrangements and, as Sofia put it, 'give them time to pack.' To which they all started some social media chat without Willow with hash tags like #inserteyeroll #needsaweektopackforthreedays #divamuch.

"You know you're all going to be thinking about what to pack for the next few days and you can thank me for giving you time for the preparation." Waving her flute glass, Sofia demanded, "Fill her up!"

"You lush," Willow teased.

"Why thank you, *mija*. Very nice of you to notice," she mocked, grabbing her disheveled hair and posing in her wrinkled clothes from the night before.

"You know, you look like an absolute train wreck," Skylar admitted.

"Uh duh. But at least I'm a spicy train wreck," Sofia winked seductively. "Cheers ladies. To toe curling kisses, panty changes, hot dates," pointing suggestively at Willow, "and a fun weekend."

"Oh, come on. What did we miss?" cried out Piper, slowly dragging in a half-asleep Harper.

Sofia quickly recapped them with her supersonic, no breath needed, Telenovela, dramatic replay of the morning.

"Opening Scene: Sink blows up," she stated, whipping her body around the stool flinging her arms out. "Luna and Willow race to save the ladies restroom from the horrors of its raging waters. They're both miserably drenched and cold."

Skylar and Zoila join in with, "ta, ta, taaaa."

"Enter Levi and Colt to rescue the damsels in the distress. Luna escapes the wanton looks of Levi only to be snared by his arms and ravished in a toe-curling kiss, leaving her with a love bite to remember him by." Sofia placed her hand over her forehead, as she leans into Luna, swaying dramatically. Luna fought the smile teasing her lips and she pushed Sofia off and grabbed her drink.

Sofia balanced herself upright and climbed on the bar, crawling on all fours towards Willow. She wrapped her arms around Willow, pulling her into a hug with an award worthy performance. "Leaving Willow alone with Colt and his uncontrollable hunger." She clutched Willow's face, making it pucker in a childlike fashion and wiggled her eyebrows. "They continue to eye-sex each other," roughly she shoved her face back into her chest and hugged her closely, "Until she gives in and agrees to go out with him."

Sofia stood up on the bar and lowers her head dramatically. "End scene."

They rewarded Sofia with loud obnoxious whoops and whistles, clapping loudly.

Harper and Piper stared at each other, unsure of what to say. "What in the world? How long have you all been up?" Harper asked in wonderment.

They stared at the obscene, blaring red lights of the clock. Willow noted the time, 6:14 a.m. "One hour," she stated.

They each turned and faced the clock and flicked it off. Why? Because that's what awesome girlfriends did.

Chapter 5

Pink Exits and Indoor Tornado

Colt arrived home, quietly opening the door. He removed his running shoes in the mud-room and hung his keys on the fish hooks made specifically for his keys. Everyone in the house knew Colt was prone to losing his keys. It wasn't that he didn't think they were not important. The issue was Noni would grab them and place them in an undisclosed location just to piss him off. His grandmother pulled some pretty crafty pranks in her golden age and taking his keys when they were not in the safety zone as she described it was one of them.

Among other things.

Like hacking his phone and snapping pictures of her posing with her cronies (again her words) with their duck faces.

He loved his grandmother. Her spirit and live-life-to-the-fullest attitude was what he believed kept her going strong. That or the fact her pink hair gave her some secret magic powers.

Add his four-year-old niece, who was a reincarnated mini version of his Noni, would both outlive him.

The smell of fresh buttery biscuits assaulted the air from the kitchen. The sounds of a tiny pounding stampede echoed upstairs above the kitchen, followed by heavy strokes racing down the stairs. Preparing for the attack, he crouched down, bracing for the tiny misfit heading his way. The little misfit flew through the kitchen door, jumped into his arms, giggling loudly midair.

"Uncle Colt. Uncle Colt. Guess what?"

Each time he looked into her sea-green eyes with her long lashes, he melted into a puddle of putty. She reminded him of his sister and of the times life could be cruel as well as rewarding.

"What is it, honey bear?" He called her honey bear after Lucy's favorite cartoon character.

"Noni is going to put pink exits in my hair to match her."

Not liking where this was going, because any idea with Noni was never a good thing and anything relating to color was definitely not good.

Last time, Noni got a Henna tattoo on herself with her cronies and they ended up getting washable tattoos for Lucy. Of course, they did not mention it was washable. She told *him* it was a legitimate Henna which caused him a coronary attack, high blood pressure, and a migraine that lasted three days.

It then followed up with changing Lucy's room from a soft taupe color to rainbow bright colors because every little girl needed to have color in her room and glitter walls. Which had to be followed up with changing the carpets because the cronies did the master craft glitter project themselves and did not cover the carpet floors appropriately.

There were still remnants of glitter fluttering around the house till this day from a project done six months ago.

"What do you mean pink exits?"

"Extensions, honey. Extensions. Don't worry, Colt, they're detachable."

Right on time. Cue in the pink hair misfit.

"Good morning, honey," she said, giving him an affectionate squeeze on his shoulder.

"There're fresh biscuits and honey in the pantry."

"Is that why there're biscuits?" he asked, still holding onto his little smiling rebel with butterfly lashes.

"Oh no you don't. You don't get to flutter your pretty little eyes at me, honey bear. Not this time." The little deviant held on tight, giggling as he struggled to place her on the floor. He looped her around towards his back, walking over to the cabinet to grab the honey and a fresh biscuit.

"Can I get one too, Uncle Colt?" she asked sweetly.

"No, you little deviant fairy," he teased.

Still giggling, she wiggled her way up his back, partly choking him till she was hanging on piggyback style. "Please, Uncle Colt?"

He poured honey over the sliced biscuit and brought it up to give her a bite, only to pull it away and take a bite of it himself.

"Hey that's mean," she pouted.

"No, what's mean is you trying to con me into getting pink extensions with your pretty green eyes and sweet Uncle Colts."

Her tiny arms hugged his neck tighter, choking him while he tried to swallow the biscuit. "Please, Uncle Colt. It's only for the summer. Pretty please."

I'm in so much trouble. He dropped the biscuit on the counter and looped her back around staring into her eyes. "You want this, honey bear?"

Her little brown locks bobbed up and down

enthusiastically. He looked at Noni, who was secretly smiling behind a cup of coffee that said, 'Noni always wins.' "How much is this going to cost?"

"Nothing for you. I bought them at the store for kids. They're hair clips you can clip on and off. They're not real extensions, Colt. That's absurd. You can't possibly think I would put real extensions on a four-year-old," she said, insulted.

"Wouldn't put it past you," he muttered. Leaning his head against Lucy, "Alright, honey bear. Pink exits it is."

She wrapped her little arms around Colt's neck and squeezed tightly. He leaned down and put her on the floor, smiling into her emerald eyes. Completely lost himself in them, thinking of his sister, Clover, Lucy swiped his other biscuit and took a bite out of it, racing away from the kitchen.

"Why you little…"

"And you fold, like a cheap suitcase," mocked Noni.

Hands on his hips, he shook his head, conned by a four-year-old. Man, he was a sucker for his niece. Like he was for her mother.

He missed her.

"That little girl has you wrapped around her tiny little pinky finger tight, you can't seem to unwind yourself from her will," laughed Noni. "What fun I'm going to have with her."

"Keep it up and I'm shipping you to a home," he threatened teasingly.

"You wouldn't dare, Colt," lowering her cup of coffee, the worried lines crinkling the corner of her eyes. "You know I wouldn't survive a day in one of those places. You can't do that to me. Oh, the horror," she cried out dramatically, laying a hand over her forehead and the other over her heart, giving an award winning performance.

Colt grumbled and grabbed the rest of his one-sided biscuit and polished it off. He reached for a second one, peering behind him as the sound of a beguiling little fairy floated through the kitchen. He narrowed his eyes and searched for the little deviant, pointing a warning finger at Noni, who raised her hands.

Quietly, he slid behind the kitchen door, patiently waiting for his niece.

She slowly crawled in, placing a tiny finger over her lips, communicating with Noni to remain silent as Lucy slowly crab crawled into the kitchen. Noni pretended to silence her lips and throw away the key, continuing to drink her coffee.

As soon as Lucy made her way past the door, Colt reached down and grabbed her, throwing a laughing Lucy into the air.

"I've gotcha, you little thieving fairy."

Noni laughed and rinsed her coffee cup out and placed the biscuits on a plate.

Colt split the biscuit and gave Lucy his other half as he sat her on the counter, still holding her hostage. "That's all you are getting. Bread and Honey."

"That's the best jailbait food ever!"

Choking on the bread, he looked at his niece.

Where did she learn these things?

"Jailbait? Where'd you hear that?"

Her soft smile over the biscuit in her mouth answered his question.

He looked over and caught Noni trying not to laugh.

"What?" she asked innocently. "It was on a TV show we watch."

"Which TV show?"

"A funny one."

"How about we avoid watching shows with jailbait as the subject matter and instead watch that fairy movie again while I'm out?"

"Excuse me? You're going out again tonight?" Noni questioned.

"I had to work yesterday, which you are aware of." He wasn't sure if he wanted to fill her in, but knew she would find out either way. "And I have a date tonight." One he was looking forward to.

"You have a date? With who? Where did you meet her? Do I know her?" questioned Noni.

"Is she pretty? Does she like fairies?" wondered Lucy.

"Alright, alright," grabbing Lucy, he safely lowered her from the counter. She raced to Noni, who quickly sat down at their small dining table and pulled Lucy onto her lap.

Both patiently waited for his answer.

He groaned. "I met her last night. She's one of the owners of the Martini Girl Bar. " He glanced at Noni, dreading the look in her matching sparkling hazel eyes that resembled his.

She was planning.

Shit.

"She's beautiful, Lucy. I'll ask her tonight if she likes fairies."

"Ask her, Uncle Colt. It's a deal breaker if she doesn't like them," she said, slicing her arms across the air making her point.

"How do you know what a deal breaker is?"

"I watch TV, Uncle Colt. I learns lots of stuff."

Jesus, I'm in so much trouble.

****

Tornado.

A freaking F10 Tornado blasted through the closet doors and tossed all of Willow's clothes onto the floor, bed, dresser, and every other space it could find, all while she searched for something to wear.

She looked at herself in the mirror, shuffling between her off the shoulder Pink Floyd retro T-shirt or a silk peep-hole deep purple blouse.

Decisions, decisions.

You look beautiful in anything you wear, encouraged Halo.

You want to impress him? Open the door in a pair of stilettos, a la nude, suggested Tails.

Willow ignored her inner voices and tossed both blouses on the bed. She pulled out a silver halter top and a gray baggie t-shirt with a cutout of a heart. She would need to rock her neon pink strapless with the gray shirt. She waffled between the two shirts again. The heck with it. She ran over to the closet and tripped over her discarded towel and turned over hamper.

Wretched tornado.

In a hurry, she found her black wedges, juggled on her feet as she put them on. She reached into her drawer and found her neon pink strapless, resembling a bikini top. She snapped it into place and threw the gray t-shirt over. Side to side, she turned and watched the cutout show off the pink bra and some decent cleavage. Satisfied with the look, she grabbed her brush and dried her hair, flipping the ends out, giving her hair some sort of body.

Her recent highlights shined bright in the bathroom

light. Pleased with her hair and outfit, she quickly grabbed her minimal cosmetic bag and finished her look with a soft smoky eye and pink lip gloss.

Earlier in the morning, Sofia had grabbed her phone. She found out that Colt had sent her message after Willow had given her number. His message was a simple, 'now you have my number too.'

"Text him. Tell him you'll meet him today," Sofia had urged. After downing three mimosas, Willow's liquid courage provided her enough gusto to text him.

Willow—*Want to get together today around 3?*—

After hitting send, her courage faded to the ultimate 'what did I do' moment. Epic freak out mode. "Great, he's going to think I'm desperate!"

"Uh, no way. He's into you," Sofia continued encouraging her decision.

Her phone had beeped shortly after with his reply.

Colt—*I'll pick you up at 3*—

Which upped her epic freak out mode to Def-Con-Five in two point five seconds.

Her place was a disaster. She had cleaned up the bed, completed her two loads of laundry, and vacuumed the rooms. After mopping the floors and getting the house smelling like a lemon grove, she'd looked at the time and saw it was quickly reaching 1:00 p.m. Proud she was on time, she'd taken a shower, washed her hair, shaved many areas, because, hey, you never know. Once she made it to her closet, she had frozen. "Oh, my God. I have nothing to wear!"

Hence the F10 massive Tornado leaving her bedroom in utter chaos.

The clock now read two fifty-five with Prim buried beneath an avalanche of clothes, her long tail swishing from underneath. "Prim, come on, girl. Let's get you fed." The sudden movement of clothes rustled around her bed till a furry head peaked from under her blouses and covers. "Meow."

"I know. Mommy's freaking out." Willow cooed to her fur baby, and carried Prim to the living room, closing her bedroom door and containing the unnatural disaster.

They walked together to the kitchen pantry where she kept Prim's food and poured it into her bowl where it stated, 'I'm the princess in this house.' One last rub down, Willow looked down and made sure no cat hair clung to her clothing before she washed her hands.

She blew out the candle on the kitchen counter and prepared her small clutch purse. The sudden sounds of heavy footsteps outside her door caused her to pause.

With shaky hands she smoothed her hair down and inhaled a calming breath.

Her heart fluttered.

She waited.

The confident, solid knock on the other end of the door beckoned to be opened. She licked her lips.

Breathe, Willow, reminded Halo, fluttering her wings.

Tails remained unusually quiet.

She unlocked her side and opened the door.

Oh my! Halo fell back.

Oh, hell yes! Tail stood up on her other shoulder.

"Hi," Willow said breathlessly. Her eyes drifted over him. The shadow of his beard gave him a rugged aura. His dark brown hair, still moist from his recent shower, glistened in the sun. His green eyes shone brightly against the charcoal button-down shirt paired with dark denim jeans and black biker boots.

Deep breath, Willow, Halo whispered.

A slow smile teased Colt's lips, tempting her to no end. A shiver coursed through her as his eyes appraised her from head to toe.

He keeps staring at us like that and we're going to need a change of panties, moaned Tails.

"Um, let me get my purse."

They definitely needed to go.

"Yeah, but first." Powerful arms snaked around Willow's waist, pulling her flush against him. A slight gasp escaped her lips. His soft green eyes darkened with anticipation.

She licked her lips.

His eyes lowered.

She threaded her fingers through his hair, and he captured her lips. Slowly, tasting for the first time. His lips were warm and smooth. Her soft sigh allowed access for his tongue to teasingly slide against her lips. She opened for him. The hint of mint teased her tongue.

Willow locked her arms around him tighter, as he slowly backed her up against the door's edge, deepening the kiss. One of his hands reached over, running through her hair, the other feeling its way down her back, pulling her closer.

Heaven.

She was sure she had found heaven in his kiss.

Slowly he pulled away, ending the kiss, and leaned his head against hers. "I needed that."

It appeared Halo and Tails were short-circuited.

Utterly silenced.

So was she.

"Ready to go, darlin'?"

Still not able to compile words together, she nodded

and made an incoherent noise while grabbing her clutch purse. Amusement sparkled in his eyes. They locked her door and walked down the stairs. He held her hand. A new experience for Willow. She was sure she rocked a goofy smile all the way down.

He opened the door to his black truck. She slid her shaky hand against the softness of the leather, enjoying the feel, slowing down the rushing impulses and shock waves thundering around in her body. Spurts of lemon and fresh clean pine drifted through the cab. In the back was a child's booster seat buckled securely with a fairy doll sitting inside.

He reached over the center console and grabbed her hand, rubbing his thumb over hers as he drove them out of the alley and into the main street, staying connected to her. "You like seafood?"

Her eyes brightened with pleasure. She loved seafood.

"Yes."

"Portside Grill sound good?"

"I love that place."

"Me too," his smile widened in approval, carefully maneuvering through traffic and crossing the Lion's Bridge.

The warm weather brought many tourists out into St. Augustine with its historical sites, trolley rides, and ghost tours. It filled shops and restaurants with walking traffic. Crossing the bridge usually brought its challenges with traffic but when traveling in a car with working A/C, it didn't seem so bad.

They found parking and walked over and secured a table outside near the water. Colt sat on the same side of the bench with her, placing an arm around her shoulder as they scanned the water on the marina. Boats sailed in and out of the docks. Pelicans and seagulls flew around in search of fresh catch the fishermen unloaded.

"Hi, I'm David. I'll be your server today. What can I get you?"

"You want a drink? Appetizer?" Colt asked.

Shyly, she responded, ordering a frozen drink, keeping it light and simple while Colt ordered a draft beer.

"If you can provide me with your IDs, I will put these in for you," he said, checking their licenses. "Any appetizers?"

"You pick," he stated, looking to her.

"Conch fritters?"

His eyes drifted down to her lips and back up, warming all of her insides. "Sure, darlin'," he murmured.

After their ID's were handed back, their waiter disappeared with their order. Colt placed his arm back around her shoulder, pulling her into his side.

Warm.

Safe.

How could this feel right so soon? It scared her.

"So…" she started, hearing him chuckle.

"So…" he replied.

She turned slightly in his arms, tipping her head to the side. "You have a kid?"

His face remained neutral. Willow worried she may have overstepped. Although she hoped she had not. She was a rip-the-band-aid kind of girl and got to the point of things. Might as well get through the hard part.

Their waiter arrived with their drinks rather quickly and placed them on the table. "Your conch fritters should be out shortly. Would you like to order now or wait till after they are out?"

"We'll wait till after," Colt replied, dismissing him. He took a sip of his beer and nodded. "A little girl. Four years old. Lucy. Part of that long conversation I told you about."

Halo swooned and Tails remained quiet, sending Willow silent interrogation questions, most of which she ignored.

"That's a fun age. I know Beck's daughter is eleven. She's a blast to hang out with." Not sure how to ask the next question, she took a sip from her drink. "Do you and her mom still keep in touch? I mean, obviously you do, since you share a kid together. I just meant—"

"She's my niece," he cut her off.

"Oh." See, this was why she did not listen to the little devil on her shoulder.

"Like I said, part of that long conversation I was telling you about," he said.

Willow watched his eyes sadden slightly.

Crap. Way to go!

Once the conch fritters arrived, they ordered their meals. This was a challenging part for Willow. She loved seafood and their shrimp platter was amazing. As in the best shrimp platter ever, which included Hush Puppies galore. Then there were the amazing fish tacos and their scallop dish was divine.

Ugh.

"Know what you want?" Colt asked, closing the menu.

"Everything," she replied honestly.

Colt threw back his head and laughed. "How about we pick something we both want to sample and we can share?"

"Really?" This was completely unheard of for her. He must have unicorn blood.

"Yeah. I'll get the Scallops with Veggies."

Veggies?

"Shrimp Platter and Hush Puppies. But I am not eating any of your veggies," she stated in a matter-of-fact tone.

"No Veggies." He placed his order with an extra side of Hush Puppies.

"So…" he started, mimicking her from earlier.

She giggled at his sense of humor. "So…" she encouraged.

"How did you come up with Martini Girl Bar?"

"My girlfriends." She smiled thinking about it. "I worked as a bartender throughout college. The bar was originally called The M Bar. Mack was the original owner of the place and he hired me on when I was going to school. I hustled and learned the tricks and trades of bartending. Took classes and attended several conferences. I realized I was great at it.

"Originally, The M bar was a beer and whiskey bar. Nothing else. When I started working behind the bar, my friends came into the place. It was hysterical considering the bar was mainly an all-men's bar. There was nothing feminine about it. But the guys they didn't seem to mind us girls hanging out. The old timers were real charmers. I mixed drinks for the girls and before long, The M bar started serving more than beer and whiskey."

"Is that where you got your name?"

She grabbed her drink and took another sip, enjoying the sweet and tangy taste of the pineapple and spiced rum. "Yeah. Mac was the one who nicknamed me Whiskey. He said I had eyes like warm whiskey. Old man was a flirt, and a poet." She blushed, remembering Mac. He was a sweet man, and she missed him.

She continued, "When he wanted out, I bought the bar and turned it into The Martini Girl Bar. I told him what I wanted to do, and he laughed at first, but then thought it was a great idea. A lot of the original patrons stopped coming when Mac sold the place. Many of them go to The Punch Bar now." She growled the name of the hated bar. It was because of Curtis Merk she had lost those loyal customers.

"I've been to The Punch Bar," he said. "It's alright. It's been a while since I've been there but they don't have a setup like yours, but the music has always been pretty decent there."

"Yes, well, unfortunately, I'm a little biased considering the reason I lost all of the original customers of Mac was because douche bag Merk lied and said I stole the M Bar from him. That did not sit well with them."

"You're kidding." Colt said with disdain, his face slightly flushed.

"Trust me, it took some time to get them to realize that I did not steal The M Bar. But by then, they had moved on to different pastures and, well, I wanted to put it behind me as well. They come in occasionally during the day for our Noon Hour. Wes and Beck get a kick out of them when they come in. Besides, everyone in the industry knows Curtis is a snake."

"Noon Hour?"

"It's our Happy Hour at noon. We serve Happy Hour from eleven to one and then again four to seven."

"Well, hell, I didn't even realize you were open at eleven in the morning."

She swallowed her drink and enjoyed a conch fritter. "We are closed only on Mondays. Wes and Beck usually work the earlier shifts, Levi and I do most of the closings and then we alternate days off, covering each other when we need more time. We all work on Fridays. It's our busiest day, as you saw for yourself, and Saturdays are as busy but with fewer theatrics."

"Are you working tonight?"

"Unfortunately, I am. I close again tonight. But I don't have to go in till seven. Levi will cover for me till then," she quickly added, hoping this would soothe any disappointment. "Just in case I didn't say it enough yesterday, thank you again for bailing us out. You really were amazing."

She enjoyed watching the smirk on his face form. With a mind of its own, her hand reached out and caressed the side of his cheeks, feeling the roughness from his unshaven beard. "You didn't shave."

His eyes turned a darker shade of green. He reached out and grabbed her hand, turning his head and kissing the inside of her palm, shaking his head no.

"I like it," she admitted.

"Good to know," his mouth quirked with humor.

"Fried shrimp platter with hush puppies for you, my dear, and scallop dish with veggies and a side of hush puppies. Is there anything else I can bring you two?" David gingerly chimed in.

"No, we're good." Colt's scowl gave poor David an obvious answer. He turned back to Willow. "Did your girls all make it home alright?"

"Yes. They're such train wrecks. After you left, the girls stayed up and planned a little getaway this weekend. We haven't taken a vacation in forever. It will be nice to take off for a few days."

"That's cool. Where are you going?"

"Depends on who you ask. I'm sort of leaning towards the Keys. We have to see if Luna can get the time off. Her job is the more complicated one."

"How did you all meet? You all seem tight."

She moved her plate towards his. They shared and ate off of each other's dishes like an old habit. "I've known Sofia the longest. Since we were in kindergarten together and she stole my pink glitter pencil box. We hated each other so much. The teachers forced us into play groups until we were in second grade. Then, when we could choose our own partners, we ended up picking each other and I've been stuck with her ever since."

"Reminds me of something Lucy, my niece, would do," he chuckled.

"Zoila is Sofia's cousin. She's an ER Nurse. I met her in high school when she moved to St. Augustine, from Miami. Skylar and Piper, believe it or not, are sisters."

"No shit. They look nothing alike," he said, completely surprised.

"That's because they are both adopted," she quickly added. "They were in the same foster care home and the Zales didn't want to separate the girls since they were close."

"That's awesome. Few people would take on two kids that aren't siblings."

"Eric and Elaine Zales are complete gems. They've always treated Pip and Sky like they were truly their own kids. They didn't see race or age with the girls. They saw two little girls in need of a home and that's all it took for them to go for both of them."

"What about Harper and Luna?"

"Harper and I met in Junior High. We clicked right away. She's easy to get along with. Fab and I basically took her under our wings. It took a bit for her and Sofia to get along, but in the end, they did. Luna is a recent addition. And when I mean recent, I mean she was the last one to join the group. We met her in High School. She was born in Boston, but her parents were professors at the University. They moved back to England where she was raised as a child. She came back to the states her freshman year of high school."

"That explains the accent. Levi's a sucker for an accent."

"Noticed that too, huh?"

She received a nod and a wink from him. She kept the acclaimed affirmation in her mental file folder for later.

"And last, there's Fab. I've known Fab since middle school as well. Fab, Sofia, and I were always close. We knew of his sexuality before he was comfortable to admit it. When he did and realized we didn't care, he felt a complete weight lift off his shoulders. Sofia and I were with him when he came out to his mom. She said to him that as long as he continued to do his chores, respect his elders, and mind his manners, she didn't care if he turned purple, farted rainbows, and married a unicorn."

Colt choked on his beer and laughed. "Alright. I have an important question to ask you. And I need the honest answer."

His serious tone put her on edge. She licked her lips nervously, taking the last sip of her drink. She turned and provided her full attention. "Fire away."

His eyes slanted, cautiously watching her.

"This is really important, Whiskey, or do I call you Willow?"

She thought about it. She didn't date often, but when she did, they all called her Whiskey. With Colt, she wanted something different.

"Willow," she simply whispered.

That meant something to him. It was in his eyes. Gentle and some indefinable emotion.

She would give him that.

It was his.

He leaned forward and tucked a stray hair behind her ear. "Alright, Willow, how do you feel about fairies?"

Surprised by the change of subject, she stared at him, wondering if he was serious.

"Like I said, it's important," he reassured.

"I think fairies are clever and possibly the coolest in the Fae world."

His arm pulled her closer, and he leaned down with a swift kiss. "You'll do."

Halo and Tails screamed, *Yes!* And high-five each other.

For once, she was on the same page as them.

Chapter 6

Confessions (Batteries Included)

Oh L'Amour, sighed Halo
Le sigh, mocked Tails. Sort of.
Willow was pretty sure her little deviant side was caught in Colt's charm as well.
Seriously, you two. We need to focus. Willow chided herself
But he's so dreamy.
And HOT.—
We are hopeless, she thought to herself.
Like a sinking lifeboat in a stormy sea, said Halo, whom she was pretty sure had hearts circling her little halo.
With raging hormones. Jump his bones already, urged Tails, who no doubt had either a naked Colt or their trusty vibrator circling her little devil horns.
Both.
Cheese and rice.
"Do you think we have time to make one more stop?" asked Colt, jostling her out of her pervie thoughts.
After their delicious meal, they'd sat on the marina and talked more about her friends and some of their adventures. Well, anything within the Pink Book of Girl Code that could be disclosed. During their conversations, they talked of places they traveled and where they would

like to go in the future. Colt shared he would like to take Lucy up north to the mountains to see waterfalls and snow. She had never left the state. Willow mentioned taking her to the amusement parks in Orlando, and he'd cringed at the thought.

"I've thought about that. I'm thinking I might have to take her soon. Dreading it."

"If you go before she starts school, you can go during the week. Off-peak season. It will be less painful than going during the summer or holiday breaks. September might be a pleasant month," she had suggested wisely.

"Good point. Guess you'll have to come along with me."

She'd liked the idea of spending time with Lucy and him. She smiled shyly at him. His warm hazel eyes were full of promises as he asked to make one more stop.

Now, she wondered where they would go next. "Sure, I've got time. What do you have in mind?"

"You talked about the lighthouse. I've actually never been. Want to go?"

"Wait. What? You live here and have never been to the lighthouse? How's that possible?" She turned to face him and quickly pulled out her phone.

"What are you doing?" humor laced his question as he drove.

"Checking to see if they have any events tonight. Sometimes there are weddings, and they might be closed."

"Beautiful and smart."

Her eyes drifted up towards his, catching his wink before she confirmed they were in the clear. Once they arrived the short distance, he parked under the shaded gravel lot, asking Willow to stay in the truck. He looped around the front and came to her door, opening it for her, helping her down, and holding her hand as they started their approach to the front entrance. Colt purchased two tickets, arguing with her when she attempted to pay for the tickets since he covered dinner. "Not happening, baby," was all he said, giving the tickets over as they walked to the gardens.

They walked the small trails, enjoying the shade. At the end of the trail, they located an area where kids could play on a wooden pirate ship with a tube slide by the waterfront.

"Lucy would love this. She watched some fairy cartoon who was a pirate and for months she walked around yelling at Noni to walk the plank. It was the funniest thing."

"She sounds adorable," said Willow. Her heart warmed when Colt spoke of his niece.

"She's a handful. It was a rough change," he said, sitting down on a nearby picnic table. Willow sat next to him. He looked at the pirate ship, a long-lost look came across his face when he spoke next.

"My sister had drug issues," he paused, taking a moment before he continued. "We tried to get her help and for a good while, it seemed to work. She got clean. She got a job. Got a place for herself. I was gigging more with Blue Nitro then. We traveled up and down the lower east coast. Anywhere from Daytona to Charleston. We got noticed and things were looking up for us."

His eyes looked over at Willow. "Clover, my sister, she came out a few times with us. The guys all knew her. Knew she was untouchable. We signed up to play at these small-town county fairs. There were other no name bands like us, all starting out. We bonded with 352 Fury. We always played sets after them or them after us. Kixx, he's the singer, liked to smoke before he goes on stage. Relaxed him, he said. Clover was into Kixx and before you know it, Clover was into whatever Kixx was into. Then it progressed from smoking to shooting up shit."

She sat back, feeling the pit in her stomach weigh her down.

****

"Not gonna lie darlin', Blue Nitro, we weren't saints. But the one rule we had was no drugs. That was one hard rule we all had, and they did that for me because of my sister. They knew what went down before, with her, and knew she would be around us. My brothers stood by me and made sure that shit would not touch her."

"Till Kixx," she finished.

"Yeah. Till Kixx. He said he didn't give her anything besides smokes. I didn't believe him. Never did. Still don't."

"You suspected nothing? I mean, you saw how she was before. Did she not act the same way?"

Colt lowered his head, wondering that himself over and over. How he missed the signs. Why did he not see it? "I caught her smoking once and ripped into her," he said, continuing in a quieter tone. "She freaked out and apologized over and over. I was such an ass that night. Even the guys thought I might have gone too far. Man, I was furious with her. I fought Kixx that night. Nearly got us kicked out of the fair, which pissed off my band mates. I never saw her smoke after that. Never saw her stoned or high. Nothing. After a while, she stopped coming around the band, suddenly stating her job had given her the project she was excited to work on. I-I believed her. She talked up this job all the time. I bought it, of course I did, thinking we were back on track and she's good. You know?"

He stood up, not able to sit still any longer, needing to move. "Blue Nitro's popularity picked up. I checked in with her daily. Then it turned into weekly, with our gigs building up and getting busier. We started traveling further north into Tennessee, back down the east coast and as far west into New Orleans. Then Noni, my grandmother, got into a severe car accident. Broke her hip and clavicle. She punctured her right lung and needed more stitches than a rag doll does to stay together. I rushed back, thinking I'm about to lose the only parent I've known my whole life and then-and then see Clover. Or what used to be Clover. She was thin in baggy clothes, sunken eyes, stringy hair. I knew. She was hooked again. I couldn't look at her. I couldn't stand the sight of her. And the worse part of it, she knew. She stood there and told me since I was there, she could go. And left. And I let her. I didn't see her again after that."

"I'm sorry, Colt. I don't know what to say."

"Nothing to say, baby. Addiction is a bitch. You can fight all you want and even beat her. But she's always there lurking."

She placed a warm hand on his chest. "She was pregnant with Lucy at the hospital, when you saw her and Noni, wasn't she?"

"Yeah. A month later, she overdosed. Someone from the complex she lived in found her door wide open and she was on the floor. They called rescue, and they rushed her in. The neighbor was the one who mentioned she might be pregnant. One nurse had a thing for Kai, the bass player in Blue Nitro, and she called him. She recognized Clover from school and found a picture of me and Clover in her purse. At least the neighbor provided them with something to go by.

"My sister didn't have shit in her apartment. Not even a bed. Lucy was premature at six months. She was born an addict. I thought we were going to lose her, too. She fought through. Named her Lucy after Noni's favorite TV show. Her middle name is Hope, like my sister," he said, drawing his arms around her.

"Beautiful name," she simply said, wrapping her arms around him. She rested her head against his chest. "What about your parents? Weren't they around to help?"

"My mother lives out west somewhere with her husband and two daughters. I don't have any memories of my father. He split after Clover. Nadine, my mother, never spoke of him."

"You don't speak to your mother?"

"No. Nadine may have given birth to me, but she's not my mother. Noni, as much as she drives me crazy, she's my mom." He shook his head. "Come on, enough confession of dark times for one day," he joked lightly, pulling her face back up to his, seeing her tears. "No crying baby."

"Is that why you left the band? Because of Clover and Noni?" she asked quietly.

"I didn't leave the band. The band left me."

"Why would they do that?" she hissed.

"Blue Nitro got signed up for a record deal. It was an enormous opportunity they couldn't pass up. Problem was, I couldn't leave Noni and Lucy in the hospital to go to Nashville to record, and they wouldn't wait for my shit to settle. I still had to bury my sister, get Noni into rehab, and Lucy was an unsure bet. My family needed me. Levi tried to talk to his brother to hold off. To talk to the agent and tell them what was going on. But Maverick didn't think they would listen, and apparently it wasn't worth the risk to pass up the deal. The band voted. And I was out."

"That's why Levi and Maverick don't talk?"

"Part of it." Colt shrugged, looking down into her warm eyes. "There's bad blood there. It's not my story to share. Levi's had my back from day one. Maverick did too. But the dollar signs blinded him."

Her face reddened in anger on his behalf. Something he found cute. "Easy darlin'. I can see the wheels of revenge turning. No need for them. I've moved on and they have too."

"I'm entitled to be upset for you, Colton Royce. They should have stuck by you like Levi did. Remind me next time Maverick is in town to add arsenic to his beer."

"I'm pretty sure that's illegal darlin'."

"You're right. I'll add a laxative instead," she amended.

He tightened his arms and buried his nose in her smooth hair, enjoying the feel of her and smell of fresh lemon and coconut. He couldn't remember the last time he laughed this much on any date. Her antics and empty threats were charming. "You are not adding any laxatives to anyone's drinks. You hear me, little hell raiser?"

"I make no promises," she replied.

"Jesus. Remind me not to piss you off." Colt walked down the pathway they came through earlier and crossed over to the lighthouse. He stood in front, asking someone to snap a picture of them before they walked up the spiral stairwell of two hundred and nineteen steps to the top. Red bar rails surrounded the top deck. From every round focal point, the view was breathtaking.

Willow leaned back against Colt, his arms encasing her, providing her some of his heat from the heavy salty breeze blowing in from Matanzas Bay. They watched seagulls soar above. Trees swayed on the coast as boats sailed by. She zoomed in with her phone, snapping pictures of the view and then flipping the camera option to take a selfie with him behind her.

They listened as the historian spoke about the history of the lighthouse and its glory years. They followed the informal spokesman down the spiral staircase, where he told a tale of a mysterious being who haunted the lighthouse. Colt smiled as he wiggled his eyebrows at Willow. "We will have to do a ghost tour on our next date," he said.

"Nope. Not happening."

"What if I promise to be by your side and protect you the entire time?" he assured her, giving her his do-it-for-me look with his sea-green eyes.

Willow shook her head rapidly. She pointed her finger at him. "Don't give me that sexy look, Colton Royce. It will not work."

He stopped walking down the stairs, ignoring the historian as people squeezed past them down the stairs. "You think I'm sexy?" he asked, an amused grin forming.

"That's beside the point. I don't do ghost tours, or scary movies, or haunted houses, or spooky trails, or jeepers, creepers corn mazes. I mean, seriously. Why? Who does that?"

He raised his hand. "Because it's fun. Guess Halloween is not your holiday."

"I love Halloween. I'm just not particularly into all the other stuff that usually comes along with it."

It wasn't every day Colt met an enigma and Willow was one hundred percent an enigma. How one person could love Halloween but not like the scary aspect of the holiday was beyond him. "Man, and here I thought you and I had a fighting chance," he teased.

"Yeah. I guess it's a deal breaker huh," she tossed back, glancing around the stairwell. She reached over, her finger skimming the top of his belt, sliding around his waist. "That's too bad. I'm a sure bet."

Eyebrows raised, he tilted his head down, eyes sharp as the air thickened around them. He tightened his grip around the rail, letting her take the lead. Her slight touch traced the band of his belt casually with trembling hands, slipping slightly into his waistline to tease.

Her warm brown eyes shone up at him shyly and teasingly. He deserved Saint Hood for not doing half the dirty things crossing his mind. Her hands linked around his waist, caging him against the rail while she raised herself up on her tiptoes. Even though he lowered his head a little to assist. After all, he was a gentleman.

Feeling her soft lips brush his, coaxing him into a deeper kiss, he relented and released the rails, sacrificing the Saint Hood nomination. His hand cupped the back of her head. Fingers wrapped in her lush hair, deepening the kiss, tasting her sigh. He was lost in the moment, forgetting where they were, or caring if someone would find them or if the ghost that haunted the lighthouse was into voyeurism.

"You're killing me here, baby," he said, coming to

his senses quickly. The sounds of chatter echoed from below. "Let's get out of here."

They skipped the museum and the shop, passing by any more history lessons and ghost stories. Colt opened his truck door. She turned to him before climbing in and quickly placed another kiss on his surprised lips. "Just in case I forget to tell you, you give good first dates," she said.

"Date's not over," he assured her, kissing her until he was the one left panting.

****

"You ladies better talk."

One thing all the girls knew not to do was get Fabulous Fab out of her fabulous mood. And Fab, in her striking yellow tube top and ripped up jeans with leopard four-inch heels, was fabulous and fuming. "How is it y'all have a sleepover, English Tea Cakes get a hickey, you little miss thing go out with Pistol, and I don't get told about any of it by any of you? I have to find out by a Panty Dropper."

English Tea Cakes, AKA Luna, exploded. "I'm going to kill him."

"Oh no, you ain't. You ain't touching one of my boys. They've got my back and I've got theirs. In a platonic way, of course," she giggled. "But that ain't my point. Why didn't I hear this from you? Am I not a Martini Girl?"

Cheese and rice.

"Of course you are," cried out Willow.

"Girl, you know you are," stated Skylar.

"You will always be a Martini Girl," soothed Sofia.

"Well then, why didn't you call me?" she demanded, crossing her arms with pursed ruby red lips and an arched eyebrow.

Best thing to do in the situation was tell the truth. "Everything happened quickly."

Willow recapped the geyser episode in the lady's restroom. To which Fab threw her hands up, calling out their "plumbing needed to get handled stat." They quickly jumped on a plan to get the plumbing revamped sooner than later.

Colt might know someone, Halo whispered.

He can work on our plumbing, muttered Tails.

She ignored her internal cheerleaders, who had abandoned her earlier at the lighthouse parking lot, and explained how Levi and Colt came by unexpectedly. Fab's eyes lit up, already knowing more details than possible, leaving Luna squirming in her seat. "I'm going to give English Tea Cakes a pass since I know what happened with her. I want to know about you, girl. You haven't said a word since Pistol dropped you off and sucked your face senseless."

"WHAT?" yelled Sofia. "He kissed you?"

"Girl, it wasn't just any kissed. Pistol took a goodbye kiss into overdrive and then some. It looked like they would combust right there in the parking lot," Fab snitched.

With an open mouth and crazy look, Sofia grabbed Skylar's arm and started yanking. "*¡Ay Dios Mío! ¿Te cambiaste los pantis? Cuentamèlo todo, mija.*"

"English Sofia. We can't understand you," Skylar said, trying to unhook her arm from Sofia's grip. "And let my arm go before you pull it out of socket."

"Well learn dammit," she folded her hands and batted her lashes before rapidly translating her questions. "Did you change your panties? Tell me everything."

Willow covered her face with both hands. It was true. After Colt dropped her off, he opened the door like he had done all day and kissed the common sense, the logical and the illogical, out of her. She hadn't wanted it to end. She'd even invited him upstairs, but he declined. "As much as I want in there and trust me, baby, I do. There's not enough time right now for what I have in mind."

She, however, did not expect Fab to see them and then rat her out to the girls, well except Zoila, who was on shift tonight at the hospital and Piper who was on her way, an hour ago—that girl took forever to get ready—and Harper who was MIA.

"It was toe curling," Willow admitted. "He's…ugh…he's sweet and funny and sexy as hell. Lord, he can kiss."

"EEK," Sofia squealed loudly, yanking on Skylar's arm again.

"Girl, I will cut you," Skylar threatened Sofia with a matching glare.

"Are you seeing him again? Wait? Are you finally going to have S, E, X, with him?" ignoring Skylar, Sofia asked spelling out the obvious word.

Willow's already flushed face brightened more.

"*Ay Dios*. That means you will have to retire *Cho-Cha Loca*," she said sadly.

Willow bit her lip hard. Lord, she loved Sofia. Luna and Skylar shared a confused stare before Sofia and Fab chimed in laughing.

"No, she don't. *Cho-Cha Loca* can always join in on the fun, girl."

Sofia bobbed her shoulder length wild hair in agreement, her chocolate eyes rounded as if they gave her the winning numbers to the Lottery for the next ten years. "This is true."

"Um, who is coco loca?" asked Luna.

"*Cho-Cha Loca*," corrected Sofia. "It's her vibrator."

"Wait, you named your vibrator crazy pussy?" Skylar whispered, worried someone would discover this important load of information.

"Oh, you know those words," teased Sofia.

Before Willow could begin explaining the logic behind the crazy name bestowed by the crazy Sofia, she interrupted.

"Do you own a vibrator?" Sofia, with a raised eyebrow, asked Skylar and Luna. "If not, don't worry, Fab and I will hook you up. *Mija,* please add two *Cho-Cha Locas* for delivery stat," she said to Fab, who dramatically whipped out her phone and began typing while smacking her lips. "Now with great pleasure comes great responsibilities which means once you use it, your *cho-cha*," she said pointing to their lady bits, "goes *loca*," finishing her explanation while crossing her hands politely on her lap as if she finished telling them how to bake the world's best flan.

"Hence the name *Cho-Cha Loca*, ladies. You should both be getting a package delivered to you on Monday. Batteries included. Merry early Christmas." Fab stated, and gave Sofia a high-five.

"You're welcome," Sofia sassed, snapping her fingers.

Chapter 7

Underground Poker (must be fifty-five and older to play)

After dropping Willow off, Colt returned home to check on Lucy and quickly change. Saturday afternoons and nights were busy, and he had told Willow he would stop by, since she was still shorthanded from Cody and Lizzie. Albeit, that was the reason he gave her. Deep down, his only reason for risking the inquisition from Noni was to spend more time with Willow.
She was different.
Refreshing.
It hit him hard how easily it was for him to speak to her. Easy it was to be with her.
Laugh with her.
Just be.
He had kissed her senseless again and forced her to walk up the stairs alone without him, not trusting himself from crossing the threshold and into her place. Colt waited till she was safely inside before he'd driven off and headed home. He parked his truck in the driveway next to Noni's obnoxious yellow convertible Volkswagen and two other familiar vehicles.
Now, he looked down at his deflated crotch and mumbled, "That's one way to take care of you."
The house smelled of Noni's brownies and

chocolate chip cookies. The sounds of a poker chip and the bets being called out from the kitchen floated down the hallway.

"Check."

"Check."

"Check."

"I'll raise you by ten." That's his Noni. The shark.

"You old senile witch."

"Did we win, Noni?"

"We sure did, honey bear. You count all those chips for Noni. Practice your numbers, darling girl." He located the underground poker table surrounded by Noni, with Lucy on her lap, and her cronies in the center of the kitchen dinner table.

"Look, Uncle Colt. I'm practicing my numbers," she said, holding up poker chips.

"I see," slicing his eyes at Noni.

She arched her eyebrow at him. "How did it go?" she asked, smiling like a cat who swallowed the canary.

"How did what go?" asked Rita, who, at the moment, was still staring daggers at Noni for taking the pot.

"Colt had a date," Noni informed them.

"Huh, did you strike out? You're home early," Rita said, taking a quick hit of her oxygen before she grabbed the cards and dealer chips.

"Jesus, Rita," he said, pointing over at Lucy. "I didn't strike out." He reached the refrigerator and grabbed a bottled water and snagged a brownie. He pulled up a chair between Helen and Noni and grabbed Lucy, placing her on his lap. "Hey, honey bear. You behaved for Noni?" He ran his fingers through her new pink extensions. Sorely admitted to himself that they were cute on her.

"I sure did. I even helped Noni with the brownies," she announced proudly.

"Check."

"Check."

"Raise twelve," Noni called out.

Rita grumbled, checking her cards. "I'll call your saggy sweet cheeks."

Helen and Candice easily folded.

On the flop, a five of spades, five of diamonds, and three of clovers turned. After the raise, Rita burned one card and turned a king of hearts. They patiently waited for Noni.

"I'll raise another twelve," she said, tossing in her chips.

Colt watched the cards keeping his face neutral, holding Lucy as she shared the brownie he was eating.

"Why are you home early if you didn't strike out my dear boy?" she asked as they waited for a grumbling Rita to count her twelve chips into the pot and take another hit of oxygen.

"Hey, honey bear, want to go down to the beach and collect shells before it gets dark?" he said instead.

"Yes! Oh, can we? Please, Uncle Colt. Please."

"Yeah, little one. Go get your sandals and beach bucket," quickly releasing a squirming four-year-old from his lap. She raced up the stairs to get her beach items. He turned to the nosy pink haired elder, narrowing his eyes at her. "Like I told Rita, I didn't strike out. She works tonight. I'm planning on dropping by later to help at the bar."

Rita burned another card and dropped the river card. A five of hearts.

"Well, what if I had a hot date tonight?" Noni asked with huge, innocent eyes.

"Cancel it, since *you* agreed to watch Lucy for me," he called her bluff. "Rita, you doing alright over there?" he asked, concerned that she was overly quiet. "Do you need more oxygen?"

"I'm fine, boy," she snapped back in her usual charming, grumpy attitude.

"Making sure cause I'm not giving you mouth to mouth if you pass out here," he teased, winking at her.

"You better. I die and I will come back and haunt you every time you are with a lady friend doing the horizontal tango," she warned him.

Well that sucked.

"That's right, Rita. You tell him," cheered Noni.

"Nice, ace and nine. That's a good bluff," he said as he got up and walked over to Lucy, who raced downstairs with her mermaid bucket and shovel.

Noni gasped. "You little shit."

"All in," Rita said through her oxygen mask, smiling victoriously.

"You can't go all in, you twit. I have to place my bet first," Noni stated.

Rita shrugged her shoulders. She waited and chuckled when Noni folded. "Helen, help me out and bring those chips over, will you, my dear?"

"Candice, hand me your cane," Noni said, getting up from the table. "I'm going to beat the living shit out of my grandson."

"No can-do. This is my new cane. You are not breaking it in," Helen said, winking at Colt. "Go, handsome. We got her."

"Love you ladies. Drive safely home. You drive me

crazy, Noni, but I love you darlin'. See you in an hour."
****

Noni fumbled with her cards as the two loves of her life walked out of the house.

Drive him crazy.

Pish posh.

He was the one that drove her crazy.

Constantly telling her what to eat and drink. Take walks. Made her get up at God awful times of the day to do trails with him. He even bought her a bike with a basket in the front. His logic, "You can ride around with Lucy. It's excellent exercise." Exercise was torture created by the spawns of hell. She was convinced of that and yet he seemed to enjoy his morning runs.

Every day.

The boy needed to get laid.

"He's done such a great job with Lucy," Helen said.

Helen Tucker was Rita's caregiver and loyal friend to them all. She was kind and sweet. Nurturing. And the youngest of them at fifty-four.

Rita Brooks was the crabbiest, most obstinate person in the world. Talk about pain in the ass. Rita's picture would be next to the definition. Rita was the oldest of the group at eighty-two. She was healthy except for her legs were giving out and she required help in getting up and down from her chair, and the extra oxygen she usually indulged in.

Last, there was Candice Williams, Noni's closest friend. Candy and Noni went to school together and were at each other's weddings and divorce parties. After their cheating husbands left them for younger women, they bonded even more and have remained close ever since.

Candice stood by Colt when Noni was in the car

accident that nearly ended her life, and at Clover's funeral.

Noni thought of Clover. A sadness washed over her. She wished Clover would see what a beautiful, bright, and full-of-life little girl Lucy was.

"Yes, he's been amazing with her. You know Lucy asked me today if she thought Colt would be alright with her calling him Daddy instead of Uncle Colt."

Rita's eyes misted when she replied, "I don't think he would ever have a problem with that."

"No, he won't," Noni agreed.

"Why does she call him Uncle Colt instead of Daddy?" asked Helen.

"Colt wanted her to know her mother. Lucy has a picture of Clover in her room and since Clover is Colt's sister, it was easier to remain as Uncle Colt instead of Daddy."

"I think it's sweet she wants to call him Daddy," Candice said.

She nodded her head, taking the dealer's chip and cards and passing them to Candice. "Your deal."

Candice called out to Helen like a pro in a Vegas casino, "Small Blind," then to Noni, "Big Blind. Ready? Place your bets, ladies. Stakes are high and mama wants a new pair of shoes and matching handbag."

****

The salty breeze whipped across Lucy's hair, blowing wild like her, racing down the shoreline of St. Augustine beach. Her bare feet flipped the sand backwards, leaving a confused trail as she twirled around.

Colt watched amused, sitting on a beach towel with his jeans rolled up. Her pink glitter sandals and his shoes lay next to him. He held her mermaid beach bucket while she chased the seagulls like a little Pomeranian.

Thinking about the fluffy dog made him chuckle. She would love the little thing. Something for him to think about. The timing would be perfect. Lucy was older and could learn responsibility as well as grow up with the pup.

Plus, he was financially stable. His custom woodwork was picking up with more clients. He was making decent money on the jobs he currently had, and he had the money from Blue Nitro's payout from the band. He'd saved those funds, mainly because he was angry with the band for forcing him out. He did not want to touch the money, but he'd made amends with most of the band and made peace with their decision.

Whether he would have made the same decision, he was putting it behind him.

"Uncle Colt, look what I found," she dashed back to him, showing him part of a smooth marble oyster shell. "It's treasure," she said excitedly.

His brows rose in amazement. "Well, you better put this in your bucket. You want to look for more?"

She nodded enthusiastically and dropped her treasure into her mermaid bucket and went down to the shoreline in search of more. "Come on, Uncle Colt. You needs to help me."

He quietly laughed and walked down to the shoreline. They looked around, finding different shades of oyster shells. One shell caught his eye. "Look here, honey bear," he pointed out as the wave washed up.

"Oh." Her little gasp tugged at his heart. She carefully picked up the small purple shell, softly rinsing the sand from the bottom. The lavender hues inside glistened from the water in contrast to the outer purple ridges of the cockle shell. "Do you think it's a mermaid treasure?" she quietly asked, worried as if the wind would carry her secrets back to the ocean.

"I'm not sure, little one, but if it is, I think the mermaids left it there for you to find it," he whispered back.

Her round, bright green eyes sparkled with excitement. "I'm keeping it forever. It's the bestest treasure ever."

He leaned in and kissed her forehead, carefully placing the shell in her bucket as they went searching for more mermaid treasures. They found three more small purple shells, two black shells, and four shark teeth. They filled the bucket with various colors of oyster and cockle shells.

"I gots so much treasure!"

His head tilted back as he laughed at her excitement. They collected their things and headed back to the truck. He stopped at the shopping strip nearby their house. "Let's get some ice cream and take it home and eat it in front of Noni."

"Yeah!" she said with a wicked smile.

The bell chimed as he pushed opened the door to Chill Out Creamery. The decadent smell of chocolate and vanilla enveloped them immediately. Lucy hurriedly ran to the glass and stared at the variety of ice creams. "Hey there, Lucy girl, what can I get you?" asked Amy, the owner of the shop. Amy served the creamiest, most delicious, most sinful ice cream known in Anastasia Island.

"Hi Ms. Amy," Lucy cheerfully greeted. "I gots lots of treasure today," she said. Colt snickered and stood back as Lucy attempted to perch up on her tiptoes and whisper to Amy, who was leaning over the counter, "Mermaid treasure," she whispered.

"No way," shouted Amy, a teasing smile forming on her face.

"Shhhhhhh," Lucy quickly said with a finger over her lips. "You can't say nothing. They're a secret."

"Oh. Got it, Lucy girl," she reaffirmed, reaching over with her pinky finger and locking it with Lucy.

Colt covered his mouth with his hand, hoping he would not break out in laughter over their conversation. "Hey, Amy, how's it going?"

"I'm good, Colt. How are you? How's Ms. Noelle doing?"

"Noni's good. Running an underground poker table at the present time with her cronies."

"Yeah, and guess what, Ms. Amy? Noni was winning lots of shits! And I practiced my numbers with them," she said proudly.

He pinched the bridge of his nose, reconsidering sticking Noni in a retirement home. "You want a grandmother? I'll sell her to you."

"I'll pass. But thank you for the offer." Amy said, laughing at him with a pitiful look. "Guess that's one conversation you will need to have soon before she starts school."

"Oh yeah. That one's going into the books for sure." He looked down at Lucy, who admired the ice cream. He tugged on her pink extensions. "Which one are you taking with you, Potty Mouth?"

"Hey, I don't gots a potty mouth," she defended innocently.

"Shits, is a potty word, little one," he corrected.

"Nah uh. Noni says it all the time, and she says that is what she won. Even Auntie Helen asked Auntie Rita about her shits and how many she had."

He covered her mouth with his hand and lowered his eye level to her, ignoring Amy's clapping and laughter. He glanced around at the other patrons, who sat down at the tables. Some with amused smiles and another with her hands over her little one's ears. "Honey bear, you were counting her chips. Not shits."

Her eyes opened like saucers, realizing her mistake. He lowered her hand and her lip tremble. "Am I in trouble for using potty talk?"

"Come here, Lucy," he picked her up and cradled her. "You're not in trouble. Noni's in big trouble. But not you."

She shook her head, but kept her arms wrapped around his neck.

"Hey, Lucy girl, pick out your ice cream and I will add an extra for you. No charge," Amy offered.

"For reals?"

"For reals," she confirmed. "You too, Colt. Looks like you need it."

Lucy picked out her favorite ice cream. It was a rainbow of bright colors that would no doubt stain every article of clothing on her little body. Colt stuck with chocolate and brownie mix and in the end, he grabbed a cup of Noni's favorite ice cream. He placed Lucy back on the ground with her rainbow bright ice cream.

"Thanks, Amy. See you around."

"Sure thing. Say hello to Ms. Noelle, and I hope she keeps winning all those shits."

He threw one hand in the air while juggling two ice-cream cups and the door with the other. "Don't encourage this. Seriously, I won't sell her. I'll give her to you. Free. I'll even provide free delivery service and she bakes great brownies and chocolate chip cookies."

"I've got enough sweets here to last me a lifetime. Later, Colt."

He grumbled his goodbye and grabbed a bouncing Lucy, buckling her into her booster seat. Her purple, pink, blue stained lips tilted up in a radiant smile, showing off green, yellow, orange stained teeth.

Jesus.

Before he pulled out of the parking lot, he shot a quick text to Willow.

Colt—*Thinking of selling my grandmother*—

Colt—*Know of any buyers in the market for one?*—

Three dots appeared immediately. He placed his phone on the clip on his dashboard and waited. Then they disappeared. His phone suddenly rang.

He placed the hands-free in his ear, answering her call. "Hey darlin'."

"I might know a buyer, but what is your asking price?"

"It's negotiable." He caught her soft laughter over the chatter in the background. "You busy tonight?"

"It's picking up. We had another person quit today," she said, resigned.

"You're kidding. Did they go to the Punch Bar too?"

"Yep. Looks like Douche Bag Merks is making promises of grandeur. He's hitting up all of my newer employees. My seasoned employees know the score. Those that have left were because they actually joined corporate America or are saving lives somewhere or went back to school. And even then, they sometimes come back for seasonal employment. Levi threatened to go over there and have his version of a talk with Douche Bag Merks. Which is not happening."

"Why not? He's right. Hell, I'm going to go with him."

"No. It's business. It's shady business, but business none the less. My sister, Mila, she's moving back into town. She's going to be filling in one spot and my mom will help as well. They've done this before. We'll manage."

He made a mental note to touch base with Levi. "I'm on my way back to the house with Lucy. Once I get her settled, I'll come by to pull a shift tonight. Tell me what you need, and I'll get it done."

There was silence on the phone for a few seconds before she whispered back, "You don't have to do that, Colt. I mean, you can come in for a drink or hang out. But you don't have to pull a shift."

"Baby, I know I don't have to. But I'm doing it, anyway. I'll be there probably in an hour. Hopefully, by then, I'll have sold Noni, and her cronies will have disbanded."

"Her cronies?"

"Yeah, she was in the middle of a poker game at our kitchen table when I got home from dropping you off. High stakes."

"Oh man. Guess I'll get a T-shirt ready for you when you get here."

"See you when I get there."

"Bye, Colt," her sultry voice shot right through him, sending alert messages all the way down south.

He tried hard to stay relaxed. He thought of mermaid shells and the soothing ocean. Warm sand and a cooling breeze. He wondered what it would be like to have

Willow there with him. And what she would look in a bikini.

May-Day.

May-Day.

"Uncle Colt, is Noni going to get in trouble for potty talk?"

And *that* did the trick. Thinking of Noni always ruined the mood. "Don't worry about that, honey bear."

They arrived home, and he noticed one car gone. Lucy bounced inside, still eating her ice cream. A marble of colors dripped down her chin and shirt in blue and purple hues.

"Lucy, what happened to you?" said Noni.

"Hi, Noni. Uncle Colt and I stopped for Ice Cream. Ms. Amy gave me an extra scoop too, cause I'm not in trouble for potty talk. But you are," she said happily.

"I beg your pardon?" Noni asked, feigning innocence. "Colton. Explain," she huffed.

He grabbed his ice cream, now smoothie, from the bag and placed Noni's cup in the freezer while Lucy bounced on her lap. He flipped a chair, straddling it backwards as he scooped up a half-melted portion of his ice cream.

"You little shit," she said.

He pointed his spoon at Noni and swallowed the ice cream. "That's why you're in trouble, for potty talk."

"I will have you know, Colton, that I am sixty-nine-year old and can say shit as many shitty times as I feel like saying it. Do you hear me, you little shit shitter?"

He took another bite of his ice cream and looked at Lucy, giving her a little wink. "You see? Potty talk." Her head bobbed up and down.

"Oh, hush, Helen," Rita snapped as she walked in

shortly after. "I've taken four shits today already. Those shitty pills have the inside of my saggy ass cheeks on fire like the fourth of July."

"Jesus," he whispered. Appetite lost, he placed the cap on his cup and put the rest of his ice cream in the freezer. "You done with your ice cream?" He watched Lucy jump off of Noni's lap and toss her empty cup away. Thank goodness Amy's two scoops were small. "Let's get you cleaned up and into bed. Say good night to Noni and Aunties"

Lucy quickly hugged them fiercely. One thing about his little niece, she was a hugger. "I'll show you my treasures tomorrow. Uncle Colt has to wash them for me," she said to Noni.

"Alright, honey bear. I'll be up there shortly to tuck you in."

Lucy skipped her way up the stairs to do her routine. Colt walked out to follow her and stopped at the kitchen door. "Noni, for the record. You're seventy-two, not sixty-nine. Get your age right."

He braced for any artifact to fly through the door, including a cleaver, and stopped on the first step. "There's ice cream in the freezer for you," he added, smiling, knowing she was still grumbling while opening the freezer door.

"Colton?"

He turned mid-way from the staircase.

Please don't throw a cleaver.

"I love you, Colton. Even if you are a shithead."

"Love you too, Noni. Even though I plan on selling you to the highest bidder."

She slammed her foot down and slanted her eyes at him. "You wouldn't sell me."

He shrugged his shoulders. He looked at both her hands. No cleaver. Only the ice cream and a spoon. Good.

"Watch me," he teased.

Chapter 8

Clichés

Who in the world placed the scotch with the red wines? Why was the vodka mixed in with rum? The stock room was a train wreck. Someone had carelessly placed the extra supplies of glassware in the lower racks, when they should have been placed in the cabinets in the office. All the tequila should have been together like one big happy family. Not mixed in the gin family.

Stupid, stupid Lizzie.

Willow never wished ill will on anyone, but she wouldn't mind if Karma paid that girl a visit.

I can make that happen, whispered Tails to Halo. *She's my second cousin.*

Willow reorganized the tequila shelf, putting the bottle she needed for today's drink to the side. She made a mental note to come back for reorganization duty before her OCD sent code reds to her anxiety.

Ugh, why is this brandy with the white wines?

Carefully, she secured the brandy. What else was down here?

She bent over searching the shelves.

"Jesus, you're killing me."

Oh my.

Oh yeah. Tails sat up, grinning.

Willow snapped straight up quickly and turned,

knocking her elbow into the shelf, toppling the tequila bottle.

With quick reflexes, Colt caught the bottle before it shattered on the ground. "Jesus. Are you alright?"

Her elbow throbbed as she rubbed it, blushing at her clumsiness. "You scared the Holy Spirit out of me."

She ignored his lame attempt at not smiling, dimples still teasing his handsome face into a grin.

"What are you doing back here, anyway?" She asked, her elbow still smarting from their collision with the shelves.

"Fab told me you were back here looking for some tequila? Something about pulling out her hair because of margarita and her complex ass. Threw me in for a loop, considering she's bald as a baby's backside." A confused look crossed his face.

Leave it to Fab and her dramatics. Pointing towards the bottle he saved, "We're running low upfront and there's a birthday party out on the patio. They want Marg-tinis which are margaritas in martini glasses. I needed to get more tequila and glasses for the shrimp and guacamole we're serving them. I got caught up in here. It's disorganized and my OCD is going nuts."

She followed his gaze. The storage room was large enough to hold their supplies and overflow of liquor. Like bottles of wines no one ever drank. It was sturdy with wooden shelves and stocked with different arrays of alcohol.

"Are you talking about the scotch bottle mixed with the white wines?"

"Yes. See? It's a complete disaster," she said, pointing at the misplaced bottle.

He reached over and grabbed the scotch, placing it

in its appropriate section. Still holding onto the tequila, he walked closer to her.

"You changed your shirt," she mumbled. He wore the Martini Girl Bar T-Shirt she set aside for him. The beginning of a smile tipped the corners of his mouth as he slowly closed the door behind him with a resounding click. He stalked her.

Oh my, he looks quite dashing, gushed Halo.

Yum, Tails said, licking her big ruby lips.

"I appreciate you giving me the black and white shirt and not the black and hot pink glitter."

"I don't know. I think hot pink glitter would be a good look on you," she teased, slowly backing up against the shelves. "Um, you realize we are in the storage room?"

His gaze was as soft as a caress. "Go with it, Willow," he taunted her, his lips teasing the side of exposed neck. Tails cheered her on for wearing her hair in a messy ponytail. A slow shiver raced down her spine with anticipation.

She reached up, gliding her hands over his broad chest, feeling the fit of the t-shirt and the contours underneath. Willow slid her hands over his neck and through his hair, enveloping him in her arms.

"You two are the epitome of a cliché."

Colt groaned, leaning his head against hers.

Willow counted backwards as Tails exploded into a ball of flames, cursing Fab. "Girl, you know I don't do well with margarita. You best get this over with quicker than quick."

"Got it, Fab," she said, still giggling.

"Two minutes Pistol and then your mine. Make it count, handsome." Fab winked at him, grabbing the bottle of tequila from his hand, and re-closed the door.

"She does not do well with tequila," Willow explained. "I better get back out there." Her feet moved backwards away from the doors, following Colt's lead till she was up against the shelves again. "Colt," she whispered his name.

"I have one minute and forty-five seconds left with you. You heard her. Let's make it count darlin'."

****

"Yo, Fab, where's Whiskey?"

"Levi, what do I look like to you? I'm no one's keeper in this establishment."

"True. But you still know where everyone is at all times."

"She should round those doors any second or I'm going to go back to that storage room and pull her out of there by her luscious ponytail."

Willow rushed through the doors, ignoring Fab's smirk and Levi's curious stare. No doubt her messy ponytail was messier than usual and her full lips swollen from Colt's kisses. Not to mention her face was flushed, and she was pretty sure Colt left her a sexy little love bite. Oh, and let's not get started on her panties.

"Here are the glasses for the shrimp and avocado. Does Wes need anything else for the order?"

This was a big step for them. The Martini Girl Bar was just that, a bar. They served no food. Although they'd had their license and kitchen inspected for production, it was one step they hadn't moved forward on. The birthday parties. This event would either make them or break them in that aspect.

Colt placed the additional bottles of tequila and triple sec on the bar and unloaded them onto the shelves.

"Keep one of each out?"

Fab cringed at the devil's drink, as she referred to it. The smell of tequila alone would cause Fab to toss up her life all over her five-inch leopard heels. And that would be unacceptable. "If you could leave them out, that would be great. Preferably anywhere away from Fab," Willow joked.

"Amen," Fab said with hands on her stomach. "Wes has things under control and he knows how you want the food served. He's got it," Fab reassured her. "Pistol, you're with me once you finish. Let's get these glasses over to Wes to wash and set up. We have fourteen ladies to ensure they have a Fabulous Fab time."

"I'm not sure I'm going to be good as a waiter."

They all laughed at his assumption. Levi joined in, slapping him on the back. "Think Fab is going to have you play acoustic outside, brother."

"Ah, that I can do." Relief shone in his eyes.

"Let me grab you a guitar," Levi said, walking back behind the stage.

"I didn't know Wes was your cook," Colt said to Willow.

"We are trying something new. And Wes went to culinary school. He's amazing at preparing gourmet meals and owns a food truck, Slider Up. It's the one that sells mini burgers. So good. We talked it over with Wes. He agreed. And now we are starting small, like the one today. Sort of testing the water before we go bigger and bring in menus." She realized she was rambling but continued on, "I've thought of expanding. The building next door is for sale. I would love to buy it and expand into a dining area over there."

"Again, smart and beautiful. I think I like you,

Willow," he admitted.

"What can I say? I am pretty likable," she replied shyly. "I haven't told my partners about the building next door yet."

He wrapped a loose strand of hair behind her ear. A habit that she liked he was forming. Warmth crept up her neck, shadowing her cheeks. "You are definitely likable. Don't worry, I won't say anything."

"Thanks, Colt," she whispered.

"Pistol. Change of plans, handsome. Levi's going to play acoustics. Wes needs you in the kitchen."

"Wait, why do I have to play?" growled Levi.

Fab crossed her arms over her yellow tub top, showing off her fit arms. "Listen here, Viking, everyone knows the cook runs the show in an establishment. That cook is Wes Banner. And Wes Banner is telling me he wants Pistol in there sorting plates. Then that's what is going to happen."

"No need to get your panties twisted," Levi defended.

"As if I'm wearing any," she said without batting her long lashes.

"Still don't get why I have to play?" he grumbled, passing Fab.

"Because you end up eating all the fucking food," yelled out Wes from the kitchen.

"No I don't," Levi yelled back.

"Is it always like this?" Colt asked, catching Willow's sharp movement as she moved on to mixing her Marg-tinis in one hand and salting the glasses with another.

"Not always. Sometimes they get nasty and insult each other." There was a trace of laughter in her voice.

"Good luck in the kitchen, handsome."

He playfully tugged her ponytail and winked as he followed Fab.

Willow sighed, eyes following Colt.

"You got it bad, Whiskey girl," Levi whispered from behind her.

Yes, she did.

"Apparently, you do too," she whispered back with a wink.

****

"Alright, Banner. What do you need? Or do I call you Chef?" asked Colt.

Wes chuckled. "Nothing formal here. Let's get the glasses prepped and then we can serve up the food."

Colt worked alongside Wes, cleaning out the glasses and prepping them on the trays. He watched closely as Wes added two scoops of the fresh made guacamole, three jumbo shrimp, and three corn chips in red, yellow, and blue.

"Got it?"

Colt raised his eyes to Wes. "You want me to do that?"

"Man, I remember you worked at the pizza shop. Those pies were the shit. If you can make those pies, then you can do this."

"I was sixteen," Colt said nervously.

"Wash up. I can't have Levi in here. He eats more than a tank of hungry sharks."

Colt followed orders and washed up thoroughly. He grabbed the dish rag and hung it from his pocket, matching Wes. He used the scoop and followed the instructions from Wes and completed his first martini glass, cleaning up any smudges on the rim.

"Nice. We need to make thirteen more."

"Got it." They worked side by side, Colt scooping in the guacamole and Wes adding in the shrimp and chips. Once they had all fifteen glasses done, Wes showed Colt how to call in for a waiter to pick up. Within seconds, Vet hurried in and grabbed the first tray of food and returned swiftly for the second tray.

"We give them about fifteen minutes and then send out the next order. Grab those oval plates there and let's set them up on the trays."

Colt reached over and grabbed the warm dishes, placing them on the tray. He remembered his restaurant days and inspected each plate, making sure they were fully clean.

Wes noticed and smiled. "In the center, draw a line in the middle with the sauce. Then we place three small crab cakes next to each other like this. Add a lemon wedge and kale and your good to go. Got it? We have to plate these quickly since these need to go out warm."

Colt nodded, understanding. He got to work quickly. Once the first tray was ready to go out, he called for pickup and went back to finish the second. He finished the second tray as Vet walked back in, returning the martini glasses from the first appetizer. Vet picked up the trays for the second round.

Colt washed his hands and placed the dirty dishes in the washer as the music from the radio snuck in from the window.

"What's next?"

"Waiting to see if Vet brings in anything else. That's all that the tables ordered at the moment."

"What are you making, then?"

"Steaks."

"For who?"

"Us," Wes said, grinning.

Hell yeah, thought Colt. He wiped down the counter, keeping it clean along with the serving utensils.

"Need anything from upfront?"

"No, I'm good. Make sure Whiskey's set. I'll holler when they're ready."

"Thanks, man."

Colt left the kitchen and ran right into Lacey. "Oh gosh, I'm sorry."

"All good. Everything alright?"

"Yeah. I needed to grab more rum and tequila. They are flying off-the-shelf today. If you need Whiskey, she's in the office."

"Thanks. Let me know if you all need anything else from the back. I can run and get it for you."

"That would be amazing."

"I'll check back with you all in a few."

He walked to the office and stopped. "I've already told you no in the past, Curtis. There is no way I would ever partner with you. Martini Girl is mine." Her silence and aggravated tapping of her pen on the table notified him she was listening to whatever Curtis Merk was saying on the other line.

"You have no clue what my plans are. And it's none of your business. It doesn't matter how many employees you think you can sweep in and steal from me, or copying the aesthetic of my bar. In the end, you know The Punch Bar is nothing more than a cheap copy-cat of my bar. I know that pisses you off. So you can take that and choke on it." Bitterness spilled from her voice.

Colt stared at Levi as he walked out of the shadows. Quietly he leaned into Colt, "Paying that fucker a visit real soon."

"Let me know when," Colt said, never taking his eyes off of Willow and her upset form.

Colt knocked on her door softly and pushed the rest of it open. He walked in and closed the door shut as her phone rang again. She groaned and looked at the phone, but quickly picked up the call. "Hey sissy. I'm good and you?"

He waited for her to finish her call, seeing her smile. "Alright. That's good. I'll see you soon then. Awesome. Good. Drive safely tomorrow and text me when you get to New Orleans."

She dropped the phone to the desk and looked up at Colt with a small smile. "That was Mila. Her and mom are leaving tomorrow morning and heading to New Orleans for a few days and then here. They are going to be moving in with me temporarily till she finds a place."

"Her husband?"

"Filed for a divorce and knocked some other chick up," she said sadly.

"Sorry, baby."

"I haven't told the girls," she mumbled. "Levi and Fab know because I mentioned Mila can fill in while we are on the trip. Becks knows, well, he knows since there is history there. Wes knows since Fab and Levi tell Wes everything. But no one knows the *reason* she is moving back. Only you."

Colt walked over to her and leaned on the desk next to her. "I won't say anything."

She stood up and walked between his legs, wrapping her arms around his neck. "How did it go in the kitchen?"

"Good," he said, not wanting to talk, feeling her this close to him.

"I need to get back out to the bar," she said, leaning into him.

"Yeah," he agreed, his hands slowly wandering down her back.

"Colt?"

"Yeah, darlin'."

"Kiss me," she whispered against his lips.

His lips captured hers, feeling her pressed completely against him. Her fingers slid through the back of his hair. Her soft moan enticed him to deepen the kiss. His hands wandered lower on her back, feeling their way over her curves.

He turned them around and raised her up on the desk. His tongue traced and teased the soft fullness of her lips. She slid her fingers through his hair. Squirming closer. He pulled back and gazed into her honey eyes, drowning in them. His lips recaptured hers, more demanding this time.

Completely entranced.

"Seriously, you two are such a cliché," sassed Fab, with Wes standing behind him.

"Steaks are ready."

Jesus.

Colt reluctantly released Willow after taking a long, deep breath. He needed to get his mind and body under control. If Fab and Wes had not interrupted them, who knew how far things would have gone? He knew how far he wanted it to go and from the way Willow was kissing him back, then she was riding the same lust train as him.

"Steaks?"

Colt turned his gaze back to her, shrugging, "Banner hooked it up."

"Nice," she said, going back to straighten her

paperwork and checking her cell phone once more before walking out of the office with Colt.

Once at the bar, Fab rounded back on them, giving a knowing smirk to Colt and Willow, who blushed deeply.

"Yo, Whiskey? Need you outside for a sec," called out Levi.

"Go, baby. I gotta head back to Wes. Check in with you later," Colt said. He gently tugged her back into his arms, not caring who was watching, and kissed her slowly.

"Get it, Pistol."

He released Willow and winked at Fab, as he walked away.

****

Colt polished off the steak, relishing the last bite. "Amazing Banner."

Wes nodded with a knowing smile, taking the dishes to the sink to wash up.

Colt stood and cleaned up the table as the sounds of cheering echoed through the hallway. "Looks like Levi is getting ready to play."

Wes grunted, unimpressed.

The sounds of the guitar melody coupled with a female singing stopped Colt in his track. He looked up and caught Wes's smirk. "Go," he said.

Colt hurried to the door and caught Willow singing with Levi playing. The small crowd clapped along to the acoustic beat.

"She's good,"' Wes said from behind him.

"I didn't know," Colt admitted.

"Not much our Willow can't do, Pistol," Fab stated.

"She can't play the guitar," pointed out Wes.

Some part of Colt liked that she couldn't. "Guess I'll have to teach her," he said, the thought pleasing him,

"Please do. She fucks up our guitars every time she tries to play them," complained Wes.

As the song, 'Love on Tap,' ended, the small crowd stood up, applauding loudly. Without missing a beat, Levi began strumming the next song, 'Speechless.' His husky tone seduced the atmosphere as Willow came in on the second verse, blending in smoothly. They continued to sing to the crowd.

Willow's eyes slowly connected with his, holding his gaze till the end.

"Yo, give it up for our girl, Whiskey," Levi said to the crowd.

Levi glanced over and caught Colt's attention, nodding him over. "Birthday girl, we got a little special something for you. Martini Girl Bar style. You ready, doll?"

Unsure what Levi was planning, Colt smiled and approached them, waving to the crowd. Levi called out to Vet.

"Ladies, did you know your waiter here has a hidden talent?" Levi grabbed Vet and threw his arm around him. "Want to show them what you got?" he spoke loud enough, causing the girls to giggle.

"Let's do it."

Vet moved over to Colt, shrugging his shoulders. Fab walked over and provided him his case, which he quickly placed behind him, hidden from the table.

Colt took the guitar from Levi. "Not bad for a drummer."

"You should see what I can do with a piano," Levi said, grabbing his Cajun box.

Levi looked over to Fab as she stood next to Whiskey on the MIC. He nodded over to Wes, who passed out a tambourine to Fab and grabbed a stool for himself to sit with a guiro and scraper, ready to jam.

Levi whispered the song to the group. Vet smiled widely. He reached into his case and pulled out his all-black custom trumpet. He started the song slowly, breaking into a solo, enticing the table and drawing in a larger crowd. They caught the queue from Levi, and Vet blared out the first notes of, 'Wine, Beer, Whiskey.' The table went crazy, as did the patrons who came out to listen as Levi pounded on the Cajun box and Colt strummed the guitar in tune. Willow and Fab brought in the lyrics, along with the crowd. Wes played the guiro singing back up with Colt, who enjoyed the impromptu jam session.

They let Vet take over on the solos, bringing in his classical training with a twist of rock and country. As his last note ended, they all stood and bowed, but not before Fab moved forward and queued everyone to sing, 'Happy Birthday.'

Trixie walked out serving cupcakes in hot pink long stem martini glasses adorned with a strawberry and white chocolate shavings.

Colt leaned over to Willow, hoping enough distractions were around them. He pulled her closer to the hidden alcove and drew her in for a kiss. Adrenaline pumped through his veins from performing. "You are amazing."

Willow blinked her eyes slowly. "Think so?"

"I want to see you again before you leave on your trip. Think we can make that happen?" Colt asked.

"I'm sure I can," she whispered.

"Seriously, the two of you are such a cliché, " snapped Fab as she walked past them, shaking her head.

Chapter 9

Call Me Maybe

After another long night at the bar, a day out with the girls was what Willow craved.
Well, that and Colt, purred Tails.
Oh my.
Colt pulled his weight around the bar, assisting Wes with the kitchen. She owed him big time for all his help. She had learned he worked at a local pizza shop when he was younger. They started him in the kitchen washing dishes and busing tables. He was later taught how to toss pizza dough and could prepare a mean deep dish that could blow her mind. Something he promised he would make her on their next date.

"What are you packing for this weekend?" Sofia asked from behind a rack in the store they were currently shopping in.

One thing her best friend was amazing at was always being there when Willow needed her. The call with Douche Bag Curtis put her in a sour mood, not to mention she was worried about her sister. Sofia knew the exact things to say to get Willow out of any funk or when to be a quiet shoulder to lean on.

She was loyal and fierce. Overprotective. Even when going to the restrooms. She never, ever, ever let any of the girls go to the restrooms by themselves. Any restroom. Any…worth repeating. Her logic, a girl never know when someone was going to "woman-knap" her.

Sofia was always dressed in the latest trends and her short shoulder length hair was adorbs. Her words again. Besides her being fiercely loyal and plain crazy, she also had to pre-plan her plans for future plans.

"I have no clue. You know I don't pack till the day before," Willow grumbled.

Sofia gasped in sheer horror because she was melodramatic and belonged in a Soap-Opera. She snatched the cute top from the rack and stomped over to the shredded jeans lane.

The 'Shred' section of the boutique contained a variety of clothing with trendy tattered jeans, jackets, and evens shirts. Pip's Boutique was a unique store their friend Piper owned, and they all frequented. Which also included a thirty percent discount in addition to any sales Piper currently had going. Piper's Fall and Winter collection were coming in, which meant they were in for the Summer blow out sale.

Sofia had hurried to Willow's place, still with her rollers in her hair. Yes, rollers.

"You are taking those things off before we walk down St. George Street, right?" Willow had told her as soon as Sofia opened the car door.

"I can rock them."

Sofia did not rock them down St. George Street. Fab had threatened from the Willow's bed, to shave Sofia's head if she stepped one foot out of her white BMW with the hideous neon green rollers.

Now, Sofia stood in front of the mirror. She placed the shirt up, modeling the blouse and a pair of capri-jeans with ripped knees and frayed pockets. "Did we decide where we are going?"

Fab smacked her lush orange lips and grabbed a deep purple tank top with a long sash attached at the ends. She paired it off with a simple white cargo shorts. "We sure did. We are going to the Keys. Final answer."

After several text messages, multiple phone calls, heated face-to-face conversations and even emails, all of which happened yesterday, Fab had put her heels down and declared the Keys would be their destination.

"I thought we were doing Savannah?" Sofia whined.

"Don't you start. We are doing the Keys. *El Fin.* We agreed Savannah for the Fall. We will go in October and do the haunted tours."

"Right. You think you're going to get that one on a haunted tour?" Sofia said, pointing to Willow.

"Sure will. Especially if Pistol is there. He even said he would be down for Savannah in October."

"Wait. I never agreed to go on a haunted tour. I said I would go to Savannah but not to check out any ghost," Willow clarified.

"Even if Colt is there holding you close?" Sofia challenged.

"I'm not doing it," Willow firmly stated.

"We'll see," Sofia and Fab both said, laughing.

"And who said Colt was going on a girl's trip, anyway?"

"Uh, we did. And Levi. And Wes. And Beck," said Fab, announcing everyone.

"And who is going to run the bar, genius partner of mine, if the three of us are all gone?" Willow asked with her hands on her hips, patiently waiting for her once upon a time intelligent business partner to reappear but someone was drinking the same cool aide Sofia dipped into occasionally.

"Girl, you know Mama Jones got this. And Mama Lawson. And your sissy Mila. They can hold down the fort for one day, girlfriend. And if we need backup, I can call my cousin Mo' and she will be here faster than the Panty Droppers can drop panties."

"She doesn't even like martinis," hissed Willow. Had Fab gone crazy like Sofia?

"Neither do I, and yet here I am," Fab said, spreading her arms wide.

"*Un momento,*" interrupted Sofia. "You don't like martinis? Since when? You drink Cosmos with us all the time."

"Correction, I *chug* Cosmos with you," Fab clarified.

"You drink Lemon Drops," Willow pointed out.

"Which are also shooters, and I chug those, too."

"Who are you?" Sofia asked with her hand clutched over her chest.

"Right? How did we allow you into our circle of trust?" teased Willow.

"That's because I am Fab, and I go where I go. Plus, you would be lost and bored without me."

"Then what in the world do you drink? Please don't say beer," Sofia said, practically gagging.

"Ain't nothing wrong with an excellent beer. But I am classy," Fab said, fluttering her long lashes. "I like me some fine wine."

Sofia looked over at Willow, her eyes rounded, about to pop out of their socket. "She's a Vino Babe."

"Red or White?" asked Willow.

"Red."

"Good, cause that's pretty much most of the wine

we have at the bar. The white sells out pretty quick."

"Yeah, I know. And it's trash. Might as well be vinegar."

The Martini Girl Bar was not known for their wine. On rare occasions, they had a Vino Babe come in, ordering for a glass of red or white wine. However, that is exactly how they sold it. Red or White. Maybe they needed to look into expanding their wine selection...

"You've never said anything," defended Willow.

"Because we are a martini bar. Wine is not exactly a top priority. I know we order red and white to have in case someone like me or Mo' comes in and orders a glass, but hell, Willow, it's on our drink menu as red wine or white wine."

Sofia snickered and snorted, grabbing another blouse to try on. All while Fab continued to dis the wine options. "You can dye a shirt, dress, even stain a piece of wood with the red wine and possibly remove the dye from the shirt and dress plus the stain from the piece of wood with the white wine. It's that bad."

"Why the hell haven't you said anything? Has anyone ever complained?"

"Do you see how many bottles we have of the wine in the storage? We don't have complaints because no one orders it. Word gets out pretty quick. They come to us for the mix drinks, not for the shitty wine."

"Then speak up. We can call Luca and see what he has for wine distribution."

"Now *that* I can do. That man is fine with a capital F, I, N, E."

"Is that the bootlegger?" asked Sofia.

They all laughed. Prisco Distribution was the only distributor in the city, and Luca ran the business. He took over for his father when he passed last year.

He was young.

He was a professional.

He was hot, seductive, and luscious, with his dark hair and even darker eyes. With golden sun kissed skin and a six-foot runners' body dressed in a suit, he wreaked havoc on all breathing things.

Luca went to school with Wes and Wes recommended they stick with him. Since then, Luca renegotiated their contract. Prices remained fair and Martini Girl Bar received good quality liquor in a timely manner. The downside, Luca also distributed to The Punch Bar and there was an instance or two where deliveries were 'mixed up' with the driver.

The first one was not an enormous issue. The second one cost the bar a good penny for top quality liquor they needed for a festival happening in the city. Willow had called Luca and complained, not something she enjoyed doing. Luca handled the situation with delivering the missing liquor to them directly himself with extra bottles to make up for any losses the bar was incurring, as well as stayed to enjoy the festivities. It was the first time she saw Luca let loose and relax. He was always intense. The girls nicknamed him the Bootlegger, from when he dropped off the liquor. Luna and Sofia had mentioned he looked like a gangster from the roaring twenties, in his suit, delivering whiskey and rum in crates.

Willow continued to shop around the store and found a cute long summer dress in a pale-yellow, with a halter top, open back, and low cut front. She found her size to try it on and found the same dress in an electric blue color. She picked them both up, trying to see which color she would like better, doing her best to stay away from anything resembling solid black, solid gray, and, black and gray.

Since Pip's boutique had opened in the last three years, Willow had slowly branched into a range of different colors in her wardrobe. She had moved on to purple and blue and was slowly moving into pink and red.

The little bell over the door chimed, alerting them of Skylar's arrival, as she held a cup of coffee in her hand. Dark shades covered her almond shape eyes. Her long, black, thin braids hung loose down her back. Skylar raised her sunglasses over her head. Her face was clean of makeup with a soft hint of lip gloss across her lips. She wore small, studded earrings in both ears and a small stud in her helix piercing.

"Look at what the cat dragged in," announced Sofia, walking over and giving Skylar a warm hug, swiping her coffee cup from her hand.

"I spit in it," Skylar said, annoyed.

"Yummy," Sofia said, taking another sip before passing the cup back over.

"I swear girl. You ain't right."

"Ah, I love this song," cried out Sofia to Dua Lipa's, 'New Rules.' At that moment Fab opened the dressing room and posed against the door frame in the purple tank top with the sash tied around her small waist and white cargo shorts, singing along with Sofia.

On the second chorus, Willow opened the second dressing room in the electric blue dress singing her part of the song, swinging her hair around.

"Oh my God, you're scaring my customers away," laughed Piper, walking out to the front of the shop.

"We are your customers. You're not even open yet,"

replied Sofia.

"Hey, sis," Skylar greeted her.

"Hey, sister," she replied. "Did you go by the folks this morning?"

"Yes, they're good. They want us over for dinner sometime this week. It's your turn to cook dinner."

Piper turned and admitted, "Fab, that outfit looks hot on you. I've been dying to see someone try on that tank top."

"Girl I know. They made it for me."

"Willow, get that dress. Blue not yellow," Piper added.

"Sold," Willow said, giggling.

"Wait, I have to try on my clothes!" cried out Sofia, racing to a dressing room.

Willow changed back into her clothes, grabbing the yellow dress and placing it back in its proper location. She grabbed a Maxi dress, two cargo shorts like the ones Fab tried on, and a halter top. She placed her clothes on the cashier table to be rung up by Skylar, as they all waited for Sofia to model her clothes. After everyone raved on Sofia's choices, Piper rung her up.

"What are you all going to do?" asked Piper.

"We are meeting up with Luna for brunch. What time are you taking a break?" said Willow.

"Not sure. I have the new inventory to go through and I want to update the displays. A lot to do before the weekend escapade. Oh wait, here, give this to Luna." She grabbed a bag from behind the register. "She bought a blouse the other day, but she didn't realize she picked the wrong size. I told her I would exchange it for her when it came in."

"Will do."

"Hey, is Harper going too?" Piper asked.

"I haven't heard from her. I swung by her house last week. There was a car at her house. When I asked her about it on Saturday, she was evasive." Willow pursed her lips.

"I'm sure she is fine. It was probably some secret hook-up she has. You know she's always been a little hush-hush about her lust life."

True statement.

****

Luna arrived a bit early and collapsed into her seat at the restaurant. A bit stressed. Not to mention exhausted. She'd received a text from Sofia letting her know the rest of the girls were on their way and that they had a package for her from Piper.

Luna perked up a bit with excitement.

She'd requested a round table near the window on the second floor and ordered a spicy Bloody Mary. She sipped on her drink, reading the appetizers, when her phone chirped with an incoming text. Why anyone would not simply call was beyond her understanding.

Unknown—*You coming to the bar tonight?*—

She stared at the phone, unsure whose number it was.

Unknown—*This is Levi*—

She choked on her drink, reading the last text. "Bollocks."

Unknown—*Haven't seen you*—

Unknown—*Want to see you before you leave*—

Luna's palms broke into a sweat. Her hands shook slightly. Her face, body, entire universe became warm. All from a text.

Unknown—*Come on Love*—

Unknown—*At least tell me I'm not the only one feeling this—*

"Oh bloody hell," she groaned and placed her phone down. If he only knew how quickly his blue eyes and secret smirks or soft touches and demanding kisses drove her to have an out-of-body experience. Even his, 'Hello, Loves,' caused her to have panty changes faster than a model on a runaway show.

Unknown—*Music?—*

Unsure what he meant by that, she took a long, large gulp of her drink and replied, her phone saving his contact.

Luna—*What about it?—*

She did not have to wait long before he replied.

Levi—*Do you like it?—*

She stared at her phone as if it grew horns, arms, legs, and was ready to conquer the world with its guitar and hell raising melodies.

Luna—*Of course. Who doesn't?—*

How could she explain to someone else that she lived her life in her own personal musical? Music was a constant in her world. It's what kept her calm and centered.

Levi—*Beautiful Drug—*

"Beautiful Drug," she whispered to herself out loud. She quickly googled it while her phone chirped again.

Levi—*Think of me when you listen to it—*

Levi—*I think of you every time I hear it—*

Her heart stopped.

She swallowed the lump in her throat and pulled her wireless earphones out, playing the song.

Luna read the lyrics as the song played, enjoying the playful tempo of the song. Lost in the moment, she didn't notice the girls approaching her slowly. She replayed it again. Not thinking about what she was doing, Luna texted back.

Luna—*Call Me Maybe*—

She froze. Panic seeped in. "Oh no. What did I do?"

"English Tea Cakes, what's got you all freaked out?" asked Fab, snatching the seat next to her and hanging her oversized bag on the chair.

Levi—*Crazy, Beautiful, Sexy*—

Levi—*Call you tonight, love*—

Bloody hell.

Bloody hell.

Bloody hell.

"Breath, Luna, before you collapse," warned Fab.

"Who's texting you, *mija*," asked Sofia, taking her seat across from Luna. She grabbed Luna's drink and took a sip and smacked her lips. "So good," she grinned, pleased.

Skylar rolled her eyes but grabbed Luna's drink and took a sip as well. "Oh wow, that's good and spicy," sitting next to Sofia.

Willow pulled her seat next to Luna, placing her hand discreetly on Luna's under the table. She mouthed "Are you alright?"

Luna's enormous light blue eyes sparkled with a mixture of excitement, fear, and something else she was sure Willow would not put her finger on.

Fab reached over and grabbed Luna's drink, polishing it off and smacking her lips loudly. "Oh wow, that is the bomb."

The waitress came back, and Fab ordered a round of Bloody Mary's for the table. Extra Spicy.

"Back to the Sofia's question. Who's texting you,

English Tea Cakes?"

Luna stared back, her fingers hovering over the last message. "Levi," she whispered.

A huge grin spread across Fab's face as the Bloody Mary's appeared on the table. Fab took a sip of her drink, enjoying the savory, salty tomato mix with the extra spices.

"Did you give him my number?"

"Sure did," admitted Fab as the other girls gasped in surprise.

"Why would you do that?"

Fab turned directly to Luna and pointed her well-manicured nail at her. "He asked me for it."

Willow, Skylar, and Sofia turned to Luna, waiting for her rebuttal.

"Don't you think it should have been up to me to give it to him?"

"Wait, would have given it to him," interrupted Skylar, curious.

Fab arched her eyebrow. Challenging Luna.

"It still should have been up to me to do it," defended Luna.

The girls turned to Fab.

"English Tea Cakes, get over it. We walked in here and you were flying around in whatever cloud Viking put you on. You are welcome for that."

The girls turned to Luna.

"That's not the point," Luna stated haughtily, seeking help from Willow and Sofia. Sofia sucked on her straw between smiles, thoroughly enjoying the verbal match, as Willow stared at her drink, trying to identify its ingredients.

"You suck," snapped Luna at Fab.

"Uh no, I don't. I'm the hottest bomb. And because I'm the hottest bomb, that look he described to me thoroughly when he kissed you at Willow's will be back on your face again and again and again."

"Bloody Hell," Luna groaned.

"And," Fab said, moving Luna's hair away from her neck, exposing the faded love bite, "that will be back and possibly joined by another," she teased, wiggling her brows.

"I'm going to need another drink," mumbled a fully flushed Luna.

Willow took pity on her friend. "What did he say?"

"He asked if I was going to the bar. He wants to see me before we leave on our trip."

Fab danced to her own rhythm and laughed, snapping her fingers in the air. "Get it, Viking. Get it!"

"Excuse me, but whose side are you on?"

Sofia and Skylar sat back and laughed out loud as Fab downed her drink, placed her food order, and another round for the girls.

"*Mija*, we have to walk back, you know," Sofia complained, attempting to finish her first drink before her second much more watered down one.

"Drink up ladies," Fab continued to dance in her chair. "We got two Martini Girls who are going to get laid soon by some hot, hot, hot Panty Droppers."

Willow blushed, and Luna groaned in embarrassment. Her insecurities slowly seeping in.

"Don't," whispered Willow. Only Willow would have picked up on the sudden change in Luna.

Luna gave her a sharp nod. Her phone chirped again.

Levi—*Call Me Maybe? Really, love?*—

Levi—*Never heard that song and now it's stuck in*

my head—

Luna stared in shock at her phone. "How is that possible?" she said out loud, then looked at Sofia and Skylar. "How is that possible?" she asked again.

"What?" Skylar and Sofia asked in unison.

"He's never heard the song, 'Call Me Maybe.'"

Sofia spit half an olive out and choked on the spices as Willow grabbed a napkin to assist their dramatic friend. Skylar reached over and moved Sofia's drink before she spilled the rest, smacking her on the back. Harder than necessary.

"What's, 'Call Me Maybe?'" asked Fab casually, sucking on her spicy pickle and clearly enjoying the crunch when she bit into it. An unbelievable silence met her as five pairs of eyes, which included their curious surprised waitress, stared back at Fab.

"Do you all want anything else?" the waitress asked quietly.

"Another bloody round," hissed Luna.

"You don't know, 'Call Me Maybe?'" Willow asked.

Fab continue to arch her eyebrow and lowered her glass to the table. "No, Willow girl, I don't know, 'Call Me Maybe.'"

Sofia wildly waved her hands at Luna, still coughing and wiping her leaky nose and eyes. "Play it," she choked out.

Luna grabbed her phone and played the song softly for Fab. Their waitress brought them their drinks and lingered a little longer than necessary. Kept cleaning the same spot till the polish of the wood came off.

Once the song finished, the same five pairs of eyes patiently waited for Fab's review.

"Well," the waitress anxiously asked, and then realized she had joined a conversation she probably should not have been a part of.

Fab shrugged her shoulders, "It's cute," reaching for her glass and sipped her drink.

The waitress tossed her hands up, exasperated, walking away, deflated.

"Cute," whisper-yelled Luna.

"Yeah, cute."

"You seriously have not heard this song," Luna asked dumbfounded.

Fab crossed her arms and arched a sassy eyebrow.

"It was played on every radio station. Every day. Like all the time," Skylar said as she smacked Sofia on the back several times and shoved napkins in her face.

"What rock did you live under?" whispered Willow.

"Yeah," Sofia sniffed, blowing her nose loudly.

Fab smacked her lips and sipped her drink. "Apparently the same badass rock that Levi lived under, which explains why he has never heard the song either."

Luna's eyes bulged as she glanced at Skylar then back at Fab then back to Willow and Sofia. "You are bloody nuts," she muttered.

"Why? Cause I've never heard this song?"

They all nodded their heads including the waitress who remained close by and deeply invested in their conversation.

Fab dramatically smacked her lips and took another sip of her drink before she pointed her infamous manicured pointer finger at Luna.

"You listen and listen good Tea Cakes, like me, Viking is a badass. A badass don't listen to, 'Call Me Maybe,' unless a little pretty, sweet English Tea Cake tells them to listen to it," Fab teased, enjoying herself, humming the song. "It's catchy. Got it stuck in my head, so you know it's stuck in his head. Which means, you are stuck in his head. Well played Tea Cakes. Well played.

"Bloody hell."

Chapter 10

Tuna and Tequila

"Yo, Whiskey. Someone's here to see you?" called out Levi.

Thank goodness for interruptions. Willow was still hopeful good fortune would befall on her and someone would pay it forward and leave her one million dollars or an all-paid inclusive trip to Fiji or Alaska. She wasn't picky. Anything to take her away from the mountain of paperwork she was going through. She would rather go to the dentist than file paper.

Scratch that.

She would rather go on a haunted tour than file paperwork, and that was saying a lot.

A light breeze blew through from the patio and the opened bay windows. Kenny Chesney's voice rang through the speakers while some of their guests enjoyed the outdoor seating.

Wes had expanded his food menu, adding shrimp ceviche on a tostada, mango salsa with chips, and his take on an ahi tuna poke bowl with avocado and brown rice. It was then that she decided the ahi tuna poke bowl was her favorite meal of all time, to which Wes had laughed and stated, "Duly noted."

"Who wants to see me?"

Levi scooped up another bite of his ceviche and

tostada chip, before wiping his hands on his dish rag. He smiled and pointed over to a table in the far end corner. That smile of his meant trouble.

Willow sliced her eyes at him. She reached for a pitcher of water and walked over to the table full of older ladies. She noticed right away one had pink hair. The one who sat next to her appeared older in age with beautiful frosty white hair and an oxygen tank. Both were dressed classy and held an air of elegance, and something else.

"Good afternoon, ladies," Willow said, pouring them each a glass of ice water. "What can I get you to drink this afternoon?"

Lady Frost, that is what Willow nicknamed her, took a quick hit of her oxygen before speaking. "Are you Whiskey?"

Her smooth voice surprised Willow for some odd reason. "Yes, ma'am," she replied politely.

"Told you she would be hot," Lady Frost said to Lady Pink.

Wait. What?

"Indeed, you did," Lady Pink said.

"Think she gave up the milk?" asked Lady Frost.

"Either her milk is sweet, and he's coming back for more," Lady Pink said, sipping her water. "Or he has only had a sample of it and not the full glass."

What the H.E. double hockey sticks?

"I'm sorry. Do I know you?"

Lady Frost took another hit of her oxygen and said, "It's rude to interrupt a conversation."

Lady Pink nodded her head in agreement. "Very rude."

"This younger generation has no concept of manners," mumbled Lady Frost, picking up the drink menu.

"It's also rude to talk about said young generation in question like she is not present," Willow pointed out sweetly.

"Well, one thing is for certain, not only does she not have manners, she is quite presumptuous," Lady Pink said, snubbing her nose in the air as she placed a pair of small reading glasses on her nose to read the drink menu.

Her mama taught her to respect her elders at all times. She was also taught not to be a pushover. However presently, her little angel and devil were speechless. Neither knew what to do or how to handle the situation. Willow stood there, dumbfounded, waiting for the two crones to place their orders.

"I think I will try your Long Isle-Tini," ordered Lady Pink.

Lady Frost placed an order for their summer draft beer.

Unsure if it was safe to serve her a beer, considering she kept taking hits of the oxygen tank like she was some sort of alien who could not live in their atmosphere. "You sure you want a beer?"

Lady Frost's blue eyes turned stone cold, sending a shiver down Willow's spine. "What? You think I can't handle a beer? I've been drinking long before you could say cock."

Stunned, Willow turned and walked away from the crazy old bats. Levi stood amused behind the bar, cleaning up the area and sweeping the floor. It was the thing she loved partnering with him. He was tidy. Lacey, not so much. "What do they want?"

"For starters, you know me. You know I never spoke ill of my elders, but those two old bats are effing cray-

cray. Lady Frost wants the summer draft beer. Lady Pink wants a Long Isle-Tini."

Levi threw his head back, laughing loudly at Willow's description, wiping the tears that escaped.

"You know it's inappropriate to talk about your clients behind their backs," yelled out Lady Frost.

With her back turned to them, Willow pointed and as if saying 'see what I mean'. He grabbed a glass and poured the beer for her while she mixed up Lady Pink's drink. Long Isle-Tini was her take of a Blue Long Island Ice Tea with added sugar to the rim, garnished with a cherry. After shaking all the ingredients and insuring this was going to be one of her best drinks she had ever made, Willow poured it into the glass with blue sugar rim, topping it off with two cherries instead of one.

Take that grouchy crone.

Willow gingerly walked back to the table and stopped midway. Somehow the two crones had multiplied to four and all eight eyes stared at her.

Deep breath, Willow.

"Here are your drinks, ladies." She turned to the rest, "Hi there. I'm Whiskey. Is there something I can get you to drink? I'll bring you some water in the meantime." She put on her perfected smile.

"Hello, my lovely people. Fab has arrived on this glorious Sunday. How are we doing this afternoon?"

Thank the good Lord. Willow took her words back; she'd rather be filing instead of dealing with the old crones.

"Let me try your drink. It looks so pretty," said the new arrival in her pretty short curled blond hair. Her arm, with thousands of gold bangles, reached across Lady Frost to grab the drink, taking a quick sip from Lady

Pink's. "Oh, that's yummy. I will have one of those," Lady Bangles said.

The younger one of them all, looked over the menu and her eyes lit up. "I want a Cosmo."

Willow liked them. They weren't crones after all. "Coming right up."

"Bring some chips or something to munch on. And I want a blue drink too." Lady Frost said.

"Rita," Lady Bangles scolded in a whisper. "I'm sorry, my dear. Rita gets a little *hangry* when it passes her lunchtime."

"Is that the issue? Here I thought it was the lack of oxygen," Willow retorted. Take that Rita, AKA Lady Frost.

As she walked away from the crazy elders' table, Lady Bangles' hands clapped and jingled while Lady Junior, the younger one, snickered along with her. Willow was pretty sure she caught Lady Pink hiding a smile behind her Blue Isle. Willow might win these crones over yet.

"Now what do they want?

"Lady Frost wants chips or something and a Blue Isle. Not sure if she is going to drink the beer."

"She'll drink the beer," Levi said.

"How do you know?"

He did a chin lift to the table. Willow turned around and found the old bat practically guzzling the beer down.

"I swear, she's got to be an alien or possessed." She placed the food order for their table. Wes assured her he would take care of it and served her up a mango salsa plate and chips. She grabbed the items she needed to make the two Blue Isles and Cosmo. Fab swept by the bar, seeing the plate to be served. "It goes to the Elder's table," explained Willow as she gave Fab a quick cliff notes version of the day's saga.

"Girl, I got this," she said, grabbing the tray and strutting over to the table in her white Martini Girl Bar T-shirt and dark blue denim jeans and brown boots, the dress code of the day.

"And how are all of you gorgeous ladies doing this morning? Are we having a fabulous time?" She asked, pouring two glasses of water down with a side of chips and salsa. Fab went on, chatting along with them as if they were part of the same bushels of apples picked together.

How Fab could easily win them over, Willow didn't understand. It was obvious why Fab was the people person of the bar and not Willow. She was the brains of the business, and Levi, he was their investor. When they asked him why he wanted to do this with them, his only reasoning was, "It's smart business."

Their three-way partnership worked like a charm. They met every Wednesday to discuss any changes with the schedule, staff, as well as participation in city festivals. They discussed fresh ideas to make them more marketable. Levi was the one who thought of bringing in some local bands and renting the space by having them perform a few sets to see if it would draw in a crowd. Expanding the business was the new focus.

Fab was on board with bringing in fresh talent, but she was not giving up Fridays. Flat out, she put her high heels down and stated Fridays are Fab's nights and that tradition no one was taking from her, to which they all agreed.

Willow secretly planned for expansion. Of a different type than Levi's. It would be an enormous investment and a tremendous risk with such a large real estate deal, but she believed they could be successful. Especially if they were going to introduce food options.

The additional space would provide another two thousand square feet, as well as more parking space. Parking spaces were a gold mine. And the best part of the new place, the plumbing, was up to date. That alone was a plus in her book.

Her mind raced through the endless possibilities of expansion as a frustrated Fab slammed the tray on the bar top. "I need two shots of tequila. Make it the cheapest, shittiest tequila we have, and two shots of whatever lethal untraceable poison you got back there for the two old hags in Pink and Silver."

"Ah, you met Lady Pink and Lady Frost AKA Rita," Willow confirmed, pulling the tequila bottle and four shot glasses.

"Oh, I met them." Fab turned her blazing dark eyes and long lashes to Levi, pointing a pale pink manicure fingernail at him. "You need to control your Nana."

Say What? "Your Nana?" Willow hissed.

Levi grabbed the shot glasses from Whiskey. "I'll take care of it."

"Which one is your Nana?" Willow asked, still in shock.

"Uh, Lady Frost herself," shot back a fuming Fab, crossing her arms over her tube top, staring them down.

They both watched Levi walk over to the table, murmuring to the crones as they cackled and shot back their drink. Willow watched as he turned, waving for her to come over.

"Girl, you better take that bottle of tequila and that paring knife with you," muttered Fab, heading back behind the bar to cover for Willow.

She walked over, without the paring knife, and braced herself.

"Whiskey, let me officially introduce you to this band of misfits." He introduced Lady Bangles as Candice, Lady Junior as Helen. "Lady Frost, as you dubbed her, is Rita Brooks, my Nana," he said with a wink. "And Lady Pink, is Noelle Royce."

Something in his warning tone triggered a code red siren to sound off in her mind. *May-day, may-day... Can you hear me, Halo or Tails? Anyone? Need some help here.*

"Another round of tequila?" she asked instead.

"Aunties, this is Whiskey, my business partner. You met Fab, our other partner," he said, waving to Fab who stalked over to the table, rolling her eyes, unimpressed.

"What kind of name is Fab?" questioned Rita through her oxygen mask.

"A fabulous one," snapped Fab. "Is there anything else that I can do for you ladies this afternoon? Another round of Blue Isles? Perhaps a nutritional protein shot?

Willow's jaw dropped. Fab was not one who lost her cool, and never with customers. What in the world did these women do to her? Levi coughed, covering his laugh. "Oh shit."

"Protein shot? How old do you think we are, boy?" fussed Rita.

Oh no.

The air thickened in the room. Something escaped from the deepest part of her dearest friend that was neither a gasp nor growl. It was both. A noise only Fab made when she was unleashing her Dragon Queen's fury. Angry vibrations bounced off of her.

"Fab," Willow whispered.

Fab's hand came up, silencing her. Fab looked over at Rita and grabbed her unfinished Blue Isle-Tini and snapped her finger in her face. She then turned to Levi and demanded, "Handle it," before storming off. She tossed the half drank contents into the sink and placed the glass in the washer, passing a confused Wes with a tray of food.

Willow stared at Wes, sending silent warning messages. "Which one of you unleashed the Dragon Queen?" he asked. Quickly the three ladies pointed to Rita, who continued to complain about her drink being taken away.

Wes placed the dishes in front of the three of them and turned to take back the fourth dish.

"Wait," pleaded Candice. "Levi, honey, you know your Nana needs to eat. She becomes unbearable, and it's obvious she has reached the point of no return. Don't make us all suffer too," she said sweetly.

Levi nodded to Wes, who begrudgingly passed him the plate of food and walked off. "You owe Fab an apology, Nana. Not cool," he said. He turned to Willow and quietly told her, "I'll go check on her."

Willow nodded and stared at the misfits. "Ladies, anything else?" She moved back slightly when Noelle stood up from the rounded booth.

"Come sit," Noelle said. Her voice lost the sharpness and cattiness from earlier. She appeared earnest and genuine. Candice and Helen, both smiled at her and nodded with encouragement. Willow turned and found Levi standing behind the bar.

"Levi, you good for a bit?" she called out.

He waved her off, while he filled in an order coming

in from the patio. She sat down between a disgruntled Rita, and Noelle.

"Well, I think we got off on the wrong foot. As Levi mentioned, I'm Noelle Royce."

"What can I do for you, Ms. Royce?"

"Well, for starters, what are your intentions with my grandson?"

"Yes," commented Rita. "Are you in it for the sex, money, fame, and glory or are you harboring deeper feelings for my nephew?" she raised the shot of tequila and arched her snow-white eyebrow.

Cheese and rice.

"Rita, please let the poor girl relax before you scare her off," Candice said.

"Exactly. Put the tequila down and eat some food. It's absolutely amazing. What is it, by the way?" asked Helen.

Still shocked by the inquisition, Willow slowly reached over and grabbed the tequila Rita put down and inhaled it herself. Not caring if it would cause another outrage from the old crazy bat. "It's an ahi tuna poke bowl," Willow whispered.

"Do you need another one, honey?" asked Candice, bringing her tequila shot up to Willow.

She quickly reached for it and downed the shot and found Helen's as well. Not waiting Willow downed the third shot ignoring Helen's raised eyebrow as she took another bite of her rice bowl.

"This is amazing. Rita. Eat. Now," Helen demanded of the disgruntled woman to swallow some of the rice.

Willow stared at the last shot of tequila in front of Lady Pink, AKA Noelle. She watched Noelle's right eyebrow perk up and a sly smile form on her face. "Well,

Whiskey? Or do I call you Willow?"

"Willow. You can call me Willow, Ms. Royce. I'm only called Whiskey by the staff and patrons that know me at the bar. Outside of that, I'm just Willow."

"Willow then." Noelle raised her shot glass and took it without a hitch. "That is some shitty tequila."

Something inside Willow bubbled up as she blurted out laughing. She was not sure if it was her overwhelmed nerves of being face to face with Colt's grandmother, who she knew was an important person in his life. Or who she possibly made a complete, disastrous first impression with her and her cronies. Or the possibility the three God awful tequila shots she took were taking over her senses and causing her to be insensible during her work hours, because, who doesn't like a drunk bartender?

Yes, quite the professional.

"Hmm, I think this one has thicker skin than you both thought," chimed in Candice.

"I like her like I like this poke bowl," said Helen, doing a happy dance on her chair as she took another bite of seared tuna. "So good," she moaned in delight.

"Helen, you need to stop making all those noises over there," Rita scolded. "Making me uncomfortable here with my tuna."

"Oh, honey. I'm sure your tuna has had no feelings in ages. Better to be uncomfortable then dead," teased Candice waving her hand with a thousand bangles.

Helen covered her mouth from spewing rice, dropping her fork. The clattering sound drew the attention of some guests. Levi's gaze turned to them. Willow nodded her head, letting him know she had it covered, doing her best not to laugh at his grandmother's tuna. "Uh ladies, let's keep everyone's tuna out of the conversation."

"Oh, where's the fun in that? Not like you don't have one too," said Rita.

"Yes, well, I don't know you well enough to discuss my tuna with you, Ms. Brooks," Willow replied politely.

"We have exchanged pleasantries, and unpleasantries, and you stole my shot of tequila. You can call me Rita. Besides, you and my Levi are close and he speaks highly of you. I know enough to give you a hard time."

"Which means, in Rita's talk, that she likes you," explained Candice.

"With that said, what's my nephew Colt got that Levi don't?" Rita demanded.

"Rita, please," hissed Noni. "We are not here to find out about Levi."

"Makes no difference. Levi talks about Whiskey this and Whiskey that. Only seems right to ask why she didn't go for Levi. Don't get your bloomers in a twist."

Noelle slammed her fork down. Willow stared with wide eyes as Noelle leaned over, pointing her hot pink nail at Rita. "You better turn up that hearing aid and listen up. I have not and will never wear bloomers. You hear me, you wretched saggy ass hag."

Rita sucked in a long draft of her oxygen, fumbling a bit before she turned and leaned across Willow to face off her nemesis. "Saggy ass? Who the hell do you think you are talking to here? My ass is no more saggy than yours. Levi, tell this old bat your Nana does not have a saggy ass." She yelled across the bar, causing Levi to stop short his conversation with a pretty blonde and over pour the draft beer in the mug.

Willow slowly lowered her face into her hands, sighing helplessly. She raised her one hand high in the air to Levi, making a circling sign. "We need another round of tequila. Bring the good bottle, please."

"Amen!" cried out Candice with her bangle hands raised high.

Halo remained shockingly quiet throughout the entire interaction. She turned to an also completely stunned Tails.

Yeah. I've got nothing too.

"And can I get another Poke Bowl?" requested Helen. "So good."

Tequila and Tuna.

Who would have thought?

Chapter 11

Just Another Sunday

There were times Colt believed he did the parenting thing right. He had made sure Lucy's diapers were on straight without duct tape. He had finished a French braid without using an entire bottle of gel to hold it in place. Matched bows with outfits. Bought mismatch socks because it's the cool trend for little girls to wear, which he questioned why bother matching her bows if her socks would not match. That caused a whole other conversation of epic four-year old proportion to which she advised him he would never understand. Threw a kick ass fairy birthday party, which included a dramatic water balloon fight where his aim always shot true to Noni and her cronies.

Easy targets.

And picking out the perfect puppy from the shelter.

They had spent the day again at the beach looking for more mermaid treasure and frolicking in the water. Building sandcastles and having a picnic he packed earlier in the morning. He brought her boogie board and taught her how to stay on the small waves. She squealed as she rode down the shore. The more comfortable she became on the board, the braver she became, jumping on the waves on her own. He kept calling out to her to remain close to the shore. Despite her confidence and ability to swim, he did not want her going out too far into the larger waves.

He snapped pictures and videos of her surfing the waves. He figured might as well send pictures to Noni to show what she was missing out on and Levi, since the crazy fool was the one who bought Lucy the boogie board. After their morning at the beach, they packed up and headed in for some ice cream and visited with Amy for a bit. It was Amy who'd mentioned the shelter was holding a big Adoption Day.

"Let's walk over there."

"Oh, can we please, Uncle Colt? Please." Excited at the prospect of looking at the animals, Lucy nearly spilled her bubble gum flavor ice cream.

"Mind if we leave my truck here in the lot?" he asked, chuckling at the little ball of energy swirling next to him.

"Of course not. Take pictures of the puppies. I'm looking for one myself," Amy said.

"Will do. Save me a cup for Noni. I'll get it on the way back."

An hour later, they were signing papers on a white and black spotted furry pup with ice-blue eyes and checkered bandanna. The puppy was eight months old and full of fur. "He's an Aussie-Pom mix, and the sweetest in the litter. Such a teddy bear," the lady said from the shelter. "Here's his record. All shots are current. We've included the food we've been feeding him. He's currently going through leash training and is not a hundred percent house broken. Still needs a little work. Do you have any questions for us?"

Colt read through the medical records, making sure the pup would not need any additional treatments besides the normal check-ups. He looked over and found the puppy rolling on the floor with Lucy, licking her sticky fingers from her ice cream. His heart expanded. Yeah, he was doing the parenting thing right. "I think I got it. We good to go?"

"Yes. He's all yours."

He picked up the pup and held Lucy's hand. They walked back to the truck, showing off the new family member to Amy. "Oh my gosh, he is the cutest thing ever. Are there more like him?"

"They have lots, Ms. Amy. But he's the cutest," Lucy said excitedly.

"What's his name?" she asked, scratching him behind his ears and enjoying the puppy kisses.

"We haven't..." Colt started.

"Fluffy!" declared Lucy.

Ah, hell.

"Well, he is quite fluffy," Amy confirmed.

"It's perfect for him. Right, Uncle Colt?"

"I don't know. I mean, he *is* fluffy. But there's so many other descriptive names out there. Let's run it by Noni. She might have an opinion." He prayed his grandmother this one and only time would be on his side. Who was he kidding? Poor pup was going to be stuck with Fluffy. Colt shook his head.

"Noni is going to love the name Fluffy. You'll see," Lucy said assuredly.

"Well, either way, he's adorable. Better get going before Noni's ice cream melts."

He packed up his little clan, buckling up Lucy in her chair and securing the pup in the front seat next to him, as Colt made his way to the pet store for supplies. Once inside, Lucy's female DNA kicked into fifth gear, filling up the cart with so many things the pup would never need, including a ski jacket and purple rhinestone collar.

"Lucy, he's not going to need any of these things. Here, we'll get him a ball and a frisbee for the beach. You can pick out one of those squeaky toys there and a rope. We can get him the furry pillow bed thing in brown. We need his water and food bowl." He walked by the food and grabbed a bag of puppy chow, along with some teething snacks. He switched the purple rhinestone collar for a blue harness with a retractable leash. As they walked down the toy aisle, the pup barked wildly and whined.

"What is it, boy?" Colt picked the pup up, making sure he did not catch his little paw in the cart. He wiggled fiercely in Colt's arms. He placed the pup on the ground and watched the pup scramble to the chew toys bottom shelf, pulling a rubber chicken and shaking it around, making the chicken squeak obnoxious loud with its eyes bugging out.

"Look, Uncle Colt. He likes the chicken."

"I see that," he chuckled, picking up the pup and squeaky toy. "Guess this is the toy you want." He secured the pup back in the cart in his furry bed and watched him circle around till he collapsed with the chicken next to him. "Alright, little ones. Let's get going."

Colt arrived on time for both a four-year old to barrel inside to use the bathroom and a whining pup to use the patch of grass outside for his needs.

"Put Noni's ice cream in the freezer," He reminded her before the door shut on her. Colt glanced over at the unfamiliar parked car, while he waited patiently for the little fur ball to sniff around the new surroundings and finish his business. Colt still refusing to acknowledge the pup as Fluffy.

"Need any help?"

The sound of Willow's smooth voice drifted from the doorway. Turning, he found her shuffling her feet.

"Come on pup," he called and walked over to her, only stopping till they were eye to eye. "Hey," he whispered, leaning in and brushing his lips over hers. His gaze was eye level with hers.

"I promise I'm not a stage five clinger or have a stalker fetish," she quickly explained, "But your grandmother and friends stopped by the bar and, well, they needed a ride home and refused to take a paid car service. I can't remember if it was Lady Frost or Lady Junior who said they may get taken to some port to be shipped off to an island and sold to a merchant who will sell them as sex slaves or something. Levi had an emergency at Haze and had to rush out, which left Fab and me and, well, Fab is pissed at Lady Frost, so that left me to drive them home. Lady Pink said to bring them here. So…here I am. Surprise," she finished, blowing out a rush of nervous air.

Colt pulled back, feeling something clawing at his pant leg. He looked down at the furry ball and picked him up. A soft, delightful gasp escaped from Willow. "Let's start over. My grandmother was at the bar?"

He noted the unconscious way she nervously bit her lip and nodded.

"And she was there with her cronies?" He asked, watching her slowly nod.

Colt reached over and brushed the back of his fingers over the apple of her blushing cheek. "I'm assuming Lady Pink is Noni. Tell me, baby, what did the

crazy pink haired bat and her cronies do?"
****

Willow made every attempt not to laugh at the situation. The initial awkwardness of an unexpected visit wore off. Not because she didn't want to see him. It was that the invite had not come from him and she was not sure if Colt was ready to have her over yet.

Willow had expressed this concern to Lady Pink AKA Noelle AKA Noni, who informed her after the fifth shot of tequila to call her Noni and she was welcome at their house as *her* guest anytime. Regardless of what happened between Colt and her. To which the brigade all cheered, "Here, here!" and took their sixth shot. Willow had stopped at her third shot. Not joining in on the action, considering she was still working.

This led a pissed off Levi to fuss at his Nana AKA Lady Frost AKA Rita, who in turn told Levi to remove the stick up his ass, which was right before he got the call from Haze, the Tattoo Parlor he owned.

Unfortunately for Willow, he rushed out, leaving her with the hell raising drunken elders. Fab completely avoided their table, handling all other customers and graciously greeting everyone with her usual sunny disposition and the occasional dagger stare at their table.

Willow observed Colt through lowered lashes. She pulled her hands out of her pockets and laid them on his shoulders.

"You mean besides finishing an entire bottle of tequila, calling Fab a boy, and asking if I have given up the milk yet and what my intentions are? Which when I got around to telling them after their fourth tequila shot that we have only been out on one date, Lady Frost, which is Rita by the way, demanded to know why I haven't done the horizontal tango with you and what was wrong with me?"

"Jesus," he muttered, shaking his head.

"It gets better. Lady Junior, AKA Helen, could not stop eating the tuna bowl. Somehow Noni and her cronies turned tuna, a simple Rated-G fish, into a Rated-Triple X should-never-be-discussed-in-public conversation fish."

"Jesus," he muttered again.

"I'll never look at tuna the same way again," she told him in a serious tone.

"Any word from your contact about buying my grandmother? At this point I'll give him a deal, buy her and I will throw in Rita for free."

Despite of levity of the situation and earlier events, she chuckled and wrapped her arms around his neck, pulling him closer. "I don't think Levi will be happy with you selling his Nana."

"I don't know. I think we might easily talk him into the deal. Hell, he might even deliver them for us," he said deadpan.

Still laughing at his threat, she watched the pup watch her curiously, giving Willow a light yap for attention. She reached a hand out to pet his soft, furry coat. "Who's this little guy?"

"Pup, this is my girl, Willow."

Her breath caught. The flutters in her stomach swarmed chaotically.

Yes, he's claimed us, cheered Tails.

"Willow, this is Pup," he said, passing him over to her.

"You named your puppy, Pup?" she asked incredulously.

"Not exactly. Lucy wants to call him Fluffy," he said, running his hand through the puppy's fur. The little guy was enjoying the attention from both of them.

"He is fluffy and cute," she said, melting as Pup gave puppy kisses under her chin.

"None of that, Pup. She's mine," he said, winking at her, causing the constant blush she wore around him to deepen.

"Ah. You're in denial," she stated.

"Denial?"

"With his name being Fluffy," she said teasingly.

Colt moved Pup to the side, pulling Willow closer. "What's it going to take to get you to help me convince a very cute, very adorable, very stubborn four-year old to change his name from Fluffy to something, anything, else?"

Clean out our cob-webs, screamed her little devil.

How is it I only hear you and not my little angel?

She's having a spiritual moment with Mr. Grey.

Cheese and rice.

Invite him over, Tails persisted.

"Well, that depends. What are you willing to do for such a favor?" she lowered her voice to a seductive whisper.

"Ask me for anything, Willow," he said. The sudden feeling they were both losing an emotional battle that neither wanted to fight came over her.

"Come over?" she asked breathlessly, feeling their noses brush against each other, as she ran her fingers through his thick hair.

Oh my, Halo spoke up. *She asked him over. It's a bit too soon for that.*

Absolutely not. Go back to your book, Tails

chastised.

This Mr. Grey is a complicated soul. I haven't even passed
Chapter four and can tell he's quite troubled.
Skip to
Chapter eight and keep your white wings out of this conversation.

Willow took a deep breath, waiting for his answer. Was she being too forward? Oh, Lord, why did she continue to listen to her hussy side?

Because I'm trying to get us some action that requires a little math—Add a bed, subtract the clothes, and divide the legs, girl. Now bat your eyelashes and suck his face already, Tails ordered.

"Uh hello, *mija*? I know you are not leaving me in here with these *vieja locas* by myself."

Curse you, Sofia!

Colt chuckled, pulling back and winking at her.

"I forgot she was here," she whispered to Colt, laughing softly under her breath. "She helped me bring them home in her car. My car has no A/C."

"Uncle Colt, we have guesses here!" his little niece squealed in delight. "Can we show them Fluffy?"

"Is that his name?" asked Willow. "I thought it was Freckles. I must have misunderstood," she said dramatically, hitting the side of her head.

"Freckles! Oh, oh, oh yes, Uncle Colt. That's perfect for him. He has all those spots. I love it!" Lucy cheered excitedly.

Colt watched Willow with wide eyes mouthing a silent, 'Thank you'. "Freckles it is, honey Bear. Go show Noni." He put Freckles on the floor, who chased after Lucy inside. "Hey, Sofia, mind giving me a minute with

Willow?"

Sofia rolled her chocolate brown eyes at them, huffed and stomped back inside, raising her voice and speaking in Spanish to Rita.

"I better get in there before Sofia commits mass murder in front of Lucy and Freckles. I would hate for them to suffer that kind of trauma at such an early age."

The sudden yank on her hand brought Willow to a stop and right back into Colt's arms. One hand tangled in her hair, the other around her waist, crushing her to him. He pressed his mouth to hers. Lips coaxed hers to open. She gasped and drank in the sweetness of his kiss.

Finally, moaned Tails

"*Vieja loca.* Sit down before you break your neck."

"Don't tell me what to do, you little imp of a girl."

Their kiss slowed, as she pulled away with a frustrating sigh.

"Yeah, we better get in there," Colt agreed.

CRASH!

"No, Auntie Rita. That's Freckles. He's not a skunk."

"Get the rabid critter!"

"Rita, stop it! It's a puppy, you old hag," yelled Candice.

SMASH!

"Helen, help Noni off the ground."

"I'm not touching her. You know, once she starts laughing like this, she ends up pissing herself."

Colt's eyes widened as she looked up into his sea-green gaze.

****

"You're a damn nurse, for Christ's sake. You've seen piss, shit, and lord knows what other bodily fluids,"

Candice scolded.

"I'm retired. I retired just so that I would not have to deal with piss, shit and other bodily fluids," said Helen.

"Oh, fuck a hornet's ass. Rita, sit your saggy drunk ass down and do not move a muscle." Candice reached over and grabbed Freckles and Lucy, placing them on the cabinet next to a wide-eyed Sofia. "Sit here, honey bear," she said, and passed the fluff ball over to Lucy. She opened the freezer and grabbed Noni's ice cream from the freezer.

"Hey, that's mine," shouted Noni from the floor, attempting to stand up.

Candice opened a drawer and grabbed a spoon, passing the cup over to Sofia. "Enjoy it," she said and walked over to Noni, who was on all fours, giggling and twerking.

"You keep that up and you're going to dislocate a hip bone," cried out Rita.

"Shut up, Rita," cried out Helen, Candice, and Noni simultaneously, causing Noni to cackle like a madwoman.

****

"What the hell is going is on?" Colt demanded.

Oh dear.

Work it Noni. Work it, encouraged Tails as she twerked as well.

Willow stood behind him, taking in the scene. Her hand came to her mouth as Rita pouted in a chair like a little child in time out. Noni was making dance moves that were not decent for any person to make at any age. Helen chewed on her nails, scared to address Colt or scared to laugh out loud in front of him. Candice waved her hand, addressing him, "She's drunk, Lord Obvious."

Sofia nodded her head, taking a scoop of the ice cream and sharing it with Lucy. "*Vieja locas,*" she muttered again.

"Let's watch Magic Mike," chimed in Helen, trying to break the tension in the room.

"Yes!" screamed Noni as if orgasming, raising herself to her knees.

Magic who? Asked Halo.

Channing Hot Stuff Tatum, Tails said twirling on a pole. *Finish with Mr. Grey and I'll introduce you to the magical moves of Channing Tatum.*

"Noni," Colt growled, and then looked at Willow.

"I need my glasses. Colt, grab my glasses. I want to watch Tatum do his thing," Rita said, shimmying her shoulders.

"Can I watch too? I want to see a magic show!" asked Lucy.

"NO," Colt cried out. "Sorry, honey bear. No. Not till you're never years old."

Lucy's crestfallen face softened Willow's heart while Colt's flushed face worried her. No doubt he was suffering from an onslaught of high blood pressure. Not every day a man's four-year-old niece got excited to watch the not so magic show of Magic Mike.

"How about I order pizza for dinner, huh?" Colt asked.

Lucy's face split into a grin.

"I'll get the movie started," chimed Candice happily as she slapped her hands together and walked out to the living room, pinching Rita's face.

"I need my glasses, dammit," Rita scolded. "You," she said, pointing to Willow. "Can you pass me my glasses since my nephew is conveniently ignoring my request?"

Willow looked around the kitchen and found Rita's purse, glasses inside. She handed them over to Rita who walked into the living room, taking a spot on the recliner, waiting patiently for the movie to start without thanking Willow.

Helen was finally successful in getting Noni off the floor with the help of Colt, who was fuming at her for letting herself get this wasted. "What were you thinking, drinking this much?"

"Oh, pish posh. I'm not that drunk. I'm not even slurring my words," she said, swaying on her feet.

"Sit down before you break something," he scolded.

"Do you want me to order the pizza?" Willow asked, walking into the kitchen. She noticed the change in Colt. His eyes darkened with concern over Noni's inability to walk straight.

"How much did she have to drink?" he asked. His tone no longer holding its usual charm.

Taken aback, Willow stared directly into his fiery eyes. Hurt clawed its way through her chest. She pushed back the feeling, hating how she quickly let herself get attached to him. "She had two Blue Isle Martinis. Six shots of tequila, of which the last two were watered down. I made sure she ate two bowls of tuna poke and plenty of chips with mango salsa," she defended herself.

"And you didn't think to stop her at any point in time?"

"No Colton. I didn't. Like any other patron who comes to my bar, as long as they are drinking and not acting unreasonable, belligerent, or vomiting all over the place, they continue to get served. However, considering I am an observant bartender as are Levi, Lacey, and Fab, we watch those who order and how much they order and make sure after a certain point we ask them how they are getting home and make calls for them if needed. Sofia and I drove the ladies home."

She'd overstayed her welcome. Willow knew it. She looked over to Sofia, who observed them, still keeping Lucy and Freckles close by. "You ready to head back?"

"*Si*," Sofia quickly said, putting the empty cup and spoon in the sink. "Alright *princesa*, let's get down."

****

"Willow. Wait," Colt called out as she walked towards the front door without saying another word.

Noni stared at Willow's back, grabbing Candice's cane she left behind and smacked him in the back.

"You shithead. Go stop her or you will regret it."

He followed Willow, stopping in the living room to yell out, "Candice, Noni is using your cane as a stripper pole!"

"Noelle Royce, you better leave my cane alone and get one of your own. Get your saggy tits in here. I'm not restarting the movie."

He found Willow about to get in Sofia's car. "Willow, hang on," he called out, stopping her from opening the passenger door. "It was a dick move of me to blame you. I shouldn't have done that."

She kept her back to him.

"Stay," he said quietly.

She turned, her eyes cast down. "I think I'm going to go. I had them all drink several glasses of water before we came over here. Helen said she would make sure they were good. Candice said this wasn't their first rodeo and they would be fine. I texted Levi and told him Rita was here. He said he's on his way."

"Willow," he whispered her name.

"I have to go check on the bar. Fab called in Lacey, but this was her day off. I have to relieve her and Fab has to leave to go with her mom. It's Sunday tradition to have dinner at their house and she cannot miss it."

"Baby, look at me," he muttered, hoping she would look up and stop avoiding his eyes.

"I better go," she said, turning around again and opening the car door.

Colt watched Sofia's white BMW pull out of his driveway as Levi's black F150 truck pulled in. Tied up in knots for the way he acted, he hated watching her leave this way. He made a mental note to call her later, knowing her invitation to come over was most likely revoked.

"Yo." Levi growled. "What did you do to Whiskey?"

Colt ran his hand through his hair. "I'll fix it," he promised.

"He acted like a shithead," yelled Noni from the porch.

"Noni," Colt warned.

"Don't you use that tone with me, Colt," she said, her voice faltering slightly at the end.

"Why does she look green?" asked Levi.

"Awe hell," muttered Colt as the devil took over Noni's body and spewed massive amounts of projectile vomit over the porch banister and into the hedges.

Chapter 12

Monday Blues over Club Sandwiches

Mondays.
They should be the day of the week where expectations were not required.
No plans.
No illusion of self-accomplishments.
Nothing.
Willow craved them like she did a taco stand on lonely nights. Except her Monday started with eyes popping open at six a.m. for no logical reason, other than her brain annoyed her all night with thoughts of Colt. More than frustrated with herself, she began her morning with Yoga, detesting Colt at this point. She ran to the vet with Prim and got her shots and a new toy. Since she was out and about, she stopped by the store, with Prim stowed away in her bag, occasionally peeking her head out to greet people, and bought a bookshelf and another new toy for Prim.

At home, she finished up her laundry and put together her new bookshelf. Lastly, she conquered the dreaded closet from the guest room, where she still had most of her books in boxes. She anchored the smaller book shelf to the wall above her other shelves. From the same closet, she found a painting she'd completed one night with the girls and another painting she'd completed with Mila and her mom. She hung both of her masterpieces on each side of the bookshelf. Pleased with the look, she unpacked the remainder of her books and cleared out the closet and drawers. By mid-morning, she had the guest room ready for Mila and her mom's arrival.

In her room, she combined her clothes as much as she could and made room for her sister. Once she had some drawer space completed, she moved into her closet and made room on one side. With that done, she cleaned the rest of her place from top to bottom. Changed out light bulbs and finished watching the season finale of her show.

Now, she thought back to last night's events. Sofia'd hung out with her at the bar. She'd helped as much as she could with serving drinks and taking a few orders. Fab left shortly after they arrived, still heated from her earlier interaction with Rita. Lacey told Willow she would stay and finish out the day with her to avoid closing alone, and they agreed to give Lacey Tuesday off instead. In the end, it all worked out.

Levi texted her later that night, letting her know he would cover Tuesday for her since he bailed out on Sunday. He'd mentioned Noni's vomiting spell and how it continued to happen most of the evening. He hadn't left till after midnight and Noni was still the color of pea-soup. Rita didn't fare off well either, but she had a cast iron stomach and was not throwing up.

Colt had text her several times, starting with a simple, 'I'm sorry,' followed by, 'Let me know when you can talk.' Willow had texted back, letting him know she would get back to him later. Things were busy at the bar. She'd half expected him to show up at the bar. Even hoped he would. Then Levi had texted letting her know the tequila devil Fab feared the most had visited Noni. Willow hadn't received another message from Colt again.

Call him, Halo encouraged her.

She noted it was close to lunchtime and wondered if he would be on break. Before she could talk herself out of it, she sent him a quick text.

Willow—*Hi*—

Willow—*How's Noni?*—

She waited, watching the three dots appear on her phone as he responded, then suddenly her phone rang.

"Hey," she answered, unsure.

"My dear, I'm fine," replied a hoarse Noni over the phone.

"Noni?"

"No, it's the First Lady. Of course, it's Noni. Who else would hack her grandson's phone."?

"Why are you doing that?"

"Because my grandson is a shithead. Now get over here. And please, my dear, bring whatever secret remedy you have for a hangover that includes nothing with the Devil's drink," she whined over the phone. "And food. I cannot get up to make lunch for myself and Colt is working and I refuse, you hear me, refuse to admit that I need him to make me anything to eat for lunch. Knowing him, he will give me moonshine pickles or something dreadful, just to spite me."

"I'll bring something to help you. Should I bring lunch for Colt and Lucy?" Willow asked, shaking her head and giggling despite the little guilt nagging her.

"That's sweet of you. He took Lucy and that wretched dog with him to get checked out at the vet. I'm sure he will bring Lucy back with either a trumpet or a set of drums and another screaming chicken for the mutt."

"Hang tight, Noni. I'll be there soon."

An hour later, Willow parked her car in Colt's empty driveway. The butterflies swirled around in her belly. She grabbed the drink carrier and feast she'd bought and walked to the front door, juggling the bags, keys, and drinks like a pro. She rang the doorbell with her elbow and cursed internally when the loud ringing bell echoed through the house.

"Ugh," she mumbled with keys in her mouth. Sounds of shuffling feet and muttering curses came through the doorway.

"You know, maybe Rita is right. You should date Levi instead, because I'm going to kill Colt when he gets home. That shithead," Noni said, opening the door wider for Willow to walk past her and straight to the kitchen.

Willow unloaded the bags and placed her keys in her pocket. "I don't think that's going to work. My friend is into Levi, even though she's in denial," she stated, taking out the carton of food, laying them out on the table in a spread designed for royalty.

She looked up at Noni. Her pink spiked matted hair stood in different directions. Mascara was smeared under her eyes darker than a raccoon. Her eyes were bloodshot. Topped off with a mossy shade of green complexion, she was the definition of a train wreck.

"Sit," Willow ordered, guilt slowly making its way to the forefront. "I didn't know what you could stomach. I brought everything from a greasy burger to chicken noodle soup. But the one thing you will definitely need to drink is this," she said, passing over the purple smoothie. "Drink all of it. It will help settle your stomach."

"Pish posh. I'm not drinking that."

"Yes, you are. No arguing about it either. Besides, it's yummy." She grabbed one cup and began drinking the purple concoction. "Hmm, so good."

Noni snatched the smoothie cup and hesitantly took a sip of the smoothie. "Where did you get this?"

"I made it. I usually drink a smoothie at home. Blue berries and bananas help with hangovers and upset stomachs. At least it does with me. And then I move to plain white rice or toast. Some people go for broke and get the greasy food. Sofia is like that. She swears by it. Hence the burger. If not, I got you a club sandwich or chicken noodle soup. Can't take credit for those, though."

"I think I'm going to try the soup and maybe half a sandwich," Noni said, cringing at the burger.

"Good choice. Save the burger for later. Where are the spoons and bowls?"

Noni weakly pointed to the drawer and cabinet and placed her head in her hands.

"Do you need any pain meds?" Concerned, Willow quickly poured some soup and served it to Noni to eat and told her to drink more of the smoothie. Willow opened the different cabinets, finding one with fresh bottles of pain killers. "How many can you take?"

"Only two," Noni said, wincing slightly and chuckling at the same time. "Seems I cannot bounce back like I used to."

Willow placed the two pills in Noni's hand with a glass of water. "No more tequila for you, that's for sure."

Noni sliced her eyes at Willow. "I'll have you know that I have been drinking since—"

"I know. I know. Since before I could say the 'C' word," Willow interrupted. "Drink your pills and water. Finish your smoothie, and then your soup. If you hold all of that down without turning like a sweet pea, then we will move up to your half sandwich. I might even let you eat the bacon."

"You cannot eat a club sandwich without bacon. That's absurd."

"Drink. Swallow. Eat," demanded Willow, taking a seat next to Noni.

"I can't say I've ever had a woman say those words to me. I suppose there's a first time for everything."

Willow choked on her first bite of her delicious smoked salmon club sandwich. "Oh my God, Noni. Let's not turn this into another poke tuna conversation."

Noni smiled and slurped her soup. It pleased Willow to see her enjoying the soup, despite her hangover.

"Have you talked to Colt?"

Willow slowly chewed her sandwich and took a sip of her drink, a sinking sensation feeling settling that she was being set up. "He texted last night, but things were busy at the bar. I tried to reach out to him this morning," she reminded the nosy pink haired devil.

"Yes, well, serves him right for leaving his phone behind. I swear he constantly leaves his phone or keys in random places in the house. Even though I bought that big wrought iron key holder that states Keys and that bowl over there for his wallet, phone, sunglasses and anything else he carries in his bottomless pockets." Noni took another mouthful of soup. "If he leaves it around the house, they are fair game."

"Like hacking into his phone," Willow confirmed.

"Exactly," replied Noni, pointing the spoon at her.

"He's a lot like his grandfather. Overprotective. Stubborn. Direct. A pain in the you know what." She sighed. "Oh, did I love that man with everything I had. Could never love another. I never even tried to."

"What happened to him?" Willow cautiously asked.

"Oh, you know. I got older, and he liked younger. He found some twit and convinced her a of a life of grandeur. I suppose they're somewhere in Maui, both getting skin cancer on their asses."

"I'm sorry, Noni."

"Oh, honey, don't be. I'm better off. I knew what I was getting into with Randal Royce. He was hot on wheels and slicker than lube when it came to smooth talking a lady. He hooked me good. Made me feel like a queen, and I loved every minute of it. Till I didn't. Now my Colt, he saw what that did to me. He was much younger then. But he knew my heartbreak. He wrote his first song about it. 'Love Lost.' That song is about my love that I lost of his grandfather's," she said, her eyes drifting into memories of her own. "It changed him. He made me a promise he would never treat a woman the way his grandfather treated me."

"You were also saying he's an overprotective, stubborn, direct pain in the you know what who will be loyal and faithful."

"Yes, you see. It's all positive."

"Got it, because that makes absolute perfect sense," Willow mumbled.

Noni took Willow's hands, gripping them sternly. "Colt told me he shared his sister's and wretched parent's history with you. He told me he felt this instant connection. I felt that for Randal, whatever the outcome of our relationship was, doesn't negate the fact Colt feels something deeply for you. Instantly. He doesn't get attached. Ever. And yet he met you, and in one night, there's been nothing but talk about Willow from that bar. I went to see who it was that caught his attention. I'm not surprised to find how beautiful you are. Or that your witty personality is a breath of fresh air. Plus, you rushed over to help me feel better when what you should have done is make a smoothie with hideous vegetables in it."

"I put laxatives in yours if it makes you feel any better," she teased.

Noni threw her head back and laughed loudly at her candor. Tears sprung from Noni's eyes. They both jumped up at the sound of car doors slamming outside and a small bark from a dog.

"I, um, maybe I should head out," Willow said, though she was rooted in her spot.

"You will do no such thing. You will sit down, finish eating your meal with me, and make up with my shithead grandson."

"Noni, we've only been on one date. There's nothing to make up."

"Sometimes, the heart knows," she said, finishing her smoothie.

Still shaking her head no, Willow braced for Colt to come through the door.

"Do you want him to make things right?" Noni asked.

Willow took less than a second to reply, "Yes."

"Then let him. The only reason he wasn't on your doorstep last night was because of me. Let me do this for both of you."

"You don't think all of this is too soon? I mean, it's crazy to feel like this, right?"

"Honey, I knew Randal was my North the minute my eyes saw him and my tuna fluttered." A wry grin spread across Noni's lips.

"Oh Lord. This is the same Randal who left you for the younger twit who is getting skin cancer on her sweet cheeks on a beach in Maui somewhere?"

"That's beside the point. Randal is a pain in the you know what."

"And you have called Colt a pain in the you know what multiple times since I've been here," Willow reminded her.

"Randal's a pain in the know what for being a blue-pill-popping, lying cheat. Colt is a pain in the you know what because he forces me to do trails in the heat, ride bike's with a basket in the front, eat brown rice, and threatens to sell me."

"I should let you know that I may have a buyer."

Noni, her eyes twinkling, slowly blinked at Willow. Noni clapped her hands together as if solving a riddle. "Well then, marry him and the both of you can be pains in the you know what together. A match made in heaven."

Amen, agreed Halo.

Hell yeah! Added Tails.

****

This was the second time Colt pulled up to his driveway, finding an unfamiliar car parked in front of his house. The older car looked well kept. He groaned, frustrated with Noni for allowing anyone to come over, especially when she was not up for the company, or him.

He retrieved a sleepy Freckles from the front seat and placed him on the grass.

"Go do your business," he ordered, watching the

puppy stretch and sniff around the front lawn, finding the perfect location to attempt the leg up position only to fall off balance and wet himself. Sighing, Colt reached in to the truck and unbuckled a sleepy Lucy, making every attempt not to wake her.

With Noni up all night sick, Lucy was as worried as Colt and did not sleep well. She'd stayed in Noni's room until late and collapsed from exhaustion. It was at that point, Colt picked Lucy up and took her to bed. Colt stayed with Noni and slept in her ridiculous lavish white chaise chair. The stupid thing had left a horrible crick in his neck.

After the thousandth gut wrenching heave, the tequila devil had left the house, leaving poor Noni wrecked. Colt pumped her with fluids and Helen warned that if Noni continued in the morning, to take her to the urgent care.

The upside, an urgent care run, had been avoided and no priest had been required to visit the house.

The soft laughter and sounds of Willow's voice alerted him of her presence.

He stopped short.

He found Noni still in her pajama blouse and pants with a house robe over her, along with her hair standing every which way, sitting next to Willow, eating soup and a sandwich. Her complexion was no longer pale green and her eyes were clearing up.

Noni gave him a knowing smile. "We have company."

He lifted Lucy a little higher, patting her on the back. "I see that," he whispered. He looked over at Willow, sensing her weariness. "You gonna stick around?"

She looked down at her hands and quickly to Noni before her eyes came back to his. "I can stay for a bit."

"Good."

He left them at the table, patting his leg again for Freckles to follow him up the stairs. He carried Lucy to her room and laid her in the bed, removing her little sandals. He placed her stuffed fairy doll in her arms and tucked the covers around her, giving her a soft kiss on her forehead before pulling the door closed.

"Your turn pup." He picked up Freckles and walked to his room, placing him in the tub and giving him a quick wash down, removing the smell of urine from his fur and towel drying him. The pup tried to bite the water splashing around him, causing more water to splash out and wetting Colt. He chuckled, making sure the pup's paws were dry, his ears cleaned, and fur brushed thoroughly.

"Alright, you little misfit. You're all set." He placed Freckles down and watched the little fur ball run to the carpet in Colt's room, dragging his body along the floor, rolling around, causing static and friction. His fur stood out all around him, reminding Colt of Noni's hair.

"He's got a lot of energy."

Colt had not seen Willow come upstairs.

"Noni asked me to help her to her room. She wanted to lie down for a bit. She ate the soup I gave her and half of the sandwich. I um…" He noticed her hesitation and the heat rise to her face, "I put the soup away and the food. There's stuff there later if she gets hungry."

He walked over to his nightstand closest to the door, turning on the night monitor on low, listening to Lucy rustling in her bed, still asleep.

"I, uh, wanted you to know that, um, I picked

everything up, and she held her food down. I also gave her pain killers for her headache," Willow continued to ramble.

Slowly he turned and stalked towards her, sensing the room alter with tension. A tension he wanted to cut through. He stood, reaching for her interlaced hands, unraveling them, and entwining his with hers. Her eyes remained on their hands as he pulled her into his room, shutting the door behind her with a resounding click of the door. Her hands shook slightly in his. He leaned his head against hers, taking in her sweet scent of lemon and coconuts.

"Tell me I didn't mess things up between us."

She shivered, releasing an unsteady breath. "You didn't," she whispered back.

He sighed heavily. Relieved. His fingers unlaced from her hands and slid around her waist while the other hand came up to caress her cheek. He lifted her chin up to meet his gaze, noticing dark circles under her eyes. Looked like he wasn't the only one losing sleep last night.

Leaning in, he pressed a soft kiss on her lips. His tongue teased lightly, keeping the kiss soft until she moaned. Then he deepened the kiss, moving his mouth over hers, devouring its softness. Her intoxicating taste and soft lips fed his hunger for more. With firm hands, he backed her towards the bed. The sudden bump warned him he reached his destination. Bracing her for impact, he flipped her around, securing her safely above him. Her muffled giggles quietly joined his, as he rolled her over onto her back and claimed her lips again.

Freckles, not one to be left out, gave a low whine, wanting to join them on the bed. Without breaking the kiss, Colt reached over and grabbed a pillow, tossing it over to the pup. The sounds of cloth tearing followed by growling, and another rip sliced through the air.

Colt returned with a growl of his own, causing another round of silent laughter to shake through Willow. He leaned over the bed, finding the little cock blocker on the ground slowly shredding his pillow. "Shut it," he hissed, groaning at the mess of cotton fuzz scattered around the floor and fluttering around the pup like freshly fallen snow.

"Oh no," Willow whispered, noticing the mess. "He's too cute," she attempted to soothe Freckles.

Freckles tongue draped out of his little mouth, with one floppy ear laid low while the other attempted to stand straight. His little head turned side to side as Willow cooed over him. Slowly, the little bugger grabbed the edge of the torn pillow and dragged it to the bed, attempting to bring it up with him, whining to be picked up.

"No, you don't," Colt said in a stern tone.

"Awe, poor little guy."

"Not happening, baby," he said, turning his attention back to her, ignoring the pestering whines of Freckles. "Where were we?" he murmured, leaning into her smile.

A sudden bark interrupted his advances.

Her fingers ran through Colt's hair. He stared into her honey eyes. His fingers caressed her cheek. Mentally he put Freckles on mute as Colt leaned forward and captured her lips again. Losing himself in her taste. His other hand freely roamed her curves. Learned every dip and luscious turn. Touched and left a heated trail in its wake.

Freckles' insistent yapping grew louder and bolder.

Lost in each other, they ignored the rebellious pup and his tantrum.

Until *it* happened.

Freckles, impatient and frustrated, grabbed the side of the sheets on the bed and tugged.

Colt leaned over without breaking the kiss and swatted at the air. Freckles accepted the challenge and dodged his hand. He scurried, scrunched low to the ground with his tail wagging side to side. Growling, he tugged on the blanket again, letting out a muffled bark. He continued to tug and sway, left and right, pulling and dragging on the blanket.

The sound of fabric shredding followed by a growl and a sudden thump against the nightstand slowly penetrated Colt's mind. He peered over and watched as the lamp on the nightstand, along with the monitor, slowly toppled over.

"Oh shit," he swore, quickly rolling over and reaching for the lamp before it met its demise, failing miserably. The lamp crashed to the ground, shattering to a million pieces. The monitor bounced once, vomiting its batteries out as it slid to the other side of the bedroom. Freckles yelped and scurried under the bed.

Colt laid there on his stomach, groaning at the mess the puppy, who no doubt was a reincarnated hound from the depths of Hell, had made. He twisted his head around as Willow laughed. Her hands were over her mouth, as she tried to keep herself quiet. Before he knew it, his door flew open. Noni stood before them in the same pajamas from earlier, her pink hair still standing every which way, and then some.

"If you two are going to do the horizontal tango, at least have the decency of doing it quietly. Some of us are trying to sleep," she fussed, eyes half asleep.

"Jesus, Noni," he groaned, face planting into the mattress.

"Oh please. Like I believe you are still a virgin, Colt. Pish posh," she said, closing the door. "And in case you forgot what you're supposed to do, you need to take your pants off." She added, then looked over to Willow and winked. "Hers too."

"Get out, woman. And take the dog with you."

"Like hell I am. You bought that hell hound. He's your responsibility. Not mine. And why is there blood on your floor?"

Colt raised himself on his arms, pushing up and glancing down to the floor. The mention of blood caused a stillness in the room. He looked over his shoulder and found Willow searching under the bed where she found Freckles curled up in a ball, licking his paws.

"Come here, boy," she cooed, "That's it. Come on. It's okay, bud." Once Freckles reached her, she picked him up and brought him to Colt. He reached over and inspected the pup.

"What did you get into, pup?" he whispered, keeping his tone friendly, noticing the Freckles ears pulled back and a pitiful whine escaped when Colt touched his front paw. "It's alright Freckles. Let me see how bad it is." He lifted the pup's paw. "It's a minor cut on one side, but this one is deep and there might be a piece of glass in it. I got to take him in."

He glanced over at Noni and watched her concerned look and behind her was a tearful Lucy.

"Hey, honey bear," he said tenderly, walking carefully over the broken debris.

"Is Freckles hurt?" Lucy asked.

"He's going to be alright. Needs a few stitches. I'm going to take him to the vet. Remember the one we took him to this morning? He was nice, right?" Tears streamed down her face as she nodded.

"Will it hurts him? I don't want it to hurts him, Uncle Colt," she cried.

He picked her up and hugged her close, leaning over and placing a quick kiss on Noni's forehead. "He's going to be alright. Promise. I need you to stay here with Noni. Make sure she eats her food and watches that fairy movie again. You know it's her favorite," he said with a devilish smile.

Noni's eyes rounded in horror, raising both her middle fingers at him.

Sniffling, Lucy pulled back from his neck. "I can do that, Uncle Colt. I'll take care of Noni."

"That's my girl," he said, placing her on the ground.

They walked downstairs together. Freckles wrapped in a towel, snuggled deep in Willow's arm, receiving soft coos and kisses from his girl. Lucky fur-bag. Colt grunted disapprovingly. Once he located his wallet and keys, he turned to grab the cock blocking hell hound and realized this was the second time Lucy and Willow had been in the same room and he had not properly introduced them.

Shit.

Maybe he should call Candice. He shouldn't leave Noni alone with Lucy. Definitely shouldn't leave Willow alone with Noni.

"Colt, maybe I should stay," Willow started. "I mean, Noni seems better, but she's still a little under the weather and—" he didn't let her finish.

"Thank you," he said, meaning it deeply. "I was

thinking of calling in reinforcements."

"No need. I've got you covered. Call me when you get an update," she breathed.

Nodding, he gently picked up Freckles and rubbed his hands over the pup's fur, placing him safely in the passenger seat. His paw continued to bleed through the towel. Colt looked back over to the doorway, giving Noni and Lucy a quick wave. "Willow, I…"

"Go. I've got this," she encouraged.

Once inside his truck, he watched Willow walk back to the porch. An overwhelming calmness washed over him, knowing she would be there when he returned. He rubbed Freckles ears again. "Ready pup?"

Freckles took the concern and rub down as an invitation to move over to Colt's lap. "Awe pup. Stay in your seat," he said, easing Freckles back to the blanket, hating the small whine coming from him. Colt watched a pair of sorrowful blue eyes stare back at him.

At the stop sign, he reached over for Freckles, placing him gently on his lap. The vet was less than a mile from where Colt was currently at. He watched Freckles' blue eyes light up and his little tongue hang out the side of his mouth in glee. "You really are a little hell hound."

Chapter 13

Vaginas Unite

Willow walked as casually as she could back to the porch. Never mind the butterflies fluttering around in the pit of her stomach. Or the sweats breaking out under her arm pits. Did she even put deodorant on? She glanced at Noni for help and found the pink hair cactus smiling.

"Lucy, this is your uncle's friend, Willow. Looks like she's going to stay with us till he gets back." Snapping her fingers enthusiastically, Noni grabbed Lucy's shoulders and leaned forward to whisper in her ear. Willow stared suspiciously at them, uneasy. Lucy's eyes grew large with excitement and her head bobbed up and down, shaking her little just-woke-up-from-my-nap curls all over the place.

Oh my. This does not look good, warned Halo.

Tails squinted her eyes at Noni, sizing her up.

Before Willow knew it, Lucy rushed over and grabbed her hand. "Come on, Willow. We gots to do this!"

Not sure what the she-devil roped her into, Willow followed curiously the little ball of energy back into the house, up the stairs, and into the little girl's colorful glitter bedroom. She sat down at a pink tea table. One colorful basket after another appeared on her lap with a variety of hair accessories, from extensions to butterflies.

Princess crowns to French combs. Hair ties to hair pins. It was never ending.

"What color hair exits do you want?" Lucy asked cheerfully, pulling out the rainbow selection of extensions.

"Do you want me to put them on you?"

Lucy's giggle sounded more like a little fairy being tickled. "*Nooo*," she emphasized. "It's for you. You're getting a make-up over. See, I have my makeup and nail paint too."

Touched and frightfully scared of the make-up over that was to come from a four-year-old, Willow sent a silent prayer for an intervention. As if the Almighty himself heard her prayer, Willow's phone rang. She fumbled with her phone, wondering if it was Colt with news already. She answered, and Sofia's face appeared on her phone.

"Where are you, *mija*?" she said in her normal greeting. Her shoulder length black hair was tied into two little ponytails, making her look younger than her current thirty years of age.

"A bit busy. I've got a little one with me," Willow said, turning the phone showing off Lucy, who waved happily back.

"Hi *princesa*," Sofia sweetly cooed in Spanish. "What are you all doing?"

Lucy climbed on Willow's lap and sat down. "I am giving her a make-up over. See?" She showed a picture she drew of a circle with multiple sticks poking out of different ends (assuming those were arms and legs). Around the circle were different colors (assuming those were hair exits), as well as two blue circles and a red blob in the middle (assuming those were eyes and lips).

"Wow," Sofia said over the phone. "Very abstract and modern." Keeping her voice serious as if she critiqued artwork professionally. Lucy continued to explain her drawing and what products she would use.

"Can I come over?" Sofia asked excitedly.

"No."

"Yes," Lucy cried out.

"I'll be right over, *princesa*," she smiled wickedly.

"I'm going to tell Noni." Scooting off Willow's lap, Lucy raced out of the room to advise the she-devil of the plans.

"You can't come over. I can't just invite you," Willow stated.

"You didn't invite me. Lucy did."

"She's four."

"So? We bonded yesterday during the fiasco. By the way, why are you over there? I thought you were giving good ole Colt the cold shoulder."

"Noni was hung over. I felt bad. I brought her some food and my magical smoothie. Then Colt came home and we—"

"Started to do the horizontal tango till all hell broke loose," chimed in Noni.

"WHAT?" screamed Sofia.

"We were not doing the horizontal tango," clarified Willow.

Noni leaned over to face the phone. "They even broke a lamp. Shattered all over the floor."

Willow groaned.

"I'm on my way," Sofia said, clearly ignoring Willow's earlier comment. Sofia secured her phone and buckled her seatbelt.

"You're not coming over," Willow reminded her

again. The phone bounced from Sofia slamming the brakes.

"Yes, I am," she said, leaning close to the phone. "Oh, wait." The phone bounced again as Sofia reversed and suddenly exited her car.

"I like her," Noni said flatly.

Cheese and rice.

Willow waited for her soon to be ex-best friend to appear on the phone. She spotted Sofia running back to the car, toting a big yellow bag. She slid the bag across to the passenger seat. Without missing a beat, Sofia leaned into her phone, still breathing rapidly, and opened a third window.

"Do not activate the call tree, Sofia," warned Willow.

"*Por supuesto que no*," Of course not, she said in Spanish. "I'm supposed to pick up Luna to meet up with you," she smiled sweetly.

Waiting for the connection to transmit, Willow caught Noni studying her phone. "How did she do that?" Noni asked.

This could not be happening.

"Noni, I will show you the ways of the smartphone," Sofia shouted through her blue tooth.

Luna's face appeared on the phone. She smiled, no doubt surprised to see Willow with a little girl on her lap and a crazy pink haired lady's head next to hers.

"Why, hello there," Luna said cheerfully.

"*Mija*, get ready. I'll be there in five minutes. We are heading to Colt's house where Willow got caught doing the horizontal tango and we are giving her a make-up over," shouted Sofia.

Luna's jaw dropped. "WHAT?"

"I was not doing the horizontal tango."

Noni snickered.

"What's a horry zonky tango?" Lucy said with a concerned look on her face.

"Horizontal Tango, honey bear. It's a dance," Noni replied sincerely.

Willow stared at Noni wide eyed before she turned to Sofia and Luna and whispered, "Hurry, please."

Luna stared incredulously at Willow, nodding her head as Sofia honked and cursed in Spanish at people on the drive over. "Luna, get your *culo* ready. I'll be there in five minutes."

"I can't wait to tell Uncle Colt I want to learn the horizontal tango," Lucy said cheerfully.

Oh my.

Tails just snickered.

****

An hour after arriving at the vet's office, they took Colt back with a trembling Freckles in hand. No amount of consoling calmed the possessed demon dog to remain calm enough for the vet to examine him. The poor assistant tried to coo Freckles with her soft voice, offering a Nirvana of puppy treats and chew toys. Unfortunately, the demon dog was no longer accepting such awards and was going for blood, snapping and nipping at her hands whenever she touched his paw.

In the end, Colt stepped in against the vet's wishes and held the angry pup close, speaking to him calmly. Stroked his ears. Held Freckles face close to his as they worked on his paw. Promised if he didn't bite Colt's nose off, he would buy Freckles another rubber chicken and give him sausage links anytime Colt cooked them in the morning. As if agreeing to the terms, Freckles licked

Colt's nose and settled down, whining at the first puncture of the needle and then finally relaxing after that.

Four stitches, an antibiotic ointment, a blue bandaged paw with bulldogs riding a motorcycle, and a new rubber chicken as promised, minus a lighter bank account, Colt placed a sleepy Freckles in his seat and called Willow with an update.

"Hey, how is he?" she quickly answered, her phone muffled. He sensed her walking away from a singing Lucy.

"Four stitches. Got to bring him back in ten days. We somehow have to figure out a way to keep him off of his foot for a little while. No running or jumping."

"Uh, the vet realizes he's a puppy, right?"

"Yeah. Should have seen my face when he told me the same thing." He stood outside of the passenger door watching Freckles sleep. They wore the poor pup out. Walking around to the driver's side, he sat down and started the truck. The noises in the background grew louder. "You girls rocking out?"

"I have a confession," she said. "But full disclosure, I tried to stop this."

He chuckled softly. Unsure if leaving her behind with Noni unsupervised was a great idea. Even in her weakened state, Noni still had cosmos powers he still didn't understand. It must have been the pink hair. No other explanation.

"What's going on, baby?"

She sighed, and his phone rang. He accepted the video option on their call and her beautiful face he was becoming addicted to appeared on the screen.

"Surprise," she said weakly, showing off her face covered in a lavender facial mask and big rollers on her hair. His eyes grew large as his hand covered his mouth. "Wait," she said. "There's more." Lucy raced over and sat on Willow's lap. She wore a similar mask in pink with rollers filling her little head.

"Hi, Uncle Colt. Look, I have a face bomb!"

Willow bit her lower lip and shrugged. Damn he was falling for her. How it happened this fast, he couldn't explain it. He wasn't sure if he wanted to. He knew watching Willow and Lucy in rollers and face bomb's, both smiling at him, made him ache to rush home.

"Uh hello. We need to do our nails. Let's go *princesa*. You're next. Oh, hey Colt," yelled Sofia from behind them with smaller rollers and a green facial mask.

"Wait!" Lucy said, running back to the phone. "Uncle Colt, is Freckles okay?"

His sweet girl. "Yeah, honey bear. I'm heading home. I was calling to let you know."

"Yay. Okay. Bye!"

They both watched her race off with Sofia, leaving Willow alone again with him. He leaned close to his screen.

"Tell me something, baby. Did you convince Noni to wear one of those face bombs too?" he asked her teasingly.

"Yep." She didn't bother denying it. "And Luna." He turned his head to the side and laughed. "And Rita, but that one was not at all planned. She showed up out of nowhere."

He started his truck, securing his phone on the holder near his dashboard. "What color are they wearing?" he asked curiously.

She tugged on her lower lip. The simple nervous act drove him crazy. He smiled as he read a notification of an incoming text from her. He shook his head at Willow. "Nothing to apologize about, baby."

Few things surprised Colt anymore. He could thank Noni and her antics. However, the picture Willow sent of Noni and Rita was one he would surely never forget. He dropped his phone and knocked his head on the steering wheel while reaching over to catch it, causing Freckles to yelp and bark out at the noise. Colt laughed. Hard. So hard, tears sprung to his eyes. He reached over and stroked Freckles. He recovered his phone and placed it back in the holder.

"Jesus, I was not expecting that."

Willow's quiet giggle caused another round of laughter. "They are having a blast," she said. Somewhere in the distance, Rita yelled at Sofia for playing the same song again. Her fussing caused a string of Spanish curses and a few *vieja loca* or crazy old ladies, as Sofia kindly referred to them. "Are you coming home soon or has all this," she said waving her hand over her face, "scared you off?"

"I'm coming home, baby. You girls ordering food or want me to pick something up?"

"We will figure it out. Come home, Colt."

His eyes darkened. He took in her eyes and parted lips. If it wasn't for the face bomb, he was pretty sure she was flushed. "On my way, darlin'," he said gruffly before disconnecting their call.

****

Still daydreaming of Colt's eyes and the hopeful promises they held, Willow heard the sudden muffled curses of Sofia as Luna tried to referee.

"Ms. Brooks, I understand your disappointment. However, as Sofia pointed out, the Blueberry Bomb is quite a lovely mask," Luna attempted to reason.

"Don't use that proper bullshit tone on me. I look like a castaway blueberry no one wants, and I am not having it."

Groaning, Willow walked into the living room. "What's going on here?" she questioned, hoping her authoritative voice would rein in the situation.

"*¡Esta vieja loca siempre esta peleando por todo!*," Sofia ranted.

Oh heavens, this will not end well, Halo chimed in.

As long as it ends and we are in Colt's bed, that's fine with me, shrugged Tails.

"What did she say about me?" Rita demanded to anyone who listened. "What did you say about me?" she turned to Sofia.

"I said you're a crazy old lady who complains about everything," Sofia translated. Her green mask now dry, she pulled on her skin as she spoke.

Rita choked on the oxygen as she inhaled. Her icy stare shifted the temperature in the room a few degrees lower. "Why, you little rotten good-for-nothing turd!" she shouted, clearly choosing her vocabulary because of the underage presence in the room, although that did not seem to ease the situation with Sofia. Thankfully Luna interjected again, holding back a green-faced Sofia and blue-face-cracking Rita.

"Ms. Brooks, I implore you. The Blueberry Bomb is a great mask, high in Vitamin A and C. I've had it myself and it leaves your skin lovely once washed off. If it's not to your satisfaction, I'm sure Sofia can remedy that with another mask treatment at her spa. Right, Sofia?" Luna stated matter of fact.

"Well, she should have said that in the beginning,"

conceded Rita with a huff.

Face-bomb crisis resolved. Luna's eyes widened in disbelief and relief all at once. They both looked at Sofia, who stared daggers at Rita and then back at Willow. "I will drink free at your bar for all eternity," Sofia stated and stormed off.

"You already drink free," Willow reminded Sofia who rose her arm up high in the sky and flipped her off as she struck a pose.

"Which one of these friends of yours is my Levi into?" Rita questioned Willow.

"Rita, leave the girls alone. They will never invite you to another girls night out," stated Noni, who sat quietly all the while painting her nails.

"Like hell they won't. I have a vagina like the rest of you. Vaginas stick together, you hear me ladies? Vaginas unite. Now which one is it, Whiskey girl? And tell me it's not the green faced turd," she whispered breathlessly before taking a shot of her oxygen.

"Rita, maybe you should ask Levi," Willow said, not wanting to out Luna who stared at Rita as if she'd grown two additional heads and three sets of horns.

"You're related to Levi?" Luna asked.

"Of course we're related. Don't you see the resemblance? He has my eyes," she snapped, showing off her icy blue eyes. Though Levi's eyes appeared to be the same color, they were always warm and inviting.

"Bloody hell," muttered Luna.

Rita cackled. "So, it's you who's caught my Levi's attention," she said, appearing to store this vital information.

"What? Of course not. That's complete tosh," Luna said, blushing more while Rita continued to laugh.

"Look, Noni, her British is showing. Tosh. That's complete tosh," Rita mimicked. "What the hell is tosh, anyway?"

"It bloody well means it's complete nonsense, if you must know. If you'll excuse me, I'll see if Sofia needs help," Luna said.

Willow sliced her eyes at the older woman and her wicked cackle. Silently warning her to behave. In the background, Lucy belted out her final lyric for the fifty-eighth time with a brush as a microphone. Her pink face turned up while she held the brush close to sing the big note at the end. She hit the note, like a cat falling into a tub of freezing water, with all her might. "Sing it, Lucy," Willow cheered on, hoping to defuse the premeditated manslaughter in Colt's living room. Willow nodded her head to Sofia, sending BFF messages only she would understand. On cue, Sofia grabbed the remote and hit replay again of the song and grabbed her other two brushes. She tossed one to Luna and stood next to Lucy as the three of them sang along again for the fifty-ninth time, all the while Rita groaned painfully.

Feeling accomplished, Willow checked on Noni and her nails as the doorbell rang. Curious, she walked to the door as Helen and Candice walked in.

"Yoo-hoo, we're here!" lilted Candice, giving Willow an embrace and air kissing Noni.

"Look who we found," Helen said. Colt and Levi walked in together with bags of food and a sleepy Freckles.

"Willow, it's time to wash—Oh, bloody hell," Luna yelled and spun, storming off back to the living room, fussing at Sofia, who laughed and came racing around the corner in her green face.

"Hey guys!" she said happily, as if it was normal to sport a split pea soup color face. "Willow, you need to wash off your mask," Sofia reminded her again. "Oh, you brought Chinese!" Clapping enthusiastically, she forgot about the spa treatments and went to the bags, helping Levi unload the bags in the kitchen.

Shaking her head, Willow shyly smiled at Colt as he gave her a wink and she walked to the bathroom. She called out to Lucy to wash her face as well. Helping the girl to the step stool, she showed her how to use the washcloth and rinse off the mask. Once done, Willow cleaned up and prepared the bathroom for the next person.

They opened the door and found Luna pinned to the wall with Levi holding her arms above her head. Levi released her slowly, "Remember, love, you run, I'll chase."

Standing still with her hands over Lucy's eyes, Willow watched Luna take deep breaths, her hands sliding over her heart. Quietly, Willow lowered her hands from Lucy's eyes and sauntered away from Luna. Silently their eyes exchanged the simple 'Are you alright?' 'Yes, I'm fine' conversation.

"Uh hello, there are others who need to wash their faces," interrupted Sofia.

Willow nodded to Luna as she entered the bathroom and closed the door. She looked over at Sofia and widened her eyes.

"What did I miss?" Sofia asked suspiciously.

Willow looked down at Lucy and smiled. Covering her ears, Willow leaned into Sofia and quickly told her what they witnessed.

"*Què?*" Sofia shouted. Not waiting for further

explanation, Sofia stormed to the bathroom door and knocked loudly.

Repeatedly.

Crossing her arms over her chest and tapping her foot like a parent who caught their daughter dry humping their boyfriend for the first time.

"Open this door right," Sofia demanded.

The door suddenly slammed opened with a half-peeled face masked Luna staring at Sofia. "Have you gone mad?"

Sofia's eyebrows rose mockingly at her. "Do you need a change of panties?"

"Oh, bugger off!" she said before slamming the door in Sofia's smirking green tea face.

Chapter 14

The Punch Bar

Colt sat in the living room with Freckles curled up next to him. Helen wiped the remainders of Blueberry bomb off of Rita's disgruntled face, while Noni returned to the living room.

"I feel rejuvenated," Noni purred. All the while, Rita grumbled about discarded blueberries and green turds. He would never understand that woman. A minute later Levi stormed by him, giving Rita a quick peck on her clean forehead.

"You smell nice, Nana," he said sweetly, pausing her quiet rant and bringing a genuine smile to her face. A rare sight to see.

"Awe, you are the best grandson any old bird can have," she returned.

Levi winked and smiled, "I'll tell my brother you said that."

"Don't piss me off, Levi Reginald," she scolded. There's the Rita Colt knew.

He sensed the change in the room. His body was fully alert as Willow entered. He just caught the four-year-old tumble weed who raced into his arms. "Gotcha," he said, tickling her. Bringing out little squeals and giggles. Releasing Lucy, she carefully sat down next to Freckles' bed. His tail wagged happily for her attention. He licked her fingers and face as she snuggled next to his bed, running her fingers through his fur. The pup released a heavy sigh of contentment.

Something warm unfurled in Colt as he watched Lucy cozying up to Freckles. Yeah, he was doing this parenting thing right. Unable to resist, he glanced up at Willow, catching her snapping pictures of Lucy and the pup. Her eyes were soft. Her face was smooth and clean of any make-up. Rollers still adorned her head. She had never looked sexier than that moment.

That look. He was falling for her.

Fast.

A shadow moved by, catching the corner of his eye. Levi nodded quietly. It was time.

"Everything alright?" Willow asked.

"Yeah darlin'," he said, standing from the couch. "I'll be back soon. Do you mind staying a little longer?" He slung his arms around her waist casually and pulled her in close.

"I can stick around," she assured him.

Unable to resist, he brushed his lips softly over hers. "When do these rollers come out?" he questioned teasingly.

She giggled and touched them. "Probably in the next few minutes. I've had them on already for an hour. I'll get the rollers off of Lucy first, and then Noni. I think I might leave Rita last."

He chuckled and kissed her again, lingering a bit before releasing her. "I'll be back soon," he whispered against her lips.

"Yo. Let's roll," Levi shouted from the doorway, staring heatedly at Luna and her brown hair cascading down her shoulders in tumbling waves, framing her clean face to perfection. Luna didn't break eye contact with Levi and blushed profusely when he winked at her as he walked out the door.

The last thing Colt wanted to do was leave Willow again, but this had to get done. Once outside, he asked Levi, "We going to Punch Bar?"

"That fucker made an offer on the place next door. Got word of it this afternoon. Wes is losing his mind and Fab is about to let loose her Dragon Queen on Curtis. I should let her, too. No one messes with Fab when she's in Dragon Queen mode. We figure if the four of us go there and confront Curtis, he'll see we're playing hardball as well. Plus, rumor has it, he's trying to recruit Blue Nitro to play a gig for them."

"What?" Fury rushed through Colt's veins. No way would Blue Nitro do that for a shady person like Curtis.

"He's offering some big payoff and even bigger venue. Said he could get strings pulled to play at the Fall Festival. You know it gets crazy with people and it's usually local bands. If he can pull off bringing in a new upcoming band like Blue Nitro, it will bring major revenue to the city. He's hoping he can cash in said favor. One like winning the bid for the place next door," Levi growled, running his fingers through his cropped hair.

"You haven't told her anything," Colt stated, knowing the answer.

"No way, man. This will break her. She's been working hard to pitch us that place. Fab and I know about it. She thinks we don't, but we've seen the numbers she's been working on. She's got everything drawn out. Hell, she even has a presentation for us. Not like we need it. Whiskey has a good eye for business. She's smart and doesn't make risky moves unless she's secure in her decision."

Pointing his finger against the steering wheel, Levi emphasized, "I know she is secure in this. I know she can make this work. Even Wes knows and he didn't want to have a storefront. He wanted to stay with the Food Truck. But he's bought in. Although he has some changes he wants to do."

Willow was smart. Colt agreed there with Levi. No doubt she would turn the new place into a goldmine, like their current bar. His chest filled with pride. "You talk to your brother? Tell him what's going on?"

"The douchebag didn't answer any of my calls or text messages. When he did, all he said was if Nana was good, that he only had a minute to spare. I hung up after that. Only has a minute to spare for his brother, who he hasn't spoken to in months. Nah, I don't need to talk to him. Handle this without him."

"I'll call," Colt simply said. He still kept in touch with Kai, the original bass player.

"Don't waste your time."

"I won't call Mav. But I keep in touch with Kai."

"That may work to our advantage. Hold that ace up your sleeves."

Colt nodded, agreeing. "What about the distributor?"

Levi turned with a raised eyebrow. "Prisco Distribution?"

Colt waited patiently as Levi thought it over, filling Levi in. "Willow told me about him. How he's a distributor and the issue she had recently with Curtis and a missing shipment. She mentioned this Luca guy handled it personally, and he wasn't a fan of Curtis. Maybe we can form an alliance of sort."

"Dude, Luca is not the type of guy you call in favors with. Cutthroat, all the way. But..." Levi paused a second, mauling over the idea.

"But what?"

"He's soft on Whiskey. That could be our advantage too," Levi treaded carefully.

Well, hell. Colt hadn't think that through now, had he?

Monday nights at The Punch Bar were relatively busy. People were scattered around the place, sitting in the sleek black bar stools surrounding the weathered barrels throughout the main floor space. The enormous neon sign shone obnoxiously bright behind the bar, mocking them as they walked in and took a booth at the far end of the room. The self-seating allowed them to sit down and study the surroundings quietly.

Once they arrived, they met up with Wes, who waited for them leisurely next to his bike. He sat there, playing a game on his phone.

"Since when you play scrabble?" joked Levi.

"Since my IQ was challenged by a cute nurse."

Colt exited the truck and rounded the front, shaking hands and back slapping his friend. "A cute nurse, huh?"

"Yeah," he simply said and changed the subject. "What's the plan? Fab stayed behind saying something about Whiskey feeding her to the sharks this weekend if she finds out about this. Beck and I are covering for them, and Mila is coming in tomorrow to get up to speed on things. Should be fun to have her around Beck again. You know how much those two get along."

"Willow mentioned there's history there," Colt stated.

"You can say that," confirmed Levi.

Sitting in a booth, they surveyed the room. The similarities between Martini Girl Bar and Punch Bar were uncanny. It was a replica. Where the curtains off the bay windows adorned the glass of Martini Girl Bar were a classy white, the Punch Bar placed masculine satin black curtains on theirs. Instead of the long square tables, they had round tables. White bar stools were black. They even set the stage up similarly. Colt grabbed a menu and scanned the specialty drinks, cursing as he read some martinis he had become familiar with.

"He's poached on every idea of hers," he said, seething.

"Check your six," grumbled Wes. They leaned over and caught a glimpse of Vet walking out from behind the stage.

Levi lowered his head and fisted his hands together. "No way he'd do this. There's got to be a reason he's here."

Colt kept his eyes on Vet as he made his way towards the men's room. "Only one way to find out," Colt said, getting up, lowering his baseball cap and following him. Colt headed to the sinks, keeping his head low, washing his hand, taking his time. From the corner of his eyes, he watched Vet finish his business and walk to the sink next to him, oblivious to his surroundings.

"Enjoying your visit?" Colt asked, turning off the water, watching Vet's eyes open wide, stunned.

A slight break of sweat appeared above his brow. Vet backed away from the sink, attempting to walk around Colt to the door. The doors swung open as Levi and Wes stalked in.

Before Vet could react, Colt snatched Vet by his collar and slammed him up against the wall.

"Talk," Colt said, ripping out the word impatiently.

"I swear this is not what you think. Levi, man, I swear. I wouldn't sell you out like this. I wouldn't sell Whiskey out," he continued to plead.

"Why are you here, kid?" Levi asked, his voice low and menacing with a distinct hardening in his eyes.

Colt pitied Vet. Part of him wanted to believe the kid, the other part wanted to rip his ass apart.

Vet swallowed hard and turned his eyes up to the ceiling.

"He asked a question," pressured Colt, shaking Vet.

"Cody. Alright. Cody," he said whispering. "Look, I swear I was going to come to you, but I needed to know for sure."

Distant footsteps and deep voices penetrated the walls. They glanced at each other and nodded. Colt released Vet and pushed him hard towards the faucet, turning it on. Colt and Levi each took a stall to hide. Wes stood by the urinal, keeping his head low as the door opened and yet still close to Vet in case he made a run for it. "Hey man, you gotta split." Cody's voice put them on edge. "He'll be here in five minutes."

"Yeah, I'm heading out."

Without saying another word, Cody closed the bathroom door and left them alone. Levi and Colt exited their stalls and Wes walked over, grabbing Vet. "You're coming with us and you're going to start from the beginning and tell us what is going on. You got me?"

Nodding and swallowing another lump of fear, Vet stared at all three and then directly at Levi. "I swear to you. I'm not a sellout." His voice cracked.

Colt cracked the door, scanning the hallway. He nodded for Vet to exit. Vet agreed to meet them at the bar. Once secured, Vet made it out without being spotted, followed by Wes leaving Colt and Levi behind. They left together without a care in the world. They wanted it known they were there. Cody caught sight of Colt right away and came to greet him with a warm smile, freezing when Levi stood next to Colt. Cody released a string of incoherent words.

"Yeah, that sounds about right," Colt muttered.

"What brings you guys here?" he asked.

"Want to speak to the big man himself, Cody," said Levi. "Got a problem with fuckers poaching on our people. And from the looks of things, our people are not the only things he is stealing."

Fidgeting under their stare, Cody rubbed the back of his neck. "How's Whiskey doing?" he asked quietly.

Before he could stop himself, Colt reached out and grabbed Cody's front shirt. "You don't get to ask about her. Understood?" Levi's hand held Colt back, releasing Cody's shirt. Colt pushed past Cody, deciding the best solution was to leave before he did something that would land him in cuffs. Aggravated for letting his temper get the best of him, Colt stormed past Wes and waited for Levi at the truck. The intimate way Cody had said Whiskey burned a hole in Colt's stomach.

He clenched his teeth.

Colt never harbored feelings like this with his Ex, Nikki. They'd dated over three of the longest years of his life. The first year was sexual bliss with every illusion the passion would never end. The second year together, things with Clover went downhill and by the time the third miserable year rolled in, Colt was drowning in constant ill contempt, never satisfied bullshit. After the band made their decision to cut him off, Nikki begged him to make things work. She wanted the rock star life. She refused to be an instant mom to Lucy. In the end, he chose his family, and she chose his meat head agent and was living not-so-happily-ever-after.

A red Lexus with loud muted music pulled into the front reserved parking spot. Curtis Merk exited the car in his designer shirt, jeans, and shiny shoes. His elaborate watch and ridiculous aviator sunglasses he wore at night made him appear more of a douche bag.

"You'd think he was a freaking Rock God the way he rolls in here," joked Wes.

Colt stared, disgusted as unwanted his eye contact clashed with Curtis who smirked as he spread his arms out and walked over.

"Well, I'll be, the nephew of a rich monkey's uncle. If it isn't Colton Royce. The man. Got to say you were the best guitarist in that band. Hell, best guitarist in town. Don't tell the guys I said that," he gushed. "You must have heard about me bringing Blue Nitro here." He stopped short and brought his hands up, covering his mouth and then clapping loudly. "Oh man. Can you imagine if I'm the reason you're reunited with the band? That would be epic."

Epic? Were we back in junior high?

Wes growled, annoyed.

"Wes Banner! Tell me you've come to your senses and are here to take over my kitchen? I mean, I'll go in there right now and tell the cook to hightail it out and it's yours, buddy."

"In your fake monkey's uncle's dreams."

"Ouch. That's harsh, man. I mean, seriously, you can have it all here," Curtis continued to sweeten the pot, adding in outrageous incentives only a sucker would fall for. "What do you say?"

Wes approached Curtis. His face slightly paled and eyes widened with discomfort as Wes loomed over the conniving jackass. "No," he hissed. "You get me? Buddy?"

What a dumbass. Willow wasn't joking. This guy was a douchebag.

Curtis took a few steps back, shrugging his shoulders and lifting his hands up in defeat. "Alright, alright. I can take no for an answer. Even if it's a stupid choice."

The sounds of boots on gravel turned Curtis's attention around, coming face to face with the ice-cold stare of Levi. Curtis slowly took a step back and walked around Levi, feeling the viking like man turn and follow his every move. Once he reached the safety of the porch entrance, he watched Colt and Wes flank Levi. "You are not welcome here," he warned Levi.

A menacing smile teased Levi's lips. "Is that right?"

"Yes."

Levi turned to Colt and then to Wes. "Wasn't aware I was unwelcome here."

"Well. Now you do. Not sure why you bother. Cody isn't going back. Try all you want. You don't stand a chance."

Levi tossed his head back, letting a loud laugh out as Colt and Wes joined in with him. "This man here got jokes," He said before containing himself. Levi stepped closer to Curtis. "We didn't come for Cody. Keep him."

"Besides, we got the best guitarist in town," mocked Wes.

Curtis's eyes moved from Wes to Colt and froze. The revelation round house kicked him, leaving him breathless and in shock. "You," he whispered in pain, pointing towards Colt.

"Me," Colt confirmed, spreading his arms out wide. "I don't want Cody back either. I got his gig. Gonna stick with it too," he said, walking up next to Levi, standing face to face with Curtis. "What we're going to do is give you a warning."

Curtis' eyes slanted and a mocking smile plastered his face. "Fellas, if you think this Good Guy, Bad Guy, Worse Guy act is going to work, you're wasting your time."

"Stay away from our bar," growled Levi.

"I don't step a foot near your precious bar and yet here you are threatening me at mine," he stated.

"That includes our people," stated Wes.

"Well, not much I can do about that. People may seek better opportunities. That includes places of employment. Free country and all," Curtis mocked, shrugging his shoulders again.

Aggravation rose in Colt's spine. His hands clenched at his side. His jaw locked tight, holding back his temper. Angry vibes swelled and flowed from Wes and Levi. No doubt, they were holding themselves back from shredding the bastard to pieces.

Colt steadily took deep breaths. Curtis was not worth the assault charges he would likely press against Colt. However, there was something he knew he could do that would warrant the satisfaction of seeing Cody squirm, as did Levi.

"Colt, make the call," Levi said.

Colt smirked. He pulled up his phone and dialed the number. "Hey man. How's it going?" He remained quiet while the other person responded, watching Curtis fold his arms. "Yeah, listen Kai, I heard a rumor y'all are playing at The Punch Bar," more silence while the person responded. "Got to say, man, know the joint and the douchebag who runs it. Not up to the standards of Blue Nitro."

Curtis' eyes sliced over, lowering his arms with fisted hands. The vein on the side of his forehead puckered with strain and his face reddened.

"No man, I'm good. I'm gigging with Levi and the guys," Colt said, continuing his conversation. "Y'all should come out. Talk to Maverick. He wants details he can ask him to call me or his bro," he said, staring directly at Curtis. "Later man."

"You can't do that," seethed Curtis.

"Like hell I can't. I can call whoever I want. Free country and all," Colt mocked in return.

"See you around. Buddy," Wes said, delivering the last blow before the three of them retreated and drove to Martini Girl Bar to meet up with Vet.

****

Curtis watched them drive off, raging at how easily they had made a fool of him. They were clueless. He turned around and entered his bar, relishing the changes his new bar manager, Lizzie, made.

She'd come to him for more hours or a higher paid position. After interviewing her and discovering she was from Martini Girl Bar, he'd made her earn her spot at his establishment. She continued to work for Whiskey and reported back to him with their routines, bar menu, staffing, and other important items for him to know. She'd copied and downloaded information from their computers and provided him with details of their suppliers. Within those documents, he discovered the plans to purchase the building next door. It was then the plans formulated to purchase it outright himself.

The M Bar should have been his. Old man Mac should never have sold it to some girl with a wild brain idea. It should have been his. Whiskey didn't know the prime real estate she sat on and the value of the building she owned. She could sell the building and make a fortune. He'd offered to buy it off her hands and instead she denied him and told him outright to his face he was a 'nutso'. Not one to give up easily, he went back again with a higher offer and she declined him. He even attempted to ask her out to dinner to woo her before giving her the ultimate offer and she'd again declined him flat out saying she would rather jump in the feeding tank with Maximo the fifteen-foot alligator than have dinner with him.

Infuriating woman.

He walked by the stage, noticing Cody strumming his guitar and changing his music sheets. "Cody, everything alright here?"

Cody looked up, eyes falling to Curtis' tight shoulders. "Yeah. Picking up the last half hour. I'm getting ready to start a set."

Curtis watched him. The only reason Cody was here was because Curtis knew it would hurt Whiskey to take him. The unfortunate fact she'd recovered as well as she did with getting Colton Freaking Royce could not be foreseen. "Nothing out of the ordinary?"

Cody tilted his head. "Not that I can tell."

Liar, Liar Cody. It's a good thing your girlfriend Lizzie is a good lay. You'd be out in as fast as Colt was from Blue Nitro.

Chapter 15

Busted

There were times Willow wondered if she'd ever wronged a person in another life. For instance, had she been a gold digger who trapped men for their wealth and left them penniless? Had she been an illustrious cat-burglar, stealing riches from the Royals in dangerous a heist? Had she poisoned the food of her village folk in some ancient pot-luck, causing the Elders to curse her for all eternity? Or was it the simplest answer? Lady Luck didn't like her and had brought her sister Karma along to wreak havoc on Willow's evening.

Eh, Lady Luck is lazy sometimes and Karma is too busy, confirmed Tails.

After cleaning up Colt's room and disposing of the glass, she placed Freckles back in his bed, administering his medicine as the bottles called for. She fed Lucy. Bathed and hair roller free, she tucked Lucy into bed for the night. Sighing, Willow glanced at her phone. It was past nine and still no word from Colt. Where was he? An errand with Levi could range from a quick beer run to a quick ass kicking somewhere.

She wandered to the living room, collapsing into an empty seat between Sofia and Luna. Both had their arms crossed and were sending silent messages to each other. Willow leaned back on the couch. "What?" she asked on a sigh, her eyes drifting to Luna for a simple answer, since Sofia would give an elaborate answer. Which would then require her mind to translate the limited Spanish she knew.

"Well, Ms. Royce was—"

"It's Noni, my dear. We are past formalities."

Clearing her throat, Luna's lips wobbled as she spoke. "Noni was recounting the earlier events while you were cleaning up and, well, Ms. Brooks asked what happened. Noni explained, and here we are."

"Listen here, none of that Ms. Brooks crap. You call me Rita. You and my grandson are practically doing the horizontal tango, so we might as well get to know each other," Rita demanded, inhaling some of her oxygen.

A deep flush brightened Luna's face. "That is complete—"

"Tosh? Yes. I know that is how you feel," Rita interjected. "Good. Don't give it to him easy. He gets easy often. Make him work for it," she chuckled wickedly, wiggling her eyebrows. "As for you," she said, pointing at Willow, "Are you a virgin? You need to lose the pants if you want the dance. Everyone knows that."

Groaning, Willow covered her face. "We weren't doing the horizontal tango," she stressed. "It was only a kiss."

The women laughed, including her traitorous friends. "Is that what you kids are calling it?" teased Helen.

"That's some kiss. They even broke a glass lamp," Candice said, fanning herself.

"You know what? How about we watch Magic Mike?" Willow asked suddenly bashful.

"*Ay Dios*, they watched that last time," whined

Sofia. She perked up off the couch and grabbed the remote control out of Rita's hand, who grabbed Candice's cane to smack Sofia with it. *"Vieja,* take an oxygen hit before you turn blue," she snapped at Rita, clicking through the channels and finding what she was searching for. She turned and shoved her face in front of Rita, who still held her oxygen mask over her mouth. "What do you know about Christian Grey?" she asked.

"Oh my goodness," whispered Helen.

You mean we can see him in person? Questioned Halo in a whisper.

And all his glory, Tails said as she stretched.

Noni's eyebrow raised curiously.

Oh lord, what is she up? Thought Willow.

Noni abruptly stood from her chair and left the room before entering back with the monitor for Lucy's room. "I've locked the front door and turned off all the lights," she said breathlessly as she sat down, turning on the monitor.

Candice looked at everyone, "Are we really going to do this, ladies? Once we see this, we cannot unsee it," she warned.

"You will not want to unsee it," stated Luna.

Rita twisted her head sharply. "You?"

"Me," Luna confirmed.

Rita's eyes bulged in disbelief. "I don't believe it."

Willow shrugged her shoulders. "Better believe it, Rita. I borrowed her books and read the series. She also bought our tickets for the movie premieres. Those were good Valentine's Day gifts," she giggled.

Luna and Sofia joined her.

"Oh my goodness," Helen said, bringing out her lace fan and fluttering it faster than normal.

Sofia, who was still leaning into Rita's chair, looked her dead in the eyes. "What do you say, Rita? Do you want to make an appointment with Mr. Grey?"

Everyone waited a second as Rita inhaled another round. "I'll pay for the movie," she said quickly, grabbing her purse with shaky hands.

"No need. I own it," said Luna.

"Well. You are quite a naughty little girl," teased Candice as the movie played.

****

After their run in with douchebag Curtis, they drove over to Prisco Distributions, hoping to meet with Luca Prisco only to be told Mr. Prisco was out of town. Levi left an urgent message, and instead they met up with Wes at Martini Girl Bar. Fab waited there with Vet, who was filling her in on what had occurred. Fab was in one of her not so fabulous moods.

"Are you stuck on stupid?" she yelled at Vet. "I should call Whiskey and tell her where you were and get you canned."

"Come on, Fab. I'm telling you why I was there," defended Vet.

"Don't matter. You know better. You stay away from Curtis Douchebag Merk."

As Colt and Levi approached the verbal lashing session, they sat down and listened to Vet's side of the story.

"As I was telling Fab," he began without hesitation, "We got our delivery today from Hoppers. The kegs were the same, but the cases of the beers seemed off. Some of the packaging appeared opened and resealed. I helped John unload like I normally do. Except this time, he was in a hurry and agitated, claiming he didn't need my help. The man broke a sweat picking up a twelve pack. He wasn't acting right. I reviewed the manifest like Beck asked. I was off three cases of beer. I thought maybe I missed it and went back in to double checked, but I kept coming up with the same count. When I went outside to talk to John, he was gone. Didn't get me to sign off on the receipt of delivery or anything. He just left," he told them, confused.

"Whose Hopper?" asked Colt.

"Hopper Brew Distribution," replied Levi.

"Thought we used Prisco Distributors."

Fab looked him over, "We do, Pistol, but only for hard liquor and shitty wine. We get the beer from Hopper," she clarified.

"Got it," said Colt, wheels turning in his head.

"What's this got to do with Cody?" asked Wes.

"I went to look for Beck. To let him know what was going on, but then Cody called. I'm not gonna lie, I've kept in touch with him, but I don't talk about the bar to him and he only asks about Whiskey," he cautiously said, glancing at Colt before continuing. "You ever get that feeling something isn't right? That's what I got when he called tonight. He asked to meet right away. Said it was about the bar and something was up. He was not down with whatever was going on and needed to let someone in on it. I met up with him after I got off, before Lizzie or Curtis knew I was there, and that's when he told me."

"Brace, Viking," Fab warned Levi.

"Cody said Curtis have been paying Hoppers to skim us on the distribution, starting with our cases. They split our primary beer cases. They hit our other cases too. The dates on the beer are past the recommended sold by dates…"

"Which means we cannot sell them at this point and have to place a rush order," confirmed Levi, slamming a hand on the table. "What cases did they split?"

"Our IPAs and Stouts."

"They split it with what? Stuff we have on draft?"

Colt watched Fab lower her eyes. He had a feeling this was not good.

"Water. They split the cases with water," confirmed Vet

"Fuck," shouted Levi.

"Shit," grumbled Colt.

"It gets worse, man," Vet mumbled. "When I met Cody earlier, he started off with small talk, but I could tell he wasn't right. He said Lizzie was talking with their bartender about shipments. Guess who's getting paid a little extra for skimming us?"

"Good old John," stated Wes.

Vet nodded. "And guess where the rest of our split cases went?"

"The Punch Bar," stated Wes again since Levi remained silent.

"I should have made him eat his teeth when I had the chance," Levi stated vehemently.

"And what good would that do, Viking? You end up in jail and then what? Cause I ain't taking on your crazy Nana that's for sho'," spat Fab.

A tiny smile crossed Colt's face as he watched his friend shake his head at Fab. A little humor lightened Levi's furious stare from earlier.

"Finish telling them the rest," urged Fab. Her eyes turned to Colt. "Brace, Pistol."

Vet sighed, rubbing the tension on his neck. "Cody

found out Lizzie is sleeping with Curtis. She denied it, but he said he's not stupid and knows she is. He needs a job, and he's hoping Whiskey will take him back. He said he should have taken his shot with her when he had a chance and is hoping he still can since Mateo is not in the picture."

What the hell?

Colt sat still, not liking the feeling coming over him. He could not remember ever being a jealous person with his Ex, Nikki, and yet the mention of Cody wanting a shot with Willow, or whomever the hell this Mateo person was, drove him to the edge.

"Too bad. He's not coming back. Colt's in. Cody's out," Wes stated.

"Agreed," stated Fab.

Colt watched Levi nod in agreement, feeling his blue eyed stare on him. Colt glanced over and watched Levi lean in. "Cody never had a shot with Whiskey," he stated, leaving it at that. However, Colt could read between the lines. Levi hadn't said the same about Mateo.

"We all have a past," Colt stated, still not enjoying this new emotion.

Vet took a deep breath. "In Fab's words, I need you all to brace for the next part. Curtis already put in his bid for the place next door."

"We know about the bid, Vet," Levi advised.

"No man. Not just the bid. He announced the other night to his staff that they were expanding, for sure. Lizzie drew up plans for the layout already."

Colt furiously bolted up from his chair as Levi stomped away. A loud banging sound from the hallway caused Fab to jump up.

"Is Cody sure it's bought?" whispered Fab, hand still over her chest.

Vet's sorrowful eyes stared back at her. "Yeah, Fab. I wish it weren't true, but he showed me the plans. That's when I ran into you guys."

Wes sat quietly, thinking. "Any chance we can put in a bid now? Maybe out bid him?"

Vet shrugged his shoulders. "I don't know, man. I know very little about real estate or any of that. But there were contacts on the paperwork. Luca Prisco's name was on there as an investor. I didn't get to see what part he played, but maybe we can start with him?"

Colt nodded, planning as Levi walked back with his left hand wrapped.

"Really, Viking," Fab said, exasperated. "How are you going to play drums, toss drinks, and fondle Luna with your busted hand?"

"It's all good," he assured her, "I'm righthanded."

Colt shook his head. "We need to go back to Prisco. He may be our way out after all."

"I'll place another call tomorrow," confirmed Levi. He looked over at Vet and placed his good hand on the kid's shoulder. "You did good. But no more visits with Cody at The Punch Bar. Stay off of Curtis's radar. Got me?"

"Yeah. Got it." Vet smiled, relieved, and then looked at Fab, "I'm not canned, am I?"

"Boy, you better be here tomorrow as scheduled," Fab stated while sauntering off.

"Head home, kid," said Wes, giving him a quick slap on the back and nod to the guys before walking back to the office to close up the bar.

"Let's roll," announced Levi.

Now here they were, at Colt's house and all he wanted was to go inside and pray Willow stayed so he could curl up next to her.

"You still have a full house?" questioned Levi.

"Looks that way. You coming in? Luna's car is still here."

"No, I'm gonna head home. Gotta think things through. You gonna tell Whiskey what went down?"

Colt thought about it. "I won't lie to her if she asks where we were. But the partners should discuss everything else with her."

Levi agreed and said he would let Fab know and hold a quick meeting before the girls left on their weekend trip. Colt waited for Levi to back out and walked into the dark house. He stopped dead in his track at the sounds of a whimpering woman...*counting*?

What the hell?

****

The credits rolled, and the living room was silent. Willow slowly turned her gaze towards Luna and Sofia, both fully aware of the moments to come in the next two movies. Noni stared, completely captivated by the television credits. Helen rapidly fanned herself while Candice quietly regulated her breathing. Rita was the first to speak out loud, shouting, "That actor is handsome," and then she took a hit of her oxygen. Luna immediately giggled, followed by Sofia and Willow.

"Amen Ms. Brooks," replied Luna.

"He is dark and twisted and yummy all at once," said Helen.

"Do you have the other movie as well?" asked Candice.

"Certainly," replied Luna.

"The Vaginas will unite again to watch the sequel," stated Rita.

"Oh my goodness," whispered Helen.

"That's it. I'm telling Levi I want the books for Christmas." Stated Rita.

Luna groaned, covering her faced as the girls laughed.

"Oh, don't fret. I'll make sure Levi knows you introduced me to the series," Rita teased.

"But it was not me who did it. Sofia, this is all your fault," Luna grumbled.

Sofia winked and smiled. "You're welcome."

"I wonder if Colt would build me an extra room?" asked Noni teasingly, watching Willow's face blush profusely and enjoying it.

"Why do you need an extra room?" asked Colt from behind them.

Oh no.

Oh yes. Break out the handcuffs and spank me rosy pink.

"Colt, you little shit," fussed Noni, throwing her empty bowl of popcorn at him.

"You know better than to sneak up on us," chastised Candice, smiling sweetly at him.

Rita inhaled her oxygen. "Levi with you?"

"No. He went home." He leaned against the door frame, tilting his head to the side. "What's with the extra bedroom?

How a man could look yummier than a Sweet Velvet Martini was beyond her comprehension. The way he leaned out of the door frame with his arms crossed or how he tilted his head when he asked a question. Wait. He asked a question. What was the question?

All eyes were on Willow, and she could not fathom why?

Oh, no. Oh, no, bawled Halo.

Oh, yes. Oh, yes, cheered Tails.

Where have you two been? She fussed at herself.

Watching the movie, responded Tails. *Honesty is the best policy,* she mocked.

Oh, no. Oh no...

Willow argued internally, feeling all eyes on her, including Colt's intense gaze. She turned to her alleged best friends, seeking help. They lowered their heads, biting their bottom lip from laughing out loud, enjoying her turn in the spotlight. She glanced over at Noni and who sliced her eyes as the mocking eyebrow rose, challenging Willow. "I'm sorry. What was the question?"

A devilish look came over him. He smiled with a spark of eroticism. "Why does Noni need an extra bedroom, baby?"

Oh Noni, you she-devil, she thought.

Noni snickered along with the rest of her hyenas. She tossed a small cushion from behind her seat at Willow, letting her off the hook.

Willow caught the pillow, staring at the wording, 'Children are spoiled here because no one will spank Grandma.' She immediately laughed and tossed the pillow back at Noni. "You wish, Noni."

Noni caught the pillow, confused until she read the wording and looked back at the Willow, her eyes lighting up and laughing. "And to think, Colt bought me this pillow," she said, tossing it to Colt.

He read the pillow and dropped it on the floor like a hot frying pan. "Jesus," he groaned.

Willow and Noni continued to laugh as Candice walked over to console Colt. She picked up the pillow and read the words and laughed, tossing the pillow to Sofia, who shared with Luna and joined in on the joke.

"Can someone tell me what the damn pillow says?" demanded Rita.

Sofia softly tossed the pillow to Rita, who faltered before she caught it, slicing her eyes at Sofia. She read the pillow and chuckled at Noni before beaming the pillow at an unexpected Sofia with all her strength. The pillow flew a little higher than she aimed and hit Sofia across the head.

"¡*Vieja loca!*" she yelled, standing up and grabbing the pillow. She returned fire with less angst and Rita caught the pillow easily.

"You started it," fussed Rita.

"I tossed the pillow to you. I did not throw it at you like a pitcher striking out a player at the bottom of the ninth inning," she said, snatching the pillow from Rita's hands, only to hit her softly on the head with it. "We are even," she said and walked away.

Rita grabbed the pillow and swatted Sofia on the ass, hard. Sofia turned around suddenly and the pillow flew to her face. "That's it."

"Pillow fight," shouted Noni like a teenager at a slumber party full of girlfriends.

"Jesus," cried out Colt, moving out of the way.

Stunned, Willow froze as she watched Colt duck and grab a pillow flying his way and dodged another, making his way to her, only to pull her down behind the couch. Pillows continued to fly and come out of nowhere, like a gremlin fed after mid-night.

"Hey," he whispered.

"Hi," she whispered back, giggling.

"So, you are not going to tell me why the extra bedroom is needed?"

"Trust me, you don't want to know."

Colt chuckled and peeked over the couch. "When you finish here, come upstairs," he said, blocking another flying cushion before it hit them, tossing it back into the ring of fire.

"You're not joining the pillow fight? I thought guys were into that sort of thing," she teased.

He smiled at her, leaning in, "You want to pillow fight with me later, babe? I'm game. But definitely not with Noni and her cronies." He waited briefly and snatched a pillow from behind Sofia, stealing ammunition from her. "Here. Get ready. I'll cover you," he said, stealing a slow, soft kiss before he tossed a pillow at Noni, smacking her in the back.

She turned around and spotted a wide mouthed Willow standing behind the couch with another pillow stating, 'In Dog Years I'd Be Dead.'

"Oh, you are getting it," grinned a vengeful Noni.

Willow shook her head, holding her pillow up as a shield.

"Wait," she stated before the flying bullet encased pillow smashed her face. The sound of Colt's laughter trailed behind him while his phone blared loudly.

After a few more rounds, the firing ceased. Both Willow and Candice brokered a truce with a reluctant Rita and Sofia. They tidied the room and sat down, exhausted from their battle.

"I can't remember the last time I was in a pillow fight," exhaled Helen, pulling her fan out.

"That's because you are an old hag and soft cushion

pillows did not exist in your time," teased Rita, leaning towards the artificial breeze.

"Oh you," chuckled Helen. "Speak for yourself, Rita Brooks. I'm a spring chicken," she said, straightening her shoulders and puffing out her chest.

Willow and Sofia whistled while Luna clapped loudly.

"Ha, more like a hundred springs season too late," cackled Rita.

Helen leaned over and smacked Rita with her fan while Rita returned her assault with a pillow. The room tensed, waiting for another outbreak.

"Ladies," called out Candice. "Behave or neither of you will be able to move tomorrow." Candice stood up and walked over to Willow. "As always, my dear, it has been a genuine pleasure." She leaned over and hugged her as she said her goodbyes. Noni stood up and followed Candice out, both secretly laughing on their way to the door, no doubt planning their next epic battle with cotton. Or worse.

Helen stood and arched her eyebrow at Rita. "I should leave your cranky saggy cheeks here."

"Like hell you will," muttered Rita, slowly making her way up from the chair and not saying goodbye to anyone. Helen turned to Willow and her friends, giving them a wink and a little finger wave as she followed a grumpy Rita down the hall to the front door.

A short minute later, Willow openly stared at Colt as he walked by them, saying his goodbyes to his aunties while on the phone. She loved how he referred to them as his aunties, even if they were not blood related. She'd learned he was close to Levi and regarded him like a brother. They'd grown up together, along with

Maverick. Of course, Levi and Maverick hardly spoke now, and Colt and Maverick had their issues as well. He'd told her it was water under the bridge, but she could tell there were still some lingering, hard feelings. "Rita is heading out. No, she's still here."

Willow continued to watch Colt walk back over, still holding his phone, shaking his head. "You know, you could call her yourself. We're not in Junior High," he told whoever he was on the other line with. "Yeah, hang on."

Willow bit her lip, trying hard not to smile. Something about his boyish frustration was endearing and sweet as he passed along the message to Luna. "You staying longer or heading home?"

Luna's pretty light blue eyes were wide and her mouth open in a perfect circle. Confused.

"I'm not spending the night. Sofia's my lift." Sofia sat next to Luna and nodded her head enthusiastically. "Whose asking?" Luna questioned.

"Who do you think?" Willow whispered.

Colt relayed her response as he tried not to smile or laugh at whatever the other end of the phone was saying. "You sure you want me to tell her that?"

Colt pinched his nose and nodded his head. "He's asking for you to go home at a decent hour. He doesn't want you ladies driving out by yourselves too late."

The impatient voice on the line called out for Colt. Luna folded her arms.

Not a good sign.

"Is that Levi?" she demanded.

Willow's insides melted at his sly smile and nod. Alright. Seriously. She needed to get her hormones together, or pounce on him and to hell with who sees them.

Oh my.

Awe yeah. Let's do this.

"Let me have the phone," Luna stated, her accent sounding more pronounced the madder she became.

"Thank God," he said, passing the phone over without warning his so-called brother from another mother.

Poor Levi. Luna marched out of the room without looking back.

"She's going to give him hell," whispered Sofia excitedly.

"She might, but she's going to fold." Colt said, sitting casually down next to Willow and pulling her into his arms. She leaned in without hesitation.

"Ugh," muttered Sofia, waiting impatiently. She perked up when Luna marched right back into the room, handing Colt his phone and leaning over to give Willow a quick hug.

"I'll call you tomorrow," she simply said.

"Wait. What happened? What did he say? What did you say?" Sofia whined.

"You're my lift. Let's go."

Willow smothered her laughter as Colt barked out his.

"*Oyè!* Are you going to tell us what happened?" cried out Sofia.

Luna turned as she grabbed her purse. "Only Pistol here told the hot Viking we were watching Fifty Shades when he walked in. Which then lead the hot Viking to tell me it was too late to watch a movie. Which I bloody well know it is. And we should be careful and drive home before it gets later. Which I also bloody know that we should be careful. But if I find myself not doing that in the next thirty minutes, the hot Viking will come over here, pick me up, take me home, and show me what a real spanking is for not listening. With that all said, we are leaving before the bloody bloke shows up," she said breathlessly.

Willow stared wide eyed as Sofia mouthed '*Ay Dios Mio*' to her before lunging for Luna. "You are so getting laid by the hot Viking and he is going to spank you," she shouted.

"Jesus," muttered Colt.

Willow giggled, leaning closer to Colt. His arms tightened around her, drawing her nearer.

"Can we please leave?" Luna whined.

"But why? Spanking is so much fun," teased Sofia.

Luna stared cautiously at her watch. "I'm calling an Uber."

Sofia raced and grabbed her things. Her chaotic moves caused her to trip over Colt's feet. He caught her midway and steadied her. "Easy, Sof. I'm pretty sure Levi won't show up."

"Yes, he bloody well will," retorted Luna.

"Fine. Let's avoid your spanking. But I bet you might enjoy it," Sofia teased.

Luna groaned and walked away, leaving behind a snickering Sofia, who blew kisses at the wind.

"Be right back," he whispered.

Willow waited on the couch. He asked Sofia to drive safely and to text when they both got home. Her heart swelled at his thoughtfulness. He sat back down next to her and pulled her close.

"I can't believe you told Levi what we were watching," she giggled.

"Actually, I was telling him what Rita was watching, but he flipped it when he learned Luna was still here."

"He's into her," she simply commented.

She leaned back and looked up into his cautious eyes, reading into his silence.

"Anything ever happened between you two?" he asked tentatively. "I got to know, babe."

She leaned forward and pressed a soft, reassuring kiss on his lips. "No. Not even a kiss," she answered sincerely. "The last guy I dated lasted three months. He was a great guy. Nice. Handsome. I liked him, but we could never connect or find time. Between his schedule and mine, it didn't work out. That was a year ago. I've tried to date again, and it's been a category five disaster," she joked. She leaned into his hand as he brushed her bangs to the one side. "I'm not good at dating," she admitted.

"Neither am I, baby," his voice was a velvet murmur. "Which means you're fucking perfect for me." He leaned in and captured her lips, making unspoken promises with each caress. "Stay tonight," he said in a low, purposeful, seductive tone.

"Yes." She let the kiss consume her, lying back with his weight sweetly anchoring her. A sigh escaped her lips as he continued to sear a path down her neck and shoulders and back up, reclaiming her mouth. More demanding. His hands roamed freely down her curves, molding to the contours of her body. She locked herself in his embrace, burying her hands in his thick hair.

The sudden sounds of someone clearing their throat broke through their clouded haze. "If the two of you are doing the horizontal tango, can you not do it on my couch?" sassed Noni.

Willow buried her red face in Colt's neck as he growled.

"Goodnight, you two lovebirds," she sing-songed her way up the stairs.

Willow bit her lip and looked up at Colt as he leaned his forehead against hers. "I'll split the proceeds with you if you help me sell her."

"Deal," she said, and sealed it with a kiss.

Chapter 16

No Shame in her Game

A soft melody strummed Willow awake, beckoning her eyes to open. She nestled deeper in the warm, lush blankets of Colt's bed and lazily drew her eyes over to the sounds. Colt's low voice joined in quietly, as his fingers plucked the strings to a familiar song.

Her breath caught. Her heart stopped.
She'd heard the song countless of times.
Sang the song at the top of her lungs, even.
But never had she listened to the words like she did when the lyrics of 'Best Shots' poured out of Colt's lips and slammed right into her.

Leaving her in some sort of Colt induced dream state. A feeling she wished she could feel every second till her last breath. A feeling she had dreamed of finding one day and she found it, lying tangled in Colt's bed, wearing his shirt, while he sang another one of her favorite songs, giving it a new meaning.

As he finished the song, Willow fought the tears from overflowing.

"Mornin' baby," Colt said quietly, placing his guitar down and cocooning her back in his arms.

She sniffed. Words lost at the moment.

"Talk to me," he said in a husky whisper.

"You sure do know how to wake a girl up," she tried

teasing, avoiding any deep emotional conversations. She needed to get her mind wrapped around what she was feeling first.

"That's one of my many ways, darlin'," his voice was low and smooth, as he nipped her ear and moved down her neck.

Well do tell, said her awoken hellion.

Please do, said Halo.

A sigh escaped Willow, leaving her feeling like she had been waiting her entire life for this moment. He drew back, eyes wandering over her as if mentally photographing her. He dipped his chin down, bringing his lips back towards her in a slow, sweet kiss.

KNOCK, KNOCK, KNOCK.

"Good morning, Sunshines," called out Noni from behind the closed door.

"Sunshines? Willow in there with him?" asked Rita.

"Oh, you two. Will you leave them alone?" warned Candice.

"Rita, get down before you break something," chastised Helen.

"Are they getting up?" asked a grumpy Rita. "Breakfast is getting cold and I ain't going to wait for them to go through rounds one, two, and three of the horizontal tango before I eat."

"Oh, to go through rounds one, two, and three again," sighed Candice.

"Rita, get down before you hurt yourself," Helen fussed again.

"Noni, what are you doing with the mirror?" whispered yelled Candice.

Colt groaned, burying his head in Willow's neck as she attempted not to burst out laughing.

"Can you see anything?" asked Rita.

"They're awfully quiet. Are you sure they're in there?" asked Candice.

Willow bit her lip.

"Jesus. It's like I'm sixteen again, sneaking a girl to my room. This isn't funny, baby," Colt growled.

Willow disagreed, but said nothing. "I think we need to get up."

"Rita, move your saggy cheeks out of the way," Noni complained.

"I can't hear anything from back here."

"You can't hear anyways, you senile hag. Move it."

"Senile? Who are you calling senile?"

****

Colt slowly rose on his arms, staring at his door, and turned to Willow laying under him. He bent over one last time and stole another breathtaking kiss before pulling away and getting out of bed. He leaned over and tossed the covers back over Willow, giving her a wink before grabbing another spare shirt. He stood in front of his doorway, raising his hand up in the air, and counted down to three before he swung open his door.

"Seriously?" he asked Noni, who was on her knees with a mirror she was trying to sneak under his door. Candice stood behind her with Rita, trying to squeeze in between them to see and hear what was going on. "Rita, you should not be upstairs. How did you get up here?"

"Boy, I put my right foot in front of my left, just like you do."

He leaned out of his door and looked at Helen, who stood mid-way on the staircase, arms crossed and fuming. "Oh, she can put her right in front of her left going upstairs, but she can't do the same coming down,"

Helen said, knowing the challenge it would be to get Rita to come down the stairs.

Willow giggled. He looked over his shoulder to find her trying to stay covered under his sheets.

"Ya'll mind giving us a few minutes to get dressed without an audience?"

"You better hurry. I made my homemade biscuits with sausage and gravy," said Rita.

"Do you need me to help you get her down?" Colt asked Helen.

"No. I'm dragging her stubborn butt down these stairs one way or another," Helen said, annoyed.

"Well then, since there's nothing to see, we'll meet you downstairs," Noni said unphased.

Helen waved her one finger at Colt like she always did.

As they disbanded, Colt closed his door again and turned to see Willow lying flat on her back with her hands covering her face, body shaking. "We need to find a buyer soon," she said, causing him to toss his head back and laugh.

****

After her morning, the last place Willow thought she would end up sitting down for the last two hours, was a car dealership. Not any car dealership. Oh no.

Once Colt got a good look at her classic Honda and provided his manly advice, which entailed putting Milly to rest because it was a safety hazard to his woman, other drivers, and the ozone layer, he decided it was time to car shop. At which point Willow reminded him Milly still had a few more miles in her. To which he disagreed full heartedly and called Milly an atmosphere killer who needed to be taken off the streets immediately. This left

Willow stunned as she hadn't realized Colt was such an advocate for the ozone which led them down another discussion of clean energy. Recycling. Living off the grid, which she gave him a hard no on living without a bathroom and running water or toilet paper.

It was during this enlightening discussion that Sofia called. As soon as Sofia learned of Colt's plans to car shop, she proceeded to tell him about her cousin Vicente and how she'd been after Willow to come into his dealership. Sofia agreed to meet them there and confirmed Vicente was working in the morning.

"Baby," Colt called out to her.

Willow sat inside Vicente's office, sulking. She hated car shopping.

This was torture, whined Tails.

Can we drive the red car? Asked Halo excitedly.

Willow turned to Colt, frowning, arms crossed, and ignoring the flip in her stomach as he smiled at her knowingly. "Want to test drive one?"

She stood from the chair and walked past him, continuing to ignore his grin. She looked at the cars in the showroom. All shiny and new. Lavish with all the bells and whistles. No doubt every window worked without a problem. The trunk was not possessed, and opened and closed when it was supposed to. The radio picked up every station.

Cheese and fancy rice.

"What's causing you not to trade in?"

She shrugged. "My dad gave me the car when I was in high school. I don't have a lot of things left of him." A sad smile pulled at her lips. "He was such a minimalist. He could live off of three T-shirts, one pair of shorts, and flip-flops without a care in the world as long as mama and his girls had everything we needed." She looked out the window to the old beat-up Honda, knowing it was time.

"Awe, baby," Colt said in a low voice. "I didn't know." His arms came around her as his lips pressed sweetly to the side of her head. "You want more time with Milly, then we'll figure it out. I'm sure the ozone can manage another year or two with her around."

Willow leaned in and smiled before brushing a soft kiss against his lips. "I don't think she has another year or two in her. I'll be surprised if she makes it another month."

Colt pulled her close. "I know it's hard to let go of things of those that are close to us. No matter what you do with the material things baby, you can't lose the most precious things about them and that's the memory of them."

Willow slowly drifted her eyes closed, leaning into his strength. "Perfect," she whispered.

Sigh.
Purr.

"*¿Mi Amor?*"

Willow peeked over Colt's shoulder as Vicente walked towards them with Sofia hot on his trail. "I have a few cars you might like. They're within your budget. Two of them are brand new and one is a used car. However, it's in excellent condition with minimal mileage."

"The last one has a sunroof," Sofia said, bouncing on her heels clapping.

Willow's interest perked up at the mention of a sunroof.

"Want to check them out?" Colt asked.

Yes, yes, yes, chanted Halo.

Awe yes, said Tails, pulling out her cat eye sunglasses.

After Willow looked over the new cars and the fairly new crossover with the sunroof, she selected the crossover and test drove it. She immediately fell in love with the car. Right down to the wine-red color and charcoal interior. Vicente let her take the car on I-95, where she opened the sunroof and all the windows and blared the radio while enjoying the feel of a smooth ride. She didn't hesitate when she returned to the lot, and negotiated a sweet price on her new car. She cried when Vicente offered her five hundred dollars on Milly and said he would like to purchase it for his son to learn to drive, and fix cars. Once her emotional farewell was over, she named her new car Red, thanks to Lucy who Sofia face-timed and showed off the car.

Colt drove them to Willow's place and Willow sat in the passenger seat, reading her manuals, and pushing every button she could find. As they parked, a blue Santa Fé pulled up next to them. Willow turned to Colt with excited eyes. "It's Mama and Mila!"

She couldn't rush out of the car fast enough to get to them. Willow pulled her mom into a tight hug, refusing to let go. Tears sprang to her eyes and slowly edged over, flowing down her face. She buried her face tighter into her mom's shoulder. Inhaled deeper. Anchored herself to the moment. Remembered her mom's perfume and scent. "I've missed you so much, Mama."

Her mom embraced her tightly. Her voice softly cracked as she spoke, "My Whiskey girl. It's so good to see you again, honey." They slowly released each other and laughed at their tear-stained faces. Willow looked over and found Mila. Crying. She released her mom and rushed over. Not caring about the ugly sobs that escaped as she enclosed her sister in her arms and held tight.

"I…am…ha…p…py…y…you…are…h…h…home…", she happily sobbed.

"Me too," whispered Mila quietly.

"Those two might need a minute or five," Willow's mom said to Colt. "I'm Emily Lawson. Whiskey's mama."

"Colton Royce, ma'am."

"Well, aren't you a cutie pie? Did we catch you all at a bad time?"

"No ma'am. We were on our way back from car shopping."

"Shut your pie hole. Tell me you talked her into getting rid of that death trap."

"Mama," Willow called out, still hugging Mila.

"Did you?" her mother asked, ignoring her.

"Yes ma'am. This is her new car."

"Hallelujah. Praise the good Lord almighty. You actually got rid of that torture ride from Satan himself you called a car."

"Mama," Mila scolded.

"It was daddy's car," Willow reminded her.

"Yes, honey, but your daddy wanted to get rid of it and get a Vespa, of all things." Her mother's dramatic eye roll made hers look like an amateur. "My husband, loved the breath out of his hippie heart, but a Vespa?"

Willow groaned and lowered her head on Mila's shoulder. "You alright, baby?"

A sudden gasp from her mom caused Mila to roll her eyes again and Willow to grumble.

I like Mama Lawson.

Me too, agreed Tails.

Willow, still holding Mila's hand, afraid if she let it go, her sister would suddenly disappear, approached Colt.

"Colt, this dramatic Southern crazy woman is my mother, Emily Lawson. Everyone calls her Mama Lawson at the bar."

Her mother cut her eyes at Willow.

"This is my older sister, Mila," she dragged on the word older longer than necessary.

"I still look younger than you," Mila teased. "Hi, Colt. Nice to meet you."

"Colt, do you like fried chicken? I make a mean fried chicken and since you talked some common sense into my daughter on getting rid of that heap of a car, I'm making it for you tonight," she said before going to the trunk and grabbing her bags.

Willow and Mila shared a secret smile. The smile where one sister reminded the other 'she's our momma.'

"I've got the rooms ready for you all and made space in the closets."

"Thank you, sissy." Mila turned to grab her bag and took the keys from Willow to open the front door.

"Are you sure you want to stay?" Willow asked Colt.

"And miss fried chicken? Not a chance, baby."

"Do you want to go pick up Lucy?"

Colt stopped.

"It would be a wonderful distraction for Mila," Willow quickly added.

He still said nothing.

"I understand if you think it's too soon for her to meet my family."

"No, baby. It's not that. I love how you want to include her."

"Of course. She's your little girl."

His kiss smothered her last words. Standing on her tiptoes, she returned his kiss with just as much urgency.

Someone cleared their throat behind them.

"It's like *I'm* sixteen again," Willow muttered, repeating Colt's earlier statement.

"Mama," Mila scolded again.

Willow reluctantly released Colt and he grabbed two suitcases "Which one is Willow's room?" He asked.

A confused look crossed Mila's face briefly before she recovered. "It's upstairs on the third floor to the left."

Willow braced, waiting for her sister to jump her once Colt started hauling his load up the stairs.

"He doesn't know where your room is?" asked Mila.

"He hasn't slept over."

"So you're not hitting that?"

"Mama!" both Willow and Mila shouted simultaneously.

"What? That is what you all call copulating these days. Or is it tapping ass? Wait. Does tapping ass mean you tap someone on their ass?"

Please don't let Colt overhear this conversation.

"Lord heavens, please tell me it does not mean you are having—"

"Mama!" they yelled again.

Heavy footsteps caught Willow's attention as Colt walked down the stairs, holding a purring Prim in his arms. Lucky cat. He exchanged a smile with her, then shook his head. Her mother continued to stare at her and Mila, who turned away and grabbed another bag, muttering something about crazy mamas and technology.

Willow stared dumbfounded at Mila's departure and braced herself.

"You better answer me, Willow Mae Lawson."

The blood drained from her face along with her soul, only to have it shoved right back into her body.

Tails, will you stop with your cackling? This is serious. We need to help Willow explain what tapping someone's buttocks means, chastised Halo.

Tails composed herself. She glowed brightly with delight at the situation and whispered, *Honesty is the best policy.*

"Google it, mama," Willow snapped, ignoring her laughing she-devil as she turned to Colt, catching him hiding a smile and a slight blush himself.

"I'm going to head home and grab Lucy, unless you need me to stay behind."

"Do you want me to drive you home so you can bring your truck?"

"How about you drive us back after dinner?"

Willow smiled, reading between the lines and his smiles. If she drove him back after dinner, she would have more time with him before she headed back home. Lord, it was like she was sixteen again, sneaking time in with her first boyfriend. She handed him her keys and walked him downstairs, letting her inquisitive mother know he would return for dinner.

"Mama, are you seriously looking up the meaning of tapping ass?" Mila asked. Willow groaned and counted to ten.

Welcome home Mama. Welcome home.

****

As Colt pulled out of Willow's driveway, he called

Noni to let her know of his plans. What should have been a simple request to get Lucy ready for him to pick up turned into a fifteen-minute debate over the phone, where he told her she was not coming over with Rita, Helen, and Candice to meet Willow's mother and sister.

"And why not? We're your family," Noni whined.

"I know, Noni. I'm sure Emily would love to meet each one of you, but right now might not be the best time. Alright?"

"Pish posh. This is the best time to meet. I can bring the brownies I baked along with a salad I could throw together. I'm sure the girls can whip something up as well for dinner. I will time face with them."

Time face? What in the world? "You mean Facetime?"

"Yes," she cried out happily. "Sofia taught me how to do it. It's amazing."

Colt groaned. "Noni, how about we make a deal?" he said, knowing this would catch her attention.

"I'm listening."

"I bring you with me tonight to meet them with Lucy. But only you and Lucy."

He waited a minute before she spoke. "We have an accord," she said in her most obnoxious pirate accent. "Lucy and I will be ready by the time you pull up."

"I doubt it," he grumbled, pulling up in his driveway.

Once inside the house, it was total chaos. Noni tossed him the lettuce head, tomato, and cucumber before reaching for the knife. He pulled it from her hand before she tossed it at him, too. "Go get ready. I'll make the salad."

He chopped the lettuce. Diced the tomato and sliced

the cucumber, placing everything in the bowl Noni had laid out. He added some olives and croutons. He sealed the bowl and grabbed Noni's homemade vinaigrette from the refrigerator.

His phone buzzed in his pocket.

Willow—*Bring Freckles. Mila wants to meet him*—

Colt—*You sure? Prim won't freak out?*—

Willow—*No way. She thinks she's a dog*—

Colt laughed and grabbed a small can of dog food to feed Freckles and his leash.

Colt—*Will do. Be there shortly*—

Colt—*Noni is coming too*—

Willow—*This should be fun.*—

Again, he smiled at his girl's witty humor. Fun was an understatement.

"Honey bear, are you ready to go? Uncle Colt is leaving."

"I'm ready. I'm ready," Lucy squealed back as she ran down the stairs in a pink glitter dress and matching pink glitter shoes with fairy wings and her pink exits. Freckles trailed behind her, somehow sporting pink glitter as well on his fur and not caring. She brought along her pink unicorn tote bag, which included all of her make-up over items.

"Honey bear, you don't need to bring this with you," he said.

"But maybe Willow's sister will want a make-up over too," she whispered.

He found it hard to say no to her. This was one of them. When her eyes were soft and her voice tender. "Alright, little fairy. But if Mila doesn't want a make-up over, then you need to understand."

"I'll understands, Uncle Colt."

He looked up and found Noni smirking at him. She dressed in a simple black button-down blouse with a chunky silver necklace. Deep blue jeans and a pair of silver sandals showed off her hot pink toenails. Silver stud earrings and multiple bangles hung from her arm. She wore her grandmother's wedding ring on her right hand and a ring with Colt, Clover, and Lucy's birthstones on her left hand. The two rings she always wore for as long as he could remember after her divorce from his grandfather.

She carried a large purse an airport would consider as carry-on luggage. He would never understand why since it only had her wallet, phone, key, and small umbrella in it, but didn't bother to question it.

"Ready?"

They both nodded and grabbed items from the kitchen to head out. He transferred Lucy's booster seat from his truck to Willow's car and secured her and Freckles in the back. Noni made herself comfortable in the passenger seat, pushing the buttons and opening the sunroof with glee. She snapped a duck face selfie with Lucy in the background smiling ear to ear and Freckles tongue hanging out.

Colton sent Willow a message, letting her know they were on their way.

"Are her mother and sister visiting?" asked Noni.

"No. They moved back."

"That's fantastic news. I'm sure Willow is ecstatic."

Colt nodded. "In case the mood is off, Mila is having some marital issues. It's why she moved back. It's pretty bad, Noni."

Noni remained quiet.

Colt glanced over quickly and noticed Noni's

demeanor change. He reached over and grabbed her soft hands and squeezed them gently. "She's going to be alright, Noni."

"Of course she is," she sniffed. "I'm sure Willow and her mother will be there for her. And you will. But I will as well. And so will Candice and Rita and Helen."

"Noni," he attempted to console her.

"I swear, boy, some men are not worth the salt of a good woman's tears."

"Don't go in there with some wild pink haired ideas of yours. You hear me?"

"Pish posh," she muttered and remained quiet till they arrived at Willow's.

He leashed Freckles as Noni grabbed her luggage purse and salad bowl. She insisted on being the one to hold on to it. Colt brought the rest and followed behind her as she trudged up the stairs. He gave her a few seconds to catch her breath before he allowed Lucy, who would not stop bouncing on her heels, to knock on the door.

****

Willow opened the door and a bowl of salad landed in her arms. A little fairy bum rushed by with Noni trailing behind, straight to her mother and sister.

"Look, Willow, I brought my make-up over stuff for your sister?"

Willow giggled, catching the faint glint of humor in Colt's eyes. "I'm sure she is going to enjoy it, honey bear," she said. "Go on up. I'll introduce you to her. If you have blue exits, then she's going to love it."

Lucy squealed happily and raced up the stairs.

"Hey," Colt said quietly.

"Hey," she replied.

He placed Freckles down and grabbed the salad bowl from her. She leaned in for a warm kiss. "Missed you." His smile was as intimate as their kiss.

He brushed his nose against hers, as she enjoyed his playfulness. "Head's up. Noni is feeling Mila's separation. I had to warn her in case things were off."

"Ah. That explains the salad bowl pass-off. Noted."

He nodded, and they both walked upstairs and stopped short. They found Mila and Lucy sitting on the floor, with blue exits ready to be put in her hair. Mila was murmuring to Lucy, sharing secrets as they giggled quietly.

Noni stood next to her mother with a sneaky smile.

"All night?" her mother repeated.

"All night," Noni confirmed.

"Willow Mae Lawson. You mean to tell me, when we arrived, you were getting home from being out all night?"

Willow groaned. "Mama, you realize I'm not sixteen anymore."

"Whiskey girl, there is no shame in your game."

"Hey, I wants to learn to play the game too," cried out Lucy.

"Mama," chastised Mila.

"And I'm going to learn the horry zonky tango too," Lucy said proudly.

"Noni," growled Colt.

Willow glanced at her sister. Mila covered her mouth with a twinkle in her eye, shaking her head. Their mother raised her eyebrows and sliced her eyes back at Willow. "No shame in your game, missy," she repeated.

"Oh mama."

Chapter 17

Dragon Queen, Ex's and Oh No's

"That's it. I am opening my own bar here in this oasis and never returning home," declared Fab, strutting down the gravel road of Robbie's Marina towards the quaint marketplace in her hot pink, strappy maxi dress and matching sandals.

Willow stepped out of the driver's seat in her new blue backless dress, enjoying the feel of the salty air and South Florida heat. The girls wore similar attires except for Sofia, who proclaimed she was vertically challenged and wore a colorful short romper. The drive had been long. The day longer. They began their road trip at four a.m., which required Willow to be up at three a.m. Which meant some of the girls spent the night at her place to avoid the short commute and gain the extra minutes of sleep or they would be up at two a.m. because…well because they're Divas and that's how Diva's rolled.

They agreed, from the beginning Willow would drive and Fab would ride shotgun, as ordained by Fab herself. Skylar, Zoila, and Luna would ride in the second row with few luggage pieces stowed away under their seats. Sofia, Harper, and Piper occupied the third row, as they were the shortest of the group, with the luggage behind them. As on many road trips, everything started with a flare of excitement. However, by the time they reached I-4, approximately one hour into their drive, Skylar had threatened Sofia three times. Harper's phone would not stop ringing, causing Zoila, who was trying to catch up on sleep from working the night shift, to almost throw the phone out the window.

"If you all don't calm your tits, I swear to the Almighty baby Jesus I'm gonna unleash my Dragon Queen on all of you," snapped Fab.

Willow had bit her lower lip. The Dragon Queen had awoken, and no one interfered with Fab at that point.

"Harper," Fab barked, "Move and sit behind Sky before she kills Sofia and that way Zoila doesn't kill your phone." Harper giggled as she stood and bent dramatically over the seat to swing her shoulder-length blonde hair between Zoila and Luna and shoved her butt in Sofia's face to sit in the middle.

"If I hear another complaint from either of you, I'll tell Willow to pull this car over and ditch you on the side of road. Have I made myself crystal clear?" Fab asked with unwavering authority, raising an arched eyebrow, waiting for anyone to challenge her.

"Yes, mother dearest," sassed Luna, causing a ripple of giggles to erupt from the back seat.

"Fab, put your Dragon Queen away," shouted Skylar.

"She wouldn't have to show her face if the third row wouldn't be showin' out," Fab lashed back. "Who is blowing up your phone, blue eyes?" she asked Harper, waiting impatiently for an answer.

All eyes turned to Harper, including Willow, who glanced from her rear-view mirror back before returning to the drive. "Work stuff. Sorry, I'll put it on silent," she grumbled quickly, sending a text and putting her phone away. She mouthed sorry to Zoila, who made a childish face and stuck her tongue out before blowing a kiss and turning back around, leaning against Luna's shoulder.

The drive had remained uneventful. Well, as uneventful as it could be with the eight of them cooped up in a rented SUV. After avoiding the mini death threats, the, "she's touching me," and, "I need to pee," or, "can we listen to music?" or even better, "Ugh I hate this song," to which, "I love this song," contributed to a sequel of the Dragon Queen to appear and another menacing threat of leaving them on the side of the road. In the end, Willow had to pull over at a rest stop, where bathrooms, drinks, and chocolate were available for everyone to calm their tits as Fab demanded.

Munching on her chocolate bar, she looked at her phone and the time. It was past seven thirty and Colt would be up. The thought of hearing his morning voice spurred her fingers into action.

"Hey, baby," his voice was thick from sleep.

"Did I wake you?" she asked, feeling a little guilty.

"It's alright. Prefer waking up to you as my alarm."

She blushed, remembering their night together. His hands and lips. The way they explored every inch of her.

"You're thinking about it too." His husky voice cloaked her with warmth.

She covered her face with her hand, heat spreading down her neck, no doubt shining brightly. He chuckled over the phone. "Where are you, darlin'?"

"We are at a rest stop in West Palm Beach," Willow said. "We stopped before the Dragon Queen consumed the souls of the maidens."

"That bad?"

"Oh yeah. I have never been so thankful to be a

designated driver." She told him about the third-row incident and then the sequel, which led her to pull over at the stop for a mental break. "I better let you get ready. The girls are about done and we need to get back on the road."

He remained silent for a few seconds before he responded. "Yeah, I need to get going too. Got to finish up a stain job for a client."

"What did you build this time?"

"He had an old canoe. Belonged to his grandfather. He wanted me to see if I could restore it, but some planks rotted. I saved most of it. I converted it into two pieces and turned them into sides tables. He said he was going to use them as bookshelves. I'm sanding them down and staining then delivering it later today. They came out pretty badass. Thinking of making me a pair for the office."

"They sound amazing. Send me pictures when they're finished. I would love to see them," she said excitedly. "I'll, um, I'll text you at the next stop."

"Yeah, baby." There was another moment of silence. Willow tried to interpret it. "Fuck," he whispered. "Happy you're on this trip with your girls. Know you've been looking forward to it and deserve it. But *damn* if I didn't wish you were here in my arms instead."

Her breath hitched. Every word coursed through her. "Me too," she admitted.

"Go have fun, darlin'," he said before ending their call.

Still giddy, she did a quick check in with Levi, not caring about the time and waking him up. He answered his phone on the first ring. "Don't tell me I have to bail all of your asses out already," he said in a deep, sleepy grumble.

"No, I'm checking in."

"You realize we're not even open yet. I got this. Get off my phone and send me a picture of Luna in her bikini."

"Creeper."

"Not denying it," he yawned loudly. "We good then? Gotta get some sleep. My partners took a couple of days off and left me alone. Had to call in reinforcement to cover for them."

"Whatever. Fab made sure you had plenty of coverage on the schedule."

Levi laughed and groaned loudly as he stretched and shuffled around on the bed. "I know," he admitted. "Colt is stopping by to help. You got a good one there, Whiskey."

"Yeah," she sighed happily. "He makes it easy, and it scares the hell out of me, Levi."

"Easy is a good thing, doll. Nothing wrong with easy. You find easy, you hold on to it."

"When did you become the guru of love, life, and hacks?"

"I'm not just a sexy, tatted beast," he teased.

She smirked. What a goof. She reminded him of the shipments coming in, to which he grumbled "I got it," before telling her to enjoy herself and to send a picture of Luna. Feeling sorry for the sap, she took a selfie with Luna and sent it to both Colt and Levi.

Willow—*Maybe a road trip for the four of us in the future?*—

Her phone beeped a few seconds later with a response from Levi first, followed by Colt.

Levi—*Hell Yeah*—
Colt—*New Orleans anyone?*—
Levi—*Bro, plan it. I'll check our schedules*—

She reminded them they would need to first let Luna know of the plans to which they both stated she was responsible for inviting her, since it was her idea. Great. Somehow, the next three and a half hours of driving should give her time to come up with a plan to break the news to Luna Cassel about her upcoming travel plans. Road trips are grand.

****

Colt sat at the bar showing off the pictures he received of Willow throughout her trip to a disgruntled Levi. After the fifth photo, Levi tossed a rag at him and demanded he begin his shift and wipe down the bar tables and get ready for happy hour. Smiling, Colt placed his phone away and happily got to work polishing off the table tops down to the bar stools. Once proclaimed spotless by the sergeant himself, Colt replenished the garnishes, making sure there were plenty of olives and coriander spice for the Spicy Dirty Martini Specials.

His phone alerted him of an incoming text. He chuckled at the silly picture of Willow strangling Sofia and then smiled warmly at the beautiful picture following of Willow posing by the water with the sunset behind her. Colt saved the picture on his phone as Mila stormed out of the storage room.

Mila had wasted no time in finding work. She looked into working at Pip's Boutique during the day and evenings at the bar. Their mom agreed to work day shifts at the bar and cover when they were short on weekends. She also offered to assist with the filing and paperwork, which all three partners readily agreed to hand over to her. Thank goodness dinner had went well after the walk of shame conversation ended. Colt won Mama Lawson over with his charms, and Noni became Mila's number one supporter. They shared a bottle of wine together, along with several tears.

Before he left, Colt had carried Mila upstairs to bed for Willow, where she tenderly tucked her sister in. Lucy fell asleep on Willow's cozy couch watching a movie, snuggled with Prim on one side and Freckles on the other.

It was at that moment, Colt realized why the luggage purse was being used. Noni had brought old pictures of Colt over to show off to Willow and her mother. Which made Willow's mother bring out old photos of her to share.

Colt and Willow had left them to their devices and snuck away downstairs and hung out with Levi and Wes. They chatted for a bit before sneaking away to the office and made out heavy before heading back upstairs for him to collect Noni, Lucy and Freckles. Willow rode back with them. She helped him settle Lucy and Freckles and said her goodnight to Noni before heading downstairs to head home, but not before he'd captured her lips again for another deep, searing kiss.

The sisters had many things in common, which included their taste in good food, wicked sense of humor, and loyalty to their family and friends. However, Colt learned the difference between them was Willow was a Martini Girl and Mila was a Vino Babe or Wine Girl. The other difference, Mila and Beck could not be in the same room together for long periods of time. As in, no more than ten minutes. He learned meetings were cut short when the two were in the same room before the tension imploded around them. Levi and Wes found it hysterical. Colt stood on the fence, unsure of his feelings.

Now, his eyes followed Mila as she stomped past the bar, ignoring him and down the hallway to the restrooms. A short second later, Beck came out and poured himself a shot.

"Gonna take a walk. Be back before it gets crowded," he said and left.

Colt glanced towards the restrooms, teetering on whether to check on Mila or give her space.

"Yo," Levi shouted as a white T-shirt flew over the bar, interrupting his thoughts. "We wear white tonight," he said. Nodding, Colt changed out of his black Martini Girl Bar shirt from his previous shift and replaced it with the fresh T-shirt. He added the dish rag to his back pocket and continued to restock the glasses for the night, along with a few other specialty glass drinks. He glanced towards the hallway, waiting for Mila. He would give her another five minutes, then go check on her.

Colt had learned both Willow and Levi kept the bar clean and organized since they worked with hundreds of complex drinks. He understood their logic and kept it up to keep the night running smooth. He stocked the last set of glasses. The sudden sounds of a familiar voice raised the small hairs on his neck to an agonizing scream.

"May I have a glass of wine?"

Nikki Busche.

Of all the bars in the city, she stepped foot into this place. Grinding his teeth, he turned to face her. There was a time her shiny green eyes and striking red hair would have left him dumbstruck. Hell, it did leave him dumbstruck. For three years he was dumbstruck on her, like a man dumbstruck on fool's gold. She hadn't changed one bit. Her eyes were still shiny green and her hair was still strikingly bright. Her porcelain skin was clear and radiant. She looked happy to see him, and he was not buying it for a minute.

"What do you want, Nikki?" he spat out harshly.

She pulled back as if struck. "Such hostility, Colton. Is this necessary?" Her sweet southern twang, laced with hurt, softly spiraled around him. Irritating him more.

"Cut the act. What do you want?"

"You know, you used to buy into my sweet and soft," she smiled wryly and leaned over the counter. "I want…"

"I got this Colt." Turning, he found Mila walking over, wrapping her serving apron around her thin waist. Her white Martini Girl Bar shirt hung off her one shoulder, showing off a nickel size tattoo of a bird flying with a string holding onto a heart.

"What can I get you?" Mila asked Nikki, staying close as he watched the front door open and Beck walk into the bar laughing with a pretty, tall blonde. He signaled two with his hands towards Colt.

"I'll take care of it," he said to Mila who at the current moment stood stone cold silent watching Beck and his newfound friend.

"Uh hello, am I going to get my drink or what?" asked Nikki, waving her hands in front of Mila.

Colt bumped Mila with his shoulder while he poured two beers for Becker. "You got her?" he asked with concern.

"Yeah, um, yes. Sorry. I'm good. What did you want to drink?" she repeated to Nikki.

Colt walked away and brought Beck his drinks, placing them on the barstool where they sat, slamming his a little harder than necessary. "Not cool, Beck." Then he returned to the bar.

Bits and pieces of Nikki and Mila's conversations floated back to him. " Let me get this straight. You don't have a Merlot or a Pinot Noir," Nikki asked.

"We have Red. We have White," Mila simply replied. "If you want a red wine, it's not Merlot and definitely not Pinot Noir. Your pick."

He watched Nikki study the menu with utter distaste, finding it amusing.

"Whatever. Ridiculous wine menu. Is there a martini that is glutton free."?

"One glutton free martini coming up," Mila snapped with a smile.

Colt quickly grabbed the drink shaker and prepared his own concoction shot, keeping a close eye on Mila, making sure she was not adding any laxatives to Nikki's drink. Not that he believed Willow would actually keep laxatives in her bar. At least he was pretty sure she didn't keep laxatives in her bar. He needed to do a sweep and confirm there were no laxatives before the sisters sent someone to the toilet for the foreseeable future.

"Here you go. That will be eight dollars and fifty cents. Are you starting a tab or pay as you go?" Mila asked.

"What the hell is this?" shouted Nikki at the beautiful rose gold glass filled with ice, topped off with two cherries and an orange wedge.

"Oh, don't worry. The cherries and orange are glutton free. And see, it's a smiley face," Mila said proudly, shrugging her shoulders and smiling.

"Colton, what the hell," cried out Nikki.

"Are you opening a tab or paying?" asked Mila

again, ignoring Nikki's outburst.

Colt stopped mid shake, doing his best not to point at Nikki's incredulous face and laugh obnoxiously.

"Is this a joke, Whiskey? I can't believe this is the type of customer service you provide here," Nikki said, arching her eyebrows and staring down at Mila. "Colt, this little thing is your new fling? Talk about a trade down."

Colt could feel the scales of the, 'oh shit meter,' tilt by the way Mila stared at Nikki. He was pretty sure if Mila was a superhero she would shoot laser beams from her eyes and blast Nikki through some portal to another dimension.

Man, if only it were possible.

"Excuse me?" Mila hissed.

Colton put down the shaker. The full picture formed before him for Nikki's reasons being at *this* bar. Somehow, word must have gotten back to her. He had moved on, and it was not something Nikki apparently approved. "Nikki, I think it's best—" Before he could finish his warning, Mila interjected.

"Uh, hold on, lover," she said lovingly to Colton, leaning in a little closer but still keeping a small distance between them. "Trading down? Is that what you think my Colt is doing?" she asked Nikki.

Nikki laughed, tossing her head back dramatically, running her painted nails across the bar top as if she were playing piano keys. "Honey, you've known Colt for what? A minute? I had him for five years"

"Three," he corrected with a growl.

Nikki pursed her lips. "Huh. Felt longer."

"No shit," he growled again, watching Beck walk over to the bar, picking up on the tension.

"Five. Three. Doesn't matter. It's more than you've known him, Whiskey. I've had him longer in my bed. And believe me. A man like Colton doesn't date a woman like you," she sneered distastefully, "Small tits, skinny, and a Plain Jane all around. Sorry honey, but you are a trade down."

"Enough, Nikki," Colt lashed out sternly.

Mila outright laughed in Nikki's face, clapping loudly and wiping the fake tears from her eyes. "Ah, poor little strawberry fake-cake. That's what you think is a trade down? My small tits and natural beauty? Oh, honey. I pity you. I pity you because life has been ripping you off. My small tits," she said grabbing them fully, causing Beck to stop dead in his tracks, "are a natural handful."

Colt covered his mouth with his hand. From the corner of his eye, he caught Levi walking in on the last part of the conversation. "Awe hell."

Mila continued to rip into Nikki as they watched a redness seep into her skin, slowly rising from her exposed chest to her neck and up her cheeks. "As for me being too thin, well, I guess I'm just lucky. I get to eat everything I want. All the protein," she said turning to Colt and seductively sliding in front of him, leaning into his body and forcing his arms to wrap around her, "whenever I want. Nothing goes to waste. While you live in an unfortunate, vain world where life fucks you over with tasteless supplements," she said, leaning over the bar, making sure Colt stood behind her, squeezing his hand, hoping he received the message not to move from his position. "I bet," she said breathlessly into Nikki's face, as Mila bit her lower lip, slowly rotating her hips and letting out a low groan, "you wish you were this

Plain Jane right…this…second." Straightening back up, she released Colt's hand and placed them on the bar. "Eight-fifty," she repeated.

Colt took a step back and stood next to Mila. "Pay or leave," he demanded.

"Got to tell you, Strawberry fake-cake, this natural red glow you are sporting is pretty bright," Mila mocked.

Nikki stood up abruptly, crying out awkwardly, not realizing Beck was behind her. She turned and looked back at Colt, slanting her eyes and stomping out as quickly as she could on her heels.

Feeling the tension of the room release, Colt took a deep breath. His eyes rose, meeting Beck's, who kept staring at Mila. Colt turned to Mila as she grabbed the lonely fancy rose glass and ate the cherries and orange slice. He smiled at her, shaking her head.

"Produce are expensive," she said defensively, finishing the orange slice and tossing the peel away. They stood quietly for a second before making eye contact and then laughing at the situation.

"Which one of us is telling Willow what happened?" she asked.

"I'll tell her."

Mila glanced at Beck and looked away. "Handle that for me?" she asked quietly.

"Will do," he said.

Colt walked over to Beck. "Need another round?"

"No. I'm done tonight. What the hell was that with her back there?" Beck asked accusingly.

Colt leveled his gaze, controlling the sudden anger rising. Beck had three inches and twenty pounds on Colt. The man was solid, and no one messed with Beck. Colt's inner Hulk rose to the challenge. "You got something you want to say?"

"You're with Whiskey. She goes out of town, and you got Mila hanging all over you. Bending over for you."

"Wait. How much did you have to drink? Are you serious? Did you not clue in on what was happening?"

"It ain't right, man. You gave me shit for bringing in the blonde and yet here you are making moves on Mila."

Colt stepped back. Levi and Mila began their approach after Beck exploded. Colt raised his hand to make them stop. "I've got this," he told them and turned back to Beck. "Let me make this clear to you. I'm not making moves on no one. No one. Got it?"

"Didn't look that way to me," Beck said, tossing back the rest of his beer before slamming the mug down.

"I'll call bullshit," Colt said, leaning in closer to Beck. "Whatever you and Mila got or don't got going on, that's between you two. You want me to stay out of it, then I will. That's all you had to say. But don't spin something out of nothing to fuck me over."

Colt waited, watching Beck stare him down. "Stay out of it," he warned Colt, then stormed away, passing Levi and Mila to the office.

Colt grabbed the empty mug and placed it with the dishes to wash, wiping down the counter and topping off another order for Vet, who was working the courtyard tonight. "Sunset is awesome tonight. I've become everyone's personal photographer outside," he whined, waiting for his drinks.

"All part of the service," Colt reminded him.

"I need two Cosmos and a Lemon Drop. You gonna make those?" Vet asked, laughing.

"One second," grumbled Colt. "Mila," he called out, interrupting her conversation with Levi, "Can you make Cosmos and Lemon Drops?"

She smiled at him knowingly and patted Levi on his arm, nodding before heading to the bar. "What were you making earlier?" she asked me.

"Something for us," he said.

"Nice," she whispered enthusiastically, reminding him of Willow.

"You sound like your sister."

"She gets it from me," she smartly replied with a smile.

Finishing his beer order, he watched her make the drinks, taking in the amounts she poured and the liquors she used, learning.

"These are Willow's favorite," she said, finishing up the Lemon Drop and handing it over to Vet. She whipped up the Cosmos faster than Colt could keep up with and poured them into their glasses, sending Vet off to serve his patrons.

"You're as fast as Willow," he said.

"She's faster," Mila admitted.

Colt grabbed the chilled shaker and two shot glasses. He poured out his drink.

"It's pink," Mila said, giggling.

"Yeah," Colt said with humor. "Experimented with some mixers and alcohol the other night and came up with this."

She took a whiff and closed her eyes. "Tequila. Strawberry Liquor and something else."

"Good nose."

"It's not laxatives, right?"

Colt barked out a laugh. "Hell no."

Loving Whiskey

Still smiling, Mila raised her shot glass to Colt, "Thank you for making my sister happy."

"Thank you for pissing my Ex off," he said in return.

"Oh, that was fun," she said wickedly. "Cheers."

"Cheers," swallowing his shot, he watched her take her drink and make a face. "Need a chaser?"

"No," she said between coughs, "I'm good."

"So you think the red wine is shit?" he asked, grabbing the shot glasses and rinsing them off.

She snorted, reminding him of Willow. "It tastes like vinegar."

Colt chuckled, enjoying this relaxed version of Mila. He grabbed the shaker and poured another round of his concoction as Levi approached.

"Hell yeah. This your drink from the other night? Pour me one bro."

He poured three small shots. Colt and Mila laughed at Levi when he coughed after shooting the drink. "How much tequila did you use?" Levi grabbed the first beer bottle he found and chugged it.

"Wuss," Colt whispered to Mila, who continued to laugh.

Levi flicked them off, grabbing his dish rag and hanging it behind his back pocket. Mila went around the inside of the bar, checking on the customers, making sure everyone was good. Playing the role of Fab. Most customers were outside with the beautiful sunset and cooler evening. Colt relaxed, enjoying the steady stream of busy and no drama.

Until Noni arrived.

"Ladies, this is the lovely Mila I was talking to you all about. Mila, this is Helen, Rita, and Candice. *My* Martini Girls."

"Actually, we are more like the Vintage Girls," Candy chimed in.

"Who are you calling Vintage?" Rita protested.

"Don't mind her. She's naturally crabby. Get her a drink and some chips and she'll be fine," Helen said.

"This way ladies," Mila said sweetly, walking them closer to the bar towards the reserved table. "Whiskey and the girls are out of town and since you are all Honorary Martini Girls, well, you get their spot. Right. Next. To. The. Bar."

"Oh my. This is such a treat. Do you see this, Rita? We are in a VIP section," gushed Helen.

"Nothing exciting about this table," muttered Rita, reading over the drink menu. "Menu is the same as before,"

"Oh hush. Why are your bloomers all twisted up? Is your sugar low? Did you forget your meds?" asked a semi-concerned Candice.

"Come now, Candy. Let's not ruin the evening discussing Rita's twisted bloomers. The horror," mocked Noni, wide eyed, sipping her glass of complimentary water.

"I'll give you twisted bloomers, you saggy ass hag," mumbled Rita.

Colt greeted the crazy bunch. "I get that it's a full moon, but why are you crazies out and about?" he teased, giving each of them a chaste kiss on the cheek.

Candice and Helen smiled sweetly. "Sugar, we had to get these two out of the house before they destroyed your kitchen. Our game of monopoly started off hot and feisty like a man should be, and ended up full of ugly vendettas in play and future pillow smothering like I wish I could do to my ex-husband," explained Candice.

Colt shook his head as Mila brought back chips and mango salsa for the table, refilling their glasses of water, listening in on the conversation.

"We moved on to Pictionary, figuring it would be safe," Helen said. They both looked at Rita on one side of the table and Noni on the other, who stared daggers at one another. "Well, that didn't go well either," she said, covering her mouth to hide her snort.

Mila joined in on the giggle, refilling Rita's glass.

Sighing heavily, Colt stared down at his grandmother. "What did you do with Lucy?"

Noni's icy stare turned to him, slicing him in two, if it was possible. "I left her locked away in a closet with a half a bottle of water and five skittles to hold her over," she snapped sarcastically. "Where the hell do you think I left her? She's with Amy. They are making homemade ice cream and lollipops. I'll pick her up on the way home," she stated, flicking the menu and sliding her reading glasses on before turning her attention to the liquor options.

Sighing again, Colt turned to Mila, who shrugged her shoulders and continued to pour water.

"My dear, do you know how to make those vibrant blue drinks?" asked Helen to Mila.

"Oh yes. Willow, I mean, Whiskey," corrected Candice with an exaggerated wink, "she made this blue martini that was sinfully divine."

"Aunties, I think you need to be a bit more specific for Mila to make the drinks for you."

"Long Isle-Tini," confirmed Mila. Impressed, Colt smiled. He should have known Mila would know right off the bat the drink his aunts referred to.

"I remember Willow coming up with the drink and

the color. She was extremely excited about the color," she told him. "It's like a Long Island Ice Tea with a Willow twist." That was his girl. Taking an old fashion drink and classing it up with style.

"And yes, Levi and I can make them. As a matter of fact, I think it's time Colt here learns how to make a few martinis."

Rita immediately tossed the menu down. "I'll take a beer," she stated flatly.

"Me too," stated Noni.

Candice and Helen scolded both ladies and turned to Colt. "We will be your tasters."

Colt turned his attention to Mila, no longer impressed. "Don't worry, I'll send videos to Willow as well," she teased.

Chapter 18

Happy Endings

Willow stared out at the blissful sky, enjoying the peaceful breeze off the beach as the palms swayed lazily. Eyes closed, she inhaled the salty scent of the beach mixed with the coconut fragrance of her new lotion and sighed heavily at ease. She looked down at her clear bag full of shells she'd collected for Lucy, all in different sizes and shapes. The colorful array glistened against the last few rays of the sunlight, as the sun slowly eased its way down the endless horizon. She'd thought of Colt and Lucy often during her stay at the Keys. Every chance she could, she took pictures and sent a text to Colt, only to receive a response within a few seconds from him.

Willow stood up and brushed off the sand, collecting her shells, and walked back to her room. In the distance, a small wedding continued its celebration. The bride's long, white, and simple yet elegant dress flowed against the groom's linen attire, a shade darker than her, as he stood next to her. Both were barefoot on the sand while the officiant read their vows. A little girl stood between them, holding both of their hands in a similar dress as the brides. It was small. It was intimate. It was simply beautiful, and it tugged Willow's heartstrings. From the distance, the groom leaned in and kissed the bride as the little girl cheered happily, dancing around them slowly.

The newlyweds laughed loudly as the groom picked her up and carried her down the aisle, holding his bride's hand. Willow smiled happily at the couple.

Caught up on the magic of the moment, she found Sofia standing on the beach, capturing the same beauty. She frowned as she walked closer, taking in her best friend's stance. The tense way Sofia stood. Her shoulders closed in.

"Hey," Willow whispered.

"Hey," Sofia sniffed miserably.

"Beautiful wedding."

Sofia wiped her tears, swallowing the large knot in her throat nodding her head.

"What's wrong?" asked Willow, worriedly.

"He married her," she simply said. Tears flowed down her cheeks again. "I can't believe it. He married her."

Willow stared dumbfounded at Sofia. Code red signs flared brightly in her head. "Sofia, you're freaking me out."

She remained quiet, lost in her own thoughts, tears streaming down her face. "The beautiful ceremony, with the perfect bride in the romantic beach wedding dress and groom in his matching white linens, matching his perfect little girl," she said, her voice breaking at the mention of the bride and little girl, "*that* beautiful wedding belonged to Fernando." Her sorrowful brown eyes turned up to Willow, reflecting her shattered heart. "The perfect bride is his *wife* and the little girl is his *daughter*," she whispered painfully, closing her eyes as if she could shut off and escape the reality she had just witnessed.

Willow immediately reached out and wrapped her

arms around Sofia, holding her close.

Cheese and rice.

"Let's go inside," she told her.

Sofia shook her head. "I need a minute. I don't want them to see me like this."

Willow turned her head, knowing the girls were behind, witnessing the same, "Take your time," she whispered, holding Sofia tight and signaling for Fab to handle the girls, although she gave Luna a knowing look. This look was specifically for Luna to insure Fab did not release her Dragon Queen on Fernando and his new happily-ever-after. No reason they should go to prison for a lying, cheating, shade of a man like him.

Sniffing and clearing her eyes from tears, Sofia pulled herself together like no one else could ever do but Sofia herself and slapped on a happy, fake smile. "Okay, I'm ready. Let's go get a drink."

"Honey..." Willow said.

"Please." Sofia's voice quivered. "I need my girls and a drink, or four of them."

"You got it."

****

The music blared out of the speakers as Luna, Harper, Skylar, and Piper belted out, 'Jesse's Girl' on the karaoke MIC while Willow, Zoila, Fab, and Sofia sat at their table, enjoying their third Piña Colada.

"We need another round of *Rumchata*," shouted Sofia.

Zoila raised her eyebrows to Willow and Fab, well aware her cousin was on a mission to numb her heartbreak.

"My liver needs you to slow your roll on the shots, not to mention my shorts. I'm about to bust out of them with these drinks," complained Fab.

Sofia waved their waitress over and pointed to her shot glass, motioning for another round.

"Let's get some food and water while we are at it," mentioned Willow, grabbing the menu and deciding Fab's shorts would have to endure the high carb intake Willow was about to order.

After the song finished, the girls returned to the table, polishing off their drinks to have it replaced with the yummy shooter. They all groaned as Sofia snickered, raising her glass for a toast. "To the best group of girlfriends any girl could ask for," she said rather choked up. "And may his cock be useless as a flashlight to a blind man," she exclaimed with venom.

"I'll drink to that," cheered Fab.

"Amen, *Prima*," smiled Zoila.

"Say it loud, girl," hailed Skylar and Piper simultaneously.

"Here, here," stated Harper.

Cheers, Halo and Tails hiccupped.

Willow and Luna raised their glass to Sofia, both solemn, "Cheers," Willow simply stated, downing the sweetness of the milky drink.

Sofia lowered her glass and bounced to the Country melody as the next group began singing. "What song is this? I like the beat," she asked Willow.

Willow smiled widely. "It's called 'Bra off.' Listen to the words."

The girls listened closely to the group while they carried on the tune, but mostly, they listened to Willow sing the lyrics. Once the chorus began, Sofia gave her first genuine smile and laugh of the evening. "I love it," she said, pulling up the lyrics to the song.

They gave the group a standing ovation for their song choice, all the while eating the arrays of dishes Willow had ordered, from grilled salmon with mango salsa and sticky rice to spicy wings with a side of blue chips to mozzarella sticks with south-western spring rolls. They devoured the food and ordered another round of Piña Coladas.

Their waitress came over and slid next to Willow. "A little birdie or two or five told me you have a bar and you can sing. Want to give it a go?" she asked cheerfully.

Willow swallowed her drink and coughed, trying to avoid the brain freeze and choke to death hazard, all the while ignoring the snickers from her traitorous girlfriends.

Sofia bounced up and down in her seat.

Fab grinned mischievously, pulling out her phone in preparation.

Luna shrugged her shoulders and smiled.

Harper continued to drink without a care in the world.

Skylar and Piper high-fived each other.

And Zoila gnawed on her lower lip, feigning innocence.

What the H. E. Double hockey sticks. Traitorous hussies.

Do it. Do it. Do it, chanted Halo and Tails with a fruity drink and umbrella in their hands.

"Sure, I'll give it go," Willow said and stood up, squinting her eyes at her friends before going to the stage. The MC introduced Willow to the crowd as she quickly scanned the songs and found one for her girls.

Especially Sofia.

"Hi," she said to the crowd. "This song is for my

Martini Girls, but also for anyone who's ever had a bad day."

She didn't need to look at the words, as she knew this song well. It was her go to song when she was having a shitastic day. 'Sway,' by Danielle Bradbery. She removed the MIC from the stand and took over the stage. Fab shouted, "That's our Whiskey girl."

The song ended and the crowd exploded, chanting for Willow to sing again.

Willow laughed and bowed, walking back to the stage to put up the MIC. The MC stopped her. "Do you want to do one more? Crowd loves you."

She looked over at her table and watched her girls all cheering and hollering for her to do one more. Sofia stood in her chair cheering the loudest as Zoila stood next to her, ensuring her crazy, semi-drunk cousin did not fall down. Zoila shrugged her shoulders and giggled as Fab helped get Sofia down, giving Willow a thumbs up to do another song.

"One more," she told the MC. She took the MIC again, hearing the crowd cheer her on. She flipped through the song selection, finding what she wanted and picked the song she knew well again. The country beat of, 'Keep Up,' boomed through the speakers as Willow quickly sang the witty lyrics of RaeLynn. She watched the girl group from earlier walk to the front and begin a line dance to which her friends got up to learn and joined in. Before Willow knew it, several others were joining in, dancing right along. Fab stood up and recorded the whole thing as she continued to enjoy her drink at their table and cheering everyone on. The song ended and another loud round of applause broke out. Fab stopped the crowd from leaving and got a waitress to snap a picture of everyone together. She quickly distributed the photo to those who wanted it and posted it to the MGB website and social media. "Networking, ladies. Hey," Fab proclaimed.

Willow sat back down and polished off her drink, hearing her phone beeping. Fab started a group chat with the Panty Droppers and they were in full force.

Wes—*Go Whiskey*—
Levi—*Rock it Whiskey*—
Beck—*Kill it Whiskey*—
Colt—*That's my girl*—

The end of Colt's text had a heart emoji inserted.

Levi—*Seriously bro? A heart emoji?*—
Wes—*GIFF of Christian Soriano saying "So Cute"*—
Beck—*GIFF of a Linda Blair throwing up everywhere*—
Colt—*GIFF of a Middle Finger flashing*—
Levi—*GIFF of a hairy man bending over*—
Wes—*My eyes! My eyes!*—
Beck—*Sick Bastard*—
Colt—*You have issues*—
Willow—*GIFF of Mila Cunis laughing hysterically*—
Fab—*GIFF of Jesus rolling his eyes*—.

Willow drank the water brought to her and enjoyed the next round of shots ordered by the other Girls' table. During the night, they combined their tables and took pictures together, tagging each other on their social media platforms and exchanging numbers. Fab made sure the other girls had the address to the bar. The other girls made sure Fab had their contact in Nashville to visit. Future plans were pre-planned and new friendships were formed.

More pictures were taken.

More tags were uploaded.

And in the end, the other girls left with fond memories of a karaoke bar in the Keys with new friends and the Martini Girls had new friends with a new girl trip pre-planned in their future.

****

After the carb overload, they paid their bill and went back to their hotel where they sat on by the pool.

"Men suck," sighed Sofia.

They remained silent, waiting for her to open up. It didn't take long before she rapidly fired her emotions.

"I mean, they really suck. I should have known he was a cheating *cabron*. All the signs were there. I'm the stupid woman who didn't see it."

"You're not stupid, *prima*," consoled Zoila.

"No, just blind," mumbled Sofia.

"What signs do you think you missed?" asked Willow.

Sofia sat up straight, then changed her mind and stood up, swaying, before raising her hand. "First," she said, pointing her finger, "He would call at specific hours. Not at a random time. Nope," she said, nodding the same finger. "Same time every day. three o'clock on the dot and nine o'clock on the dot."

"Random much," Skylar pointed out.

"Not for him. It's his work schedule or so he claimed," she said, using quotations on claim. "And I would get a text at seven thirty in the morning. Nothing more. We would talk during those times for about half an hour and then radio silence till the next time slot." She paced back and forth. "It should have been the first clue.

Next," she said, holding her second finger, "his social media does not have any post, pictures, or anything. Just his name. He would like my pictures and post and occasionally send me a random message during those specific times if he could not talk."

"Did you check to see if he had any friends or anything on his account?" asked Piper

"No, *mija*, I didn't. It looked like a brand-new account and he did not have time to put a photo and jazz up his profile. He even told me he was not sure he was going to keep it. He only opened it to see if he could find me," she mumbled. Waving her hands frantically in the air, she paced again. "Which I know is complete bullshit. Lying *cabron*."

Fab smacked her still painted cherry lips. "I'm thinking I need to place a call to my guys so they can pay this man a visit."

Willow immediately reached out to stop Fab as Sofia jumped towards her as well.

"No," Willow hissed.

"You can't," Sofia said at the same time.

"Why the hell blazes not?" Fab demanded, confusion written all over her face.

"He's a cop," Sofia whispered.

"Oh, damn," muttered Skylar.

"Well, it does bloody well complicate things," Luna chimed in.

Still not deterred, Fab brought the phone to her ear and asked. "Need to know, handsome, how illegal is murder?"

"We're doomed," cried Harper.

"Orange is not my color," whispered yelled Piper.

They watched Fab roll her eyes and smack her lips

again. "You do you and I'll do me, Viking. I'll let you go." She hung up the phone and looked at Sofia. "Apparently, it is really illegal to murder someone, so that's out." A shadow of annoyance crossed her face.

Willow stared at Fab before blurting out, "NO SHIT!" The girls gasped. Willow had cursed. She never cursed.

Sofia's eyes crinkled and lips wobbled. She bent at the waist and let her laughter rip through her. She pointed at Fab. "This is why you will always be our ride or die."

Fab looked her over, a knowing smile formed on her lips. "And don't you forget it."

****

It was later in the evening, after everyone settled, Willow's phone beeped with a text from Colt.

Colt—*Do I need to bring a shovel and an alibi?*—

She couldn't help herself. She chuckled and typed before deleting her message and called instead. He picked up on the first ring.

"Please tell me you are not running from the law?"

"Nope. I'm still a law-abiding citizen."

"Good, baby. So, who is on the murder list?"

Willow explained what happened and how broken Sofia was over it. "The thing is, she hadn't said much about him since spring break, but I guess she fell hard for him."

"She dodged a bullet. Men like him don't deserve a good woman like Sofia. I don't know her well, babe. I know that's what you're thinking, but she's your best friend and from what you have told me, she's got sweetness anyone would crave to keep. He doesn't deserve her."

She loved that. Loved the fact he stood up for Sofia

and got her even though he didn't know her.

"I still don't get why he went out of his way, though. It's not like they could see each other or anything. They live in different cities. Us watching him get married was an unlucky freak of fate."

"Who knows? Only he does. Some people want it all, regardless of what damage it can cause to the other person kept in the dark."

"I know. Sucks. I've never seen her so broken, like she was on the beach tonight. And what sucks? I caught the wedding thinking how beautiful it was and didn't realize their beauty was tearing my best friend apart," she chokingly whispered.

"Don't cry, darlin'. You can't cry. Not without me being there."

She sniffed. "How did I get so lucky?"

"This is our shot, Willow. I'm not wasting my chance with you. I'm keeping you, baby."

"Good," she leaned back against the bed, wishing again for him to be next to her. "I got the video of you making your first martini. Not too shabby, Pistol." She giggled as she remembered the intense focus while he poured the different liquors into the drink and waited nervously for Candice and Helen to critique his drink. After giving him his praise, Rita and Noni immediately ordered one for themselves. Mila had even caught his dramatic eye roll.

"Yeah, wasn't too bad," he laughed back.

"Mila said you made your own mixed drink, too. She thinks we can turn it into a martini."

"I'm sure you can dress it up,"

"Maybe I'll call it 'The Pistol,'" she teased. "I can add salt and sugar around the rim of the cup with a strawberry garnish."

He laughed.

"You think I'm joking, but I think it's going to be my next special on Friday."

"I can hear the wheels spinning from here," he teased.

"You have no idea," she said teasingly. "I totally have a plan for Friday."

"What time are you all heading out?" he asked her softly.

"First thing after breakfast. We should be at my place in the later part of the afternoon."

"Are you working when you get back?"

"No. I'm off tomorrow night. I'll check in and will see how my mom and sister are doing."

"Call me when you get home."

"Will do," she replied, smiling.

"Is the hotel nice?" he asked out of the blue.

"It is. Our patio opens to the pool."

"You sharing a room?"

"I'm in a suite with Fab and Luna. They actually took the master room with the two queen beds. I have the smaller room with the twin bed."

"Are you alone?" his voice lowered an octave.

"Yes," she replied, feeling suddenly shy.

"Good. I wanted to try something with you."

"What's on your mind?"

"Good old fashioned phone sex."

She bit her bottom lip from laughing loudly and covered her face with her hand. The warmth creeping over her body kicked into overdrive.

"Is that right?" she asked.

"Yeah, baby. Let's start with the basics. What are

you wearing?"

A giggle escaped her lips as she laid down anticipating their productive conversation.

Chapter 19

Too Much Drama for Mama Lawson

Once arriving back from their girls weekend trip, Willow could not wait to see Colt. As soon as she dropped everyone off and turned in the rental, she pulled into her parking spot and sent a quick text letting him know she was home. She received a quick response, letting her know he was stuck in traffic after delivering an order, but would hopefully be home to see her within the hour. She grabbed her bags and made her way upstairs to the loud voices coming from behind her door.

"It's not your business anymore, Beck."

"The hell it's not. Daryl is going to eat you alive if you go back alone."

"Honey, listen to him," her mother pleaded.

"I'm not going back alone. I have an attorney. He's making the arrangements to meet with Daryl and his attorney to go over everything. You are concerning yourself over nothing!" Mila hissed.

Willow opened the door warily, peeking in from the bottom of the floor. "Is it safe for me to come home?" she cautiously asked.

"Oh thank God," Mila said rushing down the steps. Willow opened her arms, embracing her sister tight. "Get him out of here," Mila growled in her ear.

"I can hear you, woman," Beck called out from the

top stairs.

Blushing profusely, Mila slit her eyes to Beck and stared and Willow, "I'm going back to the bar. I left Levi stranded. We'll catch up after you get him out of here," she said and hurried out of the apartment.

Willow stared at the closed door and then up the stairs at Beck. Slamming her bags down on the ground, tossing her hands in the air, she asked, "What the 'eff' Beck?"

"Willow, don't use foul language," scolded her mother, passing an amused Beck as she came down the stairs to help Willow with her bags. "Beck is only trying to help. Your sister is being extremely difficult."

Beck folded his arms over his puffed chest, raising a challenging eyebrow at Willow. "She didn't seem difficult. She seemed conflicted," she emphasized, walking up the steps and staring right at Beck. "Wonder why, Becker James Reed."

"This fucker is going to play her. You and I both know that."

"Why don't you scold him for his language?"

"Hush, Whiskey girl, and listen to him," her mother growled back, moving Willow's luggage to her bedroom.

Throwing her hands up again, Willow leaned against her kitchen counter. "Start from the beginning," she said, picking up Prim and giving her lovable cat some much needed cuddles.

"He's tracking her down, Whiskey. He knows she's here."

"We aren't hiding her, Beck."

Nodding his head, he grabbed one of Willow's hands and pulled her over to the window. "He has someone following her everywhere. Wherever she goes, that fucker follows her. He's taking pictures and reporting back."

Stunned, she pulled the curtain closed and looked up at him, shocked. "WHAT?" she whispered yelled. "How long?" she kept whispering, walking to the other window and drawing the curtains closed.

"Don't think he can hear you," he muttered. "From what I can tell, he's been following her from the first day. Recognized him from the bar the first night she covered. Then noticed him pop up whenever she worked. Again, when she was at the grocery store or at the bank."

"You were following her, too?"

"I followed him," he pointed out.

"No. You followed her, which he was following her and in turn you were following him too," she sassed back, making a point.

"Jesus Christ, woman, you are missing the whole point here," he said, exasperated.

"Mama, Beck is using the good Lord's name in vain," she yelled out.

"Whiskey girl, stop giving him a hard time and listen to reason. You and your sister are both so stubborn sometimes," she cried out.

"I swear, you can't do no wrong in my mama's eyes."

Beck shrugged his shoulders. "What can I say? Mama Lawson loves me."

Sighing, she released a struggling Prim to the ground and stood in her living room. "What do we do? I mean, it's not like she's doing anything illegal. She's not the one having an affair. What's his end game?"

Willow pulled back the curtain. The stalker-snitch

sat diligently by his car. Waiting.

"Mila said she wants nothing from him. Not a dime."

"She told me the same thing even though she has plenty on him to wipe his a—*butt* clean," she quickly correctly.

"Mila told Daryl about us. At some point when things got ugly between them, she told him about us. Guess he thinks…" he sighed, shrugging his shoulder. "Hell, Whiskey, I don't know what he thinks."

"That she came back for you. To reconnect. Start over."

He shrugged his shoulder again and stared blankly at nothing.

"Would it be such a bad thing, Beck? I mean, I would make a pretty cool sister-in-law," Willow gently teased.

A brief laugh escaped him as he stood and looked out the window again, next to her. "Christ," he whispered and raced down the stairs.

Willow glanced outside, catching Mila giving her stalker hell as Levi held her back. "Oh, no."

"What is going on? Why is everyone slamming doors? And why are all the curtains shut?" asked her mother.

Not answering, Willow followed Beck down and reached Mila, who was hysterically yelling at the stalker to stay away from her. "Why are you following me? You think I haven't noticed you? Stay away from me, creep!"

Willow reached for Mila and grabbed her, holding her sister's shaking figure as the determined man snapped pictures, uncaring of the distress he was causing, until he caught sight of the ominous figure slowly making his way over to him. The man lowered his camera and gulped, unsure of what to do.

Willow and Levi looked back as Beck made his way over. "Might wanna run," Levi warned.

Beck pulled Mila out of Willow's arms. Gently, he cradled her sister in his arms while carrying her inside. The sounds of the camera snapping paused his stride.

Oh no.

"Make sure he doesn't leave," he growled.

Beck took her sister inside the bar, not caring who watched. Willow turned, stunned. With speed faster than a viper, Levi grabbed the man by his shirt and slammed him against the side of the building. "Told you to run. Too late now. Whiskey, grab his camera."

"Y...you ca...can't do that," he said, struggling against Levi's hold.

"Watch me," Levi growled back.

Whiskey reached out to grab the camera when the sound of her window from her apartment above opened.

"Yoo-hoo," cheered her mother sweetly from the second floor before dumping a bucket of ice water out the window.

Willow and Levi jumped back in time to avoid the chilled waterfall, before her mother poured another bucket of water with flour mix in it over the man. "You leave my daughter alone," she shouted, and slammed the window shut.

The water boarded man stood chilled, powdered, and soaked. Angry, he reached for his ruined camera and stared at them before fear appeared in his eyes as Beck made his way over to him.

"Camera," Beck growled between clench teeth.

He handed the camera over, and Beck removed the

digital card, tossing it to Levi. "You mention any of this to anyone," he said menacingly, "and I'll ghost you myself. Understood."

The man quickly nodded his head and inched away from the wall, making his way back to his car. The sudden sounds of the window above opening were the only warning he received before a flying grapefruit flew by his head.

Followed by an apple.

Then an orange.

He quickly opened his door and secured himself safely as the fruit attack continued on his car.

"Mama!" cried out Willow while Levi and Beck laughed at the cowardly stalker, who took cover from the fruit attack. "Can you please stop throwing out our groceries?"

"Is he gone?" she asked sweetly, peeking her head out the window, seeing the taillights of the car. "Oh, thank heavens. I was dreading having to toss out the chicken breast next."

"Yes. Thank the good Lord you did not toss out the breast," Willow mocked.

"Whiskey girl, this is not a time for sarcasm. Beck, please bring my Mila upstairs and stay for dinner. Levi, you are welcome to join us as well. I'm sure Colt is on his way. I'm making fried chicken. And Whiskey, we need flour," she said before shutting the window.

"Man, I missed Mama Lawson," Levi said, still smiling, glancing at the mess on the alley. "I'll get this cleaned up," he said.

They walked in together while Willow grumbled about going to the grocery store for flour after returning from a long drive. "Awe hell," whispered Beck.

Willow stared at the redhead who was giving Mila a snide smile. Willow ignored Beck and walked behind the bar, standing next to Mila. "Are you alright?" she asked quietly.

Mila gave a sharp nod yes, never taking her red-rimmed eyes off of the redhead. "This is Nikki Busche," she told Willow.

Willow turned and looked Nikki over. "Colt's Ex," she whispered, more to herself.

"Yep," stated Mila.

"Colt's not here," Willow told her.

Nikki raised her eyebrow, about to reply, and stopped when the door open, watching in fascination as a tall, dark, and handsome drink of water walked in with golden eyes and hair shaved down to the skin. His badge flashed around his neck with his dog tags, dressed in all black. "Hey, Willow. Mila," he called out, nodding at Levi and Beck.

Willow stared at Mateo, surprised to see him. He had called her before she went on the trip and provided the attorney's name he recommended for Mila. They reached out to him together and went over the situation, explaining Mila's predicament with funds. The attorney assured them not to worry about the money. They would include a costs award in the divorce.

"Hey, Mateo," Mila replied quickly.

Ignoring Mateo, Willow continued to stare at Nikki's mocking smirk. "Why are you here, Nikki?"

"To see Colt, of course," she plainly stated. "We have something to discuss and we could not discuss it the last time I was here."

Tails cracked her knuckles while Halo massaged Tails's shoulders in the corner, preparing for the match.

Down girls, she thought to herself.

"Hey, why don't you take Mateo to the office?" Mila suggested.

Mateo arched his eyebrow and looked over at Levi and Beck, who both nodded their heads to follow through. "Sure. I can wait in the office."

Raising one hand in the air to silence everyone, including the entire world, Willow leaned over the bar and pronounced each word clearly, "Colt is not here. And you are not welcome here. Do we understand each other?"

Whistling low, Mateo lowered his knowing smile at a menacing Levi stare. "She never got possessive with me," he stated.

****

"Good to know," Colt said with a growl as he walked in, watching the standoff between Willow and Nikki.

"What are you doing here again, Nikki?" he said, his eyes straying to Willow, catching her blink and then the blank stare after he acknowledged seeing Nikki once before.

"Well, isn't this interesting?" Nikki said, licking her lips as if her secret was too delicious to withhold. "Did you know your sweet Whiskey is having a secret tryst with this luscious beast of a man? Caught them earlier together. He was carrying her in like a precious treasure. Such a tender moment," she said, covering her mouth with one hand while the other was over her heart.

Colt looked over to Mila who stood frozen, never taking her eyes off the red-haired devil.

Mateo slapped his hand loudly on the bar, mockingly laughing. "Sorry, but there's no way Whiskey would sleep with Beck. No offense, man."

"None taken," Beck answered, staring at Mila.

"Whiskey and Beck are more like sister and brother," Mateo continued. "Mila and Beck, totally different story," he said, fighting back a smile.

"I know what I saw," Nikki assured him.

"What exactly did you see?" asked Willow.

Nikki sashayed over to Beck and jabbed her finger in her chest. "I saw him carrying Whiskey into the office," she declared, pointing at Mila.

Willow tilted her head, confused as Mila lowered her face hiding her smile. Beck had both his hands on his hips, shaking his head and staring at the floor, smiling. Levi appeared to find something fascinating on the ceiling.

"You saw Beck carrying *Mila* into the office?" Willow clarified.

"No. I saw Beck carrying *Whiskey* into the office," Nikki said, exasperated.

Willow pointed to Mila. "Her?"

Colt bit back his laughter.

Nikki nodded and pointed at Mila with an exasperation that stated nothing more than 'duh'.

"This is Mila," Willow clarified. "I'm Whiskey."

Mila snickered, not able to hold back the small snort, and covered her mouth. This led for Beck and Levi to snicker and Mateo to whistle again.

Nikki turned to face Colt. "What the hell, Colt?"

Colt raised his hands up. "You assumed she was Whiskey."

Nikki turned back to a smirking Willow. Mila snorted again and turned around with a mumble, "sorry". Slicing her eyes at them, Nikki smiled beguilingly. "I guess I'm not surprised. You were a part of Blue Nitro and they always did like to share. Remember that night? You, me, and Victoria," she said seductively.

"Why you little instigating twat," shouted Mila, making her way over the bar as Willow raced around. Mateo reached over and grabbed Willow by the waist, holding her back as Beck raced over and caught Mila from attacking Nikki.

Nikki danced away, laughing, enjoying the moment, disregarding the doors opening to the bar.

"What the hell is the Dragon Pussy doing here?" demanded Noni. "Rita, hold my clutch. Candy, give me your cane."

Nikki's eyes stared in horror as Noni made her way over to her. Nikki raced behind Colt, grabbing him by his shoulders and hiding behind his back, pressing close to him.

"Jesus, Noni, don't complicate things," warned Colt.

Willow growled. Yes growled, watching Nikki feel up Colt, and tried to pry herself away from Mateo.

Halo and Tails both sneered.

"You know, you never got this hot and bothered when another woman had her hands on me," teased Mateo.

"Will you let me go?" she snapped at him.

"I already let you go once," he told her honestly.

"Mateo," she whispered softly.

"Go get your man," he whispered back sadly.

"She's out there for you. I promise she is," she told him, feeling his arms release her. She raced over to Colt and grabbed Nikki, shoving her away from his back, as Willow stood in front of him.

"I think it's time for you to leave." Willow stated.

Nikki turned to Mateo and pointed at Noni and Willow. "I want to press charges," she shouted.

Candice and Helen gasped as Noni bellowed, "Why, you little shit."

"Will you do something?" demanded Nikki, terrified Noni and her cronies would get a hold of her, finally.

Mateo sat at the bar, grabbing the beer he poured for himself. "I'm off duty," he informed her and turned on the stool to ignore the show.

Nikki stomped her foot and shouted at Colt to help her.

"Noni, stop it. Levi, control your Nana," Colt warned again. He turned to Nikki, eyes stone cold. "You are not welcome here. I told you to lose my number. Told you not to call me. Not to come looking for me. Told you I wanted nothing you were offering. You wouldn't listen. I'm going to make this perfectly clear. I do not exist for you." His ice-cold tone caused a shiver to race down Willow's skin.

She stood next to him, entwining her fingers in his. "Get out of my bar," she said sharply.

Nikki crossed her arms, refusing to accept defeat, never noticing the sudden ambush from behind her.

SPLASH!

The sudden tsunami coming from the swung bucket splattered all over Nikki.

"Mama," Mila and Willow cried out.

Oh my, giggled Halo.

Yes, cheered Tails.

Sputtering, Nikki looked down at her drench clothes covered in bubbles.

"Careful, darlin'. The floor might be slippery for those heels," warned their mother sweetly.

Mila's face planted into Beck's chest, as she felt him vibrate from silent laughter.

Willow turned her head, leaning into Colt. "I swear we are going to end up on the news somewhere."

Sighing, Colt looked down at Willow, ignoring Nikki as she slammed the door on her way out. "I was going to tell you," He assured her. "Figured it was a conversation to have face to face instead of over the phone."

She looked into his eyes, seeing the truth in his statement. "I believe you," she told him.

"Whiskey girl, this is too much drama for your mama," she said, heaving the empty bucket back towards the apartment, "and will someone get me some freaking flour!"

****

Colt paced back and forth in the office, staring up at the ceiling as they waited impatiently for Luca Prisco to answer the phone. Two weeks. Two entire weeks they had waited for him to return their call while Prisco had remained radio silent. Dodging every visit, phone call, text. He ghosted them every moment. "Mr. Prisco will be with you momentarily," said the receptionist.

"You said you were going to tell Willow about this two weeks ago. She's been back from her trip, and you still have said nothing," he flat out stated, running his hand through his hair frustratingly.

"She's been dealing with a lot," Levi calmly said.

"I know what my girl has been dealing with. I've been by her side the whole time. What I don't need is for her to be blindsided by this."

"Pistol, things are complicated with Mila. Whiskey got her the attorney and you know Daryl is not making things easy. Mila had to go back to Texas to complete the divorce because he would not have it any other way. Which set off Mama Lawson, which then set off Willow," Fab said, attempting to soothe out the tension. "Beck is fit to be tied and is making his way to Texas as we speak, which set off Mama Lawson again, which has set off Willow again. Things are a bit crazy."

"I know," muttered Colt.

"The attorney Mateo recommended will do right by Mila. He's good. She'll be taken care of. Plus, Beck's not gonna let her get fucked over."

Mateo's name sat heavily on Colt's shoulder. Sensing it, Levi put him at ease. "She made the call before you came into the picture. Trust me, he's not in with her anymore."

"Yeah. Pisses me off he could have been," he admitted.

"Look at you, getting all caveman. Willow, my woman," mocked Fab. "That's hot, Pistol," she said, batting her long lashes at Colt.

Shaking his head, he went back to pacing and staring at the ceiling.

"Reginald," said a deep voice over the phone.

"Prisco," replied Levi. "We need to talk."

"So I've been told. We do this in person."

"What time?"

"Half hour. Martini Girl Bar."

Levi looked up to Colt and over to Fab, both nodding. "You got it."

"Reginald, make sure Ms. Lawson is there," Luca Prisco said before disconnecting the phone.

"Shit," Levi sighed.

"Well hot damn," heaved Fab. Colt stared at the phone and turned towards the door. "Pistol, wait it out."

"I will not let her get blindsided," Colt turned to them, warning them again. "You tell her what is going on. All of it. As her partners, it's the right thing to do."

"Or what?" challenged Levi, with a knowing smirk.

"Or I tell her as her man."

"Whooooheee...Hot. Hot. Hot, Pistol," Fab stated, fanning herself.

"Tell me what?" Willow asked cautiously from the doorway.

****

Two weeks later, here Willow was in the middle of another shitastic storm. Shortly after the water boarding incident with the stalker and Nikki, Mila's attorney called, and they planned for her to meet and complete the papers.

Mila's plan was to complete the paperwork and pick up a few items from the house she left behind. Rent a small truck and make the drive back, stopping once again in New Orleans for the day.

However, Mila never informed Beck of the arrangements which set him off. He immediately made plans to go out there and set things straight. His exacts words to Mama Lawson.

"What do you all have to tell me? Is it Mila? Beck?" she asked worriedly.

Colt reached out and wrapped his arms around her, his eyes going to Levi and Fab, who were all sitting in her office. "No, baby. They're good. In fact, Mila threatened to take his balls and strap them to the hitch of the truck."

"Oh. Well, that's lovely," she said.

"We need to talk, Whiskey," Levi told her.

"Girl, come sit down," Fab stated.

This does not look good, Halo worried.

Tails sliced her eyes at Halo.

Levi looked over at Colt. "You mind? This is a business meeting."

Colt stared coldly at Levi. "Fuck off, I'm staying."

Both Halo and Tails relaxed slightly.

Willow's eyes bounced back between them both and then to Fab. "What's going on?"

"A few weeks back, we found out some information we did not like. We found out someone was skimming our liquor." Fab quickly interjected before Willow could say anything. "It's been rectified."

Pausing, Fab looked over at Levi for support. He looked at Willow, who had nothing but concern all over her face.

"What is it Fab?"

"We know about your plans to buy the place next door," Levi stated.

Willow licked her dry lips, uncertainty sinking in for the first time. "I…"

"It's a brilliant plan, Whiskey. We are all on board," confirmed Fab. "Wes wants to buy in."

Sighing deeply with relief, she turned to Colt with a radiant smile and faltered. She turned back to Levi and Fab, "So what's the problem?"

They both looked at each other uncomfortable. Colt reached for her hand. "They have sold it."

Her stomach coiled into knots. "What?" she whispered. "When? How?"

"We found out a few weeks ago they sold the place.

It's under contract," Fab stated.

Lowering her eyes, her shoulders slumped over slightly. "Oh. Well then, who knows? Maybe the contract falls through. Maybe I can still put in a bid for it and be a backup. Worst thing they can do is say no, right?"

"There's more darlin'," Colt warned.

Levi rubbed his forehead. "Levi?"

"Curtis Merk bought it. *He* has the contract on the property."

Chapter 20

The Bootlegger

Deep breath. Deep breath. In and out, chanted Halo while Tails furiously stomped back and forth on her shoulder, erupting into a ball of flames before cooling back down and returning to stomping on her shoulders.

Willow stormed out of the meeting. Out of the bar. Past the open veranda and next door to the empty building. She slowly envisioned her dream diminishing and warping into a new version of the Punch Bar. An unsettling heaviness weighed on her chest as her stomach hardened. She closed her eyes, refusing to see what was to come.

Warm arms wrapped around her from behind. "Sorry darlin'."

She nodded her head, not able to form words. She turned in Colt's arms, burying her face in his chest, breathing him in deeply. They silently stood there, unaware of the time passing. "I had so many ideas and plans," she whispered. Her breath hitched.

"Tell me about them."

She pulled back and looked around the open courtyard. "I wanted to grow the bar and remove the wall dividing both courtyards to make it one large one. I thought of adding a couple of pergolas with lights and outdoor dining furniture. Over there," she pointed to the trellis, "those plants are Morning Glory flowers. I wanted to add some couches and a fire pit for people to hang out and sit and enjoy them."

"I thought of catering more towards wine in the new building since we don't at Martini Girl Bar. I figured it could be something Mila could help us with, and Fab. Fab loves wine."

Surprise reflected in his eyes. "Fab's into wine? Thought she was a Martini Girl."

"Shocker, right? She's a Vino babe like Mila. You think you know people and BAM," she jokingly said, a sad smile forming on her face. "We should go. I'm pretty sure we are trespassing."

Colt pulled her back into his arms. "Are you alright?"

"No," she answered honestly.

"You are correct, Ms. Lawson. The both of you are trespassing. However, I'm not a fan of the red and blue lights. I won't tell, if you won't," said a deep voice from the gate.

Colt and Willow turned to find a tall, well-groomed young man in a tailored gray suit and white button-up shirt standing confidently with his hands in his pockets. His trimmed dark hair glistened in the sunset. His dark eyes held an acuteness like no other.

"Luca," whispered Willow.

Colt straightened, watching a smile form on the man's smug face.

"Hello, Willow. A pleasure to see you, as always," he said, slowly crossing the gate towards them. He reached out his hand and introduced himself to Colt, making eye contact with him and slowly raising Willow's hand up to his lips for a slow kiss. "I believe we have a meeting to attend to, my lovely. Your partners are waiting for us."

She looked up at Colt, wariness easing in again. Drawing another deep breath, she followed Luca back to her bar, not glancing back at her lost dream.

"I'll be right behind you," Colt said gently. She swallowed the sudden lump in her throat and escorted Luca inside.

Colt—*Need to activate the Martini Girl call tree—*

Sofia—*Sorry, hombre, but only a M.G. can do activate tree—*

Luna—*...—*

Colt—*It's an emergency.—*

Sofia—*You can't activate an emergency M.G. call tree and not tell us what it is about Pistol—*

Luna—*...—*

Colt—*Building sold. Bought by douche bag Merk.—*

Sofia—*GIFF of a woman overturning a table—*

Luna—*...—*

Colt—*Do it—*

Sofia—*Activating—*

Luna—*Bloody hell!—*

Ignoring the alerts from the text messages, he silenced his phone and met up with them, standing behind Willow and next to Levi. Fab sat next to Willow while Luca Prisco sat across from them all.

"Well, Reginald, you called this meeting," Luca began.

Colt eyed Luca inquisitively. Levi and Colt had discussed how they would tactfully formalize their approach. "A couple of weeks ago, we learned we were being skimmed by Hopper's," Levi started. "Long story short, the mess was sorted out with Hopper himself, but it's left a sour taste in our mouths. Trust has been broken and we are branching out. We use your distribution center already for hard liquor. Thinking why not our beer too?"

Luca remained stoic and unmoved, "You're going to put all your eggs in one basket? It wasn't long ago we had a similar situation with my distribution on some cases of liquor as well occurred, if you remember. For transparency, I am pointing out I had a similar issue as well."

Fab cleared her throat and raised her hand at him, "You did. However, you were the one who pointed out the error before we did and you sorted out the mess the same day plus provided additional samples and cases for us on your dime. We are a small bar compared to many. The loss we would have taken on the error of those cases would have hurt us. You took action and owned up to it."

"It's about trust Luca. We...we trust you," Willow stated matter of fact.

A small flinch crossed over Luca's stoic face. However slight it was, Willow made a direct blow.

"This is business, Willow. What you have is smart business. Monopolizing all of your demands to one distributor is not smart business. What if I go under?" Luca pointed out.

"Are you?" challenged Colt.

Luca's dark eyes glared at Colt.

Willow leaned forward and spoke with more confidence. "Luca, we know your company is worth us taking a risk merging our distributors to solely you. Your warehouses are closer, which means if we are in a pinch, we can always drive there and order on demand if needed. You have comparable prices, although your

IPAs are overpriced and Porters are underpriced," she stated raising both hands as he raised his eyebrows at her, "My opinion and observation, however, we can discuss it during contract."

Colt stood amazed as his girl snapped right into business mode. Impressed and slightly turned on by her take charge attitude.

"And here I thought you were unaware of the issues at hand, Willow. I thought they did not inform you of the mishap with Hopper or of the sale of the building. But I can see I am wrong," said Luca.

Shit.

Her eyes faltered, lowering to the ground, but came back up. "No, you are correct. I was made aware of Hopper's today and was not fully aware of the plans to move all of our demands to your distribution." Pausing, Colt encouraged her to continue. "But I trust my partners and if they believe this is the best move, then I support them."

A sigh of relief escaped Fab.

"As for the building, it's an unfortunate situation. I thought I still had time to bid. It's a missed opportunity on my part for not jumping sooner on it but I have a Plan B in place." She shrugged her shoulders as if losing the building was nothing more than a mere thought and not a hopeful dream of expansion.

"I see," Luca said. Colt saw what Luca saw. The style and feel of the place. Minor details from the simple succulents sitting on the distressed charcoal oak writing desk with its heavily blocked splayed legs and slat accents. A copper mug, typically used to serve Moscow Mules, held an array of pens and pencil next to a carousel of picture frames, full of photos. A closed laptop sat in the middle and tray with paperwork and envelopes on one side, with a simple sign reading, 'Shit To File'. "The sense of urgency to meet with me was to merely discuss the renegotiation of your distribution contract? I find this lacking and underwhelming in more ways than one."

"Our contract was part of the reason," confirmed Levi.

"And the other?"

"The bid on the property," confirmed Levi.

"Interesting," he stated with a calculated arched eyebrow. "Tell me, Willow, earlier, outside, you said you wished to extend this facility. However, focus more on the wine instead of martinis, which is what your bar is known for."

A soft gasp escaped Fab as she turned to Willow, surprised.

Willow turned to her partner in crime, biting her lip nervously, "I thought about what you said, Fab, and I agree we should expand our wine menu. I think we can do it and with Wes' menu we can upscale the place to a more wine and dine location. I thought of doing different flights for higher end liquors like whiskeys and tequilas." She glanced at Levi, catching his thoughtful look and an encouraging wink and nod from Colt before she continued with her thoughts of the courtyard. "I think with us having the courtyard in between as a more relaxed hang out and keeping Martini Girl Bar as is. We up-scale the new place for wine and flights, and we can have a successful trifecta."

Luca nodded and pointed to Willow. "I agree. I believe you would have a trifecta in your hand. But the problem remains, they sold the property."

"Yes. I have a plan," Willow flatly stated. "I will

have to rework the figures to see financially how much it would be for the business, and I know personally it will be a hit for me. But I will do it if my partners are on board."

"What's Plan B, Whiskey?" asked Levi.

"Expand up," she simply replied. "There are three floors in this building. I have two more floors above that we can rework the square footage and expand into, making the second floor our wine bar and possibly the third floor, opening it all up to a courtyard if we can get permits for it."

"But then where would you live?" asked Fab, concern etched on her face.

"I would have to look for a place. Mom and Mila too."

Colt stared at Willow. His eyes slowly slid to Fab, who stared back at him and then back at her friend.

"We would still have a Trifecta in our hands, Luca, regardless of who takes over the building next to us. We made this bar successful. It's the hottest place for people to come and hang out and drink kick ass martinis and listen to kick ass music. We are adding a menu and cross our fingers fixing our crappy plumbing." As the words flowed out of her, she gathered her confidence.

"Preach girl," snapped Fab.

"What Whiskey is trying to tell you, Luca, although the rumors are that Curtis Merk is the new owner for next door, I know you are a silent investor. In the end, Merk will not be successful next door to us," Levi simply said.

Luca tossed his head back and laughed. "You think an imbecile like Curtis Merk would bid and win a development like the one next door? Not likely. Merk never stood a chance. Honestly, he was never a contender in the race to begin with. Oh, he knows the right people and talks a good game, but that's all it is. Talk," Luca said, waving his hand in the air.

"You, on the other hand, Willow, I like you," he said boldly, staring directly at Colt and smirked. "I respect a beautiful mind, especially when it's attached to a beautiful woman like yourself. You surround yourself with smart people," he said, pointing to Fab, Levi, and Colt. "You know how to take care of those who work for you. You're intuitive in business and know how to make something out of nothing work. I wouldn't concern myself too much about the upcoming business opening next door. From what I have learned, an investor bought the property and is holding it. Searching for an opportunity, I suppose."

Willow looked to Levi and Fab, her wheels spinning, and turned back to Luca. "Do you know this investor?"

Luca merely shrugged his shoulders. "I suppose I do."

"Would you be willing to share that information with us?" asked Colt impatiently.

"Maybe," replied Luca.

Slamming his fist down, Levi looked him dead in the eyes. "Name the price."

A knowing smile formed on Luca Prisco's lips, causing their backs to straighten.

"My price is nothing more than dinner with Ms. Lawson. What do you say, Willow? Eight o'clock, tonight, work for you?"

****

No way in hell was Willow going out with Prisco. The thought better not even cross her mind. Not even for a second.

"Bro, calm down." Colt paced back and forth, ignoring Levi and, for once, a wary Fab after Willow asked to speak with the self-righteous poacher on her own. "She will not take his offer seriously."

Damn right she won't.

"Who does he think he is, anyway?" fumed Colt mostly to himself.

"He's Luca Prisco. Warned you he was sweet on Whiskey, brother."

Yes, Levi did. It did not mean Colt was going to stand by and let some smooth talker worm his in to get his girl's attention. "It doesn't mean a damn thing. He knows she's with me. He saw us next door, and he thinks he can ask my girl out and I'm going to stand by and not say anything?"

Seething, he waited impatiently, waiting for the office doors to open. Mentally forcing them to exit. As if the hinges felt his nonexistent powers, the doors opened and Luca walked out. "See you tonight, Willow."

What the hell?

He walked past a stunned Levi and stormed into the office.

"Tell me you did not agree to the date," he demanded. Her uneasy eyes and fidgeting hands told him all he needed to know. "You're kidding me, right?"

"It's not a date, Colt. I promise it's not. It's…"

"Bullshit. He's wanted you from day one, and this is his way of getting it."

"Colt, please just listen—"

"No. I'm not buying it. You know how many times Nikki called and showed up at the shop to see me? I ignored every single one of them. Not because I want nothing to do with her. I did it for you. Out of respect for you and what we are trying to build together."

"That's not fair. You cannot compare a meeting with Luca with your Ex."

"I can when the endgame for both of them is the same shit. She knew I moved on and she wanted to cause problems. He knows you're with me and it's not stopping him from making his play and cause problems too. You want to know why? Because entitled assholes like him think they can have anything and everyone they want and you're playing right into his hands."

Stunned by the accusation, Willow stilled. "Honey. I need you to trust me. I know what I am doing."

Shaking his head, Colt turned and strode out, leaving a torn Willow behind. He grabbed his keys and wallet from the employees' lockers and strode to the front of the bar.

"Leaving already?"

Colt turned and found Mateo sitting at the table, having a beer. Internally he growled at another one of his girl's admirers. He ignored Mateo and walked out of the bar.

"You're Colt, right? Willow's man?" Colt turned on his heals and squared off with Mateo. "Look, I don't want to start trouble."

"Then what is it," demanded Colt.

Mateo lowered his hands and shook his head. "You look like you could use a drink."

Colt raised an eyebrow, unsure, as Mateo smirked at him.

"Come on. There's this hole in the wall around the corner. Mostly cops hang there. Fish and chips are pretty good, too."

Colt followed Mateo, and found himself with the other man in a small dive bar with a round of beer and a steaming fresh batch of fish and chips.

"We didn't even order," stated Colt.

"No need. They know what I get and I always get the fish and chips."

Colt cut through the first fish and took a bite, enjoying the savory flavor of the batter and flakiness of the fish.

"Told you," joked Mateo. "The cook here is an old timer. I don't know what he adds to the batter. Whatever it is, rocks."

Colt leaned back on the stool, relaxing a bit. His earlier conversation replayed in his head.

The hurt look in Willow's eyes.

"Jesus."

"Yeah," acknowledge Mateo. "So, you fucked up?"

Colt took a swig of his beer, swallowing a large gulp of bitterness and regret before the waiter replaced the empty one in his hand with another.

"Did she tell you about us?" Mateo asked.

"I know you guys dated," he begrudgingly admitted.

Smiling, Mateo took a swig of his beer. "Yeah. Dated. If you can call it dating."

"What's that supposed to mean?" growled Colt.

"Not what you're thinking," admitted Mateo. "We barely saw each other. Timing sucked. I was always working a case and with her bar hours, it was difficult to get together to even go out on a date. I think we probably went out four times the three months we supposedly dated," he said using quotations on the word dated. "Straight up, I liked her. Would have liked to see where things would have gone, but it was never in the cards for us."

"No offense man, if you liked her like you say you did, you would have made time to see her. Spend time with her. Move the universe for her. I'm thinking you may not have liked her as much as you thought you did." Colt drank deeply again, watching a silent Mateo stare back at him.

"And you're this man?"

Colt leaned forward, eyes never wavering from Mateo's. "Make no mistake. Willow is my girl. I'd move Heaven, Earth, Hell's Fire, and the whole fucking universe for her without hesitation."

Mateo tilted his head to the side. "Good. Then how are you going to fix things?"

Collapsing back in his seat, Colt dragged his hand through his hair. "No clue."

"Start by apologizing, then work your way to groveling," teased Mateo. "But make sure I'm around when you do."

"Jesus," Colt said, not realizing a smile teased his lips as he drank his beer.

****

He left.

Willow couldn't believe Colt left without letting her explain. Did he not trust her? She was not going on a date. She told Luca she would go tonight, but only if her business partners were there. They made decisions as a team and he agreed. She stormed after Colt to give him a piece of her mind when Levi told her he was gone.

"What?"

"He left with Mateo."

She threw her hands in the air and groaned. "Great. My current boyfriend, who, mind you, is super pissed off at me, is bonding with my ex-boyfriend. This only happens to me."

Powerful arms came over her shoulders. "Never seen Colt lose it like that, Whiskey." Levi said. "Not even with Nikki. I'm being real with you. I found out my girl made dinner plans with some smooth, young, good looking rich dude who I know wants in her pants. I'd lose it too."

Sagging against him, she buried her face in her hands. "It wasn't like that," she retorted. She moved in front of Levi, stabbing him with a sharp finger. "I agreed to the dinner, with one exception. You know what the exception is, Levi Reginald? No, you don't." She said heatedly, not letting him guess. "And neither does Colt, because he didn't give me a chance to explain. He doesn't trust me to do right by us."

She stormed off, heading back to the office, only to turn back and stare at Levi. "You need to be ready by eight for dinner. Your butt needs to be there, as does Fab," she said, slamming the office door rattling the glass on the bar.

****

"What the fuckity fuck, Viking?" hissed Fab.

Shrugging his shoulders, Levi began to send a quick text to Colt.

"Don't do it, Viking," warned Fab.

"He needs to know we messed up. We all did."

"Excuse me? We? Oh no, Viking. You and Pistol did. I did not accuse her of going off and agreeing with the hottie bootlegger's date. Y'all did, because y'all didn't stop to think our Whiskey girl can handle things when it gets tough. I knew our girl had it under control. Like Willow said, get your ass ready for a business dinner."

Resigned, Levi walked back down to the hallway, deciding to make his amends.

"Wes," shouted Fab. "I know you were not a part of the invite, but you're getting one. Be ready at eight tonight if you want in for the proposition next door."

Wes wiped his hands, confused and amused. "Who is going to handle the bar? Beck's not here and neither is Mila."

"Vet. Front and center, sugar. You and Lacey got to handle things tonight. You on board?"

"Yeah, Fab. We got this."

"Good. I'm getting Mama Lawson to come down and handle guests and I'll ask Mo' to come by and help as well. I'm sure y'all can handle things for a few hours." Fab snapped her fingers as if she resolved the world's problems. The front door open and she smiled hugely. "And see, we solve our problems. Martini Girls are here. Hey!"

Sofia hurriedly walked over to Fab. "What do we need to do? I have my dad's truck and shovels in the back."

"Girl, I already confirmed it's illegal to whack someone. *No bueno.*"

Growling, Sofia pouted and crossed her arms. "Fine, but I'm keying his car next time I see it."

"I'm going to pretend I did not hear that," sighed Mateo, walking in behind her with Colt.

"I said nothing," said a denying Sofia.

"Sure, you didn't," teased Mateo, nudging her shoulder with his.

"Where's Willow?" asked Colt.

"Office," Fab snapped back, pointing her long-painted nail at him. "You need to stand in line. Levi is back there groveling first."

Sofia turned to Colt and back to Fab. "Why is he groveling?"

"Whose groveling?" Luna said, rushing in breathlessly, dressed all in black as well, attempting to catch her breath. "Bloody hell."

"Where were you? I went by to pick you up and you were not home?" complained Sofia.

"I...told you...I...would meet...you...here," she said, still catching her breath. "Lord, I need to get in shape. Did you not get my message?"

"What message? It was taking you two point five years to text back and I still have nothing."

"I left you a bloody voice mail."

"I don't check those. I must still have my phone on silent. You seriously need to get better at texting," sassed Sofia.

"Why are you two dressed like wanna be ninjas?" asked Wes.

Luna pointed to Sofia and shrugged her shoulders, ignoring her lack of texting skills comment.

"Don't change the subject. Why are Levi and Colt having to grovel?" Sofia asked.

Fab rolled her neck and stared at Levi as he walked back down from the office, quiet and regretful, "Because they were acting like fools."

Sofia stormed right up to Colt. "What did you do?"

"But you activated the Call-Tree," stated Luna.

Fab's eyebrows raised high. "Well, Pistol, that might put you back in her good graces."

Colt ignored them all as he walked past Levi.

"She's hurt," he heard Levi whispered.

Colt nodded. "I'll fix it." He walked down the short hallway to the end, where the office door was slightly ajar. Nudging the door open, he found Willow standing behind her desk, staring at the shelves he'd installed for her and the pictures she had recently added of them and of Lucy with Freckles.

He entered her office quietly and closed the door unnoticed and came to stand behind her. She stiffened in his arms. "I do trust you, Willow," he whispered to her. He felt her shaky breath leave her body and inhale a deep breath. "I'm sorry darlin'."

****

Willow closed her eyes. Levi had whispered the same apology to her. One she knew he meant deeply. But he at least stood by and let her explain. Colt had left.

She turned in his arms, staring into green eyes she realized she loved. Feeling her eyes well up with tears, she placed her hands on his chest and pushed back gently. Swallowing the knot forming in her throat, she separated herself from him. "I have to get going."

"Willow," he whispered.

"Please, Colt. Not now." Willow walked past him and grabbed her messenger bag. She placed the plans and proposal inside along with some other items such as menu ideas, drinks, and expansion note she had. She went to grab her keys when the sudden pull on her elbow forced her to turn around and slam into Colt.

"What are you—"

His mouth covered hers hungrily. His hands slipped up her arms, bringing her closer, encircling her tightly around her waist with one arm. While the other dug through her hair. Her lips softened under his as she returned the kiss and bound her arms around him. A soft moan drew her deeper as he nipped and tugged on her lower lip. Her tongue slid against his, deepening the kiss until they both drew apart for air.

"I'll be here when you get back," he said huskily, brushing his mouth over hers again, deepening the kiss once more before slowly withdrawing and walking away.

Willow stood still, staring at the open door. Her fingers brushed her lips. "Wow," she whispered to herself.

Oh my, whispered Halo.

More. I want more, begged Tails.

Snapping out of her Colton kiss trance, she grabbed her bag and keys, and closed her office. She made her way down the hallway as Fab barked orders to Vet and Lacey. Once done, Fab turned to Luna and Sofia and gave them their duties along with a t-shirt to change into. "Colt, are you staying or leaving?"

****

Colt's eyes remained on Willow. "Staying," he replied.

"Good, then get with Wes on what food needs to be prepared. Keep it simple tonight. Sofia and Luna can be your runners. Mo' is on her way here to help Lacey."

"What if they ask me to make a Whiskey Martini? I don't know if I can make martinis like Whiskey," Lacey asked.

"Manage it," Fab said. "Whiskey has the recipes there for you. Take your time and handle it. You got this, Lacey," she encouraged. "We won't be long. Colt's here. He's been working with Mila on mixing some martinis."

Fab stared at the skeleton crew they were leaving behind. "Handle the bar while we are out. You work for us for a reason. Colt, prepare your drink. Lacey, change the name on the board. It's The Pistol. Promote it like it's the last drink in the world. Colt can show you how to make it. Rim has sugar and salt. Garnish it with a strawberry. Short leg martini glass."

Wes went over the menu, keeping it simple for Colt to manage. Luna and Sofia quickly changed into their fresh shirts and began prepping the tables, wiping down the tables with glasses and returning the glasses to the washer. They worked quickly as Mama Lawson made her way down, preparing for the evening.

Willow kept her distance from him. Raised a wall between them. Levi told Colt they would all be going to the meet with her later. She'd agreed to meet Luca only if her partners went with her.

He was a complete ass for not letting her explain. Not giving her a chance. Colt hoped after the meet she would still give him a chance to work things through. She hadn't requested him to leave on sight. Yet. It gave him a small glimmer of hope. He thanked Mateo for earlier, had even mentioned for him to stop by if he could for another drink.

"Ready?" Levi asked them.

Wes grabbed a bottle of water and placed his phone in his back pocket. Fab grabbed her large handbag and keys. "I'm driving," she announced. Willow stood still for a second, still watching him. He walked over to her slowly.

"You good?" he asked.

She shook her head no, taking another deep breath.

"Hey, you got this," he said, hoping to encourage her. Her eyes still stared into his. "Baby, what is it?"

She swallowed and blinked. "You'll be here when I

get back?"

He leaned his head against hers. "You still want me here?"

She quickly nodded her head without hesitating. Releasing a breath he did not know he was holding, Colt gently placed a kiss on her lips. "Then I'll be here."

She slowly released a long, shaky breath.

"Go, darlin', before Fab releases her Dragon Queen on me," he said, and winked at her.

"Please make sure the ninjas don't get into trouble," she teased him, before leaving the bar.

Chapter 21

The Meeting

The ride to Prisco Distribution was tense and quiet. They sat together, each lost in their own thoughts.

Willow reviewed her proposal for the fifteenth time, knowing her bottom line was the same number it was the last fourteen times she'd reviewed it.

Halo kept her focused and calm on the upcoming meeting while Tails sent images of Colt and their searing kiss they shared in the office or of their night together before her trip. Snap shots of his hands roaming over her freely. The way his lips tasted her greedily.

Ugh!

She needed to focus. She slammed the folder shut and began reviewing the documents over again for the sixteenth time.

"Whiskey girl, you know those numbers are not going to miraculously change no matter how many times you review them," snapped Fab from her driver's seat.

Willow cut her eyes over to her old friend, ignoring the chuckles from Wes as he continued to play on his phone next to her.

Levi turned and winked at her. "It's all good, Whiskey. We got this." His eyes turned to Wes. "You still playing Scrabble?"

Wes ignored the stares from the girls, as he

considered his next move. "Still being challenged by a pretty nurse," he simply replied.

Fab smiled knowingly and drummed her fingers on the music on her steering wheel. As they pulled up on Prisco's road, she slowed down. "We all know what our plan is, right?" A worried Fab was uncommon.

Willow reached over and placed a calming hand on Fab's shoulder. "Like Levi said, we got this."

"Damn straight," concurred Wes, fist pumping the air as he took the lead in the game, only to have his short-lived victory squashed by his pretty challenger and a two-letter word. "How the hell does she do it all the time?" he questioned as the 'You Lost' flashed brightly on his phone. A message appeared 'You've been challenged. Do you accept?' Not one to turn down a challenge, he accepted. This was his third attempt to beat the pretty little nurse.

"She beat you again?"

Wes growled, annoyed at Levi. He ignored the notification, letting him know it was his turn. He would have to think about his strategy. "We there yet?" he asked impatiently.

"Just about," whispered Willow. She disregarded the bantering between Wes and Levi, unsure who they were referring to. Her mind was preoccupied with the upcoming meeting, and of Colt. She gave into her little devil and shot him a quick text.

Willow—*Hey*—

Unsure how busy they were, she silently prayed he would reply quickly. She released her breath as three dots appeared.

Colt—*Hey baby*—
Willow—*Wanted to check in*—

Colt—*Everything's good. It's picking up*—
Willow—*Oh, good*—
Why did it seem like they were having an uncomfortable conversation? Maybe she should say nothing else.
Colt—*Willow?*—
Willow stared at the text. *Text him back,* cheered her little inner voices. She replied as her phone rang.
"Hey," she answered in a low voice.
"Hey."
Muffled sounds and low background conversations came through the phone as Colt shuffled around. "Talk to me, Willow," he said, finding a quieter place.
Willow hesitated. "Are we good?"
"I hope so, darlin'. Cause if you tell me we aren't, then I'm doing everything I can to fix things to get us back to being right between us. What do I got to do to put your mind at ease, baby?"
Willow smiled softly, feeling the tears tease her eyes. "You just did."
"Good," he whispered to her.
"You know I think I'm in like with you," she said teasingly.
"Good to know," he chuckled over the phone. "Cause I'm pretty sure I fell in like with you the moment you ran into me on day one."
Her breath caught and her heart skipped a beat.
Halo grabbed Tails and shook her roughly, screaming from her the top of her little angelic wings, *He really likes us!*
"Baby?" he asked, humor lacing his voice.
"Uh yeah…sorry. I think we are here," she said.
"Alright, darlin'. Call me when you're finished."

"Okay, Colt."

"Hey, Willow?"

"Yeah?"

"I like you, baby," he said, causing her insides to melt and tears to spring up again. Her little angel fainted and her little devil sat down, speechless, on her shoulder, fanning herself.

"I like you too. A lot," she shyly replied before disconnecting the call. Willow stared at her phone, feeling her heart throbbing. She looked back out the window and noticed they were parked. Three pairs of eyes stared at her with amused smiles on their faces.

"You guys are so cute," mocked Wes.

"Walking cliché," muttered Fab, grabbing her purse and exiting the car.

Willow glanced at Levi, catching his smirk and wink. "Shut up," she muttered to him, exiting the car as well, ignoring Levi's laughter.

They walked together, the four of them. United. Levi informed Willow he'd updated Beck on the issue. Beck was, in his words, pissed he was not there to make sure shit was handled. To which Levi replied they could handle it only for Beck to reply with an emoji of a flashing middle finger. Levi followed up with a picture of a hairy man in a string bikini bending over. To which Beck stated Levi was a freak and needed to get laid. Willow outright laughed, tears springing from her eyes. The knotted tension tugging and contracting in her stomach, eased as she read the exchange.

As they continued on their way to the front of the building, a few cars were parked in the lot. None they recognized, except for the black slate Audi they knew to belong to Prisco himself. Wes stared at the car, admiring the sleek look. "Got to admit, the dude's got good taste in cars."

"Surprised you like the car. Thought you were more of a truck guy," said Willow.

"I am, but I appreciate a badass car when I see one."

They walked up to the front wooden door and entered the lobby. They were greeted by a receptionist who immediately showed them into an office with shelves filled with different bottles of liquor on the side and the Prisco Logo on the other side. A large monitor flickered on with a black screen, stating pending connection as the logo floated around the screen.

"Ever wonder why the logo is a turtle?" asked Wes.

"My sister," Luca's voice came through the opened doorway as he entered, with another gentleman. "She loved turtles. Specifically, sea turtles."

For once, they all glimpsed a small part of the man that was Luca Prisco as he spoke of his sister.

"This is Alec Prisco, my cousin and attorney. He will join us today. I see you brought another guess with you, Ms. Lawson."

Stunned by how quickly he turned back to the businessman they knew him for, Willow glanced at Wes and back to Luca. "Yes, this is Wes Banner. He would be our chef and partner in this new proposition."

Luca shook Wes's hand and arched an eyebrow at Willow. "Another partner?"

Wes shook Alec's hand. "Problem?"

"Banner? You wouldn't be the same Wes Banner who owns Slider Up?" asked Alec.

"The Food Truck?" asked Luca, surprised.

"One in the same," replied Wes

"Hands down, best burgers," praised Alec.

"Ms. Lawson, you continue to surprise me with the talent you surround yourself with, my lovely," Luca said, impressed.

"We all have our talents, Mr. Prisco."

"So, it seems. Come, let us sit down and discuss plans for the new building."

Fab glanced at Levi curiously and sat next to Willow. Wes sat next to Fab and Levi pulled the seat on the opposite end of Willow, enclosing her in within her partners. Willow withdrew her plans and sketches from her bag, along with the proposition and marketing data. As she mentally prepared for the beginning of her speech, the doors of the office opened.

"Ah, you are here. Good," Luca stated.

Willow could not believe her eyes as they followed a smug Curtis Merk walking into the office, shaking hands with the Prisco's and sitting next to them.

"Look at that. The MGB crew is here," said Curtis. "Where's the Rock Star? Did he bail out on you all like he did his band? Typical."

Willow placed a hand on Levi to keep him from standing.

"What is this Luca?" demanded Levi.

"Earlier today, you all asked to meet with the investor. I am the investor. With that said, Mr. Merk has been aware of this tidbit of information for some time. How he came of it, I am not clear. We will get back to that soon," Luca said as Curtis cleared his throat, losing some of the smugness he wore when he entered. "He provided some exceptional plans and a promising proposition for the building. One I have looked over and memorized since the classy establishment he was presenting pleasantly surprised me."

Alec reached into his briefcase and provided Luca with a file and contents and passed them over to Willow, who sat right across from him.

As he continued to speak of the plans, Willow nervously opened the folder, blinking rapidly. Confused. They were *her* plans. The same ones she had brought in for today's meeting except for a few modifications she recently made to the courtyard.

But it couldn't be.

Could it?

"When I arrived earlier at our meeting, Ms. Lawson described vividly the transformation of the courtyard. You can only imagine my surprise of hearing her speak out loud the words of the plans provided to me by Mr. Merk. Is that not ironic, Mr. Merk? How you and Ms. Lawson share the same vision, right…Down…To…The…Flowers," Luca stated, eyes sharp and focus on Curtis.

Willow flipped through the paperwork, noticing places where she would add notes were exactly the same but in a different handwriting. Levi grabbed Willow's documents and flipped through them, noticing they were the same documents.

"Earlier, Mr. Banner, you asked about the turtle. I mentioned it was because of my little sister. She believed they were good luck. When I took over for my father, I hated the logo he had. It was a snake. My cousin and I agreed we needed to make changes, and we began with the logo. We decided on the turtle for my little sister, Elisa, and we severed ties with the snake."

"Where did you get these?" Willow asked.

Before Curtis could make a move, Alec moved with lightning speed, kicking Curtis's chair from under him and slamming him on the table.

"You will answer Ms. Lawson because in this situation, Mr. Merk, you are the snake," Luca stated flatly.

Levi stood up and sauntered around the conference table, keeping his eyes focused on a whimpering Curtis.

"Answer her," growled Levi.

Willow looked back down at the papers and shook her head. "Lizzie," she whispered.

"Say what?" Fab said, leaning over Willow's shoulder to look at the document.

Alec pulled Curtis' arm higher, causing him to cry out. "Answer her," Levi said, leaning closer to his face.

"It was Lizzie," confirmed Willow. "He doesn't have to answer. She writes her, 'I' with a heart. It's how she signs her name and apparently how she writes wine on the paperwork as well."

"Well then, one mystery solved. On to the next. Mr. Merk, shall we discover the easy way or the hard way of your knowledge of the building's finances and my investment in it? Do tread lightly. Alec has been working out and has a bit of a Hulk complex," he joked as Alec squeezed Curtis' arm tighter.

"Ahhhh, it's, uh…was, uh, public knowledge," panted Curtis in pain.

"Tsk. A snake and a liar. Not good qualities. If I say so myself, wouldn't you agree Alec?"

"None," Alec said, pulling tighter on a squirming Curtis.

"Prisco, y…you said t…the building would be mine," Curtis claimed.

"Release him, Alec." Luca waited for Curtis to compose himself. "My exact words to you were the proposition provided to me was promising and something I would like to further discuss. This proposition," he said, picking up the file, "does not belong to you. Therefore, any further discussions will not be held with you. And like I did with my father's logo, I am severing our contracts and negotiations. I will no longer be distributing to The Punch Bar."

"You can't do that. We have a contract."

Alec leaned over and provided another folder to Luca. "Our contract is month to month. Ah, as Ms. Lawson pointed out, signed by Lizzie with double hearts. You received your delivery for this month and since I am not completely ruthless, we will make your delivery for next month. However, afterwards, you will need to find another distribution center."

A thought flashed across Luca's face. "I wonder, could Lizzie have accessed our records somehow like she did Ms. Lawson when she was here to sign your contracts? It would have been the only opportunity for her to get this information." He turned to his cousin. "Let's run the security tapes. See if we find anything now that we know what or whom to search for, Alec?"

"I should sue you," Curtis said, pointing his finger at them all.

"Careful, Mr. Merk. I am going to assume you are having a moment of hysterics, however, my patience only goes so far."

"This is bullshit. I have Blue Nitro on the hook to perform opening night. She can't get that. What she has is a washed-up guitarist who was kicked out of the band for being weak. And now you want to sever your contract with me, when I can make that dump of a building into a goldmine?"

"You are such an idiot," Willow stated.

"That's not nice of you, Willow baby," mocked Curtis.

"I was going to call you stupid, but I don't like the 's' word."

"Still not nice, baby."

"You're right," she sighed dramatically. "I need another word besides idiot and stupid."

"Douche bag," called out Fab.

"Dumbass," stated Alec.

"Whiny bitch," Wes said, snapping his fingers.

"Fuck face," said Levi.

"Dick head," Luca said, shrugging his shoulders before joining in.

"Asshole," said the voice from the monitor as Maverick Reginald's face appeared on the screen.

"Mr. Reginald, thank you for joining our call. I apologize for all the miscommunication, but we needed to clear the air. As you can see, there was a bit of a misrepresentation." Luca smiled.

"I see. Don't know where douche bag, dumbass, whiney bitch, fuck face, dick head, asshole Merk thought Blue Nitro would play for him. I never agreed to it," Maverick confirmed, taking a sip from his cup, lowering his sunglasses. "S'up, little bro."

Levi stared at his big brother, still unsure how to reply.

"Tried calling you back. You never answered," Maverick stated. "Got a message from Prisco. I didn't know you were involved in this mess. Would have jumped in sooner."

Levi remained quiet. Still shocked.

"Yeah. Good talk, bro," Maverick chuckled. "I'll

call Nana later this week. We good, Prisco?"

"I believe we have everything we need. I appreciate you taking the time to call in. I understand you have a busy schedule. Good luck on your upcoming tour."

"Later," and just like Maverick, the lead singer of Blue Nitro, had appeared on the screen, he disappeared as quickly.

Willow looked over to Curtis, as he stared at the dark screen, "Bet you wish you would have stuck with idiot, huh?"

****

"You still haven't given him the necklace*? ¿Pero, que tu espera, mija?*" Sofia turned to ask Luna.

"You realize I do not speak Spanish."

"WHAT ARE YOU WAITING FOR?"

Shrugging her shoulders, Luna glanced up and caught Colt listening in. "I don't know." It hurt to watch Levi walk out to the meeting and ignore her.

Oh, it really hurt. Luna grabbed a stool and sat down. She pointed a clear manicure nail at Colt. "This stays here, understood?"

Colt shrugged his shoulders and winked at Sofia as he continued to fill in her order.

"I don't even know what necklace you are talking about."

"She bought Levi a necklace while we were at the Keys. What I want to know is why she hasn't put on her sexy panties and given it to him yet."

Colt tilted his head, curious.

"Bloody hell, you are worse than a chihuahua in heat," Luna began, taking a moment to calm her shaky nerves. "I stopped by Haze when we got back. Actually, I stopped by here first, but Vet said I missed him and he was on his way to Haze to close up. I've never been to his shop, so I figured why not? When I got there, his truck wasn't the only one in the parking lot. I thought nothing of it. I walked in but a girl came out from the back, barely wearing anything to begin with."

She stopped to catch her breath, knowing her emotions were showing. "And when I mean barely anything, I mean a lingerie model had more clothes on then her. I wasn't sure if I interrupted something or if I was too late," she sadly whispered. "I said I was lost and in the wrong place and ran out as quickly as I could before he could see me. I haven't spoken to him since we've been back. I've been avoiding him every chance I can. To the point he texted me, saying he would not text me anymore."

Sofia stared at Luna in disbelief. She leaned heavily into Luna, embracing her tightly and nearly toppling them over. "Men suck," she said.

"Hey," complained Colt.

"Shut-up", both Luna and Sofia said simultaneously.

Colt shook his head and poured a shot for the girls. A purple something or other he had seen Lacey make. "Here, drink this. Sofia, order up."

The girls downed the drink. Sofia gave Luna another quick squeeze before grabbing her tray to take outside.

Colt slowly approached Luna. "So you know—"

"Don't. I've come to terms, I'm not for Levi," said Luna.

"You're selling yourself short," Colt continued. "Straight up, Levi might look like he plays the field, but it's not his style. He's into you. For all you know, this mystery woman was getting a body piercing or ink. Just saying you might want to ask him. If you're not into him, then let things be. But don't sell yourself short, Luna. Any man would be lucky to have you. And Levi, he's one of the good guys."

Luna's eyes glassed over, wondering if she misread what happened.

Colt turned to Luna, mixing another round of the Pistol drink.

"Thank you," she said softly before getting up from the stool. "I'm going to check on Mama Lawson."

****

For the past two hours, Colt watched time slowly tick away. He now understood Willow's love/hate relationship with the obscene red blaring clock. He glanced at his wristwatch and his phone for good measure. Still no messages since the meeting began. He grabbed another drink order and quickly filled the beer glasses and placed them on the counter for Sofia as she chatted with Luna.

His eyes trailed to Luna, worried about her. The girls were slowly worming their way into his life. Shaking his head, he knew he was in for a lot of drama. But as long as he had Willow, he would take it.

As he continued to fill orders, he hummed a tune in his head. Slowly, his fingers played imaginary chords as a melody came to life in his mind and the hook of the song developed rapidly. He reached for a pen and napkin and wrote as quickly as he could, the words flowing out onto the paper. He looked around at the dying crowd.

"Mo', can you cover for me? Ten minutes tops."

"You got it, boo."

Colt walked behind the stage, grabbed his guitar, and created the melody aloud. He tweaked his initial words and chords and replayed the song from beginning to end. By the time his ten-minute break ended, he had a rough concept of a song.

He'd never written a song this quickly before. Not even his first song with Blue Nitro. He ran his fingers through his hair. Staring at the lyrics. He folded the napkin carefully and placed it in his wallet for safety. He placed the guitar back in its place. He stopped at the sight of Willow.

"Hi," Willow said shyly. "You jamming out all by yourself?"

Colt reached out, wrapping both of his arms around her, pulling her closer to him. "Something like that," he said, kissing her forehead. "Everything work out with Prisco?"

"About that," she said hesitantly. "Looks like you may need to put in more hours because you are looking at the new owners of the building next door."

"Congratulations, baby," he said, spinning her around.

"Luca is going to remain a silent partner since he technically bought the building. We agreed to bring him on with a slight cut to the profits next door only, and in return we, the Martini Girl Bar, gets discounted prices on the liquors. One hand washes the other. Plus, he cut ties with Curtis. Turns out Lizzie stole my plans. Somehow, she hacked into our computer and got them. Luca was checking his security footage to see if she did the same at his office. I told him I would not press charges, but I don't think he is going to let her off the hook so easily."

"No, I don't think he would."

Willow relaxed in Colt's arm, releasing a sigh. "There's still so much to do next door. Inspections.

Remodeling of the kitchen. Plumbing. Ugh, the plumbing. Hopefully, it's nothing like this one. Hell, I still have to fix the plumbing here. Ordering furniture. Hiring staff."

Colt took the liberty to kiss her softly. "It will all work out, Willow." She relaxed in his arms again. "Dance with me," he said and led her to the middle of the stage. He twirled her around and slowly guided her into his arms, rocking side to side to a melody he hummed and sang quietly to her.

"It's not every day we feel this obsession,
To a love poured neat to near perfection."

He continued to drawl them to the melody he'd worked on earlier as the lyrics came to life.

"She's fiery and smooth, with amber eyes
Boy, she steals my breath by surprise."

Willow's breath hitched as she listened to Colt sing to her. Pulling back, she looked up into his eyes. He saw the same emotions mirrored in her own.

"Colt, I think I more than like you."

"Good to know, Willow, because I know I more than like you."

She tipped her head up, offering her lips. He took her sweet kiss, feeling his chest tightening. He poured his feeling into the kiss, losing himself in her taste and arms. He pulled back, whispering softly against her lips, "More than like you, baby."

She smiled against his lips and kissed him again. "More than like you, too."

"Seriously, you two are so freaking cute," mocked Wes, batting his eyes.

"Cliché, I tell ya," grumbled Fab.

****

Levi nodded at Vet and Lacey as he walked down the hallway to the office. He needed to get into the computer and see what safety measures he could put in place to avoid any future hackings, and place some security cameras. A conversation with Beck he was not looking forward to. He stopped short at the door, catching site of Luna filing documents as Mama Lawson filtered through files from an old cabinet they were exchanging out.

"Who needs manuals of a dishwasher they no longer own? This is ridiculous. You would think my daughter would get with the times and go paperless."

"Mrs. Lawson, I don't think it's Willow, per se. I believe it might be more of a Fab issue. She keeps every document known to humankind. But at least she's organized."

"Oh, for heaven's sake, look at this. A manual for a Zenith TV. Zenith? Please tell me there is not a box full of cables with input/output somewhere around here or I am losing my everlasting mind."

"I'm pretty sure Whiskey has a box somewhere in storage," Levi said. He brushed a light kiss on Mama Lawson's cheek and nodded curtly at Luna.

"Oh, for heaven's sake," she grumbled again.

Levi chuckled and grabbed the rest of his things. He needed to get out of there quickly. Being this close to Luna was bound to drive him crazy. She'd cut him off and he had no clue why.

A man could take a hint. He gave her the space she obviously wanted and backed off, much to his disappointment. Never had a woman crawled into his mind and dug their way into his every thought, dream, and breath.

It was insane how much he craved to hear her voice.

See her face.

Taste her lips.

He needed to get out of here.

"You ladies need anything before I head out?" Anything? He thought to himself. Come on, Luna love. Give me a sign. Any sign.

Exasperated, Mama Lawson glared at him, throwing up more aged manuals. "This is ridiculous Levi. Absolutely ridiculous. Where's Fab? I need to give her a good talk to."

"Oh no," Luna whispered.

"Front bar, updating the crew on the meeting."

Mama Lawson stormed out, leaving them in her wake in awkward silence. He casually leaned over and picked up the tossed manuals and placed them next to Luna, who sat on the floor. "Need anything?" he asked quietly, keeping a slight distance from her.

****

Luna breathed in shallowly. She raised her eyes to meet his blue wary ones. "Good thing she did not find this file of receipts from three years ago. She would really box Fab's ears out," she said, hoping to lighten the mood.

A faint glint of humor came into his eyes. He tugged on a rogue strand of her hair teasingly and stood up. "Take care, Luna."

It shouldn't hurt to watch him leave, but somehow it was wrong to leave things the way they were. Her chest was bursting. *'Take a chance,'* a little voice whispered in her head.

"Levi, wait," she said, standing uneasily.

He turned and waited.

Patiently.

"Um, I...bloody hell," she mumbled nervously. Her breath seemed to have solidified in her throat. A cold knot formed in the pit of her stomach.

"Rip the band-aid, love," he told her.

"What?" she asked, confused.

"Sometimes the best way to say what's on your mind is to come out and say it," he explained.

Right, she thought to herself. Rip the band-aid. So be it.

"I like you, Levi," she confessed shakily, raising her hands to her mouth, shocked she said the words aloud. Bloody hell. She ripped the band-aid alright.

He stood stunned. He took a step towards her and stopped as her eyes widened. She placed one hand up.

"But I can't be with someone like you."

"Someone like me?" his tone was smooth, yet edged with steel.

"It's just," she said, fumbling nervously again.

"It's just what?" His jaw thrust forward, tensing. Cold eyes sniped at her. "Think I'm not good enough? I don't fit your mold?"

Luna's eyes widened in disbelief, feeling nauseous. "No," she cried out, "That's not it at *all*."

"Christ, thought you were different. Had me fooled, that's for sure. I was a little walk on the wild side. The tattooed guy who you suddenly realized mommy and daddy won't approve now that they're coming in for a visit. Is that it?"

She stared at him, surprised.

"What surprises you more? That I know about your parents coming into town or that I know your reason for suddenly turning up the cold shoulder?"

"But that's not it at all. Yes, my parents are coming into town, but that's not what this is about."

"Then what, Luna? Why shut me out?"

"Because I bloody saw her," she said sadly, tears pooling in her eyes. "I saw her at Haze, and I won't be with someone who is seeing someone already. I won't be made a fool of. "

Levi stood cold still, his eyes icing over. "Saw who, Luna," his voice hardened.

She shrugged and looked away.

"Eyes, dammit," he growled. "You give me your eyes when you try to accuse me of something. You saw who when?"

She swallowed the sudden knot of regret. "The night we came back from the Keys, I went to Haze to look for you," she said awkwardly. "It was late. The door was open, and I knew you were about to lock up. I walked in and saw a woman walk out from the back. She was scarcely dressed. Her lipstick was smeared and, well, she looked…"

"She looked what? Say it." He demanded.

"She looked like someone thoroughly shagged," she said, watching his stormy blue eyes turn colder than she ever thought possible.

"And you immediately thought it was me?" he asked incredulously. He raised his head and closed his eyes. "Ask me, Luna. Ask me who she is?"

Luna swallowed another lump. "Who was she, Levi?"

"Moxi. Ask me if I have fucked Moxi? Go ahead, Luna. Ask me."

The tears pooled over and traced a fast river down her cheek. "Have…have you slept with Moxi?"

"Not slept…fuck."

Closing her eyes, she took a deep breath.

"Yes," he answered honestly. "Ask me how long ago."

Luna shook her head and grabbed her purse, storming past him. Levi reached for her arm and swung her around, holding her close. "Ask me how long ago?"

"How long ago?" she hissed at him, angry at herself and at him.

"Ten fucking months ago," he said, slowly releasing her. "Ten. Months. Luna. Moxi and I were passing time. Nothing serious. I stopped fucking her the day, *the very same day,* I laid eyes on you."

Luna inhaled a shaky breath.

"Ask me, Luna. Ask me if I was with her that night at Haze?"

"Levi…" she whispered.

"Ask me, dammit," he roared back.

"Were you with Moxi that night at Haze?"

He stared at her furiously. He leaned in, inhaling her scent, ingraining it in his mind. "Why the fuck does it matter when you already believe I was?"

Her breath caught, leaving her with her self-doubt and regret as he stormed past her. Luna collapsed to her knees, hugging her purse as the floodgates opened, and the tears overflowed. "What have I done?" she murmured to herself.

"Luna?" Sofia slowly pushed the office door back open and came to kneel next to her. "Luna?" she asked again.

"I messed up Sofia. I messed up so bloody bad," she said again, leaning into her friend's embrace.

Chapter 22

A Girl Name Whiskey

"Where are my Martini Girls at tonight?" asked Fab, hyping up the Friday night crowd. "And where are my brave men at?" she asked, followed by another explosion of howls and deep cheers.

Luca Prisco sat at the bar, enjoying the show and a Spicy Martini. He chewed on the stuffed olive with jalapeno and drank the spicy citrus concoction, letting the ingredients all explode in his mouth.

"So, what do you think?" asked Willow.

It had been three weeks and four days, and Willow could not wait any longer to catch up with Luca.

"The drink or the show?"

She arched her brow and crossed her arms.

"The drink is phenomenal. The show is fantastic as well," he said reassuringly.

"I know," she said proudly. "I meant about the final plans."

"Ah, those, my dear, are all set and turned in. Didn't you notice the cleanup process beginning? There is not a lot to be done over there. Inspections have all passed. Even the plumbing," he teased. "We should be able to open doors by mid-October. Most of it's cosmetic. Good thing you have a boyfriend who knows a few things about construction."

She smiled, thinking of all the help and strings Colt had pulled to get people out to work on the building. They'd gotten lucky in that there were no structural damages. Most of the changes they were making were in the kitchen and bathrooms. They wanted to keep the old charm of the building and add some of the farmhouse elements the Martini Girl Bar had. Barn doors were being installed to the patio to match the current bar. Paint colors were going to remain the same, dark wood with white furniture. Pops of dark green and dark blues would decorate the area. They agreed to make an area for tasting and tapas. Flights of whiskey, tequila, beer, and wine, along with appetizer size food elements.

"Trust the process, Willow. We will be up and running in no time." Luca had stopped referring to them all so formally however, he refused to call her Whiskey, which pissed off Colt in the beginning until he realized Luca was doing it to purposely piss him off. Which had pissed Colt off even more. At which point, Willow stomped over to Colt, dragged his head down to hers and kissed him thoroughly in front of everyone, including Luca Prisco. To which Colt kissed her back for good measure by hiking her up higher in his embrace, ignoring the catcalls and whistling. Afterwards, Colt got over his issues with Luca Prisco.

Well, sort of.

Willow nodded to Luca and served up another Spicy Martini, still replaying the smoldering kiss in her head.

"I don't think I can do another one. These are dangerous."

She laughed as she mixed up another drink order for the Martini Girl table. "I'm sure you can do one and then some."

He smiled wickedly at her and winked, drumming his fingers to the beat of the music as Colt strummed his guitar during his solo performance. The crowd erupted in applause as the song ended.

"Did you find the recording of Lizzie?" she asked.

"I did. But it wasn't her who broke into our computer. It was an employee who is no longer employed and probably wishes he had never heard of Lizzie with double hearts and Prisco Distributors."

Willow stopped mid shake and tossed her head back, laughing. Ever since Luca had become a silent partner, they'd all gotten to know him a little and although he was still scary in a hot Greek mafia sort of bootlegger kind of way, he had a wicked sense of humor. She leaned forward and looked around, causing Luca to raise his dark right brow. "What about Curtis?"

"Ah, Douche-bag Dumb Ass Whiny Bitch Fuck Face Dick Head Asshole Merk, well he still has a pulse, my lovely. From what I hear, Hopper is his distributor and is costing him a penny or two. The Punch Bar is still there and I believe Cody Mills still plays for him. Speaking of which," he said, drumming his fingers, "Any chance of bringing him back to the Wine Girl Bar?"

Halo put down her book of Fifty Shades Darker and stared at Luca, surprised, while Tails conjured up a fireball to toss it at him. "Yeah, I don't think that will go over well with everyone."

A knowing smile formed. "I had to ask."

****

From the stage, Colt's eyes lingered on Willow as she interacted with Luca. Slowly, he was getting over his animosity towards Luca. Not much, but slowly. The

Panty Droppers finished their last set of the songs, killing it as usual.

"Ready, Pistol?" asked Fab excitedly. "Everyone is here."

Colt steadied himself and nodded, glancing over at the band he considered his brothers. They all gave him a nod and got back to their places.

"Martini Girl Bar," called out Fab, "We have some announcements to make. As your Diva hostess, it is my duty, my responsibility, my obligation to keep you all informed of trends, changes, additions, and events. With that said," Fab said, taking a pause while the crowd snickered, "New Trends. Y'all got to check out Piper's boutique. My girls' clothes are on point," she said, pointing towards Pipe and spinning in her new outfit. "As for changes, we got a few coming up, but one current outstanding news, we got the plumbing fixed. Can I get a, 'hell yeah'!"

Colt stood back and laughed, catching Willow's eyes, and smiled. He winked over at her as she blew him a kiss.

"Addition. Additions," Fab said, tapping her ruby red nail to her matching red lips. "Have you all met Luca Prisco?" The crowd shouted back their 'No's.'

"Luca, stand your fine ass up," Fab called out. "Y'all give it up to Luca Prisco who has joined the Martini Girl Bar Family. Not only did he join us, but we are expanding and opening the Wine Girl Bar next door."

Luca stood up and acknowledged the crowd and quickly sat down, shaking his head and taking another sip of his drink.

"Yes y'all. That means we will actually have the good shit next door and not wine that taste like vinegar."

Luca spat out his drink at Fab's description of their current wine selection.

"I've given you an update on trends, changes, additions. What am I missing?" she said dramatically, confusing Willow.

Multiple people from the crowd shouted, "Events!"

"Ah yes. Events. This is technically an event for us here. See, it's a personal event. I'm going to let Pistol take over."

"Recently, I received a call from a buddy of mine to fill in for some guitarist who walked out on their band. I turned it down," he honestly said. "Only to call back within the hour and tell him I'll take the gig."

Colt kept his eyes focused on Willow as he spoke. "It was supposed to be a temporary gig. A way to earn extra money to help support a four-year-old going on sixteen and a grandmother who still believes she's twenty-one." He shrugged and smirked at her.

"You're welcome." Levi yelled out from his seat at the drums, causing Colt to laugh as the crowd did too.

"These lyrics poured out of me in seconds, as did the melody. Can't say it's ever happened to me before." he looked back up at Willow and smiled at her lovingly. "The song is called 'A Girl Name Whiskey.'"

****

Willow's breath caught. She stepped around the bar and walked towards to the center of the room, not caring if she blocked anyone's view. Her heart and soul beat at the slow rhythmic sound of the drums and Colt's guitar. His deep voice flowed from the MIC as he sang the lyrics:

"See you standing there

A vision of beauty so unaware
You consume my mind, body, and soul
I'd give it all to you to have and hold
It's not every day we feel this kind of obsession
For a love poured next to near perfection
I'm taking my shot and hoping she'll kiss me
Because I fell in love with a girl name Whiskey.
Oh yeah, because I became in love with a girl name Whiskey.
Cause I fell in love with a girl name Whiskey
I've got nothing to lose,
No Excuse, oh, oh, oh
I'm putting my heart out there
Taking a chance without a care
She's fiery and smooth with amber eyes
Boy, she steals my breath by surprise
I'm taking my shot and hoping she'll kiss me
Because I fell in love with a girl name Whiskey.
Oh yeah, because I fell in love with a girl name Whiskey.
Cause I fell in love with a girl name Whiskey.
And every day my love grows more
And every day my soul soars
Because of you, I'm finally home
A place where my heart will never be alone.
Oh yeah, because I fell in love with a girl name Whiskey.
Cause I fell in love with a girl name Whiskey.
Oh, because I fell in love with a girl name Whiskey."

Tears streamed down Willow's face as she listened and remembered the melody and words he sang to her almost a month ago the night they danced. He strummed his guitar as his husky voice sang the lyrics sweetly. As the song came to an end, the crowd erupted around her.

Her eyes never left Colt as he walked down the stage towards her. She threw her arms around him, ignoring the crowd, and kissed her man. "I love you too," she whispered back, feeling his arms tighten around her.

"Got to ask you something?" he whispered in her ear.

She pulled back and looked into his sweet moss green eyes.

"It's important."

She bit her lower lip and nodded. "Hit me with it."

"How do you feel about a trip with Lucy and I to the mountains in search of fairies?"

She tossed her head back and laughed happily. "Best kind of trip any girl could ask for."

Colt lifted her and spun her around till she faced the hallway entrance to see her mom, Noni, Candice, Rita, Helen, and Lucy, standing with tears shining brightly and smiling.

He pulled a ring out of his pocket and brought it up between them. "I love you, Willow Mae Lawson. I knew I wanted you the moment you ran into me on my first day. You were immediately embedded in my every thought. Everything about you lights me up. Marry me baby."

The gorgeous oval cut diamond sparkled under the bar lights. Her heart thudded. Overjoyed.

"Yes. I love you. Colt," she said hugging him. "You're the one I've been waiting for."

A high squeal torpedoed towards them as Lucy raced over into their arms. Colt picked her up into his arms, holding her in their embrace. "She said yes," Lucy exclaimed happily.

Halo blew her nose for the sixth time, shedding happy tears and circling hearts around her head, while Tails dabbed the corner of her eyes and drew in deep breaths.

"Whooooheee, y'all, so much excitement. Our Whiskey girl is engaged to our Pistol," Fab called out from the MIC. "But we have one more event. For those of you who don't know who this precious little diamond is. This is Lucy. Go ahead Lucy," Fab encouraged.

Colt and Willow looked at each other and back at Lucy as her little lips quivered and shy voice broke through the silence, "Can I call you daddy?"

Willow laid her head on Colt's shoulder. More tears rushed out. She glanced over and caught the eyes of the band and their eyes, tender and soft as they watched this little girl bring Colt to his knees with the small little request.

"Awe, honey bear," he whispered, resting his head against hers, catching his voice as it broke from the overwhelming emotions. "I would love that."

Halo let out a loud wail and another round of tears. *He is perfect.*

Tails lips wobbled. She took one look at Halo and collapsed on her partner in crime. *I'm overwhelmed with feelings.*

Oh, contain yourself, Tails.

Lucy squealed again in delight and tossed her little arms around Colt. "That means you will be my new Mommy," she said happily, throwing herself into Willow's arms.

Willow laughed and cried, hugging Lucy tightly, and sweetly showered her with kisses on the forehead.

"Does this mean I gets another grandmother?"

They smiled at Lucy. "Yes, honey bear. Willow's mama will be your grandmother and Mila will be your aunt."

"I gets an auntie too?" she asked excitedly. Lucy leaned back, staring at her new found parents, pleased with herself. She quickly turned in Willow's arms and sought Sofia, her new bestie. "Sofia," she called out over the crowd.

"Hi, *princesa*," Sofia said, waving happily from the table, tears streaming down her face.

"Will you be my auntie too?" she asked loudly.

Sofia clapped excitedly, "*¡Si, si, si!*"

The girls at the table rushed them at once, clapping and pulling Lucy from Willow and Colt's arms. Mila immediately hugged her sister and Colt, congratulating them and welcoming Colt to the family. She still wore the blue extensions Lucy had placed in her hair and matched them with blue glitter nail polish. "Ladies, can I hug my niece," she asked with tears of joy in her eyes.

Sofia reluctantly released Lucy only to grab Willow in a tight hug. Luna wrapped her arms around them both, and, slowly, all the girls created a small circle around Willow. Fab reached over and grabbed Mila, bringing her in close with Lucy, who couldn't stop smiling. "Martini Girls forever ladies."

"Forever," they all said united.

"Now hold on a second. We need to be a part of this as well, dammit," complained Rita.

"Oh Rita," sighed Helen.

"Let me see the ring," asked Candice excitedly. "Oh you chose good, Colt. I'm proud of you."

"Of course he did. We were there to help him," Noni

said proudly.

"Jesus."

Willow giggled as her mom came over and hugged her tightly, and then Colt. "You took Noni with you?" she asked.

"And Rita. Trust me it was not by choice. It was either take them with me or let Noni paint her bedroom red. Not sure where the hell she got that idea from."

Sofia and Luna stared in shock. Willow couldn't control her burst of laughter. "Don't ask."

"Wait," they heard Lucy call out from Mila's arm. She whispered something in Mila's ear who smiled at her and nodded, 'yes,' enthusiastically at her. Lucy squirmed with delight with the newfound information. "Can *all* the Martini Girls be my aunties?"

The sudden rupture from all the women imploded in the room. They took turns taking her in their arms, loving up Lucy, making plans on spoiling her, to which Mila said, 'she would be the true aunt and would do all the spoiling,' until Fab joined in and said, 'no one can spoil a princess like she could.' Which then set off Sofia, who proclaimed, 'she was Lucy's bestie and would be the one to do the spoiling.' Which turned into another issue between Mila and Fab. Skylar and Piper thought they could make their plans to win Lucy over and made promises of taking her to the theme parks. Only to have Luna proclaim, 'she would not condone such behavior around little Lucy and that she would have to be a proper auntie and take her to the beach and search for mermaid treasures.' As soon as Luna said this, Lucy's eyes widened with excitement, to which Harper jumped in, stating, 'they should all go to the beach in search of mermaid treasures ceasing the battle of who can spoil

Lucy more.'

Willow turned to Colt, eyes shining with humor, love, and promises. "You sure you're ready for all this?"

"As long as I've got you," he said, leaning in for a kiss.

Willow smiled happily, "Here's to forever, Colt," she whispered, sealing her promise with a kiss.

A word about the author…

Gracie Cooper was born in South Florida to a large, loud, rowdy Cuban family where Sunday dinners were as sacred as the dominoes played every evening. She currently resides outside of Saint Augustine with her husband, two sons and a miniature schnauzer and continues Sunday dinners and rounds of dominoes with the family. http://www.graciecooper.com

Thank you for purchasing
this publication of The Wild Rose Press, Inc.

For questions or more information
contact us at
info@thewildrosepress.com.

The Wild Rose Press, Inc.
www.thewildrosepress.com